WAR HAMMER

NATE TEMPLE SERIES BOOK 8

SHAYNE SILVERS

Shayne Silvers

War Hammer

Nate Temple Series Book 8

Formerly published as The Temple Chronicles Series

ISBN: **978-1-947709-06-5**

© 2017, Shayne Silvers / Argento Publishing, LLC

info@shaynesilvers.com

DEDICATED TO AMY BETH WALKER NOLAN...

Amy was a great friend. Her input helped me polish the man known as Nate Temple into the hero we all love.

But she was taken from me before her time, so this book is dedicated to her, one of my original readers. We'll drink absinthe some day, Amy, and I'll dazzle you with tears and laughter as I share the rest of Nate's story...

*You guys are not just readers. You are my family. Without your love, input, advice, and support, I couldn't make these stories as raw as they are. **Memento Mori**. Don't waste a second of this precious thing we call life.*

Consider this the beginning of Phase 2 in the Temple Chronicles. Things are about to get... interesting. Without further ado, let's see what that rascal, Nate Temple, is up to, shall we?

CONTENTS

The Nate Temple Series—A warning	1
Chapter 1	3
Chapter 2	8
Chapter 3	12
Chapter 4	16
Chapter 5	21
Chapter 6	26
Chapter 7	30
Chapter 8	35
Chapter 9	40
Chapter 10	45
Chapter 11	50
Chapter 12	55
Chapter 13	60
Chapter 14	66
Chapter 15	71
Chapter 16	77
Chapter 17	83
Chapter 18	89
Chapter 19	96
Chapter 20	101
Chapter 21	108
Chapter 22	113
Chapter 23	117
Chapter 24	121
Chapter 25	126
Chapter 26	129
Chapter 27	134
Chapter 28	139
Chapter 29	145
Chapter 30	149
Chapter 31	157
Chapter 32	161
Chapter 33	167

Chapter 34   172
Chapter 35   177
Chapter 36   181
Chapter 37   187
Chapter 38   191
Chapter 39   195
Chapter 40   200
Chapter 41   207
Chapter 42   214
Chapter 43   219
Chapter 44   226
Chapter 45   229
Chapter 46   235
Chapter 47   243
Chapter 48   248
Chapter 49   257
Chapter 50   261
Chapter 51   266
TEASER: NINE SOULS (TEMPLE #9)   275
TRY: UNCHAINED (FEATHERS AND FIRE #1)   282
TRY: WHISKEY GINGER (PHANTOM QUEEN DIARIES # 1)   288

MAKE A DIFFERENCE   291
ACKNOWLEDGMENTS   293
ABOUT SHAYNE SILVERS   295
BOOKS IN THE TEMPLE VERSE   297

THE NATE TEMPLE SERIES—A WARNING

*N*ate Temple starts out with everything most people could ever wish for—money, magic, and notoriety. He's a local celebrity in St. Louis, Missouri—even if the fact that he's a wizard is still a secret to the world at large.

Nate is also a bit of a...well, let's call a spade a spade. He can be a mouthy, smart-assed jerk. Like the infamous Sherlock Holmes, I specifically chose to give Nate glaring character flaws to overcome rather than making him a chivalrous Good Samaritan. He's a black hat wizard, an antihero—and you are now his partner in crime. He is going to make a *ton* of mistakes. And like a buddy cop movie, you are more than welcome to yell, laugh and curse at your new partner as you ride along together through the deadly streets of St. Louis.

Despite Nate's flaws, there's also something *endearing* about him...You soon catch whispers of a firm moral code buried deep under all his snark and arrogance. A diamond waiting to be polished. And you, the esteemed reader, will soon find yourself laughing at things you really shouldn't be laughing at. It's part of Nate's charm. Call it his magic...

So don't take yourself, or any of the characters in my world, too seriously. Life is too short for that nonsense.

Get ready to cringe, cackle, cry, curse, and—ultimately—*cheer* on this snarky wizard as he battles or befriends angels, demons, myths, gods, shifters, vampires and many other flavors of dangerous supernatural beings.

Like any epic tale, Nate's journey starts out with a noble cause...

To find a cure for a reptile dysfunction.

Because dragons have come to St. Louis...

∾

DON'T FORGET! VIP's get early access to all sorts of Temple-Verse goodies, including signed copies, private giveaways, and advance notice of future projects. AND A FREE NOVELLA! Click the image or join here:
www.shaynesilvers.com/l/219800

FOLLOW and LIKE:
Shayne's FACEBOOK PAGE:
www.shaynesilvers.com/l/38602

I try to respond to all messages, so don't hesitate to drop me a line. Not interacting with readers is the biggest travesty that most authors can make. Let me fix that.

CHAPTER 1

I glanced over my shoulder at the fidgety vampire. "Ready?" I used the microphone built into my helmet to speak to Alucard. My visor was up, but our helmets were connected via radio.

Alucard sighed. "I guess so." His voice sounded tinny since we were so close to each other.

I turned back to the front door, repositioning myself slightly on the back of the idling ATV. "Yahn should be out any minute. I texted him five minutes ago. Be ready to floor it."

"There are so many ways this can go wrong," Alucard complained.

"It's just a little fun. Calm down," I scolded him, rolling my eyes. "Is everyone else ready at the tree?" I asked.

He grunted. "I think so. I still don't know why we're doing that either. It will be fun, sure, but don't we have more important things to do?"

I grunted. "I *know* we have more important things to do. But we can't *do* them yet. Things like this will keep everyone's attention occupied so we don't kill each other out of sheer boredom."

"If you say so," he muttered. At least he sounded mildly interested in our upcoming fight. But he was such a drama queen sometimes, especially of late. The sun shone down on us, and it was surprisingly warm outside for this late in the year. Underneath Alucard's melancholy, I could sense that the weather had perked him up a little. Being a Daywalker vampire, he still

3

had instinctive fear of sunlight, even though it now gave him power. He didn't need blood anymore, just a dose of UV to power up. Still, some old habits were hard to break.

The front door of Chateau Falco – my mansion – began to open, and I grinned as a figure stepped into view. My target was Yahn, and he was about to be hazed into my family – a welcoming rite of passage – since he had done so much to assist during the war with Indie and her Greeks.

I glanced down, the motion awkward with my helmet, and pressed the buttons on all three of the leaf blowers beside me, which were aimed directly at the door. As each kicked on, thick clouds of blue powdered paint – which I had packed inside the tubes of the leaf blowers – launched directly at the open doorway, pelting the unsuspecting dragon. I let out a triumphant cackle as I stared at the cloud of paint. "Take that, *Mr. I'm so cool because I'm invisible and stuff!*" I mocked in my best high-pitched Swede impersonation. "Welcome to the family!" I hooted, turning off each leaf blower – now empty of their payloads.

As the leaf blowers powered down, I heard a very different sound than I had anticipated.

Not the feminine shriek I had expected from Yahn, but two feral snarls of outrage. One a spitting hiss, and another a deep, foreboding growl. My stomach clenched, and I didn't need to see through the cloud to realize I had made a very, very big mistake.

"You're dead!" Gunnar roared, just as Talon screeched, "I'm going to kill you!"

"Alucard, go, go, GO!" I snapped, kicking the leaf blowers off the back of the ATV and grasping onto the cargo bars at my hips.

"Shit! That's not Yahn, you fucking lunatic!" the vampire said, shifting the ATV into drive.

"Fucking right, it's not!" Gunnar snapped, lunging from out of the cloud of colored paint to tackle me, his fancy new eyepatch glittering in the sunlight – because the werewolf only had one eye. His usual glorious, long blonde hair was now completely blue, as was his entire body, transforming him into the world's buffest, tallest Smurf. As he took his second step, he hit the trip-wire I had set up with make-shift grenades of more powdered paint. Three massive *booms* overpowered his shout in an explosion of green paint that blasted the area like mortars had just struck my mansion.

The silence was deafening, and even Alucard hesitated as we both stared at the shifting cloud.

"Wow! Like, totally rad. Paint party!" I heard Yahn call out cheerfully from beyond the open doorway, apparently having been behind Gunnar and Talon, thus escaping the hazing I had carefully prepared for him.

I heard a pair of very low, menacing growls.

"Fucking *GO!*" I reminded Alucard at the top of my lungs. The vampire slammed on the gas right as Gunnar emerged from the cloud of smoke, and our tires squealed on the driveway. I cackled triumphantly as Gunnar fell short, a massive, green and blue vision of murder. "See you at the tree!" I slammed my visor down, just in case Gunnar saw fit to shoot me from a distance.

"What the fuck, Nate?! I thought you were trying to get Yahn?" Alucard hissed into my earpiece.

"I was! I thought you told everyone else to be at the tree already!" I argued, watching as Gunnar decided to run after us, much faster than most humans could. He hadn't changed to his werewolf form, because that would leave him naked during our upcoming game at the giant white tree that dominated the grounds of Chateau Falco, my ancestral home.

And paintballs wouldn't feel good striking naked flesh.

Talon wasn't far behind, silver eyes glinting in the sunlight as his were-cat-like form tore up dirt and leaves in his pursuit of absolution.

"The wolf is slightly unhinged, if you forgot, and Talon is a certifiable psycho. He was much better as a housecat. And in case you forgot, cats *hate* getting their fur dirty. Why didn't you check who it was, first?" Alucard growled into his headset.

Talon had been disguised as a Maine Coon the entire time I had known him. Up until I decided to take him to the Land of the Fae, which had been when he revealed that he was much more than just a talking housecat. He was now a bipedal werecat warrior – imagine a Thundercat from that kid's cartoon – and he went by the name Talon the Devourer. The only other thing I knew was that he was the Fae version of a killing machine.

I shrugged. "I was too excited. It didn't even cross my mind because, you know, everyone else was *supposed* to be waiting at the tree!" I shouted over the sound of the engine.

Alucard grunted noncommittally. "Don't try to blame this on me." I stared off into the distance, noticing that the laborers working on the wall surrounding my property had paused to stare at the sound of explosions and the clouds of colored smoke wafting through the air. Also, they were likely wondering why three figures were now chasing an ATV across the grounds. I waved at them, and they quickly resumed work, probably not sure if one of the helmeted figures was the man who had hired them.

We skidded up to the tree to see a bewildered assortment of people staring at us, already decked out in their paintball gear. Two of them were teenaged girls, creeping ever closer to that mystical age when they presumed the world would be handed to them on a platter – eighteen. They were stunningly attractive red-heads named Aria and Sonya, but we just called them the Reds – both for their hair color and their color of dragon. They could use mind control, like all shifter dragons, and their crimson irises flashed in the daylight, their horizontal pupils contracting as they stared past me, shaking their heads. "What the hell was that?" they shouted in unison, studying the still-present cloud of smoke drifting near the entrance to the mansion, and the two figures tearing after us. Yahn jogged behind them, grinning excitedly.

The bastard. He had no idea how much time I had secretly put into setting up that trap.

Alex was leaning against the trunk of the large white tree, shaking his head in disbelief, not sure if he should be smiling or seriously concerned about the monsters racing our way. He was tall, dark-haired, and broody, but he was also wildly naïve at times. We had saved him from the Fae not too long ago, the prisoner of one of their fabled Changeling operations – where they kidnapped a human child and switched it out for one of their own. They got power from this, and I still hadn't verified how long Alex had been a prisoner, but we were slowly nursing him back to mental health, showing him that not everyone was a monster.

Basically, letting him be a kid again.

In a way, I had kind of adopted him, because his parents had been murdered.

I very bravely repositioned myself so that the ATV was between me and the approaching psychopaths. Yahn ran after them, faster now, but still grinning like a big idiot – enjoying himself.

But the two ahead of him were not enjoying themselves. They wanted revenge.

Gunnar, the alpha werewolf of St. Louis, and Talon, a seriously deranged cat-man from the Land of the Fae. Both were very, very good at killing things that annoyed them.

"Nate, why did you paint-bomb the two most unstable beings here?" Aria asked, grimacing at the two rainbow-skinned nightmares.

"And why, oh why, did you *let* him do this, Alucard?" Sonya, her sister, added.

I still hadn't decided which was their most dangerous forms – as red, fire-breathing dragons, or as two mind-controlling teenaged girls. And they had Alucard – their stand-in dad, since their mother had been killed – wrapped around their fingers.

Alucard grimaced. "He was trying to get Yahn, but Gunnar and Talon came out first."

"Well, that sucks," Alex said, uneasily. "They're not *really* going to kill us, right? They look pretty serious…"

"Play it cool, Alex," I said, backing up to stand beside him. I leaned closer, verifying the Reds weren't watching. "Channel four," I told him, tapping the side of my helmet to switch to a different frequency. He did the same, plopping his helmet down over his head.

"This it?" he asked into the headset, his voice carrying over the communications channel.

"Yep. Let's make sure Alucard is ready. I don't think Gunnar is going to want to give us any time to set up."

I cocked the pistol in my hand and – without warning – shot Alucard in the back of the helmet. He shouted, spinning to glare at the Reds. They instantly pointed at me, laughing inside their helmets. Alucard turned to glare at me, and I waited until the Reds weren't looking to flash him four fingers and then tap my helmet.

I couldn't see through the visor on his head, but I bet he wore a frowny face.

CHAPTER 2

*A*lex, Alucard, and Yahn were on my team – the green team – easily recognized by our matching, shiny green helmets. Talon, Gunnar and the Reds had blue helmets.

"You're an asshole, Nate," Alucard finally muttered into our shared channel. "Hey, Alex. You up for handing Nate over to the blue team?"

Alex laughed, and I shot him a look, silencing him.

Gunnar and Talon skidded to a halt before us, looking entirely too eager to play our game.

"You're going to pay for that, Nate," Gunnar growled, his shoulders flexing instinctively.

I lifted up my visor. "I was trying to haze Yahn. Alucard was *supposed* to have told you to be at the tree already," I said, shooting the worthless vampire a significant look.

"Intent does not absolve guilt, wizard," Talon snarled.

"Sourpuss," I muttered. Talon's brightly-painted fur bristled at that, and I saw his claws unsheathe on instinct. I waved a hand at him. "It's not permanent," I added. "Although I think the warning label said to keep it away from pets, so don't lick it off." His tail began to twitch, but I managed to keep a straight face. "You guys ready?"

"We already set up the coms channel for you," Sonya said, handing a helmet and gun to Talon. He curled a lip at the headset, but firmly placed it over his head with more force than was necessary. Aria did the same with Gunnar, who instantly checked the gun with practiced hands, and shoved the helmet down over his long hair.

"Was that the surprise you warned us about?" Gunnar asked as Yahn finally reached us, laughing joyfully at Talon and Gunnar's colorful bodies. He abruptly stopped when they shifted their glares to him, and changed course to accept his gear from Alex.

"Paint guns! This will be fun, yah?" he hooted, practically skipping from foot-to-foot.

Gunnar waited for my answer, and I shook my head at him, smiling. "No, that wasn't my surprise." I turned to Alex and motioned for him to touch the tree. "Wake up my Beast."

Alex grinned, turning to jog back to the tree. He slapped the bark with an open palm as everyone else began to shout over each other. "Wait, what?" Alucard hissed over the others. "You're waking up your Beast? The one who lives in the tree? Why the hell—"

A heavy branch slammed into the earth just to his right, and Alucard actually squealed.

I held up a hand, and the tree stilled, but I could almost feel it chuckling in amusement.

"We have a third party in the game. He doesn't have a preference for either side. He just wants to hit things. And *we* are the *things*," I said, grinning.

Gunnar popped up his visor. "Why the hell are we doing this?" he asked, studying me and the tree with his lone eye. Not scared, exactly, but wary. He also knew that as much as I liked my fun and games, I usually had an ulterior motive.

"We're getting ready to go to the Land of the Fae tomorrow. Some of the trees over there are alive. I figured this would be good practice." I pointed at the various rubble, bushes, and make-shift hiding spots I had set up yesterday. It was all centered around the tree, easily accessible by the titanic wooden sentinel. Not only would we be fighting each other, but we would have to keep an eye out for the tree's malevolent inclinations. "I also had Dean rig the area with traps, so keep your eyes open." I shot a pointed look at Gunnar and his lone eye. "Figure of speech."

Gunnar didn't comment, but he did scan the area before glancing up at the tree thoughtfully. Firm resolve slowly settled onto his face as he realized this was basically a practice run for the Fae.

Because I was telling the truth.

His fiancée, Ashley, had been fatally injured after killing Hercules a month ago. Pan – the Wild God and my live-in bodyguard – had seen the severity of her wounds, grabbed her, and then immediately disappeared. My assumption was that he had taken her to the Land of the Fae – a place where time moved differently, possibly granting him the extra seconds he needed to save her life, because if he hadn't acted, she would have died in Gunnar's arms moments later.

I glanced back at Alex, who gave me a nod. "Kai's ready."

"Who the hell is K—" Talon began.

Another tree branch slammed into the earth, and Talon jumped away, shooting his gun at the ground as he leapt. The paintballs splattered the branch, which instantly whipped back up into the canopy.

"*That* was Kai," Alex answered softly. I didn't have time to question him on it, but I sure as hell hadn't known my Beast's name. Or that Alex was on such good terms with it.

"One minute to get into position," I shouted, and began to turn away.

"Nate!" Gunnar shouted urgently. I spun at the tone in his voice, only to find a canister flying at my face. I dove to the ground and rolled just as the canister exploded with yellow paint. Then I was hissing into my headset for everyone on my team to run.

"Cheaters never prosper," Alucard offered in a dry tone as he used his vampiric speed to vamoose the hell out of the danger zone.

"Can it, Glampire," I panted, hunkering low as I ran.

I heard Gunnar shouting after us, his visor still up. "Hey, Alucard! I wanted to let you know that I had my paintballs blessed by a priest!"

Alucard stumbled, helmet darting my way as he scrambled over a stack of pallets. "He wouldn't really do that, would he?" the vampire whispered nervously into the microphone.

I shrugged. "I have no idea. But maybe now that you're a Daywalker, it won't be a big deal."

Alucard cursed, and Yahn skidded up behind a bush, laughing happily as he held his gun to his chest in an awkward Charlie's Angels impersonation.

The next thing I knew, a concussive *thump* erupted right where he was standing, and all I could see was a giant pink cloud of paint. He had tripped one of the traps Dean had laid out.

I cursed, ignoring the laughter of our opponents.

Team Temple was already down one sparkly dragon, and we hadn't officially started yet.

CHAPTER 3

I squeezed the trigger, aiming for one of the blue helmets, but quickly dove for cover as I felt something thrash above my head. A moment later, a long, thick tree branch slammed into the ground like a whip, right where I had been standing, igniting one of the tripwires to unleash a cloud of yellow smoke. Thankfully, the paint didn't get me.

Paintballs began peppering the earth to the right of me, so I quickly rolled away.

Alucard was keeping Talon pinned down, who wasn't as familiar with his gun as the rest of us, being a cat-man-thing. He was able to use his gun, albeit awkwardly, but he just wasn't used to the device, preferring up close combat in the real world. I heard him yowl as he tried to make an escape, only to be plastered with paintballs by Alucard, who chuckled into my headset.

"Kung Pao Kitty is served. Where's the wolf?" he whispered.

I laughed softly, thankful that Talon hadn't heard the comment. "No idea. Keep an eye out. I'm going to take down one of the Reds."

"Affirmative."

I rolled my eyes. "No one talks like that."

As the rules dictated, Yahn was lying prone on the ground, having 'died' before the game had even begun. Alex was fleeing from the Reds, retreating quickly as they tried to flank him, sending him further and further away from me. I dove behind a bush, wary of traps, and trying to get a bead on the Reds to help Alex, because our guns were surprisingly accurate at a distance.

He was the only Regular out here, but he seemed to be doing well, considering.

I gave him cover fire, just as the Reds both hunkered down behind a barricade.

"Grenade to the right, Alex. I'll throw one to the left. On three," I whispered into my helmet.

"Got it," he panted excitedly.

"One. Two. *Three!*" I hissed, hurling a grenade as hard as I could over my barricade. Mine came up short since he was so far away, but had the desired effect of startling the Reds just as Alex's grenade landed on the opposite side of their shelter, exploding almost simultaneously.

The Reds rolled over the center of the barricade in a dead sprint for Alex, shooting their guns on full automatic.

I managed to tag one of them across the visor, and she collapsed with a curse, rolling in the dirt dramatically. Alex stood from his concealment and began shooting.

But his gun ran empty after the third click.

A bush was between me and the surviving teenaged weredragon, but I heard her laugh. "Time to die!" she hooted.

"Heads up," Alex murmured smugly into my headset.

I blinked as a massive branch swooped down faster than any of the other attacks and clotheslined her, sending her flying a dozen paces closer to me, dropping her gun in the process. She slammed into Alucard, who had been creeping up behind her unseen, sending them both flying into a bush.

I flung my last grenade at them for good measure, because technically, they had to be painted to 'die' in this game.

The resulting thump caused a roar of anger as blue smoke covered their tangled frames. "What the hell, Nate?" Alucard snapped in my ears.

"Sometimes you have to sacrifice a paw—"

"Behind you!" Alex suddenly shouted.

I spun, lifting my gun to see Gunnar flying at me in his hybrid wolf form – a giant, bipedal white werewolf – having discarded his slower, human form to achieve his payback for the Great Leafblower Incident. But that left him without a gun, which was the only way to play the game. His stone eyepatch glinted in a ray of sunlight that pierced the canopy from above, and he looked immensely satisfied. His paws slammed against my chest, and I felt them tangle with my shirt before I flew away at the impact, my helmet knocked free from the force of the attack.

Still flying in midair, I glanced down to see two grenades tucked into my shirt. "Motherf—"

They exploded hard enough to paint my face in pink paint and bruise my chest.

Then I hit a bush, blowing entirely through it, scraping myself up in the process.

The bush, of course, happened to be rigged with one of Dean's traps, which erupted with a gallon of purple paint all over my body. Wet paint, this time. Not the powdered crap.

Gunnar howled, holding his palms up triumphantly.

Which was when a tree branch slammed into the back of his legs, cutting off his howl. He almost did a double backflip before striking the ground with a grunt onto his stomach, where he rolled painfully. Alex picked up one of the discarded paintball guns and unloaded on the wolf, hitting him in the ass a dozen times before releasing the trigger.

Gunnar yelped at the barrage.

I wiped more paint from my eyes, then stared at Alex. He nodded once at the tree, as if saying *thank you*, and the tree rattled its branches a few times as if giving him a high five. Had… Alex used the tree during our fight? Was he able to communicate with it from a distance? He had spent a lot of time near it over the last few days, whenever he wanted to get away from people. After his captivity in the Land of the Fae, he was inexperienced at social situations, and often needed alone time.

But, this wasn't something I had expected.

I had freed my Beast – an ancient, sentient being of unimaginable power – into the tree, ending my brief run as a Maker, because I hadn't liked the idea of sharing a body with such a dangerous force. The Beast had seemed perfectly content with this arrangement, even grateful for it. I didn't think he was trapped inside the tree, but that he had chosen to remain there. Because I hadn't forced him inside it – I had simply freed him. Still, he had stuck around inside the tree ever since.

Alex scanned the battlefield, and seeing no one standing, held up his hands triumphantly. "I win!"

Then he abruptly disappeared with a grunt of surprise.

I glared, noticing Yahn's handiwork. He was a chameleon dragon, and could make anyone touching him disappear. The ultimate stealth mode.

Just then, Yahn appeared from behind his bunker, sniffing the air warily, looking concerned.

I blinked, feeling a sudden wave of anxiety.

If Yahn hadn't…

"Someone took him!" Gunnar bellowed, sniffing the air as he jogged up to me. Everyone was suddenly on their feet, prancing back and forth as they tried to either catch a scent or get a bead on Alex's abductor.

CHAPTER 4

I couldn't see or hear anything that pinpointed Alex's location. It was as if he had never been here with us. The tree suddenly began to rattle, a group of its branches seeming to point in a very specific direction. I followed the motion, squinting to see something. Anything.

Unsuccessful, I closed my eyes, reaching out with my senses, my magic. I felt a primal urge tugging at me, wanting to bathe the land with fire and ice, willing to swallow up the world to get Alex back.

Wylde – a deep, dark part of me I had discovered while in the Land of the Fae – wasn't a person, per se, but a more savage, primitive version of myself.

And *territorial* was putting his feelings mildly.

He saw Alex as his family, and that family had just been taken, which meant he was practically frothing at the mouth – mad with bloodlust.

But another voice whispered inside me. Where Wylde was loud and savage, this feeling was cold, calculating, and anticipatory – and it was a very, very new part of me. In fact, I had never felt it manifest so directly before, as if trying to encourage me to listen. I had felt its power before, but never communicated with it in any way. It reminded me of a greasy smile given to a young woman at a bar during last call.

I didn't respond to either of them – not daring to give in – but I did acknowledge them as I continued facing the direction the tree – Kai – had seemed to indicate. I reached out with my magic, and felt both of the alien sensations inside me lend it strength. Not a lot, but enough to notice. I shivered as their strange powers amplified mine, but I didn't stop them.

"Hurry, Nate! I can't get a track on him!" Gunnar growled.

I risked a glance with my eyes in time to see the Reds explode into dragon form – large crimson nightmares, easily the size of three Great Danes mashed together – and launch into the sky, sweeping out over the area, heads darting back and forth as they searched for our invisible kidnapper. They were getting bigger, and scarier.

Like all my friends.

But I didn't have time to admire them right now. I closed my eyes again, reaching further and further outwards, absorbing the sounds of life around us – the growing grass, rustling tree branches, the sighing wind, and a prevailing sense of coldness that was flooding the area. An unnatural cold.

Something that didn't belong.

"Open your goddamned eyes, Nate! Do something!" Alucard snapped.

Through that alien coldness, I suddenly felt... heartbeats racing across the ground.

Far, far away. Near the wall protecting my property – a good two hundred yards distant.

I focused on the heartbeats, separating them. One set was sharp and fast while the other was lower, heavier, slower. Taking a guess, I lashed out and squeezed one of the heartbeats in an imagined fist. The Reds roared in surprise and I opened my eyes, releasing my magic. I blinked at the sudden emptiness inside me, let out a breath, and wiped some paint from my brow, staring out at where the dragons were landing. I could see Alex frantically kicking something on the ground, shouting incoherently.

I began walking towards them, accepting Wylde's proud murmur of approval, and wondering where the other sensation had come from – or gone. I let my anger simmer as I continued walking, trying to shake off the residual effects of my strange use of this new power.

Gunnar jogged up beside me, still in his man-wolf form. Talon, Alucard, and Yahn spread out beside us, looking sickened, and very nervous.

Of me.

I ignored them, staring out at the Reds who were trying to calm Alex down, now in their naked human form – having lost their clothes when they shifted to dragon form – grasping at Alex to restrain him.

Any other young man would have forgotten absolutely anything to be manhandled by two naked teenaged girls, but I could still feel Alex's heartbeat, wild, erratic, and angry. He finally slowed, allowing the Reds to guide him to the ground where they sat beside him, arms placed over his shoulders. They began to stroke his hair, no doubt using their mind control in an effort to calm him down.

"How did he die, Nate?" Gunnar asked softly, not turning to look at me, but fixing his one eye on Alex as we approached.

"I ended him," I said, without consciously thinking about it. I hadn't even intended to speak until I reached Alex and verified that he was unharmed.

Gunnar hesitated. "How? The gold light thing?" he asked, pointing at my forearms.

I glanced down to see he was right. Golden light shone from my veins, although it was fading, now. "I... stopped his life," I mumbled, not entirely sure what the words meant – or the light.

"Okay. But... there wasn't any fire or explosions, or... anything. It was completely silent."

I nodded absently as I began to jog, wanting to get away from his questions. "Death doesn't have to be so loud, brother..."

I heard them jogging behind me, but none of them had any further questions after that.

All my attention was for Alex. I had sworn to keep him safe, and had almost failed. But what bothered me the most was wondering how anyone had broken into my property, and who the hell had they been? Not many even knew who Alex *was*.

I reached Alex and knelt before him, clutching his face with my hands as I studied him, checking for injury – whether seen or unseen. Plenty of things could harm a person without any visual signs.

He returned my look, and let out a deep breath. "Thank you, Nate," he whispered.

I pulled him close, squeezing him into a hug. "I'm so sorry, Alex. None of us sensed a thing. Before or after. I almost didn't catch him in time," I whispered, my eyes burning and my voice raw. Because something inside of me felt flayed at the brief and nearly fatal encounter. Someone had invaded my home to take an innocent, and I had almost let it happen.

An innocent that I now considered family. Not my son, but in a way... my son.

And a man was supposed to keep his son safe. It was pretty much the most important job.

"Nate, stop. No one could have done better. What you did was good enough. Thank you," he said, patting my back consolingly, sensing my quivering muscles. I realized that I was fucking shaking, and that Alex was comforting *me*.

"Good enough... *isn't*," I growled, remembering one of my father's famous sayings. I slowly released him as I climbed to my feet. I let out a breath and addressed everyone. "Keep your eyes open in every direction. Alex doesn't leave your sight. Yahn, be ready to get him out of here at the first sign of trouble."

I didn't wait for a response as I turned to the body on the ground. He wore a laborer's outfit, just like the ones working on my wall. I discarded my sudden flash of anger at that fact to flip him over with my boot and get a look at his face. He wasn't one of the typical crew. This man was black, and everyone working on my wall were white Europeans – all one family.

I memorized the face, even though he was dead, and then crouched down to go through his pockets. He had obviously impersonated one of them, stealing one of their outfits. Did that mean one of the laborers was dead? I found nothing in his front pockets, but did find a folded slip of paper in his back pocket.

I unfolded it, my vision seeming to darken into a tunnel as I read.

Get the boy and get out. Or kill some of his friends. Anything. I want Temple to feel pain, to hurt, to know fear, to know failure. Exploit any weakness. He took everything from me. – C.Q.

I crunched the paper into my fist, and almost burned it to ashes at the waves of fury that suddenly crashed over me.

Alucard grabbed my fist. "Don't, Nate. Whatever it said, we might need it."

"You've got a crazy look in your eyes," Talon purred. I looked up to see his ears twitching in all directions, as if anticipating an unseen attack, but his eyes were locked onto mine. He also held his great white axe glaive – a polearm weapon with a long, wicked, slender axe at the tip. Even the metal was white. Not bone, but something alien.

I couldn't even find the humor to laugh at the paint covering his fur.

I tried to steady my pulse and regain control of my breathing before turning to face everyone. "Castor Queen wants revenge against me for taking away his Syndicate and handing them over to the Academy."

"*That's* where they went," Alucard said softly, scratching his chin. "I was wondering what you'd done with them."

I nodded. "There weren't many left. And I didn't feel like fighting G Ma over them. Most of them are criminals and will face a swift death. But I'm pretty sure some were blackmailed into service."

"What makes you think that?" Gunnar asked with a frown.

I met his eye, not focusing on the stone eyepatch that marked his missing eye. When I had healed him a few weeks ago after the battle – when I had first donned my Horseman Mask in full – the stone patch had melded into his missing eye as a permanent fixture. His claws were also the same rough, uncut diamond-like material.

Just like my Mask. My skin had turned into the same material when I donned the power.

I wasn't really sure what to make of that. Was Gunnar tied to me as a Horseman? Was I officially a Horseman now? Or was it simply a result of the family rune he had on his wrist – the rune that had first allowed him to control his werewolf form as a child – the rune that tied him to my family, and the protections that Chateau Falco granted the Temple Clan.

Had the magic of my Mask simply reacted oddly to his rune?

"Because my dad was blackmailed into helping them," I finally said.

The group grew very quiet. "We should probably get back inside," Gunnar said, shelving my comment for later. "What do you want to do with the bod—"

The body burst into flame behind me, because I was already walking away, heading back to the house, my mind a wash of dark thoughts.

"Everyone get inside. Clean up. Get some rest and some food. I've got a few things to take care of. We'll talk later," I said over my shoulder.

CHAPTER 5

I let my friends walk back to the house without me as I headed back over to the white tree where we had been playing only minutes ago.

I stared up at the tree as I approached, considering. The branches waved slowly, undulating. I stepped up to the trunk, and the entire tree slowly hunkered down to meet me, the branches sagging lower as if trying to give me a hug. I placed my hand on the trunk and focused intently, reaching out with my mind.

"Kai?" I asked tentatively.

Yes, a familiar voice responded. *Thank you for saving Alex. I couldn't reach him from within the tree.*

I knelt on the grass, wanting to maintain contact with the wood, even though I wasn't sure it was necessary. "Is that your real name?"

The entity inside the tree was silent for a time, as if considering how to answer. *In a way. It has been a long time since I considered it. I've carried many names over the years, but that one felt right when Alex asked what he could call me.*

I nodded. "I like it." I turned to lean my back against the tree. "What's up with that?" I asked, staring up above me. A very large treehouse was tucked into the branches, as if part of the tree itself. Or as if it had been there for fifty years, even though it had only appeared a week ago. "I've been meaning to ask, but no one else seems to have even noticed it."

The voice chuckled. *I like Alex. I feel like he's a long-lost brother. He is kind, even though he has every reason to be otherwise. Out of all the places he could have gone for solitude, he came to me – to my... tree. So, I helped him. I figured every boy should have a friend... and a secret treehouse,* he chuckled, the bark shifting against my back.

I smiled distantly, nodding. "That's really cool of you, Kai. Thank you." I felt the tree vibrate slightly, as if shrugging his shoulders. "Why are you still here?" I asked. "It wasn't my intention to trap you inside the tree. Did I mess something up?" I asked apologetically.

The bark grew warm beneath my back, and I was fairly certain that the being inside was mirroring my position on the ground from inside the tree itself. *I wanted to stick around. Get some rest, stretch a bit. Haven't really figured out what I want to be when I grow up, I guess. I never really considered what I would do with freedom, because it isn't typically granted to us.*

I nodded. "Well, if you need anything from me, let me know. You don't have to stay here if you don't want to."

I know. But I have my reasons. And then there's Alex... he trailed off. *Everyone could use a friend. A family.* He sounded wistful as he said it.

"You don't have to do that. Alex has friends here. He has a family," I pressed politely.

Kai was silent for a time. *I wasn't speaking of Alex. I was speaking of myself.*

I blinked, and then laughed. "Well, you're family, too. Unless you decide to go all crazy on me. You help out, do what you can to keep my friends safe, and you can stay as long as you want. Just let me know if you're going to take my tree away. I'm kind of fond of it, now."

He grunted, and silence soon enveloped us. I realized that I could no longer hear the sound of hammers from the workers outside. I looked over to see the laborers in a tight huddle, talking animatedly. I sighed, preparing to climb to my feet and figure out exactly what had happened.

Do you know how long it has been since I was allowed to play? Kai asked me in a soft whisper.

I turned to stare at the bark, placing my hand on it again. "I guess I never thought about it," I admitted. "Did you have fun today?"

He chuckled. *Oh, yes.*

I grinned. "Good, but you're required to always be on my team."

Then Alex will be on your team as well...

I smiled. "Deal. I need to go run and take care of some things. Let me know if you ever need anything, Kai. Some fertilizer or something, I guess."

The branches slowly rose back up into their normal position for a tree, and I nodded to myself. I had a new level of what I constituted as weird, and a talking tree just wasn't in it. I climbed onto the ATV and turned the ignition. Then I made my way over to the laborers, who were suddenly all watching me.

I pulled up to the broken wall and hopped off the ATV.

"Hey," I said, approaching them, assessing their progress on the wall – which had been broken in my war with the Greeks, led by my ex-fiancée, Indie.

I received very odd looks in return, and realized that I was still covered in paint. I smirked, holding my hands out at my attire and shrugging.

"Our brother is missing," Danny Regazio, the leader of the crew, said. He took off his hat – one of those ones that looked like the Fidel Castro style cap, and the sun struck his steel-gray eyes. He was thin and wiry, but I had seen him wrestle with his brothers on break. He was stronger than he looked. He was never clean-shaven, but it wasn't quite a beard either, just a thick scruff.

"Was he black?" I asked.

Danny frowned at me. "No. What kind of question is that?" he asked, clearly distraught at the situation, not comprehending my random question. I sighed. That was something, at least. It meant that the black wizard had most likely killed or taken his brother to steal the gray coveralls they all wore.

Fearing the worst, I closed my eyes and tried to reach out with my senses again. Like I had when saving Alex. Almost immediately, I felt something under one of the vans near the back of the row, away from the work-site. It was faint, but it made me smile in relief.

I ran over to the vehicle, and crawled down onto my knees. "Help!" I called out loudly, but I needn't have bothered. They had followed me as soon as I began running. I found a body tucked up against the wheel under the van, hastily stashed out of sight. They erupted in shouts of joy as they saw their unconscious brother. They pulled him out, shaking him and patting his cheeks eagerly. He was a broad-chested, hairy one. Built like a blacksmith, and currently wearing only thong-style underwear with an Italian flag on the front. I grimaced at that and dipped my head at Danny as

23

the man woke with a gasp. He stared at me, a very thoughtful look on his face.

"He was knocked unconscious," I said. "I found the man who stole his clothes, but I took care of him already. You should get your brother to the hospital just to make sure he's okay. Take the rest of the day off."

Danny took a step closer, speaking under his breath. "I would very much like to speak with this man," he said in an aggressive tone.

I nodded in understanding. "That won't be possible, Danny." His shoulders tightened in anger, assuming I had handed the man over to the police or something. I placed a hand on his shoulder, meeting his eyes. "I took care of him. He won't be talking to anyone. Ever again. I don't tolerate thieves. But you should know that he tried to kidnap a kid," I said, pointing a thumb over my shoulder. "*My* kid. I think my anger trumps what was done to your brother. No offense."

Danny stepped back, a look of profound disbelief on his face. It slowly transformed into a very dark, satisfied nod. He was impressed. "I think I enjoy working for you, Master Temple. I would consider it an honor to work on any other projects for you in the future."

I smiled. "Show me what you can do with this wall and I'll consider it, Danny," I said, pointing at the remains of the battered wall surrounding my property. The wall Hercules and his pals had destroyed a few weeks ago. Then I placed a finger over my lips, indicating silence on the matter of the infiltrator.

He chuckled. "We Italians know how to keep a secret. And how to solve problems. Your actions will be kept secret from others, but my brothers need to know the truth. Or they might decide to investigate." I nodded in agreement as he turned to walk away. As if an afterthought, he halted, turning back to me. "I forgot to tell you. I know you wanted to be kept updated on who is working on the project here." I nodded. "I had a man ask for work. My brothers have worked with him before on other projects over the last few years, but I wanted to ask you first before bringing him here to help."

"He hasn't worked here yet, right?" I asked, thinking back on the wizard who had just tried to infiltrate my home. Danny shook his head. "What's his name?" I was pretty sure I was being paranoid, because Danny had said his brothers had worked with this guy in the past. For years. Still, paranoia was only crazy when it was wrong.

"Leo Vasilias," he said with a shrug. "He's a hard worker, or I wouldn't mention it." He glanced at the wall. "And this is one hell of a job." His eyes met mine, curious, but not accusing. "We found claws in the rubble. Some blood, too…"

I waited for a time, considering my response. Danny was a Regular, but he and his brothers did good work. They had also done some work for my father at Temple Industries, and had jumped on this offer for lower than their competitors' bids, simply wanting to work with me rather than make the most money possible from a billionaire. "Why did you offer less money?" I asked.

Danny sighed. "Your father paid for his wife's surgery," he said in a soft voice, jerking a thumb at one of his brothers. "To be honest, they wanted to charge even less… But I'm a greedy bastard, and didn't want it to look like we were begging. The work is worth what we offered."

I chuckled at his last comment, nodding. Then my face grew serious. "I didn't know about the surgery."

He nodded. "I only mentioned it because you asked, and I'd rather not lie. My brothers liked your father a great deal. And he helped us when we were just starting out."

I reached out a hand, grateful for his honesty. "If you trust this Leo, bring him on. Make this the best wall you've ever constructed – in record time – and I'll add on a bonus. As well as a contract to work any future projects. First right of refusal."

He shook my hand with a pleased grin, and then dipped his head. "As you wish, Master Temple. We'll make you proud."

He winked, and then turned back to his brother. Someone had pulled out a pair of sweatpants and an extra shirt. Danny gathered them close, pointing a thumb over his shoulder at me, speaking animatedly in a low tone. I saw their eyes widen in surprise, and then respect as one-by-one they turned to acknowledge me with nods of appreciation, wariness, respect, and loyalty.

I tipped an imaginary hat at them and hopped back onto my ATV.

I looked up at the sun, and let out a deep breath, realizing the time. I was anxious to speak with some people who were waiting for me at the house. Well, they better be waiting for me at the house. Otherwise I was going to hunt them down myself.

CHAPTER 6

I sauntered through the front door – that was now coated with powdered paint – to find Dean scrubbing the entryway floor where some of the paint had made it inside. My butler scowled up at me. Dean was a little older than my dad would have been, but he didn't show his age. He was neatly dressed in a very expensive suit from Thomas Pink, because working for my family had made him what some may call a clothing snob.

I shrugged guiltily. "Need some help?"

He dropped his sponge and climbed to his feet. "The lizard keeps shedding."

I nodded. "I hear they do that," I said, trying to keep my face serious.

"But *they* aren't the size of a man, and *they* don't leave them in areas where guests could find them," he argued.

"I'll talk to Carl," I sighed. "You know he's not good at these things." Because Carl was an Elder – a reptilian monster who lived with me. His kind had been banished from the world a long time ago, considered too dangerous to walk free. And when the entire magical community agrees on a thing, you can pretty much bet that they're right. So, Carl was an anomaly. He had found his way out of his prison, and after a lot of his brothers had betrayed me, had stuck around, even defending me from them.

But he had some domestic skills that needed polishing. Like not leaving dead skin around the house. Because reptiles shed their skin.

Dean was scowling at nothing. "People will think we have a goddamned anaconda wandering loose," he muttered. I blinked, my gast flabbered at his curse, because it was completely unlike him, which meant he was well and truly past his comfort zone. "Follow me," he said, blushing furiously at his outburst, turning to head towards the sitting room to our right.

Frowning at his change of topic, I obeyed. It was always beneficial to humor Dean. Especially if he was this upset. He could very literally make my life miserable in any number of frustrating ways. Because he ran Chateau Falco like a pirate ship. For example, if I drove too fast on the driveway, I was liable to find deflated tires in the morning. Things like that.

I entered the sitting room to find a fire already going, casting the room in a toasty haze. I wanted nothing more than to just sit down and relax, but knew that Dean would very literally kill me if I got paint on the furniture.

Dean plucked up two packages off a side table and handed them over to me.

I recognized one as something I had ordered for Carl a few weeks ago. But the other package was a dark, wooden chest. Real wood, not a cardboard package. I saw an emblem carved into it – two ornate letter *D*'s. I accepted it, grunting curiously. The box looked like an antique of some kind, probably worth its weight in gold. I looked up at Dean, frowning. "What is this?"

He shrugged. "It was on your doorstep."

I stared at him, suddenly uneasy. "How the hell did it make it to the doorstep? The Guardians would have eviscerated any mailman." Because griffin sentinels guarded my home, living constructs of stone that didn't play well with trespassers.

Dean met my eyes. "There was no mailman. It was simply *there*. The Guardians saw nothing." Knowing me, he shook his head. "There is nothing dangerous about it. Falco checked."

I nodded slowly, feeling my shoulders relax slightly. My house had checked it for booby traps, which was cool. Like Kai and the tree outside, my house actually contained a Beast as well – one of those sentient beings that typically partnered up with Makers to give them godlike powers. Someone had freed it very long ago, and used my house as a giant spell to trap it. But it didn't seem bothered by this. We were kind of pals. Maybe after a life of being bonded to someone, the Beasts needed some sort of symbiotic relationship with another entity, and were incapable of living on their own.

Regardless, you could say my house was alive, and you would be kind of right.

Punctuating this, my house purred, the beams above our heads seeming to vibrate in a soothing rumble.

"Thanks, Falco," I said, staring down at the box. After Alex's near abduction, I had instantly feared the worst. That this box might contain some sort of trap or bomb of some kind. A gift from Castor Queen. I studied the box more intently, impressed at the quality. "Darling and Dear…" I read out loud. "From Kansas City." I looked up at Dean questioningly.

"Never heard of them," he said, staring at the box. "I tried researching them, but found nothing alarming. Nothing at all, in fact. Like they don't exist."

I grunted thoughtfully. Odd. It sure looked like it came from an established company of some kind. They had a custom wooden shipping box. A new thought hit me. It was almost my birthday. Had Callie Penrose sent me a gift? I wasn't sure if she knew when my birthday was, but Kansas City was her stomping grounds. She hunted monsters for the Vatican there. I tucked both packages under one arm, wanting to open the one for me in private, having no idea what it was, but kind of hoping that it was from the beautiful white-haired wizard.

Because like a schoolboy, I was pretty sure I was crushing on her. Even though neither of us had any time for that sort of thing. "Are they here yet?" I asked Dean. He peeled his curious eyes from the box and nodded. "In the Solarium. I told them you would be along shortly. After you cleaned up. Because you're about to go shower. Like the other vagrants who you let live here."

It wasn't a question.

I chuckled, nodding. "Don't worry. I wouldn't dare risk getting paint on anything."

He grunted, and then pointedly glanced down at my feet and then behind me on the floor. I looked down to find a trail of painted footsteps ending where I stood. I sighed.

"Damn it. I'm sorry, Dean," I said, using my toes to kick off the heels of each boot. Then I picked them up with my free hand and walked back to the door, setting them outside. I would pay for that. I just knew it.

I turned to find Dean only a foot away, peering over my shoulder to verify the boots were outside. He didn't look pleased at my solution, but somewhat mollified that the offending boots were at least outside his safe space. I knew they would be gone, washed, and placed somewhere he preferred before I even made it upstairs.

"Can you make sure they have refreshments while I get cleaned up?" I asked him.

He grunted dismissively. "Already done, of course."

I grinned. "Thanks, Dean. Up high," I said, holding out my free hand.

He grimaced at my hand, since it was also covered in paint, and then turned away without a word, resuming his work on the floor.

I sighed, and walked past him, shaking my head. I glanced down to see I had gotten paint all over the pretty wooden box.

Oh well. I needed to shower and talk to my guests. I didn't have much time before we needed to leave. I could almost feel the clock ticking.

Because me and a small army were about to kick down the doors to the Land of the Fae to save Ashley. Whether they wanted to see us or not. After a long talk with anyone knowledgeable on the strange Fae realm, we had concluded that it was the most likely destination for Pan to have taken her. The time distortion would have been his only hope to save her.

But per some cosmic solicitation rule, Talon had informed us that the doors would only be open to our group during a full moon. Those who had gone before could enter as they pleased – Talon, Carl and myself. But since we had a few more guests joining us – namely Gunnar to get his fiancée back – we had to follow the rules.

Tomorrow was our night to go Trick or Treating.

Wylde purred in anticipation deep inside me.

I ignored him and trudged upstairs to shower.

CHAPTER 7

*F*reshly showered, I walked the halls until I made it to the door leading to the Solarium – a large, glass room that one of my ancestors had added onto the mansion at some point. I opened the doors and inhaled deeply of the floral and vegetative scents permeating the room.

The walls and ceiling were entirely glass, and were absolutely incredible for watching thunderstorms, a favorite pastime of mine since childhood. The room was filled with plants and small trees, several fire pits, and even a small pond with fountains, giving the space a soothing, tranquil feel. The space had been furnished with comfortable couches and lawn chairs and tons of blankets and pillows. It was essentially a greenhouse, and Dean used it for such, with an entire section partitioned off for herbs and vegetables for the kitchens – which had come in handy in recent months when we had been housing a literal army here.

We still had to make trips to the grocery store, but the produce grown here had helped a lot.

I had hired a crew to install large boulders in the room, perfect for my dragon friends to lounge on when they saw fit. I had gotten the idea from Alaric Slate – the late Dragon Lord – before Raego and I had killed him.

The rocks essentially turned the room into a giant lizard aquarium. Yahn freaking loved it in here, using the area to practice his chameleon abilities to play hide and seek with us.

I walked along the gravel path, deeper into the room where I could hear voices talking faintly. I still clutched the box in the crook of an elbow, wanting to keep it within reach. I hadn't wanted to keep my guests waiting, and there was something to be said about postponing the gratification of opening a gift. I was pretty sure it was all in my head, but the box smelled like Callie, and I was forcing myself to be patient until I opened it.

I rounded a corner, ducked under some branches leaning over the path, and saw the Reds and Yahn laying out in full dragon form on the large rocks. Yahn wasn't trying to hide his colors, so resembled a candy-painted dragon – like those cars you see sometimes – a metallic sheen that shifted hues as the light hit it from different angles. As I walked towards him, his scales seemed to change colors. The Reds were nestled up against each other, and all three appeared to be napping, deep rumbling purrs emanating from them, almost making me drowsy.

I turned away to see that the other voices had stopped, and found three figures studying me.

Van Helsing – the notorious monster hunter – lounged on a chair, looking bored.

The Huntress – an ice-cold warrior with never-explained origins – fidgeted absently with an ornate, black wooden bow, caressing it lovingly. A quiver was propped up against her chair.

Baba Yaga – the nightmare old lady from Russian folklore that presumably ate children – sat stiff-backed, watching everyone simultaneously.

Well, technically, there were four people. And I use the term *people* very loosely.

Because Baba Yaga's Familiar – a house with chicken feet – lurked behind her. The house was a creature of some kind, and could change sizes, forms, and do all sorts of creepy things. Currently it resembled a giant, hooded creature with a large beak and long, gnarly chicken legs – the claws peeking out from under the worn, tattered robes.

The Familiar was cute and cuddly – in a gouge your eyes out and run for your lives kind of way. It pinned me with a look, not trying to intimidate me, but simply being its usual self.

"How was London?" I asked, trying not to cringe at the Familiar as I walked up to them and took a seat in one of the chairs. I set the box beside me, noticing their attention on the item.

Recently, I had found a secret area of my house that seemed open to only official Master Temples – ones who had been Makers – those beings who partnered up with their ancient Beasts to truly shake the pillars of the world. They were also known as Tiny Gods, and were usually hunted down by the various gods of the world to act as their tool in the world.

The best way to describe a Maker was to think of wizards compared to regular people. Regular people couldn't do magic, but wizards could do unbelievable things like make fire, lightning, and destroy stuff. Comparing a Maker to a wizard was akin to comparing a wizard to a mortal person. What Makers could do when partnering with their Beasts put wizards to shame. Literally able to *think* something and make it so.

They had pretty much all died out or been hunted down over the years.

I had been one for a short while, before a unique sequence of events had allowed me to free my Beast and ultimately put him – Kai – into the tree outside.

But the first Master Temples had been Makers, and since the house harbored one of their Beasts, she had secret rooms apparently accessible only by those she deemed worthy.

Upon discovering one of these rooms in my mansion, I had noticed a strange round table inside. A round table that rose up out of the ground when I walked by, and seemed to have a stream of liquid metal coursing across the surface.

I had heard stories of another Round Table in the past, used by some certain Knights and a king named Arthur. I had sent these three to go do some research on the story, because I had a sneaking suspicion that my round table was *the* Round Table.

Van Helsing grunted. "Well, not near as eventful as what happened here, apparently," he said, sounding annoyed that he hadn't been allowed to participate in the war that had dominated my property. I was pretty sure Van simply wished he could have had a chance to go toe-to-toe against Achilles. The two had beef for some reason.

I shrugged at him. "Shit happens. We took care of it. Your job was important, too."

The Huntress took a sip of her drink, eyes distant. She had joined them on their quest to London and other parts of England over the past several months, but at some point, my pal, War – the Horseman of the Apocalypse – had abducted her and sent her to the Land of the Fae. He'd been playing the long game, and had known that I would need her over there in order to get my friends out in one piece. Not that he told me this ahead of time or anything.

Because War was a ginormous assface. In the best possible way.

So, the Huntress had found herself in Fae – a place she had promised never to return to – and hadn't been pleased about it. I had gotten her out – well, she and Tory had gotten themselves out by kindling a small spark of true love between them – and had found herself smack dab in the middle of a war rather than returning to drizzly London. She also found herself the caretaker of Alex – the kid we had saved from the Fae.

Which was an entirely new position for the assassin. Looking after a kid, surviving a war, and escaping a nightmare. Obviously, Baba Yaga and Van Helsing had been alarmed as all hell to find her suddenly missing one day, but we had gone over that on the phone, and decided a face-to-face was necessary.

Baba Yaga cleared her throat, waiting until I looked at her to speak. She was a crone in every sense of the word. Wrinkled skin framed a very grand-motherly face, and her eyes – although appearing kind – also had a merci-less cunning to them. She smiled, revealing iron teeth. I was used to it by now, but still.

"We found no validation. We found nothing at all, in fact. No mention of what happened to the Round Table, or if it is even possible for it to be moved. Even though everyone knows the tale of King Arthur and his Round Table, none consider it anything more than a myth," she said in a soft tone. "We checked with sources from the Academy at your request, and although they weren't happy to work with us, they seemed happier to avoid your wrath," she said smiling lightly. "I wonder what you said to give them cause for such concern…"

I smiled lightly, shrugging. "I showed them my magic stick."

She smiled. "Be that as it may, we could find nothing concrete. Perhaps if you would let me actually *see* it—"

I shook my head, cutting her off. "Not possible," I said. The Huntress very pointedly didn't look at me. Because other than her, no one had physi-cally seen it. If I was right, I didn't want anyone knowing where to find it – here, in my house.

Baba sighed, holding out her hands. "Well, what next? If I could see it, I could perhaps test it," she said, trying again to wheedle information from me. Van Helsing was watching me like a tiger, trying to get a read on me, no doubt wondering where it was. Not because he really cared, of course, but because it was an unknown.

I shook my head. "Not yet. Did you try looking into the Knights themselves? Or Arthur? Hell, Merlin?" I asked.

She sighed regretfully. "No. We chased the story, not the people. We were… interrupted. By a week-long nap, if you recall. Then we woke up to find the Huntress missing."

I nodded. "She was taken against her will. I can promise that it wasn't related to your search. Just poor timing."

Baba glanced at the Huntress, but didn't offer a comment.

"War kidnapped me and took me to the Land of the Fae as leverage for Nate to do something," the Huntress admitted, sounding as if forced. Any smart man would have read the tone and realized it was now time to shut their mouths.

But not Van. The dumb shit opened his mouth.

CHAPTER 8

*V*an looked suddenly interested. "Hell of a thing to do, considering your past," he said softly. The Huntress' shoulders stiffened defensively, a subtle warning for him to let it go. He grunted. "I wasn't going to say anything else. Just… kind of a dick move."

"All things considered, I appreciate what he did, believe it or not," she said distantly, no doubt thinking of Alex. Her hand continued caressing her bow. It was carved with images of horses, war and conquest. A cobweb-thin string connected the ends, looking thin enough to break at a breath, but I knew better. The bow had belonged to Bellerophon, the Greek who had first tamed Pegasus. Anyone could draw the bow and shoot at incredible distances. The bow itself seemed to absorb all power, so that even a child could draw the string as far back as Gunnar, for example.

It was a marvel, and I saw that Baba and Van were both eyeing it curiously, because they knew it was a new acquisition, and not knowing things tended to bother them.

She noticed, and grinned. "Spoils of war…" she said. And that could have been taken a few different ways.

Van sighed, shaking his head. "Well, what's next? You already defeated the Greeks…" he trailed off, hoping for me to elaborate on the topic. When I didn't respond, he pressed. "I heard you went through some twisted stuff in Fae. Came back… different." He studied me, as if looking for telltale proof of this. "Killed Athen—"

"I'd really rather not talk about it," I said, allowing Wylde's tone and mannerisms to poke through my calm veneer. That savage side of myself I had found over there. The part of me that had shown me how to kill a god, even though I didn't fully understand it. I was pretty sure that the golden light coursing through my veins at times – and the strange power that had helped me save Alex – were related to that somehow. Because Athena's blood – ichor – had been gold.

But I hadn't wanted to play around with it, and it appeared to be fading from lack of use.

Baba leaned closer, holding out a hand to Van. "I hear Hope is in the air," she said softly.

I grunted. "It always is." I let the silence grow before continuing, not rising to what she had really been asking – about me being the Fifth Horseman of the Apocalypse, the Horseman of Hope. "I need you guys to look into the Knights. You tried the Table, now try the people."

"That… could take some time. There were quite a few of them…" Baba said.

"I'm not a goddamned librarian," Van argued. "I fight and kill things."

I met his eyes very slowly. "You do what I tell you," I warned, letting some of the wildness show through my face again.

Van paled, still unhappy, but I could see the fear in his eyes. How far dare he push me? He had heard the stories. Even been on the receiving end of some of my displeasure. But that was before I had killed a Greek Goddess. Donned a Horseman Mask.

Allegedly.

He sighed. "Fine. Can we take a few days to rest up, first? Then the Huntress can rejoin us—"

"I'll be staying here in St. Louis with Alex and Tory," she said immediately.

The room grew very silent. Baba Yaga looked thoughtful, turning from face to face to gauge the situation.

Van looked frustrated. "No offense, Baba, but your company leaves something to be desired."

She grinned wickedly, flashing her iron teeth at him. "Likewise."

"I need you to leave tomorrow. Just see what you can find. You're being paid well for this, and who knows? If you strike the right flint, you might just have the fight of your life on your hands, Van. That's why I'm trusting this to you. Between you and Baba, I pity the fool who gets in your way. I can check to see who else I can spare to help you," I added, feeling tired. But who else was there? Everyone else was kind of busy.

Van waved a hand. "No, that's fine. We don't need a babysitter. Just…" his eyes grew resigned. "Not used to taking orders."

I nodded, hoping I looked appreciative. I chose not to remind him of his past servitude to Rumpelstiltskin, also known as Silver Tongue. That had ended when I stepped into the game and abducted the little bastard. "Thanks. But I'm not giving *orders*. I'm asking you to do me a favor, because I trust you." I met his eyes levelly. "I'm also paying handsomely for your work…"

Baba smacked his arm – the instinctive gesture that all grandmothers master at some secret ritual before they received their cards. He rubbed his arm, scowling. Then again, a smack from Baba was probably more painful than your typical grandma.

I didn't know a whole hell of a lot about these three – four if you counted the lurking house behind Baba – but they had been kind of a team – forced to work off a debt with Rumpelstiltskin. They had started out as my enemies – like pretty much everyone who hung around me lately – but had soon become friends. Or maybe 'allies' was a better way to describe them.

They were each ruthless and dangerous, but they had displayed their loyalty often enough for me to at least grant them a sliver of trust. Albeit a tiny sliver.

I had redundancies in place in the event they decided to double-cross me. Mainly, that they didn't know that the Round Table resided here inside Chateau Falco. Well, the Huntress knew, but thanks to Tory and Alex, she was pretty much tied to me with chains.

Going back to the Land of the Fae had… changed her. Tory had witnessed a deeper side to the Huntress, and it had been enough to at least ignite a small spark of love between them. The beginning whispers of romance. Maybe Tory had even rubbed off on the Huntress, because the cold-blooded killer suddenly had a maternal instinct to watch over Alex by any means necessary. Whereas before she had seemed almost allergic to anything smaller than an adult, referring to them as *it* more often than not.

It was nice to see my two friends beginning that slow dance around each other. Even if it was in a burning room, like that song. Because being around me was dangerous, as recent events had shown.

I sighed, shoving that thought aside. "You guys need anything else? I'll be out of town for a while…" I said suggestively.

Baba and Van frowned at me, and then, almost in unison, their eyes widened.

"You're going *back*?!" they shouted.

I finally nodded. They might as well know the truth. Grant them another reason to fear me. "Unfinished business," I said, staring down at my inner forearm. A faint tribal design – drawn in blue ink – flared brighter for a moment, and I heard their breaths catch. It had almost completely faded by now, but anytime I thought about going back to the Fae, it seemed to get a little stronger, and Wylde's presence deep inside me climbed closer to the surface.

I wasn't going back to the Fae just for Ashley, but also because I demanded answers from Pan. I wanted to know what my blue tattoos were all about. And my connection with Wylde.

Even though I knew the Fae World was dangerous, I was hoping I had an ace up my sleeve. Oberon, the Goblin King, Master of the Wild Hunt, owed me a favor. I had taken the Mad Hatter – my great grand-whatever, Matthias Temple – out of his realm after a several-hundred-year imprisonment.

You would think this meant Matthias and I were now planning picnics, catching up on old times, family histories, and the like.

But Castor Queen – the one who had originally betrayed Matthias hundreds of years ago, causing his banishment to the Fae – had revealed that he was still alive and well…

By making himself look like me as he murdered Matthias' son, Ichabod.

Even though it had been physically impossible for me to be there when it happened, because I had been fighting Athena at the time. Matthias' emotions, obviously running hot, let him believe what he saw, and there wasn't a chance in hell he was going to listen to anyone else say otherwise.

So, not only did I have my ancestor, Matthias Temple, to worry about. I also had his arch-nemesis, Castor Queen, ruler of the now-defunct Syndicate, to watch out for.

Two Makers – the original founders of the Syndicate, who hated each other – had found a common interest… me, six feet underground.

But rather than holing up at my house and making sure I was safe, I was getting ready to go back to the Land of the Fae. The shitty part was that the last time I had gone there, I had spent what felt like two days there.

And come back to my world almost two months later.

Which meant this trip could have dire consequences if the Makers decided to come after me while I was gone, while my friends were defenseless.

CHAPTER 9

I had no idea how long it would take to find Ashley, but I couldn't afford any time-slippage like that. I could come home to find Castor Queen and Matthias Temple had partnered back up and taken over my house.

Maybe I would talk to Kai and Falco – see if there was anything they could do to keep my home safe. Since they were both Beasts, and had at one point been tethered to a Maker, perhaps they would have some insights.

Otherwise, it was a gamble I had to take.

Ashley was fast becoming Legend. She had killed Hercules, and in her moment of victory, my ex-fiancée, Indie, had stabbed her in the back. But I had gotten vengeance for that.

I noticed the looks in peoples' eyes whenever that topic came up.

Seeing me as a Horseman of the Apocalypse, complete with stone wings and a mask of pure horror, killing my fiancée in cold blood – at the moment she was begging forgiveness.

Most understood my action. Not just because I had been the Horseman of Hope – taking her Hope away at the last moment as payment for her crimes…

But the fact that I, Nate Temple, a simple wizard, would have done the exact same thing.

Not because of any personal reason, though, like most instantly assumed.

Indie had been duped, tricked into becoming a monster. We all had a part to play in that, but Ichabod Temple had been the one to fully turn her – lying to her, manipulating her, and taking her to the Land of the Fae, where she confronted a darker side of herself that she couldn't fight back against.

I had wanted to kill her for her crimes. Time and time again she had done horrible things in the name of vengeance. Ichabod made her think the Syndicate had killed her mom.

But even with all that, I may have forgiven her as a victim. Because I had shown her that her mom was very much alive, and that she had been victim to a great lie. If she would have confessed, apologized, and begged forgiveness at that moment – while her mom was shouting at her for becoming a monster – it could have all ended right there. I would never trust her again, and would have helped lock her up for the good of everyone, but I might not have killed her.

But...

That moment of clarity hadn't gone the way I intended. Well, hoped.

Indie had instead chosen to pursue her war. Immediately, cognitively choosing to pursue her vendetta out of pride. The monster was in charge.

And...

People died as a result.

Ashley had gone toe-to-toe with Hercules, for crying out loud.

And won.

But in her moment of victory, with her back turned, Indie had stabbed her in the back. Literally. Which removed all doubt in my mind.

The bitch had to die. Anything less would make a mockery of everyone who had sacrificed their lives in the war, not even considering avenging Ashley. Who could very likely be dead at this very minute, for all I knew.

Van cleared his throat, watching me nervously. "Need a hand?" he asked softly. I watched him, considering. I'll be honest. My initial assumption was that he was just trying to get out of a boring research trip. Or trying to prove how badass he was. But... there was something in his eyes. He noticed my attention, and straightened his shoulders self-consciously. "I've stood against Ashley, if you remember. She... whooped my ass," he admitted with a faint grin. "That being said, no one deserves what she got as a result of killing Hercules. Especially something so cowardly—"

41

Van cut off abruptly as a new figure entered the room on silent paws. I turned to see a giant white werewolf staring at us. He was in full wolf form, and he stared at Van with one icy, blue eye. The other was stone cold. Literally. The stone eyepatch – sans strings to hold it in place – that resembled the material of his claws that were currently sunk into the gravel walkway. He didn't make a sound.

He.

Just.

Looked.

Van cleared his throat after giving Gunnar a very respectful nod. "It wasn't right. I want to help, if you need it."

Gunnar continued to stare, so I turned back to Van. "I'll talk to him. Let's leave it for now, though. He's... rough around the edges. Understandably." Van nodded, wiping his calloused hands on the knees of his pants. "But the offer means a lot. To both of us."

I glanced back over my shoulder to see that Gunnar was simply gone. I turned back to find Baba climbing to her feet, eyes warily shooting to her surroundings, looking uneasy. Her Familiar did the same. "We'll go rest up for our trip tomorrow."

I nodded, reaching into my pocket. I withdrew two copper rings and handed one to each of them. "Please wear those. It will help me find you if I need to." They stared down at the rings with slight frowns. I had basically asked them to wear a tracking bracelet. "If things go poorly, you might be thanking me later..." I added.

They finally nodded, slipping them over a finger. Van actually flinched as the ring shrunk to fit him. Baba merely grunted, eyes calculating. I had designed them with my magic so that they adjusted to the wearer. Grimm Tech had some pretty cool stuff in the works, even though I hadn't been able to spend as much time there lately as I wanted.

"You guys are more than welcome to stay here," I said, changing the topic.

"Thank you," Baba said. "But I have some things to attend to after my prolonged absence."

"Nothing I would find disagreement with, I hope," I said in a soft tone.

Baba sniffed. "You shouldn't believe everything you hear, Nate."

I met her eyes in silence, and she took a step back. "I don't. Just half."

She lowered her eyes. "Those days are behind me. I didn't have much say in the matter, if you recall. Good riddance to the…" her eyes twinkled suddenly. "What did you call him?"

Despite the change in topic, I smiled at the memory. "Rumpled Foreskin."

She clapped, and her Familiar shifted slightly behind her. "That's it! I was in his employ during many of the stories you've heard, and so didn't have much say in the matter."

I nodded, letting my amusement fade. "Not that it matters to you, but the Syndicate is no more. You shouldn't have any problems. Not that you really did anyway. But you should still keep an eye out for a man named Castor Queen."

As one, they froze. "He died many, many years ago…" Van said, frowning.

I stared back at him in silence for a good ten seconds, and then shook my head. "Evidence says otherwise. I saw him. Here."

"England is sounding better and better," Van mumbled, shivering.

That was… good to know. That even these three – who had inadvertently worked for the Syndicate, thanks to Rumpelstiltskin – had thought Castor Queen dead. I was still a little shocked to hear he was alive. Everyone thought he was dead. But I had heard something from Athena – that Castor Queen had managed to partition himself from his Beast, never fully merging with it. Maybe that was what caused him to keep on ticking.

I wondered exactly how Castor Queen had managed to run the Syndicate from the shadows for so long. Maybe it was time for me to visit the Academy, and have a nice chat with some of their prisoners. Someone had to know something. I knew that trip wouldn't be fun. Even though they had helped me in the war, they weren't particular fans of mine. And to be honest, it probably wouldn't be a bad idea for Callie to join me. To see what the other side of the world was like. She was pretty much immune from the Academy's wrath – thanks to some secret agreement with the Vatican, but knowledge was always helpful. If knowledge didn't start an outright war, anyway.

I'd ask her about it.

Baba clapped her hands. "Since you are dozing, we may as well leave. I'm sure you have better things to do than talk to us."

I sighed. "Sorry. Just a lot on my mind. No disrespect intended."

Van grunted. "None taken. Let me know if you need my help on the other thing. If not, I'll plan on joining this beautiful broad in another dreary trip to England. Maybe we'll see if we can find anything on Avalon."

"Thanks. Keep your options open. If you seek information, be discreet. I don't want this getting out."

They nodded and left. The Familiar sniffed me as he walked past, and I saw his beak actually shift as if made of flesh and not bone. I smiled back into the deep hood, right where his eyes would be. He stared back for a long second, and finally left.

I sat in silence for a time, leaning back in my chair and staring up at the sky above. It was noon, and I had an hour until my next appointment. Enough free time to just sit and think for a while.

Before we dove back into the madness.

CHAPTER 10

J rested my eyes, thumbs tapping the wooden box in my lap. I breathed deeply, relaxing, fighting my urge to open the box and see what was inside. It was hard, because I could imagine Callie behind it all. The devious little shit.

So, it was a battle of wills, me sitting, relaxing, and refusing to open the gift.

Against my childlike desire to destroy the box in my haste.

It was surprisingly light, despite the obvious density of the wood. Not wanting to trigger anything in case it was magical in nature, I didn't dare probe the wood with my powers. Just because Falco hadn't noticed anything dangerous didn't mean that there wasn't a trap for any nosy mail thieves.

I used the rare moment of silence to consider everything.

Baba and Van would head back to England and see if they could uncover anything on my Table situation. I didn't have any real reason for needing to know it, other than sheer curiosity. But… I had grown much more interested in it after coming back from the Land of the Fae, because I didn't need to be as close for it to rise up out of the ground, now.

Before, if I walked right up to it, the stone table would rise up from the ground. But now I merely had to be within a hundred yards of it, or in the secret library itself. I had sent Gunnar into the library – or Sanctorum – to see if it was raised when I wasn't present, but he had told me it wasn't. Still, something *had* changed when I went to the Fae.

We were connected somehow.

Which pretty much confirmed that it was important. But my ancestors had been known for swiping up any trace of power to hoard for themselves. I just wanted to confirm or deny that it was the actual fabled Round Table, or if it was something else entirely.

The only one I could have asked about it was Matthias – who currently wanted me dead.

I sighed tiredly. I had hoped that all the chaos would die down after defeating Indie and her crew of Greeks. But I had been wrong. Castor Queen had found a way to enter the fray – masked in his flock of Syndicate Wizards – landing him smack-dab on my property, and cloaked from suspicion. The fact that no one seemed to know Castor Queen was still alive was both comforting and alarming. He had run the group of anti-Academy wizards from behind the scenes, much like that wizard from Oz.

I would need to check up on Chateau Falco's defenses, making sure it was safe from either of the lunatics, while I was gone. Chateau Falco must be kept safe. There was simply way too much dangerous shit here to leave anything to chance.

Then, if we survived long enough in Fae, I needed to talk to Oberon – Pan's brother, or whatever the two were in relation to each other. They were either different facets of the same person, or literal brothers. Oberon led the Wild Hunt and was king of the goblins.

Which was news to me. It seemed every time I thought I knew something, I was wrong. I had thought Oberon and the goblin king were different people entirely. But I had been wrong. Then there was the third angle.

Robin Goodfellow, or Puck, as most knew him. He also had ties to the brothers, maybe yet another facet of the same being, and he also lived in Fae.

No matter how it all panned out, I had done Oberon a service by removing Matthias from the Land of the Fae. And no matter how much I regretted how it had all turned out, I had inadvertently done Oberon a solid.

So, he owed me. Whether he saw it that way or not.

But first, we needed to find Pan – hoping he had succeeded in saving Ashley.

And I had to make sure that my friends stayed safe while there. Not just from the very obvious monsters who lived there, but from themselves.

Because going to the Land of the Fae woke up a very distant, primal version of oneself. It was what had broken Indie. She hadn't been able to remain in control, and had instead succumbed to the allure, becoming a monster, in fact.

I had gone there once, and brought my friends back safely, keeping them in control of their darker sides, but now I was getting ready to return for round two. I had come up with a crew to go with me, but I still debated endlessly on whether I should include some of them.

Gunnar was a requirement. One, because he would kill anyone who told him otherwise. Two, because it was his freaking fiancée. And the two would need their love to be able to leave again. Just in case I couldn't take us out on my own.

Alucard wanted to go as well, and since he was extremely dangerous when provoked, I agreed with him. The Fae had also expressed interest in him at one point, and I thought Alucard could use a boost of self-confidence, proving to the Fae that he wasn't scared. He was also the only one strong enough – other than me – to help keep Gunnar in line, if the wolf got out of hand.

Because going to the Fae would change us, and I might need his help if we turned on each other. Even though the obvious argument was that he and Gunnar could *both* go crazy and team up against *me*.

I also wanted to take Grimm, my pet unicorn, and his brother, Pegasus. Strictly because they were hyper-violent creatures and already very in touch with their darker natures. Also, I needed someone to fly us around so we could cover more ground, faster. And if shit really went sideways, I would need my horse in order to use my Horseman Mask to its full extent.

Talon was also coming, because he was the most knowledgeable on the place. He could control himself, and hopefully us, as well.

I had thought about taking Carl, but with all the other badasses joining me, I had wanted to keep someone here at Chateau Falco as a back-up, and everyone seemed scared of Elders.

Needing another set of wings, in case Ashley was still hurt, I had also contemplated taking the biggest virgin that God had ever created.

Yahn – my sparkly dragon.

Talon, surprisingly, had agreed with that notion. He had studied Yahn in silence for quite some time, and then nodded. *There is something about him yet to be uncovered. I think you will all be very surprised to see it. Not a darkness, per se... but something beautifully cruel.*

Coming from Talon, that was actually a compliment, and probably wasn't as horrifying as he made it sound. Because Carl and Talon could trade shot for shot on creepy comments to describe normal, everyday things.

My other concern about going to the Fae was... well, me.

Getting back in touch with Wylde, the darker side of me.

I wasn't concerned about losing myself. I was more concerned about learning things about myself that I would rather not learn. Because something very odd had happened last time I went there. I had... memories as Wylde. I hadn't checked with the others to see if they had experienced something similar for themselves, because if they hadn't, they would become even more scared of me. But Talon also said he had memories of me, which startled him considerably.

Was it just trickery of some kind?

Because Wylde wasn't *real*.

I had met many Fae while over there, even the Queens, and they hadn't known Wylde at all, nor had they heard of him. Because at first, I had thought that maybe Wylde had been some wandering spirit who had decided I would be a perfect vessel to help him escape Fae.

Despite the truth of Wylde, I needed to know more about him. Because he had helped me kill a goddess. Those odd blue tattoos that hadn't washed off my skin when I returned – seemingly drawn with Fae blood – had given me immense power. They had acted as an armor of sorts against Athena, protecting me from harm while we fought. Somewhat, anyway. And it had shocked the hell out of me to realize that I still had them, because they had seemed to disappear after I killed Athena.

Speaking of...

Killing her had given me golden tattoos of sorts, filling my veins with golden light. And as of this morning, another creepy voice hanging out in my cranium.

Long story short, what the actual fuck was wrong with me?

Everywhere I went, I picked up some new magical disease.

And I was about sick and tired of it. Granted, it had helped me out of a lot of situations, but I hated not knowing things about myself.

CHAPTER 11

*T*he only person who could answer those questions about me – because he had secretly watched over me my entire life – was Pan.

Thinking of the Wild God, I hoped his arrival in Fae – if that was where he had gone – had gone unnoticed, and that using his power to save Ashley hadn't attracted the wrong kind of attention. Or that he had used so much power that he was now defenseless.

I needed to find them. Now.

Talon had let me know that I should be able to get everyone back on my own if Pan was unable for some reason. Talon could hop back and forth at will, having grown up there. Also, Grimm and Pegasus could traverse all sorts of planes of existence, apparently, so they had a bus ticket home as well.

Which left Yahn and Alucard shit out of luck if Pan or I couldn't get them back.

I had informed them of this possibility repeatedly, but they had persisted. Yahn wanted to prove himself to us, and Alucard wanted to help Gunnar. The two couldn't be dissuaded.

Thinking of who else I might take with me, I came up with a very short list. Raego – the king of the dragons – and Van Helsing.

Raego was busy ruling a nation, though. And I didn't want to introduce him to his dark side. Because a small part of me already had concerns about Raego. When I had first met him, he had seemed slightly off in the mental department. Power hadn't helped that. He seemed... distant lately. He was also currently trying to keep his dear grandmother from asserting too much control with his subjects, which was comical to hear about. I had whooped her ass once, and she wasn't pleased about that, so we hadn't spent much time around each other.

And I was also pretty sure I didn't want to see Van Helsing's darker side, either.

I realized I was no longer drumming the box in my lap, but fiddling with a coin, rolling it back and forth over my knuckles. I put it away with a weary sigh. My Mask, given to me by Matthias. I kept it in my pocket as a coin, for ease of convenience.

The Mask let me tap into the powers of a Horseman. The Fifth Horseman of the Apocalypse, which sounded like a ridiculously poor plot for an action flick. Still, I had donned the Mask of Hope twice now. The second time had much more... noticeable results.

Mainly, that it had given me freaking stone wings.

And I had healed Gunnar from near death, permanently changing him in the process.

Which pretty much told me that I was going to be a Horseman. Whether I wanted it or not.

Just as I was considering sneaking off to try and have a chat with one of the Horsemen, I heard voices approaching from the entrance. The two red dragons stirred, and I looked up to see that Yahn was also alert, staring at the approaching sounds.

Alucard arguing with Carl.

"I don't care if it itches. Stop scratching. It's disgusting."

"Peeling off skin is pleasing to me. Always has been," Carl argued.

"Carl, we talked about this. Think about your words before speaking them. Unless you want Nate to reinstate his hand-raising rule before you are allowed to comment."

Carl hissed. "Wylde has granted me command of his minions in your absence. He, too, understands the importance of indulging in self-pleasure."

"Fucking Carl," I heard Gunnar chime in, chuckling. "And I wouldn't call them *minions* where they can hear you, Carl."

The three men rounded the corner to find me smiling at them, shaking my head. Alucard sighed. "You heard all that?" he asked, jerking a thumb at the albino-scaled Elder – a man-sized lizard person, wearing an assortment of leather straps as clothing. He was scratching his neck absently, then groaned as his eyes rolled back into his head, his second set of eyelids, flicking upwards as he blinked, peeling away a foot-long swathe of dead scales from the crest around his neck. He moaned, holding out the strip of skin before him. His tongue flickered out, tasting it. Then he flung it at Alucard, who jumped back with a disgusted sound.

Alucard flung out a hand, pointing at Carl as he shot me a pleading look. "He's fucking crazy. And disgusting. Tell him, Nate. He won't listen to anyone else. Dean almost had a panic attack when Carl licked him."

"He told me to stop pleasuring myself in public places," Carl rasped.

Gunnar chuckled again, shaking his head as he sat down heavily beside me, shoving me to scoot over or else he was going to sit in my lap. I growled and moved over, turning at a sound on my other side. I flinched to find Talon sitting in Baba's chair, staring at me in utter silence.

"Jesus Christ!" I hissed. "Put a fucking bell on or something," I said, trying to calm my suddenly racing heart.

"I am not Jesus Christ. I am Talon. The Devourer."

"Greetings, Devourer," Carl said politely, dipping his head at him. Then a thought seemed to cross his face as he watched Talon licking his paws and using it to wipe the beard of fur under his chin. He pointed a long, black claw. "He pleasures himself at least once an hour, and no one seems to care."

Talon sighed, lowering his paw. Then he looked at me. "He truly doesn't have a clue."

I nodded.

Carl flicked his tongue out curiously, as if sensing something. His head snapped to the box in my lap. Then his eyes narrowed angrily. "Poor taste," he hissed before glaring at me.

I frowned, and then glanced down at the box. Talon leaned closer, reading it. "Oh, that is very nice. I didn't even notice it. I wondered why you hadn't shopped there before."

I blinked at the two of them. "Excuse me?" I said, answering both statements with all the wit I could muster.

"Elder hide," Carl said, sitting down across from me, jerking his head at the box. "Although it is from Darling and Dear, I would have appreciated forewarning."

"Says the guy who honors his enemies by using their bones as weapons," Alucard muttered drily. He pointed at the box. "What the hell is Darling and Dear, and what is he talking about with Elder hide?"

I shrugged. "I have no idea," I said, frowning down at the box. Elder hide? "Dean said he found the box at the front door."

"You haven't opened it yet? That's not like you," Gunnar said, eyeing me.

I smiled guiltily. "I think Callie sent it..."

Carl looked suddenly protective of me. "Have you checked it for..." he hesitated, squinting. Then he glanced over at the Reds. "What did you tell me it was called?"

Straight-faced, Sonya replied. "Cooties. A very contagious toxin."

Yahn's jaw dropped open, but Carl took this as proof that it was dangerous. He turned back to me. "Have you checked it for cooties? I believe Callie is a female, and may have unknowingly contracted it. You shouldn't risk getting sickened by cooties before your journey."

Gunnar coughed, actually biting his fist. Alucard just shook his head in bewilderment, shooting a smirk back at the two red dragons. They winked back at him.

I cleared my throat. "I've checked it for cooties, Carl. We're all safe."

"Master Temple is wise," Carl said, nodding reverently before motioning for me to continue as he leaned closer, tongue flickering a few times.

I sighed, and unclasped the metal latch on the box. Then I opened it, holding my breath as I wondered again how the box had gotten to my front door. It definitely hadn't been shipped here.

Silver tissue paper was neatly folded around something inside, and a black silk ribbon was tied around it with a small card tucked underneath. I pulled out the card, and a ten-dollar bill fell onto my lap. I grinned, knowing exactly who it was from, now. I glanced at the small card, the size of a business card, and read it, my smile stretching wider.

"What does it say, man? Is it from Callie?" Gunnar growled, trying to read it over my shoulder. "And what's up with the dollar bill?"

"Use your good eye, Gunnar. It's a ten," Alucard teased. "You always pick the wrong side to leer from. It's painful to watch, honestly."

Gunnar scowled at him, but he was smiling.

I read it out loud. "See you at eight-o'clock."

Like men everywhere, we celebrated my victory with smug smiles for a few moments. Then Talon spoke up. "And the ten-dollar-bill?"

Carl chimed in. "I don't understand. Is she offering to buy your sex?"

CHAPTER 12

*T*he Reds burst out laughing, and pretty soon, everyone but Carl –
who looked confused – was joining in. I turned to Carl, shaking
my head. "I made Callie a bet a few months ago about her boss. She bet me
ten bucks I was wrong." I held up the money triumphantly. "Looks like I was
right."

"And she obviously knew you would never let her pay you, trying to
hold it over her head, so she cleverly bought you a gift and hid the money
inside," Gunnar chuckled.

I nodded, staring down at the neatly wrapped package. Callie had indeed
tried to send me my ten dollars. Repeatedly. I had returned it every time.
Gunnar reached to snatch it out of my hands and I slapped his wrist playfully, angling it away from him. Seeing the gleam in his eye, I decided I
better hurry up. I hastily untied the ribbon and tore away the paper to
reveal a sleek, white scaled expanse of leather, like crocodile skin.

I held it up, frowning in confusion.

"This is a purse, is it not?" Carl asked, idly rubbing his arms as if imagining his own skin used to make it.

"Satchel, you assholes. How many times do I need to say it? Satchel, not
purse. Hermes is the messenger god, and he fucking *loved* satchels. You're
disrespecting Hermes by calling it a purse. Men had them long before
women." They all studied me with very patient eyes, as if this were an inter-

vention. "Fucking dickheads," I muttered, turning the satchel over in my hands, inspecting it. I wouldn't have necessarily picked the color, but there was no doubt it was exquisite. It also felt very cold, as if it had been sitting in a freezer. But it wasn't stiff. It was flexible, as if broken in, but I could tell it hadn't ever been used. The strap was made of black chain – not painted metal, but something tougher, and naturally black. Almost like…

"Is that made out of dragon's scales?" Yahn asked, mortified. I glanced up to see the three dragons staring at us, sniffing the air.

"Um… maybe?"

"Someone *melted* a black dragon's scales to make a strap for a purse?" Aria asked, sounding stunned.

I glared at her. "SATCHEL!" I snapped.

"Awww, look at the wizard get defensive over his girlfriend's purse," Alucard teased.

I sighed, realizing that any reaction on my part would simply cause them to gang up on me. "I didn't think that was possible. To melt a dragon's scale. Especially not a black one…" I added thoughtfully.

Gunnar leaned closer. "I'm pretty sure I heard Raego saying that was impossible. The scale – once heated up enough – would simply turn to ashes. And when I say heated up enough, I mean like the temperature of a small sun, or something." He met my eyes, face thoughtful. "Callie buys you a…" his eye twinkled at the instant glare I shot him, "a *satchel* made from an Elder's hide and re-forged black dragon's scales… for, what? A birthday gift?" He let the silence grow for a minute as I stared down at the bag. "Are you and Callie… dating?" he asked.

I opened my mouth to argue, but then thought about it. "You are!" Alucard hooted.

I shook my head instantly. "No, that's not why I paused," I argued. "We're not. But…" I turned to meet everyone's eyes, one after the other. "This thing had to cost… a shitload of money. And Callie doesn't have a shitload of money. Not even close…"

"I stand by my claim that she is trying to buy your body for carnal pleasures. It is only logical. She will see you at eight tonight for your sex. When courting, one often spends above their means, or does an extravagant act to prove that they are worth sexing," Carl said, folding his arms stubbornly.

Alucard burst out laughing. "He's actually not wrong on that one, but I might have said it differently."

"That is because you are uncivilized, Glampire," Carl said, looking smug.

"Uncivilized?" Alucard stammered, laughing loudly. "Okay. Fine. I don't sell my sex, so I'm uncivilized—" His eyes shot over to the Reds, who looked extremely attentive. "You say one word of this conversation to Tory and I'll take away your cars."

Their eyes tightened, but they very wisely remained silent.

I studied the satchel intently. It wasn't blindingly white or anything, but it definitely wouldn't be mistaken for any other color. But again... it didn't look fresh off the rack, but almost distressed. Then I realized why. The skin it had been made from had likely been hundreds of years old. I looked up at Carl.

"How long do you guys typically live?" I asked him.

Instead of answering, he extended a claw, reaching for the satchel. I handed it over. He licked it with his tongue a few times, and Alucard actually retched. When Carl pulled away, he looked about as surprised as I had ever seen. He met my eyes, handing it back with a very thoughtful look. "That skin is over two-thousand-years old... I'm fairly certain the skin is impenetrable after that long."

I almost dropped the bag in disbelief. Talon grunted in surprise, even stopping his incessant cleaning – of his ears, this time.

"Oh..." I said, studying the satchel with more care and not a small amount of trepidation. I opened it, glancing inside, where it was dark and soft, like calfskin. Two pockets decorated the front, and a thick black buckle – that looked to be designed by God himself, etched with microscopic runes that I couldn't begin to read without a magnifying glass – would hold it closed. From the sudden thrum of energy that I felt when I touched the buckle, I was betting something magical, and very powerful was indeed inscribed there. But to be carved so small, it had to be very, very strong, or there were many different spells carved into it. I didn't know which was more impressive.

Long story short, it might be the coolest thing I had ever seen.

Gunnar nudged me with an elbow. "So, date night, eh?"

I found myself grinning despite my doubts on their assessment. "It probably is worth selling my sex for. God knows I've sold it for less." Gunnar clapped me on the back, laughing loudly.

"Well, it looks like we need to get you through this meeting so you can sell your sex," Alucard grinned.

I tensed, glancing down at my watch. Shit. He was right. I had almost forgotten about it in my excitement. "It's in ten minutes," I cursed.

Gunnar nodded, tossing a card onto the table. "Little heavy-handed, don't you think?" he asked, pointing at it.

I set the satchel back in the box, staring at the card.

The Godkiller demands your presence for tea and cupcakes.

I shrugged. "I have tiny balls. I have to overcompensate where I can."

Alucard burst out laughing, shaking his head. His eyes did latch onto my forearms, though, noticing my golden veins glowing for a moment. They did that whenever the Godkiller conversation was brought up.

"Still no idea what that's all about?" Talon asked softly, indicating my arms. His silver eyes watched me, giving away nothing.

"I have plenty of guesses, but nothing solid."

"And you don't want anyone else to know that part, I presume," Talon asked.

I nodded. "Exactly. Everyone knows more than they let on, which I understand. I'm not expecting anyone to share their every confidence, but I do expect some answers."

"Well, in demanding your answers this way, you may have offended some of them. The Old Ones are like that," Talon purred, sounding excited at the prospect of pissing off some important people. Gunnar frowned over at him, having to turn around, making it very obvious. He would need to work on his subtlety. Especially since he had a disco ball where his missing eye should have been. Discreet, he wasn't.

"Time to domi-Nate," I said.

Alucard groaned. "That's not a *thing!*" he said, sounding exhausted. "You can't just keep saying it, expecting it to just happen."

Gunnar shrugged, leaning back into his chair. "Who's staying?" he asked me, not turning to look. But he was staring at the three dragons pointedly, making his opinion clear. The kids shouldn't be here.

I smiled darkly. "Oh, they're staying. You're *all* staying. You were part of the war, and are each fairly famous as a result. This is going to be fun. You guys are going to sit here looking serious and threatening. No smiles, unless you can manage Talon's horrifying smile, the one that promises to enjoy murdering you while you sleep."

Talon snorted. "My smiles are delightful. You haven't seen the murderous smile yet. I save that one for when I use the innocent eyes to draw my victim in…"

Alucard stared at Talon, shaking his head.

I told them the rest of my plan, and although they looked concerned, they also knew that their opinions didn't really matter right now. I had called the meeting, and I was telling them how it was going to go down. If they didn't like the rules, they could leave.

No one left.

Time for Master Temple to have a meeting with the scariest fuckers on the block.

Gods.

But it wasn't really Nate Temple hosting the meeting.

It was the Godkiller, and he had a fetching new satchel from a girl he kinda liked.

CHAPTER 13

*T*he guests stared back at me, waiting patiently. They had each sworn peace while entering Chateau Falco, since it was required to prevent an instant Karmageddon – for any slights or offenses performed in the past several centuries.

None of the parties were enemies as far as I was aware, but every guest was millennia old, so who knew what shenanigans they had gotten into in their rebellious years? I wasn't about to chance that here in my home.

The Four Horsemen – cloaked and hooded – sat on one of the rocks beside the dragons, watching the gathering in silence. I couldn't see their Masks through their hoods, which was probably best for everyone. They didn't make for nice dreams.

Ganesh and Shiva sat side-by-side, talking lightly to each other, playing patty-cake with each of their four hands, increasing the tempo until it was just a blur. Then they both stopped at precisely the same instant, and slowly turned to stare at the Reds – who were watching them, amazed – with straight faces. The Reds blushed furiously, shifting uncomfortably as if they had been caught doing something inexplicably rude. Then the two gods burst out laughing, and the teenagers sighed in relief.

Shiva was in full splendor, flashing his third eye at everyone. He touched it at one point, and then used it to wink at Gunnar, indicating his eyepatch. Gunnar, not knowing what else to do, nodded back politely. Ganesh was in full elephant-man form, a crimson toned figure as large as the Minotaur, Asterion, who was calmly sitting beside him.

I hadn't seen much of him lately, except for when Gunnar, Alucard and I visited the Fight Club he and Achilles held every week to brush up on our fighting and to let off some steam. I think he still felt guilty for being on the opposite side from me in the Greek war.

Achilles sat beside Alucard, looking tense and uncertain. Understandable, since he had also been on the other side during the war. Even if he and Asterion had only been pretending to help Indie at the time. He was in his war garb, his helmet sitting beside him, resting on top of his shield and spears. His armor shone dully in the rays of sunlight streaking through the tree branches overhead.

Dean had found a way to let the animals in, so Pegasus, Grimm, Shiva's bull – Nandi – and Ganesh's rat – Krauncha – stood in a huddle, watching us with hyper-intelligent eyes. Nandi and Asterion eyed each other several times, faces thoughtful. Which was downright hilarious to me, since they were both bulls. Kind of.

Talon was playing – of all things – Cat's Cradle with Carl, barely hiding the smirk on his face at Carl's frustration with the dexterity required.

Tory was leaning back against the Reds – who were in full dragon form – and the Huntress and Alex were sitting about as close as possible to the trio as well, also using them as furniture.

I wasn't sure if Yahn was present, utilizing his invisibility skills to study my guests, or if he had left the room to practice his dancing. It was his form of meditation – to rage out to the loudest techno possible and mimic having a seizure in the privacy of his room. Whatever.

I sat on a small couch beside Gunnar. Hugin and Munin flew down from the trees around us, and perched on either end of the couch, one beside Gunnar and one beside me. They hadn't spoken yet, so I couldn't tell which was which. But it had the desired effect, sending everyone into silence.

"I'm glad you could all make it," I began, lifting my glass in cheers. Everyone did the same by reflex, and then followed my lead as I took a drink. Gunnar was first, but I made sure everyone took a sip of the tea Dean had prepared. Gunnar opened his mouth, cleared his throat audibly, and then continued to do so again, but this time there was no sound, despite him obviously trying very hard to make some.

The guests watched this in confusion, and then Gunnar casually pointed at his cup, and leaned back with a smug smile, folding his beefy arms behind his neck. I let the silence build for a few moments, until they started to realize what had just happened. Eyes suddenly shot wide, and a few began to fidget anxiously, but before anyone could grow too alarmed, I held up a hand.

"Relax. It's not permanent, and it is not an attack. You have been… sworn to silence." Suddenly hard, angry eyes latched onto me. Because I had spelled the drinks, preventing anyone from speaking for about thirty minutes. Since this was no attack – they had just seen Gunnar a victim of the same drink – they couldn't retaliate. And it would be rude for them to leave after I just told them they were perfectly safe. So… they were stuck here, forced to listen in silence.

To the Godkiller.

"You see Gunnar is experiencing no ill effects, so that is proof you will all survive having your tongues stilled for thirty minutes or so. We all know you haven't had a problem doing that in the past," I added in a dark tone. Several cheeks puffed red at either the insult or with guilt, I wasn't sure which. "I wanted to make it abundantly clear that this isn't a discussion. I have asked you here to tell you things. I don't need your opinions or persuasions, and at this point, I don't really care what either of those are. No matter how important you are, or how many people worship you…" I took a sip of my drink with an exaggerated motion, flashing the crowd of angry faces an overly polite smile. "Sucks, doesn't it? Being forced to use your ears, rather than your mouths. But this whole soiree was also designed to point out something. Plenty of you here right now have decided to not use your mouths in the past, so I thought this fitting."

I cleared my throat, and began to lay the hammer down. "In recent years, I have come against foes and forces that should have been well beyond my ability to handle. But I overcame them all with the help of friends. After the fact – almost every single time – I have learned that one, some, or all of you had held back information that could have been vitally helpful – possibly even saved lives." I leaned forward, and the ravens behind me screamed, startling everyone.

"Nevermore," I growled, just like we had rehearsed. "This is very literally the last time you will keep your mouths shut around me if you have something useful to share." With a whisper of thought – emotion, really – I allowed the golden light to flash through my arms. My eyes also flared brighter for a moment, judging by the startled looks I received.

I smirked, nodded, and then leaned back in my chair, pulling out my coin and rolling it over the backs of my fingers. I let this silence build for a few moments before stopping, as if at a thought. "Each of you is aware of everyone present. Right?" They slowly nodded, still angry, but many of them hiding their true emotions behind poker faces. These were the guilty, and unfortunately, it was almost everyone in the room. "This means that you all know exactly who heard this message, this warning. You're all aware that you're in exactly the same boat. But rather than me demanding you to give over information in front of your associates, I will allow you to come to me in private to share what information you see fit. This way no one knows who tells me what, and by not knowing what has already been told to me, it would behoove you to be utterly honest. Consider your prior omissions as a free pass. Future omissions or lies will not be tolerated. I am here to stay, a Godkiller. And… it's probably smart to be nice to the Godkiller, if you know what I mean…" I winked at them.

One by one, they returned stiff nods.

"Good. Now, Dean will hand you a list of questions and topics before you leave. Namely, I want information. Anyone with knowledge on the whereabouts of Castor Queen or Matthias Temple. Updates on the war we just won against the Greeks, and if any of the Olympians are planning something. Or if anyone has knowledge of my parents and what else they may have been involved in. There are a few other things on the list, but those are the big ones. Any questions so far?"

They shook their heads. I had to bite back a smile at Shiva and Ganesh – who were grinning at each other. Even though they were as guilty as the rest, they approved of my response. That was a start.

"Now, I know you all had your reasons to keep things from me, but that ends now. I am not an enemy, and neither are my friends. We have proven time and again that we are here to help, putting ourselves at great risk to do so. Our actions speak very loudly, if rumors are true. This is me drawing a line in the sand. Because I've been told something much bigger than all of us is coming. A war that will make everything we've seen so far look like…" I glanced at War with a faint smile, "a bar fight. We should be on the same side. Nod if you agree. For everyone to see."

One by one, although some unhappily, they all complied. I snapped my fingers and Dean entered with a tray of cupcakes. "Refreshments, if you wish," he said in a formal tone.

Gunnar reached down and took a big bite of the cupcake. A few seconds after swallowing, he smiled. "These are good," he said, dipping his head in thanks at Dean.

The guests blinked in surprise, and then each reached in haste for their own cupcake. Within seconds, a dull hum of voices filled the room as they realized the cupcakes had restored their voices. I let them do this for a few moments, watching as they slowly turned back to face me, eyes calculating.

"Now, if anyone has something they don't mind sharing in front of the others, you may do so. If not, seek me out later. But know that if I seek *you* out, answers will be due immediately. No waffling."

Shiva cleared his throat, grinning mischievously. "I like your moves, Temple. Not pleased to be on the receiving end, but we all deserved it. No matter how justified we were. You've earned our trust. But you also need to understand our trepidation…"

I nodded. "I do. That's why I'm not punishing anyone for past omissions."

He chuckled, shaking his head absently, as if still coming to grips with being coerced or forced into treating me as an equal. Then his eyes flickered to the golden light on my arms again, and his smile faded, remembering that I had earned that right. "Well," he continued. "Your friends made quite the impression during the war. Not just you, but they, as well. I was hoping to meet the one who killed Hercules…" he said curiously, eyes roving over my friends. Gunnar didn't flinch, but I could sense he was as tight as a wire. When no one else spoke, Shiva continued. "Some other time, then. Matthias Temple has sought… sponsorship. None of us have dared respond after what you did to Athena."

I grunted. That was something. Knowing that Matthias had tried to find a god to help him kill me wasn't good news, but at least it let me know he was doing something. "He thinks I killed his son, Ichabod. I can assure you I didn't. I was busy fighting Athena at the time."

"We heard," Shiva muttered drily.

"Well, if any of you talk to him in the future, maybe casually mention that I didn't kill Ichabod. If I did, I wouldn't be hiding it from him. I would flat out admit it."

Ganesh glanced at Shiva, who nodded to let him know he was finished.

"Are you a Horseman?" the elephant-headed god asked, staring from Gunnar's stone eyepatch to me.

The room grew tense at that. I glanced over at the Four Horsemen, who hadn't made a sound. They simply watched the proceedings. They stared right back at me, giving me nothing.

I turned back to Ganesh, pulling out my coin. "I think everyone saw what happened with Indie…" I said vaguely, because I wasn't entirely sure myself, and I didn't think the Horsemen knew either.

Ganesh's brow furrowed, but he didn't have any other questions.

CHAPTER 14

*A*chilles cleared his throat. "I think we're good. If we need to have a talk in private for you to... vent some frustrations, let me know when." It wasn't said in a snarky or threatening tone. Just an honest statement. I nodded, happy to hear it. "I think you know my motivations, and although guilty of what you said, my end game has always been rooting for you." This time he did smirk at the end. "You little shithead."

I couldn't hide my grin. "Thanks, you big shithead."

He nodded in agreement. "Now, from what I understand, the Syndicate is pretty much toast. You sent the rest of them packing to the Academy, where they are currently under guard. Castor Queen – who I actually thought had died a long time ago – has apparently been running their operation behind the scenes this whole time, right?" I nodded. "And he stole the Syndicate from Matthias Temple in the first place, framing him for crimes he himself committed?" Again, I nodded. Achilles grew pensive, considering this. "I would keep a very close eye on the Academy and the Syndicate. If I was either one of those two Makers, I would be angling to get back my army to come take you out. Or to take each other out." He grimaced at a new thought. "Any chance of them forgiving each other and teaming up to take you out?"

Asterion snorted audibly, both disgusted at the lack of honor that would entail, and in concern. I sighed loudly. "I sure hope not. I'd rather not have to face them together. I had hoped to get them to confront each other. But I'll do whatever is necessary."

Shiva studied me thoughtfully, his third eye seeming to shine brighter for a moment. "What's Asgard's stake in all this? They've been oddly silent in recent years," he asked, studying the ravens perched on my couch. "Does your ultimatum apply to the Allfather, too?"

"I've never met Odin," I answered honestly. "My ultimatum applies to only those gods I've personally worked with. I'm arrogant, but I haven't reached that level of pride, to think the whole world revolves around me." I smiled lightly. "Although some might argue that my level of arrogance climbs pretty high," I added, my smile stretching wider.

"The boy and his dog are a good team," Hugin cawed, offering up his opinion, even though I hadn't asked for it. As if rehearsed, Gunnar silently raised a fist my way, not even turning to look. I didn't look either as I punched fists with him. As only childhood friends can attest, we both did the explody hand motion after. Alucard muttered something full of jealousy behind us, but we ignored him.

"I'm sure the Allfather would be open to a meeting in the near future," Munin agreed.

I tried to hide my surprise at that. It was literally the first time they had said anything concrete about their master, even though I was entirely confident he had watched me battle Athena. But I didn't need anyone else to see my surprise, so I nodded matter-of-factly.

Because when in doubt, go balls out.

"Other than the two Makers, what else is on your plate at the moment, Temple? This feels very much like the calm before the storm," Ganesh asked me, caressing his broken tusk absently.

Talon piped up at a slight nod from me. "We're going on vacation tomorrow. Which is another reason Temple wanted to have this meeting. We might be gone for some time..."

The room grew brittle. "You're... going *back*?" Asterion whispered loudly.

Talon shrugged, looking bored. "Everyone keeps asking that. The place is really quite beautiful this time of year. So many lovely things to kill..."

"But why?" Shiva asked, leaning forward, ignoring Talon's remark. "Surely there is nothing of interest to you in the Fae. I imagine they were quite pleased to see you leave, as a matter of fact. After you stole the blade that could kill a god from them."

I almost blinked in surprise. They thought I had taken a blade from the Fae? I suddenly began to feel very concerned. Weren't they supposed to be practically all-knowing?

"There was no blade," I corrected. "Just knowledge and willpower. But we're not going back for that…"

Gunnar leaned closer, meeting Shiva's gaze. One eye versus three just wasn't fair, but I guessed between the two of them, it amounted to the same total of four eyeballs. "We're going to save Hercules' slayer. My fiancée. Maybe scoop up Pan if we have time," he added as an afterthought.

Asterion grunted, looking even more concerned.

"So, that's where they went…" Shiva murmured. Then he looked up. "You should know you can only go during a full moon." Then he stared at me thoughtfully. "Well, those who have never been before must go during a full moon."

I nodded. It was a step in the right direction. A god offering advice ahead of time. "Thank you. We are aware." I smiled at him, letting him know I appreciated the sentiment of him offering helpful advice up front. He winked back with his third eye. I also wanted everyone to see someone offering advice, and me already knowing the answer, which would put them on edge, hopefully guaranteeing they would tell the truth in the future, unsure if I was already cognizant.

"How are you going to work around the time slippage? Last time you went you were gone for almost two months…" Asterion asked, leaning forward.

I let the silence build for a time, hoping that someone else might offer a solution. I had researched this very question like a mad man over the past few weeks. Othello had scoured thousands of pages of lore in hopes of finding some hidden answer, but we had come up with nothing. When no one else spoke – since none of them were Fae and likely had no idea either – I spoke. "I don't have an answer to that yet. Our goal is to move fast and mitigate the effects as best we can. I have safeguards in place to keep Chateau Falco safe in my absence," I said, pointing at Carl. "The Elder, along with a plethora of other safeguards, will protect the house in my absence. In case Castor or Matthias show up."

Shiva grunted. "I don't think anyone will be stupid enough to attack your home with two Beasts present," he chuckled. At my questioning look, he elaborated, waving all four hands in explanation. "Your Beasts – Falco and Kai – are wild and somewhat free. In simple terms, do a house and tree take more effort to destroy than a human body?" he asked.

I nodded slowly, not having thought about it in that way. "Kai made it sound like he had physical limitations. That he was bound to the tree."

Shiva nodded. "Until he has fully recuperated. He can leave the tree at any point, although he would be vulnerable."

"Oh. That makes sense." Then I shot him another look, but before I could speak, he shrugged innocently, having read my thoughts or the look on my face, I wasn't sure.

"Alex told me Kai's name before we entered the Solarium."

I glanced back to see Alex nodding guiltily. I waved a hand to let him know I wasn't upset. It wasn't a secret, I had just thought that maybe Shiva might know something helpful if he already knew my Beast's name. Then again, Kai had said even he hadn't remembered his name fully until Alex asked him.

I turned to Shiva, thinking slowly and openly, not wanting to speak out loud.

Do you know about Alex's bond with Kai? Should I be concerned? I thought, hoping Shiva would catch it, since he was able to read minds.

He tapped his lips thoughtfully. "I'll think on it, but I don't see a need for alarm…" he said, causing a few others to frown. I nodded thankfully.

I met the eyes of each person in the room, unblinking. Once complete, I cleared my throat. "I'll be leaving tomorrow night. If you have anything you wish to tell me, it would be wise to do so before that time. In case I'm gone for a while. To maintain secrecy – if you find that necessary – ask for the featherbrains, here," I said, jerking a thumb at Hugin and Munin. "Just call out their name, and they'll appear." I glanced over a shoulder, ignoring their indignant squawks. "Won't you. Promptly." It wasn't phrased as a question. These two assholes needed to start earning their keep. Flying around and shitting on Talon at any opportunity was amusing, but I wanted to find out more about their motivations.

Or their boss's motivations, more accurately.

They ruffled their feathers in unison. "We will accept the cowards' petitions," they said arrogantly. I bit back a laugh at the resulting growls, but no one actually spoke out.

I turned back to my guests. "Then I bid you good day."

I remained seated as they filed out, conversing softly. I watched as they each took one of the envelopes Dean had ready for them on a silver platter. The envelope that contained the questions on my mind.

I didn't realize I was twirling my coin until a voice spoke up beside me. We were the only two left in the room, I realized with a start.

"Yes, Pestilence?" I asked the Horseman.

"Please call me Conquest. It has less nasty connotations, even if it's just a calling name." I nodded, frowning. I had heard the others call him Pestilence, so hadn't really thought about it. But I knew Famine also had a different name in the books – Strife.

"Okay."

"May I walk with you?" he asked.

I studied him thoughtfully. This made three. Three of the Horsemen had now confronted me in private. And each time one had done so, it had signified something dangerous about to start.

"Sure," I said, climbing to my feet. "Where are we going?" I asked.

"The Temple Mausoleum," he said from beneath his hood.

I stumbled in surprise, but he was already a few paces ahead. "Come on, Temple. If we're not moving, we're dying. Oh, and grab a coat. You could catch a cold out there." He glanced back at me, and I thought I could sense amusement in his tone. "We wouldn't want that now, would we?"

I sighed, shaking my head. "No, Conquest. I would rather not catch a cold," I muttered.

But I didn't grab a coat.

CHAPTER 15

*C*onquest was right. It was rather chilly outside. But because I hated being told what to do, I chose to brave the storm in my long-sleeved shirt. We walked towards the giant white tree in silence. I was curious to find out what this was all about, but he didn't seem to be in a rush to explain. In fact, so far, it seemed like he literally just wanted to walk and *not* talk.

"So…" I said. "Gunnar's eye-patch. Know anything about that?" I asked.

"Are you asking if I have knowledge of a *Fifth* Horseman?" he asked, sounding amused.

"Okay," I replied grumpily, studying his back since he was a pace ahead of me. It had been worth a shot. Since he obviously wasn't in the mood to talk, I relaxed, figuring he would get to whatever was on his mind, eventually. I saw Pegasus talking with Achilles under the tree. "Let's talk to them really quick before we leave."

Conquest simply nodded, not commenting. I frowned at his back. He had always seemed like a chatty Kathy, making casual jokes around his brothers. A new thought hit me. What if he wasn't necessarily a fan of me joining them as a Rider – a Fifth Horseman?

That could be… problematic.

The two noticed our approach, and turned to face us.

I wasted no time in pleasantries, rounding on Pegasus. "Where were you earlier? Alex was almost taken," I demanded.

He tucked his wings in closer to his back, the very definition of regal grace, eyeing Conquest warily. "I was taking a shit, if it's any of your business."

Conquest burst out laughing.

I scowled at Pegasus, somewhat surprised at his response. He had seemed so eloquent in our previous interactions. Almost noble. But he was brother to my unicorn, Grimm, who was a foul-mouthed murderer, so maybe Pegasus was simply a good actor, and being around Grimm was bringing back old habits.

"So classy," I muttered. "But I'm serious."

He arched his neck. "So was I. He was with you, so I thought I had time to shit in peace."

Achilles was coughing, unable to hide his amusement. I pointed a finger at him. "I want to know something," I said accusingly. He stilled, facing me openly. "You searched Alex when you kidnapped him, but you missed this Shit Stallion's feather. I don't buy it. But more importantly, how did no one *else* catch it?"

He shrugged. "I found it. I just didn't say anything, and in the heat of the moment, they took my word for it. When they seemed about to press the issue, I snapped the Huntress' bow to distract them. Show someone a bit of violence and they usually overlook things."

I nodded in agreement. "I'm still surprised no one caught on to you sooner."

He smiled slowly. "You didn't either, wonder boy."

I grunted at that, because he was right. I had feared the worst – that Achilles had switched sides. "I'm still confused about the blood thing. You said you didn't get blood on your blades, but I saw some on your spear and your sword…"

He tapped his forearm slowly.

I blinked at him. "You… cut yourself?"

He shrugged. "They needed to see the legendary Achilles with blood on his weapons. I obliged them. I did have to cut one or two that were particularly ambitious, but nothing serious."

"Oh…"

"Did you need anything else?" Pegasus said, stamping a hoof absently.

"Where's Grimm?" I asked, simply to keep him here for a few seconds, annoyed at his tone.

Pegasus snorted as if smelling something unpleasant. "He's breaking rainbows somewhere," he muttered disgustedly, shaking his head and causing the thick rings woven into his mane to rattle and clank together.

"Excuse me?"

"It's a hobby of his. He finds rainbows and beats on them. They... disturb him."

I turned to Achilles. "Is he serious or is he fucking with me?"

Achilles studied Pegasus. "I think he's serious."

Pegasus stretched his wings for a moment, and then tucked them down into his back, either to show off, or to find a more comfortable position. "Much like you humans need to let off some steam by punching a leather bag or starting a war, Grimm hunts rainbows and destroys them."

"But... they're not a physical thing. They're just light," I argued.

"Says the wizard who weaves starlight..." Conquest murmured.

I opened my mouth, and then let it close with a click of my teeth. Well... he *was* right.

"He enjoys stabbing pretty things with his head," Pegasus muttered. "Rainbows in particular. Now that he has his shadow wings back, he hunts them all over the worlds."

I nodded dumbly, having literally nothing to say to that, realizing that arguing would only give Pegasus the opening to ask why us humans punched a leather canvas. It was just something to do. And I didn't want to find out what *worlds* he was hunting in. I had enough on my plate.

"Is there really gold at the end of a rainbow?" I asked curiously.

"For the lucky, there are sometimes riches. For everyone else, there's impalement by a fucking lunatic alicorn," Pegasus muttered.

Conquest chuckled. "Mastercard reference. Nice."

Pegasus dipped his head self-importantly. I pondered his response. Alicorn. A winged unicorn. I hadn't really thought about that. Now that Grimm had wings again – for whatever reason they had disappeared for quite some time – maybe he really was an alicorn.

"If you two are brothers, why don't you both have a horn?" I asked.

"Why don't all siblings look identical?" Pegasus said, sounding bored.

I sighed. This bastard was a real piece of work. If Alex hadn't liked him so much, I might have decided to teach him a lesson. Prickly was the nicest way to describe him. "Well, as usual, it hasn't been a pleasure," I said. "Remind Grimm that we leave tomorrow."

I turned my back and began walking away, motioning for Conquest to follow.

I rubbed my arms at the cold, glancing over at Conquest, who chuckled. I forcefully stopped, remembering his advice to grab a coat. "Want me to Shadow Walk us there?" I asked.

An icy sensation washed over me, and we were suddenly in an entirely different place.

A graveyard.

I gasped, flinching instinctively. I saw Conquest walking ahead as if nothing had happened. "What the hell?" I hissed.

He glanced back. "Faster this way," he said in response. "We have our tricks, too. And you looked cold, so I hurried things up a bit." Then he was walking again, deftly maneuvering past tombstones towards the large structure looming before us.

The Temple Mausoleum in the Bellefontaine Cemetery.

We approached the entrance – a large door with a keypad beside it. I typed in the code as Conquest remained a few paces back, eyeing the sculptures decorating the building, because it was likely the most impressive piece of architecture – visually – in the state of Missouri, complete with full-sized statues of dozens of gods, monsters, and heroes from many cultures. The door beeped and I tugged the monstrosity open. We entered, and I let the door slam closed behind us. I turned to Conquest, losing my patience. "What did you want to talk about?"

He studied me, and then tugged back his hood. I winced instinctively, preparing to brave his horrifying mask, but was surprised to find that I was instead looking at the prettiest blonde son of a bitch the world had ever birthed. My jaw dropped open while I stared into his deep baby blue eyes.

He grinned, flashing pearly whites at me. Like a runway model, but beefier.

Being comfortable with my sexuality, I confirmed he was a Mandy – *Man Candy*. Yum.

Before I could comment, he spoke. "How are the dreams?" he asked, sounding concerned.

I blinked at him, caught entirely off guard. I hadn't told anyone about them. They weren't nightmares or anything, just particularly vivid dreams of the Fae world – which was understandable – since I knew we were soon heading back, and as a result, the place had been on my mind a great deal.

"Passing fair," I said warily, wondering how or why he knew of them.

"You must be cautious of dreams. You carry many powers, and the bleeding effect can be notoriously… dangerous."

"What do you mean?" I asked, deciding that I needed to walk. And since we were already here, I may as well pay my respects. It would give me something to do with my suddenly restless legs.

"You are a wizard. You were once a Tiny God, or Maker, if you will. You have become the Master Temple, in fact, not just by birth title. You have been cursed, and survived. More than once. You *somewhat* carry the mantle of Horseman." He leaned closer, flashing his teeth at me in a contagious grin. "And you do that *real* fucking well, I might add." He pulled back, not sensing – or not caring about – my flinch. Even his *breath* smelled delicious. I had to remind myself that this was Pestilence, and not David Beckham. "You are tainted by your Wild Side from the Fae. And you are a Godkiller. That combination is… unheard of," he said, finally.

I nodded, having wondered the same thing in the recent past. "I'm… managing. I think."

"Dreams are one of the first indicators of madness," he offered. "So, I repeat, how have your dreams been?"

I sighed, walking past statues of my fallen ancestors – great women and men alike. Conquest seemed to be more interested in them than in looking at me. "They have been very vivid. Flashbacks of my fight with Athena. And my time in the Fae…" I admitted.

"And golden light?" he asked, sounding amused.

I rounded on him. "Yeah. That, too. What is it?" I asked, glancing down at my forearms to see the faint golden glow since we had mentioned it out loud, as if it had heard us. I shivered at that.

"Killing a goddess…" he said, sounding distant, "taints you. I wouldn't call it ichor, but it's similar. You absorb some of their powers for a time. Or… some of their *essence* may be more accurate. The Wild Side of you should have protected you from it. Somewhat. It's mildly concerning that you still display the golden veins."

"You sound very knowledgeable about this. Has it happened before?"

He laughed, a chiming, pleasant sound. "Of course. You're not *that* special," he said, not making fun of me, but as if trying to politely humble me. "Although I'll admit, I've never heard of one so... susceptible to so many magical infections. You would be a *splendid* subject..."

These fucking Horsemen were going to be the end of my patience.

"Oh, please explain," I said tiredly.

"One must always watch one's loved ones for the first symptoms of madness. Even the good ones must sometimes die..."

CHAPTER 16

I suddenly felt very, very concerned, but seeing the distant look in his eyes, I simply nodded.

"I wasn't always a Horseman, of course," he said, studying the statues around us, even taking a step to glance down at one of the pedestals that contained a book of my ancestor's accomplishments. Comstock Temple. He had been a famous healer. I found it a little unsettling that Conquest – who seemed very medically inclined – had instinctively known this ancestor would interest him.

"I was an alchemist, and married to a woman much better than I deserved. We were both happy. Very happy. For a time…" he said sadly. "I was obsessed with the transmutation myth – turning lead into gold. And I missed the early signs that my dear wife was sick. Because she considered her sole purpose on the earth was to make me happy. And she succeeded. But when she began to get sick, she hid it from me, not wanting to distract me from my pursuits…"

I swallowed audibly, realizing that each of the Horsemen had truly sucky origin stories.

Did that mean the worst was yet to come for me? That I couldn't become a Horseman until I had experienced soul-crushing tragedy? I kept this thought to myself as Conquest continued.

"When it became obvious that it wasn't a passing malady, my wife sought out... treatment, telling me she was off to visit her sister a few towns away. So engrossed in my work, I heard only that I would have uninterrupted time to focus, and that perhaps I would have a solution before she returned, finally able to scoop her up in my arms and devote my attention to her fully, as she deserved." He was silent for a very long time, as if struggling with the words.

"In my obsession, I never even thought to kiss her before she left," he whispered softly. "I told myself she would only be a few miles away, likely returning before I knew it, and my newest experiment was on the burner..."

My heart shattered at the pain in his voice, and I fought the urge not to grasp his shoulder in comfort, but his face was hard, merciless, hateful... towards himself. Stating his failure out loud.

"But I didn't hear from her. For a week. Then two. My experiments had failed, and I decided I needed some fresh air, a change of scenery. I took my horse for a ride, and somewhere along the road, I realized I was entering her sister's village. Of course, I sought her out, only to find my wife was not there, having died under treatment from the local doctor.

"I met him at his home, arguing that I hadn't even known she was sick. The doctor said all the right things, consoled me in all the right ways, but I sensed something was very off about him, and I recognized several of the items in his office. Poisons," he rasped. "Chemicals with no medicinal value...

"I feigned ignorance and left, searching out the local tavern. It didn't take me long to hear that my wife wasn't the first woman to die under his care. Children, too. And not just in this town.

"I fled the city, jumping down from my horse in an abandoned field. I raged and cried out, begging for help from God, knowing that without evidence, I had no case, no proof to bring him to justice. When God didn't answer, I sought my own absolution, and wanting to punish myself further, I did this in the worst possible way – one that would torment us both." He met my eyes, madness dancing in those sapphire depths, but it was a calm, methodical madness.

The eyes of a rational sociopath. Like Hannibal Lecter.

"I befriended the filthy bastard..." Conquest actually snarled, his fists clenching. "I spent a *year* by his side, using my grief to bring us closer, to earn his trust, to get into his inner circle, because word around town said he had doctor friends with similar mortality rates in nearby villages. I shared my knowledge of alchemy with him, showing him my experiments and formulae, slowly, *ever so slowly*," he enunciated, panting, "to earn his trust. And then I began asking him if he knew what happened when certain poisons came into contact with a patient. If he had ever witnessed it. I admitted to dark fantasies, declaring that the only true way to understand medicine was to kill with it, to test its limits…

"The good doctor left my home, feigning concern, and leaving me alone for several days." Conquest looked up at me, face haggard. "Those were the longest days of my life, Nate… Wondering, waiting, *yearning* for solid proof of the dark nature I suspected. Then, when I thought I could take it no longer, and that I would have to kill him in cold blood, I received an invitation to a private dinner at his home. I accepted, and that was where I met the evilest men of my time… I ate dinner with true monsters. Wolves in sheep's wool. I laughed at their stories, their experiments, telling them I was finally ready to take that step, and put my skills to the ultimate test. To harm those who came to me at their darkest hours, those most desperate for help, and to record the entire process of the torment I would administer to them. This…" he whispered, as if having to force himself to continue, "was met with a *toast*. Every man in the room lifted his glass, and at the head of the table, I saw my wife's murderer grinning proudly, nodding both in approval and welcome. They each signed a document, confirming that I was indeed permitted to practice medicine with their unanimous support…"

The Mausoleum grew silent, and I wondered if that was as much as he was going to say. But I wasn't about to press him. No fucking thanks. I had different reasons to fear each of the Horsemen, because they were humanity's darkest angels, but I had never seen a look in the eye like I had in Conquest…

"Suffice it to say that every single man in that room grew violently ill that very night," he said with a nostalgic grin. "Except for the newest doctor… Me. I took them to a… retreat, high in the mountains. A cave, as a matter of fact. I didn't need much room, of course, because hospitality wasn't on the prescription list. I had a dozen patients to keep me company. And the last of them, my wife's murderer, shared twenty very long years with me before finally succumbing to the exotic cocktail of poisons I fed him. Because I would always do my best to heal my patients, to see how close I could bring them to death before pulling them back. I lost count of how many times he apologized for what he had done to my wife, but I made sure to have him recite his list of crimes twice a day, in excruciating detail, as one would expect from a doctor. We must maintain our standards, after all."

Conquest met my eyes, and they were red-rimmed, but his shoulders looked lighter, as if a great weight had been lifted from them. I didn't know what to say. Did I congratulate him? Apologize? Run screaming in horror? I kept my face blank, and gave him a firm nod.

Because… I couldn't quite say what I would have done in his shoes, and that troubled me greatly. Conquest didn't ask me anything, simply turned back to the statues. My response must have been the right one.

"I have never shared the details in full, not even with my brothers. Just the conclusion. That I poisoned her murderer and his associates. I don't know why I shared the rest with you… Just because you *can* do something, doesn't mean you *should*," he said, as if speaking to himself. Then he glanced at me. "One must be careful of temptation, of power, of obsessions. They usually smell of flowers and solve all your problems. But proper medicine always has a side effect, a price. Don't be conned by sugar-coated drugs."

I swallowed, and then placed a hand on his shoulder. "Tell me about her beauty," I said.

He slowly turned to face me, a single tear falling down his perfect cheeks as he smiled and nodded one time. Then he grasped my hand and tugged me down to sit beside him at the edge of the fountain that held the jeweled Temple family tree.

I listened for quite some time, giving him a brother's love. The perfect medicine.

When finished, Conquest finally cleared his throat, as if remembering why we were here in the first place. I sure as hell didn't know. I was just along for the ride, so to speak, but my heart felt scrubbed raw at his story. Still, I felt I had helped him in a small way, and the light in his eyes now blocked the madness I knew lurked in the depths of his soul.

"What I meant to say before I got sidetracked," he began, "is that you should always keep a close eye on your loved ones. You never know what demons they may be hiding, and what effect it might have. Your vampire, for instance, is incredibly ill. Did you know this?"

I flinched, staring up at him. "Alucard?" I asked incredulously. "What do you mean?"

He waved a hand to calm me. "He's spent too long trying to be some thing he is not. He is scared of his monster, and it's eating him alive," he said in a clinical tone.

I blinked at him several times. "I... had no idea," I admitted. "Well, I knew he was trying to be something better, not wanting to be a murderer, but I didn't know it was hurting him..."

Conquest shrugged. "You haven't helped him. In fact, you may have harmed him."

I tensed, my mouth dropping open. "What? *How?*"

The Horseman appraised me, eyes calculating. He finally sighed. "Everyone is so fucking scared of monsters. I just don't get it. Who is supposed to fight the truly terrifying monsters if we don't have monsters of our own?" He waved a hand, halting me from responding. "I digress. What I'm trying to say is that your friendship has made him feel he needs to become something he is not. To hide from his monster, rather than control it and put it to good use. While this sounds admirable, he is forgetting his nature. And one simply cannot forget their nature. They can *evolve*, but suffocating themselves is not medicine. Does this make sense?" I slowly nodded. Conquest sighed in relief. "Wow. Good. I thought I was going to have to fight you on this."

I grunted. "I could use some clarification. What I did to hurt, and what I can do to help..."

"Vampires are... terribly emotional creatures," Conquest said, as if that was an answer. Seeing the look on my face, he rolled his eyes. "You constantly nag at him, picking at him with your words, pranking him, yes?" I nodded.

"I do that to all of my friends," I argued, not understanding.

"And how many vampire friends do you have?" he asked, leering at me.

That cut me off short. "Point taken."

He nodded satisfactorily. "Consider also that he has been a monumental failure practically every time he has tried to be more... *human.*"

I thought about that, and realized the Horseman was absolutely right. Alucard wasn't remotely good at being human. I was curious how Conquest knew of all that, though.

"So, what do I *do?*" I asked, feeling like a shit.

He grunted. "You feed his monster, of course. Let him out of the cage. Leave a monster behind bars long enough, and pretty soon you will have an impotent creature, swamped in depression. Think about a zoo. All the animals do is eat, sleep, and occasionally procreate."

Before I could respond, Conquest suddenly stood, and resumed walking again, leaving me to either sit there or catch up.

He held out his hands at the statues around us, changing the topic as I caught up to him. "The fallen always have lessons to impart, if one knows how to speak with the dead."

I glanced to the opposite side of Conquest to study the statues, seeing them differently. I also realized we were close to my parents' section of the crypt. "What do you mean?" I asked.

"The dead keep secrets…" he whispered, voice as soft and dry as a breeze. I looked up sharply, wondering why he sounded so odd all of a sudden.

But he was gone.

"Hey!" I shouted, my voice echoing off the walls. But he didn't respond.

It was just me.

And a bunch of dead Temples.

CHAPTER 17

*G*rowling, I wandered over to my parents' section and sat down in the chair before the tall statues they had commissioned to portray their lives. I had never been approached on the details of their design, not being allowed to have an opinion. My parents had told me about this years ago, that it was the deceased's will that mattered, not the survivors. I hadn't yet designed my own statue, but it probably wasn't a bad idea seeing how things were going lately. Still, I stubbornly wished I would have had some input in their statues.

I don't know why, but there it was.

I finally steeled my resolve and stared up into my mother's marble eyes. I felt the beginnings of tears forming and didn't try to stop them. I let out a deep, shaking breath. "I miss you, mom. The real you. Not your spirit. You. I hate you guys for what you did to me. Giving me powers without ever telling me. Making deals with Pan behind my back and then dying before you could explain. Then, still not telling me about it in your death."

I sighed, still murmuring to myself, letting myself vent. This was the only time I could truly lower my guard. No one was around to see. No one was around to judge. It was just... me.

And my parents.

"Shut up, Dad. I know I could come visit you in the Underworld. Death probably has Charon on standby for just that. But... it's not the same. And I feel guilty doing it. I need to cut those ties before they break me. Popping in every now and then to say hi would only weaken me. And I can't afford to be weak right now. But you know all about that, don't you?

"And what's up with our Crest? What does it all mean? Why are the ravens on it? Were you pals with Odin, too? What other secrets did you keep from me?" I shouted, my voice echoing off the walls. "Why? Why were you friends with these guys? Why is there so much crazy shit going on in Missouri?"

After a few moments of silence, a faint smile tugged at my cheeks.

"I'm *not* being a drama queen, mom. Even the Old Ones think things are crazy."

I sighed, staring down at my hand. The emblem branded into my palm was healed, leaving behind burned skin in a perfect rendition of my Crest, with full detail.

"I killed Athena for fuck's sake, dad... And my fiancée... Indie. She's dead. Went crazy over there in Fae. But you guys wouldn't know about that. You never went there," I muttered. "Well, I'm going back. Maybe I'll bring you a gift to leave here."

I looked back up at my mom, studying her statue as tears streamed down my face like acid. She was beautiful. Elegant. Noble. And had hidden dozens of dark secrets from me.

I hated them both.

And I loved them both.

I stared at her hands, frowning distastefully at the pyramid-shaped stone in her palm. The stone copy of the Hand of God – what Indie had used to wake up Athena. I purposely avoided reaching into my pocket where I kept a small velvet bag with all that remained of the real thing – a pile of dust. Had even my mom's statue been a hint of some kind? A warning?

Had... they been *prevented* from sharing things with me for some reason?

But if that was true, someone would have had to hold them accountable to it, which meant someone out there knew the truth. Their full story.

Pan?

One of the guests I had entertained tonight?

If I *ever* found truth in that thought, I would make their last days a living nightmare.

But another thought hit me. If the stone in her statue's hands had been a long-distance message, what about the other thing in my dad's hands? I stood, approaching his statue to inspect the hourglass. What was so special about it? And anyway, this was stone.

For example, the pyramid in her hand hadn't actually *been* the Hand of God – just a replica. The real one had been with the Elders – before Indie took it.

So, was I supposed to scour the world for an hourglass? Or was it in my Armory with Pandora? Maybe I should ask.

I reached up, inspecting it closer, wanting to get a feel for it so I could pester Pandora. I would take pictures, too, but getting a personal view of it was almost more important to Pandora, because she could read my mind. Touching it was effectively a video recording. I reached up to get a feel for its size, and any specific dimension it may have.

Which meant I was caught totally by surprise when the fucking thing fell out of my dad's hands, clanging to the marble floor. I froze, holding my hands up in the air on instinct, a universal *I'm innocent* gesture. Then I chuckled nervously, still staring down at it. I was alone here. No one was about to come yell at me for breaking something, especially not my parents.

Still, her marble eyes bore into me as if she could do just that. Scoldings could happen across planes of existence – without a word spoken. Mothers were like cosmic supernovas in that regard. Supreme Beings.

But, hell, I owned the freaking building.

I stared down at the hourglass, wondering why the stone hadn't broken, and why it had made such an odd sound. Like metal. I crouched down, picking it up with careful hands, hoping I hadn't just desecrated my dad's statue for no good reason. The object was cool in my hands, and I detected a faint hum of power – muted, as if…

Encased behind stone.

Holding my breath, I tapped it against the floor, and was shocked to see a thin layer of stone chip away, revealing the dull gleam of tarnished metal. Hard, strong metal. Not copper, bronze, or anything precious, but functional. Something that could withstand the tests of time, no matter what nature threw at it.

I felt a small, eager smile cracking my cheeks, the motion creasing the salty residue from my tears. Then I began to tap in earnest at a few of the sturdier sections, and began to laugh as I watched more stone flake away in thin sheets.

An hourglass hidden in stone.

My parents had left me a gift.

A new thought hit me. I had always wondered why my parents had upped the security on the Temple Mausoleum. It was just a crypt – a final resting place for the dead – so why add bulletproof glass, motion sensors, a bank-vault door, and cameras?

Probably because they had hidden this thing here. I glanced up at the statues. Possibly other things, too. Curious, I reached up to the pyramid-shaped stone, and although hoping for it, was surprised when it simply lifted away, a separate piece from the rest of the statue, held in place by a thin layer of plaster that was easily cracked apart.

But... if Indie had used the real Hand of God... what the hell was this?

I needed to get back home. To clean these things off. Find out what they were. I realized I was staring out at the rest of the statues in the building, assessing everything. What else had they hidden here?

And since they had been dead at the time, had the sculptors been in on the ruse? But that could wait. I had a trip tomorrow. I realized I was wearing the satchel Callie had sent me, so quickly shoved the two stone items inside, backing away from the statues, studying them with a thoughtful frown.

"How long have these things been here?" I asked out loud. "Did you know, even years ago, that I would need this stuff? Or did you have a trusted friend add them after the fact. Pan?" I shook my head. "No, he would have told me. I'm sure of it." I watched my dad's statue, glaring at me as if disappointed. Now that I looked at him, I realized the sculptor had made his eyes look a little more savage than I remembered. "I think... I should double check," I said, taking a step back from that glare. "But... if they're so important, why didn't you just *tell* me about them? You were in the Armory after you died. You had plenty of time. And what are they? Why are they important? It's an hourglass and a Hand of God replica..." I trailed off, thinking furiously. Unless it was another Hand of God. But... that wouldn't do me any good. The only two Makers alive were Matthias and Castor, and they both wanted to kill me. For different reasons.

Then they could get back to trying to kill each other.

I sighed, running a hand through my hair. I had cut it back to normal after my trip to the Fae, not a fan of the longer hair, or how I had gotten it.

But I had kept my beard. Because I hadn't ever been able to wear one. Not a real one. Just a patchy excuse for a face-blanket. And since stories had spread about my bearded mug during our war with the Greeks, I had decided to leave it as a reminder for anyone I ran into.

I needed to get home and get cleaned up. I wanted to get someone I trusted to begin cleaning these items off, but I had a dinner with Callie planned, where I needed to thank her for my ridiculously expensive birthday present. Maybe find out why she had gotten me one in the first place.

With my luck, it was probably just a bribe to convince me to do something I would rather not do. Still, I felt excitement at the prospect of uncovering the truth behind the stone.

But I was acutely aware that I couldn't be sharing details about it with anyone.

Because someone hadn't been playing me straight. My bet was Pan, but it could have been anyone. Hell, maybe it was one of the Horsemen. Maybe that was why Death had allowed my parents to come back, to remind them that they couldn't tell me what I needed to know.

It wasn't that I didn't trust anyone, but I was under no impression that these people valued my feelings over their prior obligations. I knew that War believed that sometimes unpleasant things needed to be done in order to accomplish a greater good. Nothing evil, but sometimes painful. A more benevolent form of the *ends justified the means*. How the phrase had been originally intended, not the way others had distorted it as an excuse or vehicle to achieve their goals.

I was betting the other Horsemen agreed with him too, especially after talking to Conquest.

I needed to find out for myself what was so important about these two not-stone items. I found it very odd that my parents had chosen to put them here rather than their Armory – where they housed every other dangerous supernatural artifact they had found over the years.

Was that a subtle hint that they didn't trust Pandora?

Or just an added layer of security? Were these items more dangerous or less dangerous than the items in the Armory? Because their method of concealment could indicate either.

Just to be sure, I walked up to the statues and rapped on them with a knuckle, making sure they weren't hollow. I walked around them in a circle, checking all over for any levers or buttons that might reveal a hidden passageway of some kind. I even reached out with my magic, but was pretty sure they were solid, genuine statues. Nothing else was hidden on them. The only way to be one-hundred-percent sure was to break them into rubble.

And I didn't have the *cojones* to do that, or the required lack of concern for destroying the only remaining physical rendition of them. Sure, I had paintings and photographs, but there was something to be said about a statue.

I frowned at them for good measure, and then left, my mind a wash of crazy ideas.

And, over them all...

Why had Conquest brought me here unless he knew about these items? Was it just for his cryptic advice? Or had he had several reasons to bring me here?

Stupid, holy, donkey-riders, meddling in my fucking life all the time.

One of these days, they were going to get what was coming to them. But I had a date. I patted my satchel happily, surprised to find that the items didn't weigh very much. They actually felt like they weighed less than they should have, considering I had held them in my hands.

It almost felt like my satchel was empty.

I reached inside, not looking, searching for them, just to be sure. When my fingers brushed the two items, I let out a sigh. Just good balance on the bag, apparently.

The chain strap didn't even bother me, either.

All in all, it was probably the coolest satchel – both in looks and design – I had ever owned.

Callic deserved a kiss right on the mout—

I stumbled a step, realizing I was blushing at the thought. I hadn't meant it as anything romantic. But my mind raced with the thought as I continued on.

CHAPTER 18

*C*allie smirked at me over the rim of her wine glass – an excellent white I had ordered. I was more a fan of the thick, chewy reds, but a nice, crisp white was nice after a big meal. She had caught me up on most of her recent adventures, and I was still reeling to hear about some of her new acquaintances. I could tell she hadn't told me everything, but I was fine with that.

"I'm glad you like it," she said, eyes flicking to the satchel at my feet. "The last time I saw you, your satchel looked to be in pretty poor shape. I asked Darling and Dear for something a little more… resilient."

Callie was a bombshell, her narrow face as smooth as porcelain, and she knew how to make a man smile. The most distinguishing thing about her was her long, white hair, even though she was younger than me by a few years. I swirled my glass, leaning closer to speak in a low tone as I met her blue eyes. Purple flecks mixed in with the blue to create a very alluring, cool palette.

"Callie… that thing had to be expensive. You really didn't have—"

"Stop. No givebacks," she said, smiling playfully. "Now, you owe *me* one."

I nodded in defeat. "Fine." I glanced down at the bag, leaning back in my chair. I hadn't wanted to leave it with the porter, too attached to it. And I definitely hadn't wanted to leave it home, out of my sight. Not with the cargo inside. The items from the Mausoleum.

"I've never even heard of Darling and Dear before…" Then I snapped my fingers, smiling excitedly. "Carl wasn't pleased about it being Elder hide, by the way."

"Fucking Carl," she mused, taking a light sip of her wine. "You'll have to come by the shop sometime. Although I should warn you, Darling and Dear are very… quirky. But the things they make…" she said, voice trailing off in wonder.

I pointedly eyed the jacket draped over her chair, and she nodded. I had assumed it wasn't just an ordinary coat based on how I had seen her finger caressing it every now and then. Also, she hadn't checked it at the door. "What's up with the purple marks on the back?" I asked, having noticed them when I followed her to our table.

"Have you ever heard of a Gruffalo?" she asked, frowning.

I blinked at her. "There's no such thing as a Gruffalo," I said.

She studied me for a moment, eyes calculating. "Well, Darling and Dear seem to think they exist. Said my coat was made from one." She shrugged. "No offense, but I think I believe them, although I've never heard of one before."

I shook my head, disappointed to find that she hadn't heard of the children's book. Then again, she was younger than me. If anything, that should have switched the tables, as I was certain it was fairly recent, closer to her childhood than mine. Still. These leather-smiths made goods from Elder and Gruffalo hides, and were able to re-forge black dragon scales.

"So, you went grave-robbing?" she said in a smoky tone, eager to hear the details.

I shrugged. "I guess. It wasn't my intention, but that about sums it up." I had told her about my findings over dinner, because if I could trust anyone in this world, it was Callie and Gunnar. I wasn't sure why I felt that way about Callie, whom I had only known for a short time, but there was something about her naivety that drew me in. She was iron underneath, even if she didn't know it, but she was genuine to the core. Plus, she was new enough to all of this that she very literally couldn't be behind anything nefarious.

And I considered it a good investment to have an ally within the Vatican. Since Callie hunted monsters for them, I decided to put all my money on her, knowing I wouldn't be getting information from their side in any other way. Hell, I was possibly a Horseman, and I didn't want to introduce myself to them in that capacity. They might just kill me out of fear. Or lock me up.

Also, Callie wasn't really a fan of churches, believe it or not. She wasn't necessarily against them, but she wasn't drinking the Kool-Aid, either.

"What do you think they are?" she asked, eyeing my bag as if able to see the items inside.

"I don't know. But you can bet your ass I'm going to find out." She nodded, eyes momentarily locking onto mine. I saw a brief flash of wariness, and frowned. "Is everything okay?" I asked, thinking I had said something wrong.

Her cheeks blushed faintly, contrasting with her brilliantly white hair. We were sitting at a private table for four, well back from the rest of the restaurant. She had wanted to go somewhere new and exciting, and since geography wasn't really an impediment to us, I had chosen this fancy steak place in Manhattan.

I could tell she felt mildly uncomfortable, but no one else would have known it. They would have taken one look at her and assumed that she was local royalty. Callie had a way about her – able to adapt and control almost any social encounter – that was truly astounding. I didn't think she was aware of it, but it was fun to watch her in action. She was so instinctively familiar with psychology, that she could very likely convince the Queen of England that she was a distant cousin, and that it was perfectly reasonable to let her try on the Crown Jewels.

"I took out the second demon in Kansas City. Amira, the one who had been working with Johnathan when we first met," she said in a soft tone. "I… learned some things."

I waited patiently, keeping my eyes locked on her, letting her know it was okay to talk about it – or that it was equally fine if she chose not to share.

"I went back to the house. The one he took me to."

I nodded slowly, letting her share the story at her own pace. That had been one hell of a night. A demon had abducted her, wanting to kill her for something her parents had done to him. The problem was, Callie hadn't really known her parents. She had been given up at a young age, left on the steps of Abundant Angel Catholic Church in Kansas City.

"Johnathan had a secret room there. And he was especially interested in Missouri. The number of beings, gods, and Freaks residing there in recent years. Apparently, there are a lot of factions in play. You should have seen his map of St. Louis…" she said, shaking her head.

I stared at her, frowning. "What do you mean?"

"There are several gangs, or neighborhoods – little kingdoms, if you will – in both our cities."

I leaned back, nodding. "That's common. Groups tend to stick together. Safety in numbers—"

She shook her head. "I understand that, but this was *different*. It made me think of an organization. Like the mafia. And our two cities were the *only* ones he cared about. If this is common, why did he only have maps of our cities, here in Missouri?" she asked, more to herself. Then she came back to attention, leaning closer. "Anyway, we can look into that later. If I said *Hope*, would that mean anything to you?" she asked, watching me intently.

"Hope is undiscovered disappointment," I said shortly, not wanting to talk to her about my Mask, fearing her reaction and what dark suggestions the church might have put in her head on the subject.

She tensed, frowning at my tone. "Oh."

I waved a hand. "Sorry. Sore subject."

"Right," she said, still watching me. "When I was in that house, in Johnathan's secret office, I had… a vision. Of five… things riding down a giant mountain…" she said, staring into my eyes.

My mouth went dry. Me and… the Four Horsemen? "Oh?" I asked carefully.

She squinted in disapproval. "Nate, please stop. When I woke up, my partner said I was shouting *Caballarii* over and over again. That loosely translates to *Horsemen*. And I remember Roland saying something about that. About you…"

I took a sip of my drink, and then pulled out my coin. I set it on the table and slid it her way, nodding finally. "I don't think it's official or anything. At least, not yet. But that's my Mask. Of Hope," I admitted. "Consider it a job offer given to me. The Fifth Horseman."

"I recognize it," she said warily. "You carry it everywhere. It changes?" she asked, touching it with a finger.

I nodded. Then I smiled. "Just for the record, anyone else who touches it gets the living shit zapped out of them. Fun times."

She stilled, slowly raising her eyes to meet mine. "Which brings up another point… We share powers. The white magic thing. I'm pretty sure where mine comes from, and hearing your confirmation on the Horseman question, I'm about as sure as I can be on how we're connected."

I waited, wanting her to say it for herself.

"You've got access to powers granted from Heaven as a Horseman. White magic. My father was a Nephilim…"

I slowly nodded. "I think you're right. Somehow, we snuck past the Pearly Gates…" I said lightly, hoping to ease the tension.

She let out a breath, shaking her head. "What the fuck, Nate? How? We are the *last* people who should be playing with that kind of juice…"

I shrugged. "I kind of agree."

"You mentioned once that you had a friend who might have answers…" she said, staring down at her glass of wine.

"Yeah. An Angel named Eae. It means Demon Thwarter…" I added for no particular reason.

She snorted indelicately. "That's way cooler than the one in Kansas City. His name is Angel," she muttered drily. "Angel the Angel."

I burst out laughing. "You're kidding."

Her cheeks split into a grin. "I shit you not. How lame is that?"

I let out a breath. "I wanted you to come to your own conclusions before I let an Angel convince you of something. Someone else telling you what you are sounded like a really bad idea… You're the kind of person who some might describe as *stubborn*," I said, grinning at her.

I also wasn't sure how Eae would react to meeting Callie. Favorable or entirely unfavorable. And I really didn't want to see Callie kill Eae if he acted like an Old Testament pillar of dick.

Salt, whatever. Something large and phallic.

She scowled back, but finally nodded. "Yes. That was probably best." She glanced around the room, smiling at the scene. It wasn't her typical type of place, because Callie hadn't come from a family with money like I had. Her father was in the middle class, so places like this were typically reserved to a scene in a movie. "When do you think I could meet him?"

"I can set it up whenever you want, but if you want me present, it might be a while."

She frowned at that, sensing my tone. "What idiocy are you considering, now, Nate?"

I grinned, leaning back. "I need to go save a friend. In the Land of the Fae. Time moves differently over there, so I could be a while."

She blinked at me. "You're going back? You only just returned."

I nodded. "Unfortunately."

"Wait, who is in danger?"

I met her eyes. "Ashley—"

"Damnit. That means Gunnar is going, too. And probably a small army, if you're smart. Talon?" she asked, eyes distant, sounding more like a recommendation. I grunted agreement.

"We're taking the winged Mr. Eds, too. We can't afford to be gone long. Not again."

She nodded, waving a hand dismissively. "I'll check in. Make sure Falco is secure."

I squinted at her, remembering how she had taken care of Falco during the war, when I had been stuck in Fae. "That was pretty impressive how you were able to juice up my wards. Thanks."

She shrugged offhandedly. "It wasn't too hard. The house wanted me to help…" she said, blushing at the words. "We should probably get you out of here so you can get ready for your travels. I'm sure Gunnar's anxious." She paused for a few moments, debating something in her head. "Need any help?" she asked carefully.

I smiled at the offer, but shook my head. "You have enough going on. And to be honest, I'm not sure it's okay to subject you to that place." Her eyes flashed fire, slowly rising to mine. I held up my hands innocently. "Easy, Callie. What I meant to say was that I'd rather you not take over the Land of the Fae. I think it's dangerous enough over there without you in charge."

A small smile crept over her cheeks, but I could tell she didn't buy it.

Which was true.

There was no way I was going to risk taking her over there. That place was twisted beyond belief, and I wouldn't be able to look myself in the mirror if I did anything to change Callie from exactly the way she was right now. Realizing I was staring too long, I cleared my throat.

"Right. I'm sure Alex is getting into all sorts of trouble. We should go."

She nodded. "He's probably still enjoying his first slice of New York pizza. Isn't Alucard with him?"

I nodded, climbing to my feet, tossing enough cash on the table to more than cover dinner. "Yeah, but he's a terrible chaperone," I muttered. Then I remembered Conquest's advice, and cringed inwardly. I had asked him to join me on our quick trip to accompany Alex, to give the kid a taste of a normal life. And to extend a little confidence in the vampire. And here I was talking smack about him. No wonder he was out of whack. I was demeaning him at every chance, not even consciously thinking about it.

Callie slipped ahead of me as we made our way to the door of the Manhattan steakhouse, calling over her shoulder. "If Alucard's so incompetent, then why did you—"

The glass door blew inwards, striking Callie full-on. She slammed into my chest and then the hostess' podium. It crashed to the ground, trapping her legs, and she didn't immediately move.

I climbed unsteadily to my feet, surprised I wasn't injured. All I heard were screams and a loud buzzing noise in my ears as the restaurant imploded with panic.

But one thought sent a chill down to my heels. Where were Alex and Alucard?

CHAPTER 19

*J*n the seconds of chaos, I didn't immediately know what to do. Check on Callie, or try to prevent a second attack – whatever the hell it had been? I hadn't sensed anything, but unless someone had picked our restaurant out of thousands in Manhattan, and decided to place a handmade bomb directly in front of the door, right as we were walking out…

I was willing to bet the bomb was meant for one – or both – of us.

But was it a distraction or an actual attack? I heard Callie grunt, and then the podium resting across her legs simply exploded into splinters – the debris nabbed up by an instant vortex of magic – that whipped over my shoulders and out the jagged opening of the door, where I heard grunts of pain and surprise.

Our attacker, apparently.

I glanced back to see Callie gracefully rising to her feet, her eyes a polished silver shine.

I blinked, decided it wasn't relevant to our immediate survival, and then ran out into the streets where car alarms were squealing and blaring.

I skidded to a halt, feeling Callie right behind me. The street was in flames, and several bodies littered the sidewalk.

Then I heard a familiar voice shriek in protest. Alex.

Before I could take a step, a fist grabbed me and yanked me backwards.

A ball of black flame splashed into the pavement where I had been standing, melting the ground, and I realized Callie had just saved my life.

I followed the arc of destruction to see a large, ginger-bearded man snarling at me from across the street, his face a wash of splinters and blood where Callie had tagged him with the remaining pieces of the hostess' podium. He held a struggling Alex by one fist. I recognized him. Matthias Temple. The Mad Hatter. My grand-whatever. Time seemed to slow, and then Wylde screamed from deep within my soul, a primal, guttural sound that gave even my own arms goosebumps.

Not.

Today.

"Mine!" a new voice shrieked as a comet slammed into Matthias, knocking Alex free and the large ginger man into the alley. A form material-ized from within the comet, and a new face glanced over a shoulder to leer at me as he darted for Alex – who was trying to run away.

I blinked.

Castor Queen? I hadn't sensed magic, and the nondescript older man looked similar to when I had last seen him.

"I think it's safe to say we can kill both of the old dudes, right?" I heard Callie snarl from beside me, squeezing my hand one time.

"Oh, yes," I growled, squeezing back.

"Right. You take the ginger, I'll get Alex."

I opened my mouth to argue, but she was suddenly gone. She reappeared right beside Alex as a flash of silver seemed to dance around her like a quicksilver shadow. She stabbed Castor Queen in the shoulder with a back-wards thrust of a kama made out of pure energy, and he howled in both pain and outrage as she abruptly disappeared with Alex.

I heard Matthias storming out of the alley, so that the three of us stared at each other, everyone bleeding but me. The pedestrians had wisely chosen to leave the area, those still alive, anyway.

"You two fucktards really should have made an appointment, first," I growled loud enough for them to hear as I stormed across the street. A clue-less taxi driver had decided to cruise down our street, letting out an angry honk at the jaywalking wizard. So, I casually let loose a blast of air, knocking his vehicle sideways and into a building. He would bruise, but he would live. Much safer than if he got between me and my targets.

Crackling whips of power trailed on the sidewalk at my feet as I stormed closer, scorching the pavement and giving the Big Apple a few new potholes. Hell, I might have even fixed a few. I flicked my wrists as I walked, slamming the power into the road in a drumbeat, smiling darkly at the two Makers. "You two pissed off the wrong Godkiller…" I smiled, my forearms beginning to glow with golden light.

The two men snarled at me, but not before snarling at each other. Which made me reconsider. It wasn't two on one. It was… a free-for-all.

Because Matthias refused to hear me out. Maybe I could change that.

"Hey! You do know that I didn't kill Ichabod, rig—"

A wall of flame roared towards me as Matthias' eyes filled with vengeance.

I threw up a Gateway into a snowy field in the middle of Alaska that I had scouted for just such a reason, catching the flames that would have hit me, and sending them into the snowy tundra. Matthias' lips curled in fury, but they also looked mildly impressed at the tactic.

I tried again. "I wasn't even *there* when—"

Another wall of flame, followed by three more from different directions screamed towards me. This time I Shadow Walked to the other side, appearing a dozen paces away from them.

"Fucking *listen* to me—" I screamed, trying one last time.

Castor Queen joined in the attack this time. "You will pay for taking the Syndicate from m—"

Matthias spun, launching an attack at both of us this time. Seeing a golden flash near my forearms, I took a risk. I held out my palm, catching the approaching wall of flames against the Crest branded into my flesh. The flames struck a sudden shield of golden light, reflecting the power, and sending it right back towards Matthias and Castor in one concussive jet of explosive fire, slamming them both into the building.

I blinked, staring down at my hand in disbelief. "She only wants me for my pimp juice," I sang softly, slowly lifting my eyes to stare at the two startled Makers. "Not my pimp juice! I'm talking her pimp juice!" I continued, belting it out louder.

I heard Callie laugh, and then a groaning Alucard climbed out of a dumpster, shaking his head, eyes wild. "What the fuck are you doing, singing?" he shouted, eyes latching onto me. "Let's get the hell out of here!" The Makers were climbing to their feet, cursing and shouting at me, but they stopped abruptly, eyes latching onto one another.

Then they began to cut loose, trying to kill each other, messily. "My Syndicate!" Matthias roared. "You can't even keep your *son* safe, let alone the Syndicate!"

That comment right there threatened to ignite World War 3, and my scrotum was the first to attempt retreat, crawling up into my stomach.

"Right. Time to leave," Callie murmured from directly beside me. I glanced down to see her clutching Alex protectively. Alucard was racing our way, catching the attention of the two Makers. He grabbed my outstretched hand just as the Makers pointed hands at us, sensing our escape. Two midnight-black creatures flew towards us, inky black jaws opened wide, formed out of nothingness by the two mad men. I Shadow Walked us back to Chateau Falco, panting heavily as we arrived underneath the giant white tree. I searched the darkness for immediate threats.

When nothing happened, I let out a breath. Whatever those creatures had been, they hadn't managed to follow us.

The branches above us suddenly slammed to the earth, forming a protective cocoon around us. *Mine...* Kai's voice growled.

I stared at everyone, making sure they were okay. Alucard had dried blood on his forehead, but looked okay. Alex had a few scratches, but also looked fine. Callie looked...

"Damn. You don't have a scratch," I hissed in disbelief. "What the hell?"

"I have good genes," she muttered drily.

"Yeah, you do," Alucard added helpfully, openly eyeing her ass.

She slapped him full on in the face, which earned a surprised laugh from Alex. Alucard chuckled, too, not an ounce of shame.

"You don't talk to girls like that, Alex," Callie said, but she was smiling at the vampire.

I heard a chorus of growls from nearby, and noticed a contingent of two dozen wolves surrounding the branches. Gunnar's werewolves were here.

"Thanks, Kai. I think we're safe. For now," I added, shaking my head. His branches slowly rose back to normal, giving us a clear view of Chateau Falco. The wolves darted forward eagerly, sniffing us and whining in relief.

"I guess we should be asking how the hell the two bastards who hate you most in this world found us... at the same time. Far away from here," Alucard grunted.

I met his eyes, shaking my head. "I have no freaking idea."

"Thunder down under," A croaking voice called out. I flinched, glancing up to see Hugin or Munin shriek at me. Then Kai's branches were pounding into the ground as the two shadow monsters from New York City appeared out of nowhere, lunging for our group.

"Kai! Treehouse! Now!" I screamed. Without missing a beat, one of the branches lashed out to wrap around Alex's body, jerking him clear at the last second as a long set of claws slashed through the air where he had been standing. The branches lifted Alex up into the treehouse, threw him inside, and slammed the door. Then the branches began playing whack-a-mole.

CHAPTER 20

*T*he wolves darted about, snapping at the empty air as they tried to slow our attackers. Whatever the Makers had sent after us had tagged along for the ride. I reached deep within myself, trying to draw on that alien golden power, and my legs buckled. Callie was hurling glowing blue crucifixes into the air, the night screaming as they flew at the shadow monsters. One struck true, ripping right through the creature, sending it flying. But I saw it jump back to its feet, the skin forming back over the hole like oil, and it let out a dark, sickening laugh.

"Ideas?" Callie shouted at me, seeing I was doing absolutely nothing productive.

"Um…" I said, glancing back down at my hands, wondering why the golden power hadn't worked.

Alucard bolted straight into the other creature, tackling it to the ground as it began slicing through a few wolves. The wolves simply ceased to exist when struck, knocked away like sudden smoke on a windy day. Alucard slammed through the creature, skin erupting into golden light as he snarled. I blinked.

It was almost as if contact with the creature had caused him to erupt with light. The creature screamed – a wrecked, agonized sound, but Alucard didn't get up.

A trio of wolves pounced on the second creature as it glided over the ground in pursuit of, well, all of us, I guess. Probably me, but they had seemed to want Alex, too.

The wolves struck it in rapid succession, one after the other, biting down into hamstring, thigh, and stomach. But…

The creature didn't stop, and the wolves had frozen on contact.

Callie shouted, unleashing balls of fire this time.

And I took a freaking second to think – which was totally uncommon for me.

I know.

The creature shielded its face from Callie's attacks, but once the projectile struck it, tearing another hole, the creature let out another dry, rattling chuckle as the fireball winked out of existence, and the wound healed over.

I panted, calling out to Wylde to try and understand what the hell these things were, but he simply stared, confused. I glanced at the wolves who had bitten it, but they were motionless.

Then I took a step back, yanking Callie closer to me as they finally moved. The wolves slowly turned to stare back at us with jet black eyes, and their bodies also slowly shifted to black, as if oil had been poured over them. They opened their jaws to reveal black fangs and tongue.

I saw Alucard climb to his feet, stumbling woozily, staring down at his skin, which was still glowing with golden… sunlight. Light. Ultraviolet light.

I shouted at the remaining wolves as I began to weave a whole fucktillion worth of magic, guesstimating on time zones and crossing off ideas in rapid succession. "Stop attacking! Run back to the house and have Dean turn on every light we have! Help him flip every single switch you can find. NOW!" I screamed, as the shadow creature flew at us, laughing.

"Nate! What are—" Callie began, power forming in her palms as she stared at the monster.

I grabbed her around the waist and yanked her into me as I fell to the ground – just as the last creature was almost on top of us. Oh, and I unleashed my little spell. The world erupted with light as I opened a giant Gateway directly between us – easily a dozen paces wide and angled slightly up so that the creature couldn't simply jump over it.

Light from the setting sun on the coast of Malibu, California obliterated the creature in a cloud of wet, greasy ashes. I stared up at Callie's clenched eyes and burst out into a fit of giggles. She opened them, blinked at me, and then glared. I laughed harder. "Your face!"

Her hips felt decidedly pleasant on top of mine, even though she slapped me before climbing off, interrupting my victory laugh.

Alucard chuckled. "Sunshine for the win!" he said, grinning as I climbed to my feet, rubbing my jaw. "One could almost say that I single-handedly saved the day."

I opened my mouth to argue, and he shot me a very threatening glare, an ocean of madness briefly flaring up in those eyes. Something I hadn't seen in quite some time. His monster. And I again remembered Conquest's advice. "Without me, you wouldn't have known what to do and would have likely died," he said in a low tone. "Let me have this, Nate, or I'm done. No jokes. Names. Or anything." He was shaking, and I realized he meant it. He would leave me. For good.

Callie was frowning at us. I nodded, dropping my eyes. "Not even a little—"

"No. Not a word," he pressed. Then he let out a breath, and I looked up. A very faint ghost of a smile cracked his demeanor as I saw the lights from the mansion kick on all around the house, one by one. "I need you to say the following... The Glampire saved our lives."

Callie nodded smiling. "Alucard, you decadent, majestic, ultraviolet Glampire... You saved our lives. Thank you." Alucard actually blushed before turning to me.

"You totally kicked ass, Alucard!" Alex hooted from up above. "Nate did practically nothing! I was watching, and you're right." I scowled up at him. He simply folded his arms, giving me a stern look. Ungrateful little shit. He was supposed to be on *my* side.

I sighed. "Alucard, you decadent, majestic, ultraviolet Glampire... You saved our lives. Thank you." I smiled at him, for once, not even feeling like teasing him. He was actually right. I'd come up with nothing. I let out another breath, and then walked up to him, extending a hand. "Seriously, Little Brother. Thank you," I added.

He went entirely still, staring at the nickname I had used. It was what he had used to call me when we first became frenemies. He dipped his head once and then turned away, not saying a word as he stalked back to the house.

I frowned, watching him. "What's going on in that head of yours, Alucard?" I whispered under my breath.

Callie answered from right beside me. "Just a guess, but I'm thinking he feels unappreciated."

I turned to her, pensive. Callie was pretty good at reading people. "You really think so?"

She grabbed my hand and led me over to the tree, patting the earth next to her as she sat down on a thick root that had broken clear of the ground. She leaned her elbows onto her knees and met my eyes. "Nate, you really need to think about something. Can you do that for me?" she asked, face devoid of any humor.

I nodded, wary.

"I haven't known you long. Not long at all, in fact. But I've seen one thing quite a bit. You have an uncanny sense of loyalty to your friends. Willing to do absolutely anything to keep them safe…" I nodded, watching her. "But… you also expect quite a bit, which is totally fine and understandable." She met my eyes. "But you really need to understand something."

She waited, obviously wanting me to speak. "Okay," I said, leaning closer.

"Your life is fucking ridiculous," she said in a rush, leaning back as she gauged my reaction. I frowned. I opened my mouth. Then closed it, glancing down at the earth for a second. I plucked up a blade of grass, studying it intently. It was very important that I made sure it was healthy.

But it was strong and green. And…

I dropped it with a grimace, suddenly wanting to stand.

My eyes flicked all around us. On a quick estimate… hundreds of things had died here in the past few years. In this exact spot. Actually, I was pretty close to where I had killed Indie.

And where she had been killed the time before that.

And where she had been brought back to life.

Where Ashley had killed Hercules.

Where I had killed the Brothers Grimm.

Where Castor Queen had killed Ichabod – while impersonating me.

This was a field of death, and the grass was as green as ever. I shook off the dark thought.

I slowly looked up at Callie. "That's… very true," I admitted with a sad sigh.

She smiled – a heartbroken look on her face – and then she crouched down on her knees before me, pulling me to her chest as something salty leaked out of my eye-holes. By sheer force of manliness, I prepared to fight my traitorous tear ducts. Then Callie whispered in my ears, running a hand up my hair, gently combing my scalp, and ruining everything.

"It's okay, Nate. We're all alone. Alex left with Yahn a few seconds ago."

I tensed, not having noticed anyone near us. My eyes sensed that it was darker, and I realized that Kai's branches were once again forming a private cocoon around us, keeping my weakness private. How long had I knelt there staring at the stupid grass? But with that understanding of utter privacy, I broke, my armor torn away. I didn't have to be strong for anyone. Not right this minute. "I didn't want to be like this, Callie…" I said, throat raw.

Her fingers raked my scalp soothingly, and…

I let her, giving into the madness as I began to talk. I think I told her pretty much everything that had happened to me. Even things I had never voiced aloud. I told her *all the things*, folks. And in doing so, I realized that no matter how loyal of a friend I had been, I had pretty much given everyone Post Traumatic Stress Disorder for Christmas gifts.

And that maybe one, or two, or all of them were not faring so well. Including me.

Sure, I'd had the best intentions… But intent didn't matter when giving shitty Christmas gifts. Did you honestly care that Gram-Gram meant well when she got you comic book socks for you thirtieth birthday… in front of your girlfriend – who was visiting your family for the first time?

Nope.

Gram-Gram was pretty much blacklisted from your favorite relative list for a few years after a stunt like that.

Still, I had sacrificed everything to keep them safe, and they knew that. I didn't think anyone was judging me for failing them or causing them pain. No, they were thankful to have the psychopath killer for a friend. But… the knife still cut, folks. Just like the survivors of a loved one in surgery secretly despised the doctors for cutting into him.

I sighed, realizing my hands were gripping Callie's thighs, and that we were very, very close.

I had also forgotten that my face was pressed against the most glorious comfort pillow ever designed.

"Easy, Thundercat," Callie murmured, chuckling lightly. But she didn't pull back. Instead... she pulled me closer, her body contouring to mine perfectly. "Don't get any ideas. It's nap time."

I couldn't help it. I laughed, slowly trying to peel away. But she didn't let me. She pulled me back to the soft, blood-enriched grass, and I was surprised to find how soft the ground was. I spotted the blanket and pillow and scowled up at the tree.

The treehouse had no immediate use for it. You are safe beneath me. Even still, a hundred wolves guard my perimeter even as we speak. Far enough away not to hear... he added with a dark chuckle.

Callie saw my face and scowled suspiciously. "What did he say?" she warned.

"Nap time. He said it's nap time," I lied, smiling guiltily.

She continued glaring at me, but finally patted the soft earth next to her. Kai must have readjusted himself to make the exposed roots form a perfect cocoon, because it almost felt magical.

Then again, company can be everything.

I leaned back, letting out a long sigh. Callie placed a hand over my heart, leaning on her side to stare at me. Her finger began tapping on my heart, matching my beat. Which, of course, made it speed up, causing her to laugh. But I didn't pull her hand away.

"Well?" she asked in a soft whisper.

"I think... I need to give them a break. Let them know how much I care. Reduce the crazy."

She waited for a minute. "Wrong."

I frowned, glancing over at her sharply. "Excuse me?"

She shrugged, head propped in her palm as she leaned on her elbow, her white hair cresting down to the ground like a small waterfall of light. "You can't reduce the crazy. Let's be honest. That's just not possible. The world is full of crazy right now. Only one way to change that."

"So... your brilliant advice is to get me to give in to my feelings, only to, what, continue doing exactly what I've been doing?" I muttered in a dark tone, growing frustrated. "Which has only been to try and keep everyone safe from as much crazy as poss—"

She placed a finger on my lips, and then leaned very, very close, her chest brushing against my shoulder, and causing my stomach to fall deep down into the earth's core. She slowly, and very firmly pressed her lips into the finger over mine, holding them there for a moment, her eyes closed. Then she slowly pulled away, opening her eyes to stare at me from inches away.

"Show them that they *matter*. Not that you're willing to give your life to save theirs, but that *their* lives have saved *yours*."

I could do nothing but stare at her eyes and lips in rapid succession, ignoring my stupid heartbeat. And Kai's amused laughter.

"Oh," I finally whispered, wishing I had swiped a breath mint from the restaurant.

"They know monsters live inside you, and that you're willing to let those beasts loose to keep your friends and family safe. But... they need to know that you love *their* monsters. Not just when a life is on the line. But *all* the time. That it's okay to be a monster. That their monsters are just as important and valuable as your monster. Don't act guilty for what you've done to save them, like you've had to become a dark person to keep them safe. Let them see you are proud of your flaws, and proud of their virtues."

I nodded woodenly. "Callie?"

She smirked, eyes drifting up to the tree around us for a moment, smile stretching wider, and giving me a perfect view of her slender, kissable neck. "Yes, Nate?"

"Is this... you know... our moment? Our time?"

She burst out laughing, pinching my chest playfully. "No, Nate. It's nap time."

And with that, she rolled over, scooted that delicious body right up to mine, and pulled my arm over her stomach. "Shut up, Kai," I muttered murderously, ignoring Callie's laughter.

I couldn't wait to get to the Land of the Fae to kill some shit.

CHAPTER 21

*W*e had woken early to the rising sun, surprising the both of us. The cold hadn't aroused us from slumber. *Heh.* Callie quickly reminded me of our talk the night before, informing me that I had a full day to basically become a certain purple dinosaur to all my friends. Then she had left, encouraging me to take my new purse with me to Fae. She literally said this the second before her Gateway closed, leaving me to glare at empty space.

You could say that at first, my heart wasn't into following her advice. For obvious reasons.

But I had managed to make the world's worst breakfast. Dean had taken offense to this, but had sensed something in my mood, and had simply stared at me after a time. I saw him mouthing the name *Callie* thoughtfully a few times, but I somehow refrained from tossing a skillet at him.

I did drop an egg on the ground to keep him busy.

Then, remembering Callie's advice, I had sighed and bent over to clean it up before he could move. Which took some agile maneuvering, let me tell you.

Carl stormed into the kitchen as I was cleaning up, claws clicking on the marble floors. He stopped, stared at me, and hissed in surprise.

"Flesh of the unborn, coming right up!" I called out cheerfully. "I've also got pig belly, and compressed bodily fluids from a citrus demon I found lurking around outside," I said, handing him a plate of bacon and eggs, and a glass of orange juice. I ignored the startled look on his face and turned to Dean. "Get the gift. Make sure no one else sees it. If you run into anyone, just put it back and I'll give it to Elder Carl later."

Carl was holding the plate and glass, mouth open as if he'd been struck between the eyes. "You've been possessed..." he murmured, flicking his tongue out at me.

I flicked mine right back. "No, I'm just a giant asshole, and I'm realizing that I've never thanked you properly. Drink the sacrifice, for god's sake," I muttered, motioning my hand towards the glass.

He did so, taking a sip on reflex. He jerked the glass away, reptilian second eyelid flicking up over his eye for a moment as he stared down at the glass. "This is very good. Where did you find this demon?"

"We'll find you some more. Don't worry," I said, guiding him towards the table.

He sat down awkwardly, sipping his drink and eyeing me uncertainly. I sat down next to him as Dean entered the room and handed me a box. I stared down at the package Dean had given me yesterday when I got Callie's gift, biting back a smile. Then I looked up at Carl, who looked very uncomfortable all of a sudden.

"I want to thank you for being such a loyal friend. You very easily could have turned against me and sided with your brothers and Indie. But you didn't. I constantly give you shit," I said holding up a finger in warning. "And that will not change." I waited for his bewildered nod. "But I do need to do a better job of honest appreciation and thanks."

"Okay..." he hissed uncertainly.

"I'm going to be blunt with you," I admitted. "This is about the weirdest thing I've ever done, but I guess it's not all about me, is it?" I said, handing him the package, making sure no one was about to walk in. He stared down at it, then at me. "I kind of got it as a joke, but also knew you'd really like it. I had a whole big reveal planned, but it's probably better this way," I sighed regretfully.

He slowly sliced open the package to find a pair of shining red heels inside a shoebox, the biggest pair I had been able to custom order, based on the size of the boots he wore.

He jumped to his feet, hissing. "Mine!" And then he fucking *ran* from the room as if the devil was after him and his new shoes.

I blinked, slowly turning to face Dean. He shook his head in disbelief. "I... think he liked them," he finally said.

"Fucking *weird*, *right*?" I whispered incredulously.

A thin smile appeared on his face, and then he shrugged wearily. "Do you need any help creating something edible for the others?" he asked me, eyeing the eggs that were now burning on the stove.

"Damn it," I cursed, jumping to my feet. He kicked my chair just as I moved, sending me crashing to the floor.

"Stay down," he warned. "You've desecrated my kitchen quite enough already."

"What the hell is that smell?" Gunnar grunted, walking into the room with Tory and the Reds. I stared up at them from my position on the ground and sighed.

"Master Temple is trying to kill you all with his kindness," Dean muttered, glancing over a shoulder. "Apparently."

Gunnar frowned at Dean, then at me. He finally helped me to my feet, staring into my eyes like a doctor would. I slapped him away and the Reds burst out laughing.

Tory studied me. "Where's Callie? I heard she—"

Gunnar coughed pointedly.

"That you had a nice dinner with her last night," she amended lamely. "And that she helped you kill some shadow monsters."

I sucked in a breath. "Actually..." This was my chance to do right. "Alucard saved us from the monsters. But not before we lost some wolves. Because of my failure to act," I admitted, stepping closer to Gunnar. I met his eye, which was suddenly hard at the mention of his fallen packmates. I knew he had already heard, but that didn't make it any easier. "I'm sorry, Gunnar... I know that doesn't help anything, but I'm sorry."

He studied me thoughtfully, and then grunted. "Thank you. But to be honest, those three were looking to die. They were very loyal to..." he trailed off.

"Ashley," I finished. His shoulders stiffened instinctively, as if preparing to break something, but he finally nodded.

"Yes. Wulfra, to be more precise," he corrected. "They've been nothing but trouble lately."

I gripped his shoulders, staring into his eye. "I will literally die trying to get her back, Gunnar. I swear it."

He stared back, muscles bunching under my hands. "Let's try not to let that happen. I don't think she'd be pleased with that solution."

"I want you to know that I will burn Fairy to the ground to get her back," I pressed.

He stepped back, frowning at me. "Did you find out you have cancer or something?" he asked warily.

I shook my head, sensing everyone watching me. "No. Callie just helped me realize that although I may have been willing to give my life to keep you safe, I haven't been the greatest at letting you guys know how much I appreciate you," I admitted.

The room was silent. "So, your solution is to tell Gunnar that you would give your life to show him how much... you appreciate him? Isn't that the same thing?" Tory asked, trying to hide her amusement.

I scowled at her. "I'm not perfect, Tory," I muttered.

She folded her arms. "And how are you going to show me how much you appreciate me?" she asked, grinning excitedly.

"Shift just received a large donation. Several years' worth of donations. And none of the old investors have an interest in your programs any longer. Also, I want to offer my services in teaching your students how to love their beasts, not just control them."

Tory blinked at me, lifting a hand to her chest. "Oh. I thought... not that money was tight, but that there were issues in the way of you funding the school outright..." she said carefully.

"I re-prioritized," I replied, smiling softly.

Sonya and Aria stepped up expectantly. "Can you get us matching corvettes to show us how much you appreciate us?" they asked sweetly.

Tory coughed reproachfully. I spotted a blur near the adjoining living room, but I kept my face blank. "Dean? Can you get the other gifts?" I asked instead of answering them.

"Of course," he said in a defeated tone, which usually implied that everyone but me was about to experience something entirely unpleasant. Dean came back and handed everyone a wrapped cardboard box. They shared long looks with each other, unsure whether to be excited or nervous.

"Go ahead," I said, walking past them into the living room as if finished with our conversation. I listened to the sound of tearing paper behind me. Yahn and Alex materialized before me, and handed me two objects.

"What the hell?" Gunnar asked, not angry, but bewildered. Then, "Oh, shit…" His claws were suddenly out and he was tearing into his box much more urgently.

I chuckled darkly and licked the tip of the device in my hand. "It's time to be kids again, Reds. At least for the morning. Three rounds. General mayhem, then hide and seek, and then capture the flag – outside – on ATV's."

I spun and pointed my nerf pistol at Gunnar just as he tore his free. I shot him in the forehead. Since I had licked the dart first, it stuck to his skin. "Eat that, wolfi-corn!" I hooted. Then I dove behind the couch as Yahn and Alex unloaded on their victims.

The Reds shrieked with glee.

Tory and Gunnar chuckled darkly, darting into the adjacent hallway and out of the kill-room.

I saw Talon walking towards the sounds of shouting, tail twitching curiously. "Anyone who tags Talon gets fifty points!" I yelled.

Talon hissed and then fled back the way he came. I chuckled.

"Is this what kids do in this world?" Alex whispered excitedly beside me. I grinned down at him. "It is in *my* house. Whenever we can afford to," I said, ruffling his hair, momentarily reminded how close he had come to being abducted. Twice.

Alex beamed with such an innocent smile that I couldn't help return it as I watched him flee deeper into the house, hunting for the Reds.

I stared down at my gun. "Thanks, Callie," I said softly.

Then I proceeded to hunt down my family.

CHAPTER 22

*W*e had played for hours, and I can honestly say it might have been the most relaxing day of my life. Over that space of time, I had completely forgotten about everything deadly, murdery, or scary. But, obviously, at some point those thoughts came back.

Right about the time they did for Gunnar, too.

Because he suddenly realized that Ashley wasn't here with us right now.

I met his eye, nodding slowly. The sunlight piercing the solarium caught his stone eye-patch, glinting brightly. He hid his thoughts well from everyone else, who were either napping idly on the stones, or sprawled out on the couches, but he couldn't fool me.

He slowly climbed to his feet and walked over to join me on my couch. Tory was dozing in the loveseat, but her eyes peeled open at Gunnar's movement. She watched us sadly for a moment before closing her eyes again. Sneaky woman, always trying to prevent bro-outs.

"I'm going to go shower up. I take it we'll be leaving soon?" he asked me. I nodded.

"I need to speak to Alucard in private, but we should be ready to go in a few hours." Alucard hadn't been around all morning, but Dean had told me he was tanning on the roof, a favorite place of his.

Gunnar grunted, speaking softly so the younger ones didn't overhear.

"This was damned good of you, Nate. But unnecessary. You didn't need to prove yourself to us."

I grunted. "I kind of did, actually."

"We know where your heart is," he argued, but he was smiling, staring off at the Reds. Alex was leaning on Yahn, talking softly to the dragon, no doubt pestering him about his colorful scales. Alex was so unused to trust that it was fun to see him open up. He was the most curious child I had ever seen, as if making up for lost time. "You really care for him, don't you?" Gunnar asked softly. Tory shifted in her seat, obviously not sleeping.

I nodded, watching the four teenagers. They had seen the worst the world had to offer, but I had managed to give them a half-day of pure, innocent joy. "Yeah."

Tory made a sobbing sound, but tried to mask it by shifting in her sleep. Gunnar rolled his eye. Right, werewolf senses. He must have known she was awake, too. He winked at me.

Or blinked.

"Hey, Gunnar," I said. "Can I ask you a serious question?"

He was quiet for a moment, and then sighed. "Sure."

"Can you come up with a new gesture to signify winking?" I asked him deadpan. "It's hard to distinguish from your regular blinks."

He turned to face me. Then his stone eye rippled, and I spilled the drink I had forgotten about in my lap. "Jesus!" I hissed.

He burst out laughing. "How about that, asshole?"

I shivered, staring at his stone eye. "How…"

He shrugged. "I was goofing around earlier. Figured it out."

Tory snorted indelicately. "He was flexing in front of the mirror, posing. I caught the lying bastard mid-act."

Gunnar flushed crimson, and I burst out laughing. "Oh, man. That's going to stick around for a while."

Gunnar arched an eyebrow at Tory. "Maybe we should talk about you and the Huntress braiding each other's hai—"

"Truce!" Tory laughed. "She would kill all of us."

I sighed, leaning back into my chair with a big grin. "Yeah, you're probably right." The laughter slowly died down. "This was fun, wasn't it?" I asked.

They both murmured encouragingly, eyes watching the teenagers. "Just to clarify," Tory began, "and I think I'm speaking for everyone…"

"I agree," Gunnar grumbled, somehow knowing what she intended to say ahead of time.

I frowned, not following.

"We like the old Nate. This is fun, but... part of your charm is the wiseass bastard. Don't lose that. But every now and then... this is nice, too."

I glanced over at her, making sure they weren't teasing me. Then, I said, "Thank *god*."

She jumped to her feet. "I *knew* it!"

I held up my hands in a guilty gesture, and Gunnar suddenly roared with laughter. I nodded, grinning. "This was – although fun – kind of... terrible at the same time," I admitted. "I don't think I could be like this all the time. It's just not me."

Tory and Gunnar both turned to watch me, sensing I had more I wanted to say.

I stared down at my drink, my smile fading. "I think I'm just a dark person. It's not that I don't love you, but that I love you enough to do bad things to keep you safe. But..." I trailed off, thinking, analyzing my feelings, and trying to consider Conquest's advice. And Callie's words of wisdom, which were kind of the same. "It's not always about me, though. Everyone processes love in different ways, and maybe the way I sometimes show my love isn't communicated properly..." I thought about it. "I ask you guys to do some pretty uncomfortable things to show your love for each other. Namely, risking your lives. So... it's only fair that I meet you in the middle. Like, once in a while. Not a lot. Just—"

"*Jesus*, Nate. We get it. Don't ruin it," Gunnar sighed, shaking his head in amusement.

Tory waited, making sure I didn't have anything else to add. "You should go talk to Alucard."

I nodded. "Yeah." I climbed to my feet. "You all set, Tory?"

She grunted. "We'll be fine while you're gone. Just don't make it two months. Time flies when... well, I was going to say when you're having fun, but..." she mumbled. "You know what I mean. Carl and I can take care of things while you're gone, and the Huntress will keep an eye on Alex."

I nodded. "We'll be as quick as possible. I know what to expect this time. And we have rides. And Oberon owes me. Talon thinks he can track Pan, and Gunnar knows Wulfra's scent."

Gunnar growled in both agreement and anticipation. "I'll be ready whenever you are. Meet me in the Sanctorum. I'll have the others with me or they'll be at the tree."

I nodded. Tory climbed to her feet and gave me a big hug. Then she kissed me on the cheek. "Get our girl back, Nate," she whispered.

I nodded, feeling my anger flash to life. Not at her, but in anticipation of saving my friend.

She frowned. "And work on that golden eye thing. You look like a demon when it lights up."

I frowned at her. "What?"

She nodded slowly. "Ever since Athena... when you're angry, we can all see it."

Gunnar grunted, but he didn't sound bothered by it. If anything, he sounded anticipatory. "I don't care about his laser eyes. Especially not if he uses them to kill everyone who thought about harming Ashley," he said in a dark tone. "But I'll keep an eye on him, Tory."

"Thanks, guys. I love how you include me in these conversations," I muttered.

"Thanks, Gunnar. You know how he gets," Tory said, ignoring me.

He laughed. "I've known him longer than anyone. Trust me. I know."

"Hey!" I pressed. "I'm right here!"

"Don't let him come home all tattooed up again," she added.

"Well, if it's going to help, I'll let him do whatever he wants."

"*Excuse* me? *Let* me?" I seethed. They continued to ignore me, and I sensed the teenagers were all very interested in the adults' table, now. "Well, I'm going to slap some happy on a grumpy Glampire. If you'll let me, that is."

They waved their hands dismissively, so I stormed off. I ignored their amused chuckles as Master Temple stormed through his sentient house. Falco purred soothingly, trying to calm me, but it sounded suspiciously like laughter, too.

"Can it, Falco, or I'll have Dean spray pledge in your sensitive cracks," I muttered.

This time she definitely laughed, the walls quivering noticeably.

CHAPTER 23

I took a deep breath and stepped out onto the roof. It was sunset, so I knew Alucard wouldn't be on the roof for much longer, and I didn't feel like searching every corner of the mansion for him. I took two steps and froze, realizing Alucard hadn't noticed me.

"I don't care how much you love them," he growled. "Put some damned pants on, Carl. Good lord. I feel like I need a bath even knowing about this."

I smiled, taking a few more steps to find Carl lying on a lawn-chair, ass up...

Wearing his new, sparkly red heels.

Alucard had scooted his chair away, but there was only a small sliver of the roof that had the perfect amount of fading sunlight hitting it. And Carl was forcing him to share it.

"This is my safe space, Carl!" Alucard hissed, growing angrier. "Go be weird elsewhere!"

"Those filthy babies are in my sunroom, enjoying themselves."

"Then go lay out on the driveway or something," Alucard snapped.

Carl was silent for a moment as I shook my head in disbelief, trying not to burst out laughing. Alucard was so annoyed that he still hadn't noticed me.

"I don't want to get my shoes dirty," Carl said.

"Sweet sassafras," I finally burst out, mimicking Alucard's accent. "This is beautiful."

Alucard jumped, pointing a finger at Carl. "Why in the seven hells did you buy him those?!" he snapped, rounding on me.

"Because I done him wrong," I admitted, my smile fading. Not losing my cheer, but making it more genuine and less mocking, remembering my purpose here. "Carl, can you go... do whatever you do with your shoes somewhere else for a bit. We need to be getting ready, and I want to talk to Alucard. In private."

Carl looked up at me, his scaled ass glinting in the sunlight.

"You do have pants up here, right? Please tell me you brought your pants up here..."

Carl's eyes squinted, his tongue flicking out in annoyance. He climbed to his feet, snatching up a pair of leather pants. Instead of donning them, he placed the wad of clothing over his naughty bits. "Will this suffice?"

"Well, not for general hanging out purposes, but to get to your rooms, yeah," I said, trying not to make fun of him. He really didn't understand our ways yet, no matter how hard we tried to explain them to him. He had finally come to the understanding that we didn't like to see his trouser snake. But it had taken some time.

"I will take my shoes to my secret lair where I can appreciate them in privacy," he muttered.

Alucard's jaw dropped, shaking his head incredulously.

Carl was just so freaking weird that you didn't have to even be snarky to tease him. Just have a basic understanding of social etiquette. Even Alex could tease him easily, and he hadn't been around regular people for a very long time.

I held up a finger to Alucard, trying to let him know with my eyes that he shouldn't tease him. He blinked at me, cocking his head curiously, but finally closed his mouth and nodded.

Carl muttered some more as he strutted away on his stilettos. I shook my head, wondering if I should have given him something else.

But if he was into heels, he was into fucking heels, and I wasn't going to stand in the way.

Realizing how that sounded, I sighed. "Thanks, Carl. I'm glad you like your shoes."

He muttered something vaguely thankful, so I let him go. I realized I was staring at him walking away, the perfect cat walk, as if he had been doing it his entire life.

I arched a brow at Alucard, and then grinned. "Can I sit?" I asked.

He grew slightly tense, as if expecting an unpleasant conversation, but nodded. "It's your house, not mine."

I let that slide, taking note of his tone, and took a seat on the ledge, my back to a forty foot drop to the cobblestones below, a subconscious message of vulnerability. He sat in his lawn-chair, studying me warily.

"Remember that one time we were up here?" I asked casually.

"When you held me over the ledge with one hand?" he muttered. "Yeah, fun times…"

I nodded absently. "Want to return the favor?" I asked after a few moments.

He tensed, slowly turning to look at me. "What game are you playing?"

I shrugged. "Not a game. A gesture." I held out my hands. "Well, Little Brother?"

He was on me in a blink, gripping me by the shirt and holding me out over the ledge. His face was a snarl, animalistic and savage. I met his eyes, unblinking, my hands hanging freely at my sides. "Is Grimm down there, ready to save you if I let go?" he snarled.

"I sure hope so," I said honestly. "But I didn't ask him to, if that's what you mean."

He frowned, and then grunted, pulling me back to safety before shoving me away. He turned his back and took a few angry steps, shoulders bunched up as if arguing with himself.

I straightened my shirt, waiting. I sat back down on the ledge when it was apparent he wasn't ready to talk yet. And I waited.

"What is the meaning of this?" he finally growled.

I waited a few moments, hoping to impart some sincerity. Because one thing Conquest had reminded me of, was that although Alucard was a pretty suave, snarky guy, he was also very emotional. He really valued trust, loyalty, and respect. And I had shown him everything *but* respect in the last few years. Constant fighting had made me lose sight of this. As a result, he had tried to earn my respect by doing anything he could to help. And, for the most part…

He had failed spectacularly – every single time. At least, in his eyes.

He had tried managing Plato's Cave, my bookstore, and being a vampire, had been worse than useless in almost every aspect. Not able to be present during the daytime hours, and unable to touch anything even remotely religious, which was pretty much everything. Even though the merchandise wasn't Christian, the items I sold were deeply spiritual and religious to the patrons.

Which was anathema to a vampire.

Then, in a moment of weakness, he had bitten Tory. That had somehow transformed him into a Daywalker, but at the time, we hadn't known that, and it could have very likely killed her.

To make up for *this*, he had tried to help her raise the Reds. And although they loved him dearly, he had kind of dropped the ball – epically – on a babysitting weekend of his, nearly allowing them to be killed by, wait for it…

His vengeful sister, who had tricked them into coming to Kansas City where she intended to kill all of us.

Then I hadn't taken him to the Land of the Fae with me. And to Alucard, that was just another… nail in the coffin, so to speak. Another jab at his feeling of getting no respect.

Then, Alex had almost been taken this morning under Alucard's watch. The last straw.

Even though he had been there time and time again to help us, in his eyes, he had failed an equal number of times. And that bothered him. Which meant I needed to make things right.

CHAPTER 24

*L*ooking at him now, I didn't know how he had lasted this long. Or how I had missed such obvious signs of inferiority and self-loathing – such a lack of self-confidence. I really was a shit.

"Little Brother," I said softly. "Look me in my eyes."

He flinched at those words. Because it was what he had called me when we first met. Somewhere along the way, that moniker had faded away. Likely, as his sense of self-respect had diminished.

He slowly turned, looking at me with a pained expression on his face. I smiled at him. A deep, genuine smile. Then I tossed him a can. He caught it instinctively, frowning down at it.

"Sun-kissed?" he asked, reading the generic brand of the famous drink, his tone dry and not pleased. As if his hopes had just been doused.

I nodded. "I wouldn't have you any other way, Little Brother."

His fingers clenched the can, almost tight enough to crush it. "Why do you keep saying that?"

I shrugged. "Should have been said more often, Alucard. I'm sorry about that. Ask Gunnar. I'm kind of an asshole to those I care about. I guess I'm a twisted bastard," I admitted.

He waited, studying me. "Again, what is the meaning of this?"

I sighed. "Callie helped me realize something. That my methods of showing my concern might not be received the same way." He grunted.

"She's very wise."

"Just to clarify, I'm not a saint like her. I'm an asshole. But I can usually see when I made a mistake and smooth it over." I paused. "If given the chance..."

"So, this is some gushy moment to help make the emotional vampire feel better?"

I laughed. "No. I just want you to know that me teasing you is a sign of respect."

He tensed, letting me know I had hit the nail on the head. "You also tease your enemies, who you definitely don't respect."

I blinked. "Well, shit. There goes my whole spiel..." I muttered.

"Yeah..."

"I think I'm seeing how this went sideways..." I said. Alucard had been brought up in a pretty crappy home. Given the name Alucard Morningstar by his parents. He grew into that name and became a ruthless vampire over-lord, doing quite well for himself. But he hadn't liked it, and after meeting me, had seen the chance to become something better. But... my teasing had kind of had the opposite effect. It wasn't that he couldn't take a joke. It was that he already felt like a failure, and my constant teasing had only rein-forced those insecurities, driving them bone-deep.

He sat down, muttering. "I don't need your pity."

"This isn't pity, Alucard. I don't really know what it is, but I'm obviously not very good at it. I guess it's to thank you for always kicking ass. And apologizing for not telling you that sooner."

He guffawed. "I've failed at almost everything I've tried. I don't fit in like you guys. And this Daywalker shit is a constant mockery of that."

"No, it's really not. Do you have any idea how many times I've failed?" I argued hotly. "More than you have. Ten times more. Every single problem we've had is a direct result of my failure," I admitted. "But you know what?" He waited, glancing up. "You've been there every time. To back me up."

He shrugged. "I can kill. That doesn't mean I've done well. It means I'm occasionally useful."

"Aren't we all?" I argued. "Stop trying to be something you're not! I'm not as noble as Gunnar. Nor as compassionate as Tory."

"I'm a monster," he said faintly.

"Then be a fucking *monster*, Alucard..." I said, leaning forward with a dark grin.

He stilled, slowly turning to look at me. "What?"

"Stop trying to be like anyone else, and be *you*," I said. "We met you when you were a monster. You wanted to be better, but you were still happy being a monster. Somewhere along the way you tried to become something you're not. But we never asked you to do that. I'm sorry if I made you think you had to be anything different than what you are. Because I know plenty of monsters who are good. In different ways." I pointed my thumbs at myself.

He frowned, thinking deep thoughts. "That doesn't bother you?" he finally asked.

I picked up a pebble on the roof and threw it at his shoulder. "No, you lunatic. I knew you were a monster when I met you!"

He smiled faintly. "I guess so."

"Listen. You tried to become more like a bit of each of us, and failed spectacularly." He tensed, but I pressed on. "As would *any* of us if we tried to do the same. You think Gunnar could become like me? Completely? Or that I could become as sickeningly sweet as Tory?"

Alucard grinned. "No, but they have all changed," he argued.

I held up a finger. "Changed within their *wheelhouse*. Not changed their *foundation*."

He nodded slowly.

"It's not good for you, bottling up your soul. It's one reason you've been so angry lately. The only time I see you truly happy is when you forget about the crap and tease us. Or... when you're in the thick of battle." His eyes flashed momentarily as he looked up, eyes suddenly hungry. "You need to reintroduce yourself to the monster... And I know just the place to do it."

He smiled wickedly. "Cut loose. Get back to my roots..." he trailed off.

I nodded slowly. "In a way, of course. Don't let the monster take over or anything, but get back in touch with him. Hell, I've got monsters sitting inside me right now. I want nothing more than to open up to them entirely, but I don't. Still, I do *use* them. And I'm less scared of them every day, because I know *I'm* in charge. We're partners. Family. My monsters and me."

"I'll try. If you can promise me something."

"I will continue to harass you. That's not negotiable. It's... part of my monster," I argued weakly, grinning at him.

He rolled his eyes, but his heart didn't seem entirely in the humor. "Just... be my compass."

"Well, we're all fucked if I'm the moral compass," I muttered.

He grinned, nodding. "Well, you know what I mean. Maybe you and Gunnar both can be my compass."

I thought about it. "I don't think Gunnar can be counted on to be anyone's compass. Not until we get Ashley back…" Alucard winced at that. "But I might need a fellow monster to remind him who he is when we get over there. Can you do that? I have no one else I would trust more…" I said, realizing it was the truth. Sure, Talon was comfortable with his monster, but he was also comfortable with everyone else being a bloodthirsty monster, which didn't help.

"I… can do that," he finally said. "We might have to hurt him, depending on what he does."

"Sometimes that's necessary," I said softly.

"Yeah…"

"Alucard, it means something when I say this…" That caught his attention. "I don't think I could possibly have more respect for you than I do right now. Even before this talk." He frowned. I waved a hand at him vaguely. "You basically tried to become the best parts of all of us, and it didn't break you. Sure, you failed, but any of us would have. Because you didn't do it half-assed. You went all in, trying to *become* each of us. That's hardcore, man." He finally chuckled, shaking his head guiltily.

"I guess."

"But you didn't implode. I mean, you've been close these last few days, but that's gotta be a record. You lasted *years* doing this. I *might* have lasted a few days."

He nodded. "Thanks, Nate. Mind giving me some space? You're way too gushy right now."

I stood, holding out my arms and planting my feet for a hug. "Bring it in, Sparkula."

"No."

"Then no Fairy time for you," I said, teasingly.

He sighed. "Fine. But only because I want to kill some sparkly shit."

"Whatever you need to tell yourself," I said, holding my arms out wider.

He gave me a very cursory hug, but I was having none of it.

I jumped up and wrapped my legs around his hips, squeezing him in a hug that only a toddler or a military spouse seeing a loved one after a long tour could replicate. "Who's my sparkly little vampire? You are!" I whispered directly into his ear canal.

With the full force of a Daywalker vampire, he tossed me down to the ground, grimacing.

"Disgusting," he muttered.

I grinned at him, holding out my hand.

He rolled his eyes and pulled me up, but shoved me away when I tried to go in for another hug. "Give me some space, creepo," he warned, shooing me away.

"Deal. See you soon," I said, smiling to myself as I turned away.

"Nate?" he called out. I didn't turn, but I did halt.

"Yeah?"

"Thanks… Little Brother," he said.

I nodded. "Let's go kill some sparkly shit."

He laughed hungrily and I left him to himself.

CHAPTER 25

I sat beneath Kai's tree, letting out a breath. It had kind of become a favorite spot for me. Especially over the past year or so, when we'd had hundreds of people living on the grounds. I surveyed my property nostalgically. Over ten acres, most of it wooded, including this massive tree, a labyrinth, and a walking trail through the woods.

Now that I thought about it, I hadn't gone on a nice walk in years. I wondered if the paths were overgrown. I'd have to check. Maybe take the ATV out to see. But not right now.

I stared down at my arms, searching for the occasional golden light I had seen there.

I wished I knew how to consciously use it, or even had a better grasp on what it was. But I wasn't eager to feel those strange cold, yearnings again. I'd had enough of that to last a lifetime. Was the power of a god still coursing through my veins, as Conquest seemed to think?

The problem was, the only ones who likely knew the answers were, well, *gods*, and they got touchy with that kind of conversation. A brief look at mortality after a life of the opposite.

I wondered if it was a living thing inside of me, a power, a presence. Like my brief glimpse at being a Maker – those beings that willfully partnered up with a dangerous… spirit of some kind, a force of nature that could help them do things.

Like the two men currently wanting to kill me – and each other.

Matthias Temple and Castor Queen.

I let out a breath. So many had died, all because of miscommunication.

And it was about to happen again, because I knew – after my brief encounter with the two Makers in New York City – that Matthias wasn't open to hearing me out. He was back for blood. Even though the cause of both of his vendettas was the same guy.

Motherfucking Castor Queen.

And according to Athena, Castor hadn't ever fully merged with his Beast as was typical with Makers, somehow prolonging his life and staying out of the radar for any gods to take advantage of him. Which was probably for the best when it came to the future of the world, but it didn't help me out. Not at all. It just meant he was incredibly powerful.

And if I spent too long in Fae, I could return to find all my friends dead in the aftermath of their search for me. But I had to go. Ashley needed me, and I needed Pan.

I sighed, content that my phone call a few minutes ago had at least warned the Academy about the threat – that they needed to be on high alert for a jail-break in case either of the Makers decided to rebuild their Syndicate army. They hadn't sounded pleased at the news, but had at least been grateful for the warning. I was more concerned with how the two had found us in New York.

I glanced down at the coin I was absently rolling across my knuckles. My Horseman's Mask. I knew I was going to take it with me to Fae, but I wasn't happy about it. The last time I had worn the Mask it had scared the living shit out of everyone.

Including me.

Diamond claws and flesh? Wings? No thanks. But… it had saved Gunnar. Even though it had permanently changed him as a result, upgrading his claws with the same diamond-like coating.

The real question was what the living fuck was I?

A wizard. I had been a Maker for a short period. I was a temporary Horseman – because I hadn't heard any trumpets from Heaven making it official that I had signed up for the Varsity Apocalypse team. I had this strange white power that had ties to Heaven. Wylde. And now…

This Gold thing.

I scratched my cheeks, thinking.

And Callie had the same white magic – a gift on loan from Heaven like mine? But... I had also seen some strange silver power around her in New York, and she hadn't explained that.

"I'm gold, and she's silver..."

"You have no idea," a very low, bass voice murmured from out of my peripheral vision. I flinched, jumping to my feet.

Or, I tried to, but they had apparently fallen asleep, so I succeeded only in falling on my face with a loud whoosh of air. I scrambled up awkwardly, ignoring the pins and needles as I looked up, ready to fight. Because I hadn't recognized the voice, and my wards should have prevented anyone from entering my property.

Which meant that when I looked up to see a blood-red, massive, triangular nose only inches away from my face, I almost ruined my pants. Then the lips of the beast pulled back to reveal long fangs, and it let out a snort in my face. A wet, snotty snort.

CHAPTER 26

$\mathcal{I}$ scooted back with a shout, wiping the snot from my face, surprised to find it a faint crimson color. I stared up at the rest of the creature, and my mouth slowly opened in awe. Massive, velvet-covered horns decorated a gigantic head, easily ten points each, and eyes of red fire stared down at me. His nose was wet with… blood. Long, wiry, shaggy fur covered his body, and a six-inch-long patch of braided hair hung from his lower jaw, looking like a goatee. The fur bunched up into a thick mane around his neck, and his pointed ears were tucked back as if about to attack.

He had a holly wreath around his neck.

"Easy, Rudolph," the same voice said. I had completely forgotten about the voice.

A massive, one-eyed, wild-haired man stared down at me, one calloused hand resting on what must have been a reindeer's back. His beard fanned across his chest, and the mustache over his lips was waxed together in two very distinct strips that rested atop the beard hanging down his jaw. He had no shirt, and was corded with thick, hard slabs of muscle. Not the puffy kind you see in most gyms, but dense, striated, *real* muscle. His veins bulged as if he was hovering at two-percent body fat.

He wore thick, iron bracers on his wrists, and although dull, they looked expensive… and ancient. He wore fur pants, with a giant metal face over each knee, and tall leather boots that looked designed a million years ago – from dinosaur hide.

"Those look like Darling and Dear work…" I said softly, not consciously choosing to speak.

He grunted, amused. "What would a Godkiller know about D&D?"

I blinked up at him, a smile tugging my cheeks. "You might not realize how silly that sounds. There's a game about that, and it makes more sense than you think."

A single, cold, wintry eye stared back at me above leathery cheeks, and I could have sworn I saw lightning in its depths. The other socket was just scarred flesh. His skin wasn't old or wrinkled, but more like tough hide. A dark-blue, hooded cloak hung over his shoulders, clasped in front by a rune-covered silver brooch. It rippled in a wind that I could not feel.

"Wait, did you say Rudolph?" I asked, staring back at the reindeer, who stamped a hoof while continuing to glare at me, puffs of steam jetting out from his snout. "The… red-nosed reindeer? Wow, you, uh… definitely applied what we refer to as *marketing spin* on that one."

The god just watched me. I was sure I had seen him before. Up in the pavilion where I had fought Athena. Well, not in the pavilion, because he hadn't been allowed inside, but he had been seen hovering in the air as if standing on solid ground. Of course, he hadn't been alone then, but he also hadn't been hanging out with Rudolph, either.

"They're speaking with Wulfric," the man said, sounding amused as he read my thoughts.

I nodded dumbly, and then climbed to my feet. His two wolves, Geri and Freki, were speaking to Gunnar. Of course. Why wouldn't they be? "My name's Nate," I said, extending my hand, not really sure what else to do.

Two ravens cawed from up above, and I felt my eyebrows furrow. "Be careful, the bastards shit on everything."

"Just cats," the god chuckled. "They really fucking hate cats."

"Right." I glanced from him to Rudolph thoughtfully. He didn't look like Santa Claus to me, but I wasn't about to ruin my childhood by asking him. Especially not when I had more important questions. Like his name. Officially.

"You know that one already," he said, eye flickering again. With lightning.

I nodded, fidgeting slightly. Because I hadn't heard the nicest things in the world about Odin, the Allfather. "Why are your ravens on my family Crest?"

"That's a very good question," he said, petting Rudolph's thick fur.

When it was apparent that the Allfather was all-out of answers on that topic, I sighed. "Let's try an easier one. What is this gold stuff? Should I be concerned?"

He grunted. "I'm generally concerned when anything about me changes. As a rule."

"Okay," I said, growing frustrated. "Which way did you bet?" I asked, remembering my fight with Athena.

He grinned, a truly horrifying look that made me step back instinctively. Then he patted a pouch that clinked in a familiar tone. Olympian gold. I found myself smiling arrogantly.

"Fuck, yeah. Odin bet on me!" I hooted, glancing back over my shoulder, wishing someone was recording this.

He laughed. "Sure did."

Apparently, Odin wasn't much of a talker, so I pressed on, coming to the conclusion that he had come here for a reason. "Do you know what I am?" I asked, hoping that covered all my bases. "I seem to pick up magical maladies wherever I go..."

He nodded. "That's putting it mildly." He studied me thoughtfully. "Everyone should know who their father is, what he's done, and what prices he's paid. Mothers, too, of course."

Then he watched me in silence. I blinked at him. Then I began to shake my head.

"Nope. Not happening. No way—"

He burst out laughing, cutting me off. "Loki's balls!" he bellowed, throwing his hands up as he laughed harder. "You're a riot." But instead of answering me, he changed topics. "You're going Fae-side again, I take it?"

I rolled my eyes. "Please don't insult my limited, non-godly intelligence. You know whatever those two bird-brains see. You know I am."

"Watch. Your. Tone."

And Rudolph looked suddenly less-pleased, making his earlier attitude seem downright pleasant. "Sorry. Yes. I am." I paused, debating, but deciding to stand my ground on this. I wasn't walking blindly into things anymore. "Why do you ask?"

His lightning eye locked onto mine, and it felt like staring down a tornado, but I somehow stood my ground. "Where do you keep things that are important to you?" he asked. Seeing my immediate defensiveness, he chuckled. "I'm not talking about your Armory. I'm talking in general. If something is valuable, where do you keep it?"

I frowned. "Locked away? In a safe, I guess."

He nodded. "And where would you keep that safe?"

"Um… somewhere close at hand. Home, I guess."

He nodded approvingly. "Smart. Good intentions don't always guarantee good results."

I frowned at him. "What the hell does that mean?"

Rudolph lunged at my face, and I heard a shout behind me. I dove out of the way of Christmas fangs, and fell on my ass, really not wanting to throw down with lightbulb nose. When I looked up, they were both gone.

I spun at the sound of racing feet. Alucard was sprinting my way. "Nate! Gunnar wants to talk to you. Now! I think—"

"He saw Odin's wolves, didn't he?" I growled, climbing to my feet. Alucard stopped, cocking his head. His eyes immediately shot up to the canopy, but he didn't see any ravens.

"As a matter of fact, yes," he finally said. "They were fucking huge. They walked right into the Sanctorum and sat in front of Gunnar. He immediately shifted into wolf form and none of them made a sound for ten minutes. Then they were simply gone, and Gunnar shifted back to his human form. He won't talk. He just beats on the punching bag you hung up down there."

I nodded, curious. "It's time for us to go. Can you gather everyone and bring them to the Sanctorum?" I asked.

He nodded, walking beside me, obviously full of questions.

"Just… give me a few minutes. I need to figure some things out in peace."

He sighed unhappily. "I wish I could meet someone cool one day."

"Maybe we'll meet Vlad or something. The way my day's going, I wouldn't be surprised."

He eyed me for a few moments, and then jogged ahead of me.

I continued walking, mind reeling. What in the hell had that been all about?

It seemed Odin and Conquest read the same self-help books, and that the material was well-beyond my reading level. Talking of items that should be kept locked up reminded me of the items from the Mausoleum – still in the satchel at my hip.

But I didn't have time to lock them up, and I wanted them within reach at all times. Until I figured out what they were.

CHAPTER 27

I entered the Sanctorum to the sound of fists striking canvas. I glanced over to see the Round Table rising up out of the floor, even though I was nowhere near it. With a scowl, I dismissed it, hoping Baba and Van would have more luck on their second attempt to find answers.

I approached a sitting room off to the side to see Gunnar, bare-chested, and going to town on the heavy bag. Sand coated the floor where he had torn through it in places.

"You ready to get your fiancée?" I asked.

With a vicious snarl, Gunnar punched entirely through it, pouring sand all over the floor.

He turned to me. "Now I am. I'm trying to get used to this diamond crap," he muttered, suddenly extending a set of rock-like claws as his hands shifted to his wolf form, a thick white fur shooting up to his elbows.

I nodded. "We're in the same boat. We'll get our answers soon enough, I'm sure. But first, that smoking hot redhead." He grinned like a predator, his concern momentarily trumped by his eagerness. Then the look slowly faded into something darker, realizing we had some work to do to make that happen. "What were they like?" I asked in a soft tone.

He frowned. "Like family. Like a higher form of myself. A bit like Wulfra, a bit like me. Like a perfect merging."

I nodded thoughtfully. "Interesting…"

He grunted. "They wished me luck," he said in a low tone, sounding very thoughtful, and happy at the memory.

"That's it? A pep talk?"

He studied me thoughtfully. "That's all I'm allowed to say. I swore an oath…"

I frowned. Not at him, but at the entire situation. "Well, Odin wasn't as helpful. At least I don't think he was. I always meet the cryptic immortals. Oh, and Rudolph is definitely scary as fuck. He and Grimm would get along great."

Gunnar shook his head in wonder. "Does his nose really glow?"

I shook my head. "With the blood of his enemies, maybe. It was like a raw, open wound. Just blood." I shivered, and Gunnar grimaced.

"Maybe we shouldn't share that with the Reds. Or Alex."

"Good idea. Leave them in ignorance. I wish I could join them."

Gunnar frowned, scratching his jaw thoughtfully. "I thought Odin had an eight-legged horse?"

I thought about that, nodding. "Sleipnir. Wait, how many reindeer does Santa have?" I asked.

"Eight… Fuck me sideways…" he breathed, eye widening. "You think—"

I waved a hand, cutting him off. "To be honest, I'd really rather not think about it."

He nodded as he scooped up a canvas rucksack from the corner of the room, and then followed me as I walked towards the waterfall, my own satchel thumping against my hip. Talon seemed to think that we could use it to get to Fae, since it resided inside my home, and I now had a bus pass to the land of sparkly psychos. If not, we would Shadow Walk to Stonehenge and try to enter that way, like we had last time.

"Alucard should be here with Talon and Yahn any minute," I said, studying the waterfall.

"I sure hope the other part works."

I nodded. "They didn't seem concerned about it. We'll just have to see. But we'll have Yahn and Vampula to scout in a worst-case scenario."

Gunnar grunted, still not happy that Yahn was joining us, thinking him much too young.

And he was right, but we needed wings, and Yahn had been the only dragon willing to go. Raego was dealing with some dragon stuff, and had

had about enough of my associations, lately. He'd lost a lot of dragons in the war, and wasn't happy about offering up another. He also told me it didn't look good that he kept helping me. If he wanted to remain neutral to events – giving him a better vantage to discover what was happening out in the world – he needed to not be seen as my errand boy.

He had a point, but it still made me feel uneasy. Something was off there, and I idly wondered if it was related to what Callie had told me, that I had been pushing people away lately, not speaking to them in their language.

But it would have to wait. Yahn was our only choice, and his skills could be invaluable over there. Camouflage. If we needed to get Ashley out quickly, he could hide her for us until I had a second to get us all out. Because Talon told me that since I had survived the Fae Invitation, I now had the ability to bring others back and forth at will, no longer needing a key to return.

We were about to find out.

Talon, Yahn, and Alucard entered in silence, game faces already on. They met us near the waterfall, and I studied them as they approached. They each wore plain clothes and a jacket with a canvas rucksack slung over a shoulder – complete with medical supplies, food, and water. They didn't wear them entirely over their backs in case their change destroyed the straps, unable to accommodate their new forms. Because the Fae had a way of changing you. Some more than others.

Even Yahn, the normally upbeat Swede was unusually somber. Then again, he had been through a war, and wasn't entirely as innocent as he had once been. For everyone's benefit, but mostly his, I cleared my throat.

"You all saw what happened to me when I went over there. It… changes you. I mean, look at Talon. He got a new name and now has to take care of his own litter!" I said, face serious.

"Hilarious, Manling," he muttered.

I met each of their eyes, Alucard first. He nodded resolutely. Yahn didn't even bat an eye – either the best poker face in the world, or entirely committed. It would have to do. He was a big boy, and I needed to show him some respect. He could always disappear if things got crazy.

Then again… that would leave him stuck in Fae.

I met Talon's eyes, which were watching mine as if reading my thoughts. He nodded one time, and I concealed my breath of relief. Talon would get him out if things went sour.

"First a few rules. The Fae are… different. They consider anyone born on our side to be Manlings. Much like we tell Fairy Tales, the majority of them share Manling Tales. And the majority of those we came across saw Manlings as the next best thing to the bogeyman. They will still try to eat your face, but you need to understand that they see us all as monsters."

"Good," Alucard interrupted. "Let's drive that point home, shall we?"

Gunnar growled his agreement.

I nodded. "Be that as it may, we're not looking for a war. We're extracting a friend. We can't let our rage take over. It's way too easy to let that happen over there. I'll try to keep you grounded, as will Talon, because we have to remember part of ourselves – as we are here, right now. I want everyone to think about the most important thing in the world to you. Seriously, think on it. Then you're going to share with the class so we can all hear."

I waited. Gunnar didn't miss a beat. "Ashley. She's my everything."

I nodded. "That's good. I also would have accepted your best friend, Nate, but Ashley will suffice," I mumbled. He grunted, not looking the least bit guilty, but he was smiling.

Alucard stared at the ground for a few moments. "Family. My real family. You assholes. The Reds. Tory. My family of monsters."

I smiled, nodding. "Remember it. You'll need it as a totem."

Yahn was staring into the middle distance. "The Reds," he said firmly, not meeting my eyes.

Alucard turned to him suspiciously, but Yahn didn't return the look. "The Reds?" I pressed.

Yahn compressed his lips, nodding. I really tried not to smile. "Which one?"

Alucard folded his arms, scowling murderously.

But Yahn didn't immediately answer. After a few tense moments, he finally did meet Alucard's eyes, and what I saw made me shiver. There was not an ounce of fear in them. It was a raw challenge.

Talon began to clap. "Well, well, well…" he chuckled.

"Shut it, tuna-can," Alucard snarled. Then he took in Yahn up and down, sneering. Yahn didn't bat an eye. "We'll talk."

"We'll see," he said, a glimmer of a smile creeping over his cheeks. But… not a guilty smile, a possessive one.

"Fuck me," I breathed, and then burst out laughing. Before anyone could get off track, I snapped my fingers. "Okay, everyone has their totem. Now, focus on it for a few moments. Imagine losing it forever, and what you would do to prevent that." I waited a full minute. "Got it?" They nodded. "Okay, here's the tricky part. I need you to be willing to let your monster out a bit as well. Your totem will help you dance the line, but you're going to need that dark part of you, too. You might even need to rely on it at times. I know I did..."

They looked unsurprisingly uneasy at that, but gave me grim nods.

"Don't be surprised if you look different. It might be immediate, or it might come about after our first skirmish." I glanced at Talon, who shrugged disinterestedly. "Also, I'm in charge. Entirely. This isn't a power trip or a joke. This is quite literally to keep you safe. What I become over there might look like Nate, but it ain't. Wylde is my name, and I think you saw what he's capable of when he feels disrespected..." They nodded soberly. I had killed Athena, that's what.

"Let's invade fairy town," I said, and held out my hand. Gunnar latched onto it, and soon we formed a chain of clasped hands. Then I walked through the waterfall.

CHAPTER 28

*W*e entered a thicket that I had never visited before. I crouched down low, squinting at the sunlight high overhead. Which didn't do much good, because the thicket was made of glass grass. The stalks swayed in the breeze, and several crunched and shattered at our sudden arrival, but I felt everyone crouch down behind me. A quick look let me see no one had changed yet, so I studied our surroundings again.

I felt Wylde stretch out inside of me as if waking up after a long nap. Or a night of epic sex.

Home... he whispered excitedly. I let him merge with me, confident in our shared control. He murmured appreciatively at my display of trust.

Without warning, a very loud horn erupted, seeming to originate from... *everywhere*. Like an alarm had been sounded, and the grass thicket we stood in collapsed to absolute dust at the intensity of the sound. Each of us tensed, ready for an immediate fight since we no longer had any cover. Even Wylde was as tight as a spring inside me. But nothing else happened as the sound faded away.

But I certainly didn't like the timing. Not one bit.

Listening to the heavy breathing behind me, I waited, scanning our surroundings, but I found nothing alarming, even with Wylde's assistance. *What was that?* I asked him.

I... don't know, he admitted warily.

I let out a nervous breath, deciding it was past time for us to move. Especially if that horn was for us. Anything nearby that had heard the horn would have immediately come to investigate, so I figured we were fairly safe. That didn't mean I wanted to just stand around and wait, though.

"Scent," I murmured. Gunnar immediately obeyed. He sniffed the air, but as a human that wasn't much help. I cuffed his arm instinctively, feeling Wylde acting through me without warning. Gunnar grumbled, and then suddenly exploded into his wolf form.

Times about ten.

Luckily, he had tossed his bag beside him, because he suddenly towered over me, easily seven feet tall, and corded from claw to snout in muscle. Thick, wiry, matted, white fur covered his body, almost like dreadlocks in places. With his back to me, I saw that his hair was braided from his neck to his spine, and sporadically adorned with bones – like a light armor of sorts.

Some of those bones still had a bit of dried flesh on them, even though that wasn't entirely possible since we'd only just arrived. Then again, Fae World.

He turned to face me, and I nodded back in approval, realizing I was smiling. His diamond claws extended inches longer than usual from his fur. His teeth were permanently extended from his jowls, in the world's worst overbite. And his single eye was abnormally large and human, as clear as a glacier. The other was the uncut-diamond eye-patch, but it was obviously much bigger, and had a wolf-head engraved in the center. He also sported a tarnished bronze crown that was held in place by his braided fur. The fur below his jaws was also braided into one long cord.

If any of you have seen that old Ninja Turtles movie, you'd have an idea what I'm talking about. That large red-furred thing that was pals with the razorback turtle. The mutant bad guys from one of the sequels.

"Wulfric," I murmured approvingly. He sniffed the air, turning his head back and forth before turning back to me with a shake of his head, which set his bones to rattling. "She's alive," he whispered, his lone eye seeming to glisten involuntarily. Then he shook his head. "She passed not far from here, but it's faint," he added in a low, low growl. Like a loud whisper in a cavern. Soft, but impacting.

I nodded, glancing back at the others. I waited for a few moments, but they didn't shift.

Yahn stared at Gunnar in awe, likely wondering what he would look like when he changed. Part of me wondered why Gunnar had changed so easily. Was it his ties to me? Our shared family rune? Or the stone eyepatch?

I subconsciously checked the wooden disc at my throat, making sure I had the Horseman Mask. Because to get Ashley back, I would do whatever it took. Not just for Gunnar, but because she was my friend, and she also sported one of my family runes.

And… Indie was the one who had almost killed her, so it was all on me.

Alucard was grinning at Gunnar, glancing down at his arms as if hoping to will his change to happen. I shot him a dark look and a grunt. "If it's going to happen, it will be sudden. I think Wulfric's channeling me, so it was easier for him. Don't be discouraged. Take out the feather," I told the giant white wolf.

He reached into his pack to withdraw a pristine white feather. He closed his eye and said a word in a guttural growl. "Pegasus."

"Grimm," I murmured simultaneously.

The skies rippled, white and then black, and two winged horses erupted out of a haze of light, accompanied by bolts of lightning – one white and one black.

A deep *gong* reverberated through the land, as if a second giant fucking alarm had just been activated. Everyone stilled, turning to me warily as the horses landed beside us. But nothing else happened as it faded away.

I glanced at Pegasus and flinched. He was… dirty, and covered in blue tattoos. More like brands, because they could be seen through his fur with perfect clarity. His mane was still long and braided, but more wild and wiry, less shampoo commercial and more Seattle grunge.

His eyes were gold, and they actually smoked faintly, which I have to admit, was pretty unsettling. His wings flared back, and the feathers looked like they were tipped with razor blades, and one chrome hook protruded from the peak halfway down the length of each wing. The gleaming blade looked lethal – as if designed to rip someone in half without much effort.

He had fangs. Because, why not?

Talon purred excitedly.

Grimm looked the same as he always did, his peacock-like feathers sporting red, bloody orbs – that were actually wet with blood. But his wings were pure smoke and chips of obsidian stone, held together as if a dense fog of death. I hadn't really taken a good look at them because he could kind of turn them on and off at will ever since I had donned my

Horseman Mask. As if on cue, they disappeared, leaving the nightmare unicorn sans wings.

"Fairy fucks inbound," Grimm offered casually, licking his razor-sharp teeth.

I glanced up, not feeling very concerned. Instead, I felt eager. Rarawk thundered over the crest of a hill a hundred yards away, and they had riders – tiny, feathered things with bows and arrows in their hands. I glanced over at Talon, who had an ingrained hatred for the beasts.

My breath caught at that thought.

Because… that memory wasn't *real*. It was one of those flashbacks from Wylde, and it made me very nervous – again, wondering what Wylde really was. The real wrench in the whole thing was that Talon had been surprised to suddenly have new memories with Wylde, too – something he hadn't had before coming with me to Fae the last time.

Which made me think we had been spelled. Because Talon remembered his past here. It was only when he came with me that he suddenly had new memories of Wylde.

But we didn't have time to worry about that.

The Rarawk were much closer, covering the distance between us quickly. They resembled stags, complete with massive horns that fanned over their heads, the points easily several feet long. But instead of fur, their bodies were covered in a thick shell. They were usually solitary animals, loners, and didn't work in concert. Which meant these feathered archers had subjugated them somehow. They were more dangerous than they looked, it seemed.

Grimm, not wanting to delay the fun, suddenly pounded towards the oncoming attackers, neighing loudly as the glass grass crunched under his hooves. His horn tore through the first Rarawk's shell in an explosion of blue blood, coating Grimm's face, even as the others raced past him, hungry to get to the rest of us. I saw the rider on the ground, backing up as he fumbled with the bow and arrow he had dropped.

Grimm saved him the trouble, impaling him in a quick serpentine motion with his barbed forehead horn. He lifted up on his back legs, the feathered creature still stuck to his horn, and whipped his head to the side, flinging the body away as he neighed delightedly. Then he dipped down on his front legs in a bow, staring at Pegasus, as if to say, *your turn…*

Pegasus obliged, returning the gesture briefly, his lips curled back in what passed for a grin. He zipped into the air, almost straight up before tucking his wings back, and plummeting back down to the ground. The talons on his wings stabbed through two of the riders when they were still two dozen paces away from me… and then the talons tore down through the Rarawks' shells, shattering their antlers in the process, amidst shrieks of sheer terror.

The rest of the attackers scrambled, their formation broken, defining them into individuals rather than a single mass.

Grimm sniffed disdainfully at his brother before bounding in for round two. A wave of arrows was launched at Pegasus, who simply lifted his wings, forming a shield. The arrows struck it like metal coins thrown at a glass wall, splintering on impact.

I chuckled as I sat down, waving a hand in permission for Wulfric to cut loose. He slowly turned, and let out a booming howl akin to a Jurassic roar. Talon folded his arms as he approached me, watching the invaders with a derisive sneer. I could tell he wanted to kill them all, but he shot me a subtle nod of approval at deciding to sit the fight out and let my friends have play time with their new juice.

Which meant Alucard and Yahn suddenly looked very uncomfortable. Not afraid, but as if they were standing naked in a crowd. I shrugged, turning back to watch Wulfric.

He bounded straight up to the largest Rarawk, grabbing a hold of the beast's massive antlers. The beast skidded to a halt, but not of his own volition. Wulfric's back paws skidded across the earth a foot or so before halting, more glass shattering underfoot – which was pretty damned impressive. The Rarawk was at least eight-feet long and built of solid muscle. The feathered rider screamed as he shot an arrow at Wulfric's face from point-blank range. I flinched in fear, but it was instantly quelled as I realized Wulfric was… laughing.

The arrow struck his diamond eyepatch and exploded, the tip ricocheting back at the feathered fuck, slicing into his cheek in a spray of blood. Wulfric flexed and the antlers in his fists snapped off. The Rarawk screamed in both pain and outrage – because those horns were signs of his authority – his power in this place. A sign that he had lived, fought, and fucked his way through the land, growing bigger, stronger, and had never been stopped before.

Wulfric didn't much care for any of that.

He crouched down, wielding one of the massive antlers, and uppercut the Rarawk in the soft flesh beneath his jaw, piercing up through the animal's forehead.

The creature's knees wobbled, and then he fell.

Wulfric chuckled. "I made a unicorn!" He bellowed proudly.

"Too soon…" Talon murmured, but he was smiling, happy to see at least one of us embrace our wilder sides. The ones that the Fae World always brought out of those who dared enter.

I glanced up, studying the surroundings, only to find that the horses had dispatched the remainder of the attackers. Well, a few were fleeing – either Rarawks or their feathered riders – now on foot. I snapped my fingers, and without looking, the two horses pursued. Grimm lowered his head as he pounded after the feathered creatures, and Pegasus took to the sky with a single flap of his wings. He circled once, as if plotting the best way to take down the two fleeing Rarawks, and then he dove down like a hawk.

All I saw was an explosion of… shell, horn, and blood – and all I heard were horrified, begging screams. I shrugged, glancing back at Yahn and Alucard with a raised brow.

"Nothing?" I asked.

They shrugged. "I… never really felt in danger," Yahn said, glancing out at the dead bodies. I noticed some of them moving, even though they were dead, and frowned. Then I saw scaled hands were actually tugging them away. The creatures disappeared as they were pulled underground by some… things. Free dinner, I guessed.

I smiled, thankful they had saved me some work.

CHAPTER 29

I glanced at Alucard. "That… is going to happen to us?" he asked, sounding both fearful and excited. I nodded. "Wow… I didn't feel anything, but to be honest, someone could have crept right up on me and I might not have noticed. That was *epic*…" he said, staring at Gunnar in awe.

I was mildly surprised the two hadn't shifted at the first sign of attack. Last time I had visited, merely arriving had turned us into our new forms.

But we had been Invited that time… Maybe that was why it was different. I grunted, hoping that this wasn't going to be a problem – that the two of them weren't going to be liabilities.

Wulfric had kept one of the antlers, and was walking back up to us, studying it thoughtfully. I arched a brow and he shrugged. "Souvenir?" he asked, setting it down beside him.

I grinned. "Sure."

"That was… so refreshing!" he finally said. Then he saw Alucard and Yahn, and frowned for a moment. "Why didn't you come play?"

I waved a hand at him. "They will. Don't worry." I studied him curiously, then glanced at Talon, who shrugged. "You feel okay… Gunnar?" I asked casually.

He nodded. "Yeah, Nate. It felt like I had stretched muscles that had been sore for so long I couldn't remember even *having* them." He stared down at his claws, shaking his head. "Think Ashley will like it?" he asked, gesturing at his entirety.

I chuckled. "I'm pretty sure you two will get along just great." But I was mildly surprised. He had responded to *Gunnar*, called me *Nate*, and asked about *Ashley*. Not shying away from our real, human-world names. The last time I had been here, a blood-fever of sorts had taken over everyone, totally washing away our memories of our real lives. Which had made me think I would have the same problem this time. That *Wulfric* wouldn't remember *Gunnar*, *Nate*, or *Ashley*, but would instead remember only *Wulfric*, *Wylde*, and *Wulfra*.

But why was this time different?

I was leaning closer and closer to the hypothesis that we had been spelled last time. It was possible that Gunnar was simply in better control with his monster. Or that he was immune to the brain-wash due to his ties to me, with his fancy new eyepatch that matched my Horseman Mask.

Those who were already wild and savage beings in our world typically didn't have a problem remembering who they were. Carl, for example, had felt incredible, but hadn't had a problem remembering our world. Kind of like Gunnar, now.

Talon was originally from the Fae, so this was just a trip back home for him.

Studying the horses, I realized that they were also savage at heart – Pegasus merely masked it when in my world – because they were teasing each other back and forth as they approached.

"I've missed you, brother. Whatever convinced you to act prim and proper back home was a waste of years," Grimm said in a throaty rasp, licking the blue blood from his lips.

Pegasus grinned, walking prouder than I had ever seen him. As if I was seeing him in his true skin for the first time. "Maybe it was all that time with the Greeks – always trying to be sophisticated. Must have just rubbed off. But this..." he trailed off, arching his neck to glance at his wings. "Feels right. Sorry for being a dick," he said, bumping shoulders with Grimm.

Grimm shoved back, snorting. "No, you're not," he teased. "But I'm glad to have you back."

I shook my head, turning to Alucard and Yahn. It looked like they were the only ones I would have to keep an eye out for. To make sure this place didn't mess with them too much.

"Which way, Wulfric?" I asked, feeling a sudden surge of impatience from Wylde.

Wulfric sniffed the air again, closing his eye as he did. He pointed to our left, where I could see the earth rising gradually in the distance into small, rolling hills of purple trees like willows. I climbed to my feet and picked up my satchel. I studied it for a moment, considering the items I had brought with me. I had shoved the foodstuffs and water on top of the hourglass and pyramid.

Maybe when we set camp I could study them a bit more in-depth. Maybe Wylde would even have some thoughts on them. Probably not, but you never knew with Wylde.

"Let's walk for a bit, get a feel for the place. Maybe give them a chance to… adjust," I said, flicking my head towards Yahn and Alucard.

Alucard was studying me. "It's still you, right Nate? You have those blue tattoos again…"

I nodded. "Yep. We had that bro-out a few hours ago, where I told you—"

"Okay, got it," he interrupted quickly, shooting wary glances at the others. They each shared considering looks, their curiosity peaked at his obvious desire to change topics.

I grinned at his scowl. "Yahn, have you tried shifting into dragon form yet?"

He shook his head. "Didn't know if that would mess with something here. Maybe prevent me from doing…" his eyes drifted towards Gunnar, and he shrugged, "that."

I sighed. "Possibly. Let's get moving. I want you two to really try." I shot a look at the others. "Which means you guys need to hold your horses if we're attacked again." Pegasus sniggered at the bad pun. "Share in the bloodlust," I added, ignoring them.

Without further ado, Talon began walking beside Gunnar. They spoke quietly back and forth, likely trading knowledge since they both believed they could track our friends. Maybe they were triangulating the scent, or something super cool.

Me? I just walked behind them with Yahn and Alucard. The horses walked a few dozen paces off to the side, talking lightly back and forth and keeping an eye out for any signs of attack.

A thick forest stood between us and our destination, making me think it would be wisest to fly over it rather than waste days breaking through underbrush – and likely encountering a dozen different flavors of murdering things that called the woods home. Still, we would have to walk until we reached them, saving our flyers' energy.

Because two horses weren't going to be much help with five riders. I needed Yahn to change, hoping he had a shining set of wings, so he could carry Talon. I had Grimm, and Gunnar had Pegasus. There was the very likely chance – judging by what I had seen Alucard do – that he had his own set of wings, too. But if not, one of the flyers would need to carry two riders.

And someone might need to carry Ashley and Pan, depending on how fast we needed to get out, and if I couldn't simply take us home the moment we found them.

I really wanted to track down Oberon, to see if he was able to help somehow, maybe prevent a major time-shift, or lend me aid, but the problem with that was that I didn't really want to risk him saying *no* or worse, starting a fight. And I didn't know exactly where he was, because I didn't have a map. Also, it would cost *time*. Something I didn't want to waste.

So, I let the idea of visiting Oberon go, assuming that all of Fae probably knew we were here, thanks to the alarms that had sounded upon our arrival.

Which all pointed back to finding Ashley and Pan fast.

My army of savages marched forth into Fae, and all was right with the world...

CHAPTER 30

*W*e had reached the woods faster than expected, and had decided to take a quick rest while Pegasus scouted the area from above. He had just returned, letting me know that flying over the forest would be easy and fast. I had hoped so, because we had been able to see the purple fields Gunnar had indicated from our original arrival point.

Gunnar and Talon had both confirmed that the purple fields were our destination.

A faint tune emanated from within the woods, but I couldn't tell if it was from a person, or simply the wind whistling through the trees. This was Fae, so maybe the wind sounded like singing. Or maybe there were wind chimes in the woods, from whoever lived there. Or, maybe there was a band of cannibals who held singing contests. Regardless, we weren't planning on going into them, and it sounded far away, faint, so I let it go.

"You didn't see any signs of danger?" I asked Pegasus. "I'm not fond of an aerial battle."

He shook his head, mane whipping back and forth. "Not saying there isn't, but I didn't see anything on the horizon. Then again, those trees are where I would nest if I lived here."

I grunted, reaching out to Wylde, seeing if he knew anything.

Do I look like I fly? He muttered.

So helpful.

149

The distant melody sounded closer as the wind picked up. Or at least louder. But that wasn't our problem. Talon was scratching his neck absently, staring into the woods with a frown, no doubt curious about the sound as well.

But flying left us with one concern. We needed more flyers to get us over the woods.

I turned to Alucard, frustrated to see that he still hadn't changed yet. Then again, our trip had been pretty mellow. He had spent some time walking with the others, likely trying to get an understanding of what to expect. But no one had given him any answers – per my rules. No fore-warning. It just needed to happen.

Wylde had been adamant about that.

Learning first could change things.

To get the powers, you needed to let go of yourself. Let it happen naturally.

Not clinically, organized, and methodical. A spark of passion. Rage. Fear. Something. Whatever it was that made you change needed to be authentic, not premeditated.

I almost wanted to go pick a fight with something.

I was slowly walking towards the woods. Maybe that stupid fucking song—

"Yahn! What the fuck are you *doing?*" Alucard shouted suddenly, snapping me out of my thoughts.

I flinched, noticing that Yahn had torn ahead of me into the woods, ripping off his clothes in the process. I blinked. The song was on full stereo now, and I saw Gunnar and Talon shambling closer to the woods, shaking their heads stubbornly, but still moving forward. Just like I had been.

Grimm and Pegasus exchanged a look, shrugged their shoulders, and turned to me. "You might want to go check that out," Pegasus offered help-fully. "Or just leave them to die."

I reached down inside me, already running towards the singing. *Wylde, what the hell is going on?* I asked him. He grew very silent.

Plug your ears. They're already dead...

Alucard burst ahead of me, and right past Gunnar and Talon, who were now holding tree trunks with their claws sunk deep into the bark, as if trying to fight something I couldn't see. Like... they were being assaulted, mentally.

I shivered at a sudden thought. Sirens? Some kind of siren call luring us to our deaths? I scoured Wylde's brain, but he just kept encouraging me to *run*. I ignored that, commanding him to tell me how to plug my ears. I hadn't brought fucking ear plugs to Fae.

Fairy wings, he finally said, showing me something strange with my Fae magic.

Without questioning it, I duplicated it, pulling out the sound of flapping fairy wings and creating a bubble of sound right inside my ears, muting everything else around me but the rapid *thump-thump-thump*. My vision wavered as the song faded, replaced by the steady beat.

I hadn't even noticed it affecting me, but I had been walking that way, too.

Branches whipped at me as I bolted after them, pursuing Alucard and Yahn. "Stop Talon and Gunnar, horses!" I shouted. I heard the swoop of wings, and Gunnar and Talon were scooped up from the ground and into the air, shouting at their mounts in protest.

Alucard and Yahn were so fucking *fast*! How had the pudgy Swede dragon learned how to sprint faster than a vampire? Or me, for that matter. I dove over roots, small bushes, and rocks, trailing what I could see of Alucard's back.

The ground where he ran flashed golden, as if he had run through wet light.

Which was entirely possible, here. I glanced back, but didn't see it behind me. Just where Alucard ran. I huffed as I ran harder, faster, not knowing if I was too late or if I was simply racing to my own death. Then again, I had my Mask. Maybe that would save me.

Alucard suddenly disappeared from sight around a bend up ahead, and even with my fairy wings earmuffs, I could practically feel the song pulsing and throbbing around me. I dove through the branches, and skidded to a halt, almost too late.

I came to a stop at the very edge of a small cliff that overlooked a swanky pond.

You know the type.

One of those ones you see in movies. Waterfall, crystal-blue water, birds singing, rays of sunlight peeking through. Picturesque.

Except when you looked for them in real life you typically found trash, or an army of bugs, or a whole lot more mud and gunk than the picture led you to believe.

Not this place, though.

And in the center of the pond, maybe twenty feet away, was a grass covered island with several naked, blazingly hot females surrounding Yahn, ready to eat him alive, and...

I blinked. They were feeding him grapes. He was bare-chested, and several of the women were drawing things on his pudgy belly, tickling him.

He made the Pillsbury Doughboy sound. I shit you not.

And he had the brightest smile I had ever seen, totally calm and serene.

"They're going to kill him. Eat him. Sex him," a voice muttered beside me. I flinched to see Alucard, pacing back and forth, muttering furiously under his breath, his dark hair whipping back and forth as he argued with himself. "The little bastard likes the Reds. They'll kill me if I don't help him. But why should I help him? They're my girls!" I shook my head in disbelief.

"Are you really going to let him die out of trying to keep the Reds from something they want?" I asked, turning back to Yahn, who seemed to be in absolutely no danger at all.

The pudgy swede noticed me, and waved, motioning me to join him.

Was he in danger? I could bet that he was, but what did I do? If I tried to get closer, the stunning women would have ample time to kill him before I made it to the island. Right now, with me a safe distance away, he was unharmed.

The women giggled at me, and several dove down into the water, with barely a ripple as the water rolled over their breasts. They came up out of the water right beside the river bank before me, impossibly close for such a quick submersion. Their hair was perfectly slicked back, not a hair out of place, and they were able to float high enough that their breasts rested atop the water as if the pond was simply holding their chesticles as a polite courtesy.

I was already walking closer to make sure the water didn't need any help.

"Goddamn it to fucking hell!" Alucard roared, and the world exploded with golden light, incinerating the ground around us to ashes, and hurling me back into the trees. I landed with a grunt, shaking my head, realizing that the fairy wing earmuffs were simply gone, and the sirens' song had almost taken me.

Wylde struggled against it, shaking his head angrily as I climbed to my feet. I began humming loudly, not wanting to waste time using magic I didn't fully understand, but I still had a hard time focusing as I ran back to the edge of the water. Two dead bodies floated before me, and they were... utterly *grotesque*. Scaled mermaids of some sort, with crimson fangs and horned fins on their backs. Their breasts were sagging, misshapen hunks of flesh, and they stared back at me through the glaze of dead fish eyes.

The pond-bank was ashes, and a film of that soot coated the dead bodies and the perfectly blue water, turning it into a brackish-looking swamp.

I looked up to see a golden light racing towards the island, but it was struck down at the last second, and Alucard fell into the water with a splash before I could do anything. Two sets of fins zipped after him, hungry for their new meal.

Yahn stood up from his harem of still-beautiful women, and gripped one by the face, still smiling at her. Then his eyes flashed to glass, and I stared in horror as the woman he held did, too. A perfect, glass statue.

"No," he commanded, and the force of that single word rippled out into the pond in a perfect circle, slamming into the two sirens swimming after Alucard's thrashing body, which kept pulsing with golden light before he sunk back into the water as if doused – like the water was hampering his ability – whatever that was.

The shark-like siren mermaids turned to glass and disappeared under the water, no doubt sinking. I scooted back from the edge of the pond in case his power wanted to make a Nate ice-sculpture, but it struck the bank with barely a splash, halting.

I frantically searched for Alucard only to find a comet of golden light launch up from the water, growing and building until a hulking angel of fire in tattered, stained robes hovered in the air, rotating circles of gold spinning around him in a slow spin. His eyes were fire as he stared down at the island with an entirely blank face.

I turned back to see the sirens at Yahn's feet, holding up their hands adoringly, pleadingly, but no longer trying to seduce him. They were... begging.

My eyes followed their hands to see a walking being of glass staring back at them, glistening and reflecting in the light. But his skin was covered in scales – also of glass. But it was most definitely Yahn, but no longer pudgy. He was smiling, utterly calm. I shook my head in wonder.

"Who wants to experience all that is Yahn? Just the tip?" he asked in a lower voice than usual.

They begged and pleaded *yes, we would.* He grunted, and then clapped his hands. They turned to glass statues, forever frozen in those forms of worship, and forever beautiful. He stepped back, and a perfect replica remained where he had stood, as if he had also made a statue of himself.

Then he sprinted at me. Right before he hit the edge of his island, he exploded into shards of glass, and a glass dragon exploded from within the cloud, hurtling at me. Alucard swooped down to land beside me, and right before Yahn impaled me, he shifted, doing a perfect flip in the air, and landing directly before me on one knee as if bowing, but his fist pounded into the earth with another sound of breaking glass, which created a small crater before me.

He lifted his head to reveal a perfectly muscled Yahn, with absolutely no man-meat, thank god. Like a glass Ken doll. No glass phallus to speak of, which suited me just fine.

"At your service, Wylde," he said in a low, smooth tone, entirely unlike Yahn.

Alucard did the same, now a creature that looked to have fallen from Heaven, hitting every stair on the way down, but still maintaining a golden light that shone from his skin.

He, as a person, was beautiful and majestic, with a set of ruthless eyes. But he wore tattered canvas robes, like an old priest, and the hem was coated liberally with dried blood.

"Master Wylde," he said, lowering his head so that his dark hair swung freely before him. Then the two stood, staring at me.

"Totem," I said gruffly, not letting any emotion show on my face.

They blinked, and then turned to each other, considering.

"The Reds," they said in unison, and then shot each other considering looks. Not aggressive, but just... highly aware.

"Right. Well, if you need to work any shit out over that, do it here. Just don't kill each other." I folded my arms, waiting. I glanced over Yahn's shoulder, staring at the sculpture garden he had made – like his very own glass menagerie. Several beautiful naked women worshipping Yahn, the glass super-stud. I really wished I had my phone to take a picture, but alas.

I turned back to them to see that they were shaking hands. I squinted suspiciously. Alucard had feared for Yahn, so had tried to save him, activating his inner savage, even though the thought of Yahn being with the Reds deeply bothered him. But now he was calm as can be.

Yahn, in return, had no problem flirting with murdering sirens, almost seeming to control them, but fearing for Alucard, he had saved the vampire, waking up his inner Fairy. Good chances that this was a positive development, but one never knew over here.

Any ideas, Wylde? I thought to myself.

I could feel him looking through my eyes, studying the two curiously. *I think you need to stop bringing your friends here. It can't be good for the world*, he finally replied. *But I don't think you have any reason to fear. They are all much more stable than the first time you came...*

I nodded to myself. Which was an interesting development. Everyone had changed to their savage, Fae form, but hadn't gone postal like we had last time. But why? I just didn't know.

They watched me with deep, wise eyes. Which was downright creepy on Yahn, since I was used to seeing the Swedish cheerleader scared of female nudity. Well, any nudity, really. But he sure as hell looked in his element with those sirens.

"What gives, Yahn? Naked chicks are your kryptonite," I said, waving a hand at the island.

He glanced over a shoulder. "Sex is just a weapon. To win at sex, you have to serve better than you take," he said distantly, as if considering it for the first time. "And I guess I know how to use that weapon well." He burst out laughing at the words, shaking his head and holding up a hand to Alucard. "Before you get angry, no, I don't get it. I just... they were very easy to control." He shrugged.

"Aren't you a virgin?" I asked incredulously.

He shifted uncomfortably from foot to foot, reminding me of the old Yahn. "If I was, perhaps that would give me a unique perspective on the matter..." he said, not meeting Alucard's eyes.

Alucard studied him with both surprise and concern, the familiar vampire showing through. Because Yahn had admitted to being very interested in the Reds – one in particular or both, we didn't yet know – and here he was telling us he was the Fae version of Dirk Diggler. I realized he hadn't answered whether he was a virgin or not. Had he and the Reds played under the blankets?

Ho' boy. I wasn't going to touch that.

I had always assumed Alucard would be the sex monster, if it had been anyone.

"Let's go, unless you two need to out-macho each other on your sexy-time magic."

Judging from the sounds of their footsteps behind me, they didn't. I glanced back at the sound of crunching glass, shooting Yahn a scowl. He nodded, and the sound ceased as he glanced down at his feet. As if simply making it so.

I glanced at Alucard who was leaving golden footprints and arched a brow.

"Ummm…" he said, his golden-skinned face scrunching as if thinking. He took a tentative step, leaving no trail, then smiled up at me.

I rolled my eyes. This was going to be a long trip. I just knew it.

CHAPTER 31

*T*he gang was waiting for us when we returned, all on the ground, now.

Pegasus snorted. "We let them down when the songs stopped. Did you kill them or bed them?"

"Ohhh, or even *better*," Grimm growled. "Did you bed them and *then* kill them?"

Pegasus lifted a hoof, and Grimm pounded it with his own, emitting sparks.

I burst out laughing. "Jesus. You really are Bro-nies."

Wulfric and Talon were grinning, but the horses didn't seem to get it. Then everyone saw the two behind me and stared in awe. I stepped aside, letting them fawn over each other for a few minutes as I looked up at the sky uneasily. I didn't see anything, exactly, but I felt a tugging at my soul, which was never a good sign. Because tugging meant someone or something was behind it, and you didn't typically tug someone unless it was against their will.

And that feeling drew me towards the purple fields beyond the woods.

I wasn't sure I was going to like what we found there. The thing that really bothered me, though, was that Wylde seemed just as anxious. And he wasn't really scared of anything.

I sighed. But a friend needed me. Two friends.

I turned to the others to see that Yahn had already shifted to his dragon form, a crystal-clear glass dragon, much larger than even Raego – which was impressive – and larger still than his usual weredragon form. The light above shone through him, casting tiny prisms of light behind him, almost as if he had a rainbow shadow.

With friends like this, I had no end to joke material.

Especially when I saw Talon tensing as if trying to prevent himself from swatting a fly. His tail began to twitch back and forth, and I followed his gaze to see him glaring at one of the moving rainbow reflections on the ground behind Yahn as he spoke to Wulfric and Alucard.

Grimm noticed Talon's interest, and casually trotted over, curious what he found so interesting. Then Grimm saw it, and his eyes flashed silver with fury. "DIE!"

And I stared with awed glee as he charged at the flicker of rainbow-colored light.

Talon yowled. "Shiny thing! I must have it!"

Yahn, unsurprisingly jumped at the hostile shouts, spinning to see what the hell was going on, which essentially turned him into a disco ball. Talon and Grimm...

Went absolutely ape-shit, chasing and trying to catch or murder the rainbows.

I stared, open-mouthed, shaking my head. Wulfric and Alucard burst out laughing while Yahn hopped back and forth, wondering if he was being assaulted by invisible tiny ninjas, and trying to find the source of Talon and Grimm's outrage.

Pegasus let out a long, tired sigh. "He *really* hates them..." he said, indicating Grimm as his brother's hooves tore up clods of earth in his frothing pursuit of the darting rainbows.

I let them wear themselves out for a minute. As amusing as it was, we needed to get going, and one of the two were going to hurt themselves if they went after the same shiny.

"Yahn, fly up!" I shouted.

He launched to the sky with a big sweep of his wings, and the rainbows suddenly grew larger and fainter, no longer easy to locate. Grimm was panting, huffing, and glaring at the ground, searching in a mad frenzy. Talon froze, looked up at me in shame, and then straightened. I nodded maliciously. "Oh, you can bet your ass this one's getting shared…" I said with a grin.

He sighed, shoulders sagging. I snapped my fingers at Grimm.

He glared up at Yahn, then down to the ground, before letting out a snort and returning my look. "Let's go," I said.

He studied Yahn thoughtfully. "Is he the Father of Rainbows?" he asked hungrily.

I shook my head, but he continued talking anyway, not noticing my response.

"I could murder *all* the rainbows…" he said softly, as if imagining winning the lottery.

"No!" I snapped, growing concerned. "Absolutely not. They're just reflections. He's not the father of rainbows," I said, *really* needing him to understand.

"We'll see…" he said, not promising me anything.

"Grimm," I said in a warning tone. "I need Yahn alive. Killing him won't end the rainbows in the world. You know that, right?" I pleaded, walking closer.

"There's only one way to be sure…" he said distantly, pawing the earth with his hoof as he stared up at Yahn, who was hovering above us, watching us warily, not able to hear us. Grimm's wings suddenly flared into existence, and he prepared to destroy Yahn.

Pegasus suddenly slammed into Grimm, knocking him on his ass. He rolled, flipped, and groaned. After a few seconds, he climbed unsteadily to his feet, shaking his head. His eyes locked onto Pegasus, who pawed the earth, staring at his brother.

"He's not the Father of Rainbows, you dumb shit," Pegasus said. "Nate will buy you a giant crystal when we get home. It will give you *endless* rainbows. Won't you, Nate?" he said, not looking at me.

I nodded eagerly. "Yes. Absolutely. Giant as hell. Just promise you won't kill Yahn."

Grimm glared one last time. "Fine."

I let out a breath, motioning for Yahn to land, and ignoring the laughter from the peanut gallery. "Let's ride."

I mounted Grimm, Gunnar climbed onto Pegasus, and Alucard and Talon shared Yahn, looking very displeased at the arrangements. Which was just beautiful to me. Then we took off, Grimm's smoke wings lifting us higher and higher in massive sweeps. I let out a laugh of pure joy, and paid close attention to my friends, who were also grinning like maniacs as we flew out over the trees below – the first normal looking trees I had seen in a while.

"Track the horned god!" I bellowed, and Gunnar and Talon focused, staring out ahead intently, subtly speaking with their flyers until we were angling towards the purple fields. I could see our destination in the distance, and knew it wouldn't be a long flight. I stared at those fields, feeling very uncomfortable – as did Wylde – but I couldn't exactly place why. Probably because I didn't know what we would find there. Hopefully not an army of Fae holding Ashley captive…

And as we flew out over the treetops, I couldn't help but wonder how much time had passed in the real world…

CHAPTER 32

*W*e landed fairly gracefully, although Talon's legs were shaky as he dismounted. We studied the purple field around us, wary of threats, but other than the breeze causing a steady wave in the tall grass, thankfully nothing jumped out and tried to eat our faces off.

Not that they could have succeeded, but they could have tried.

The field was on a hill, and a steady incline lead up to a cliff overlooking a stone ocean – the very edge of one corner of the Fae World – unless they had islands in the distance. To our left was the beginning of a mountain range, and several boulders dotted the field we now stood in. From the sky, we had seen a large cave near the cliff's edge, but we hadn't wanted to land too close to it and startle the inhabitants, if there were any. We also hadn't wanted to be ambushed from behind if we landed at the cave – pinned against the cliff if anyone was hiding in the fields.

That sensation of unease inside me had magnified about a thousand times over during our flight, but I brushed it off as nerves. Wylde had simply disappeared deep inside me, muttering unhappily to himself over and over again.

I looked up to see that Gunnar looked on the verge of sprinting towards the cave, idly thumping his Rarawk antler into his other palm as he growled under his breath. I snapped a finger and he looked up at me, catching my warning look. "No need to rush into a trap. We're here. Let's do this smart,"

I said out loud, keeping my voice low. The group nodded, although Gunnar, of course, didn't look too happy about it.

Yahn shifted back to his glass human form and walked beside Alucard, who looked as if he was concentrating so that his steps wouldn't catch the field on fire.

We walked towards the cave, eyes alert for anything amiss, but it was about as peaceful as you could ask for. We reached the cave entrance without fanfare, and I shot a look at Talon, who suddenly ghosted ahead on his velvet slippers – which didn't leave a trail – to inspect the entrance. He kept low in the purple grass, which grew almost right up to the entrance. I saw a fire pit that had been recently used, and a single cooking pot, but again, nothing sinister. Talon froze suddenly, staring at the cave for a full minute. Then he jolted, as if forgetting what he had been doing. He slipped back our way, keeping his eyes behind him, wary of an attack.

Had we found them? As easy as that?

Talon stopped beside me. "They're inside," he said in a low purr. "Just them."

Gunnar had crept closer to overhear Talon's report, and by crept, I mean as stealthy as a giant fucking, love-sick wolfman can creep – which was not very stealthy at all. But he wasn't screaming, or on fire – which would have been only slightly more noticeable.

"I don't sense anyone else here," Gunnar murmured. "No game, no wildlife, nothing but them." That sounded strange. No wildlife? "This close, I can almost taste them..." he said, staring at the cave entrance with an almost physical need.

I arched a brow at Talon. He shrugged back. "I agree. They are alone. We are the only ones to step foot in this field in a long time." His eyes trailed off, and he looked very, very uneasy, slowly spinning to scan everything around us.

"Talon," I pressed. "If everything is fine, why do you look like Gunnar just shit on your favorite cat toy?"

He didn't answer for a few moments. "I'm... not sure. This place..." He finally sighed, shaking his head with an ashamed frown. "Perhaps I've just been gone from Fae for too long. I don't sense danger, I just feel strange here. I've felt it this whole trip, but it's worse here."

I studied him acutely, considering. He would have warned me of any dangers, but he seemed to be describing my own inner feelings. Was something wrong with the Fae World? Had we messed something up last time we were here? Or had something happened to mess with the entire world?

I shook my head. None of that mattered. Ashley was here. No danger was present, and we didn't plan on sticking around. Get Ashley, get out. That was our objective. Fae could burn for all I cared. I had other problems at home that wouldn't wait.

"Pan!" I called out, striding up to the cave's entrance, not wanting to set off any traps he may have set, and also not wanting to simply storm inside and cause him or Ashley to panic.

Heh. Panic. Pan.

I called out a second time. "Mallory!"

Mallory – in human form rather than his godly goat form – slowly stepped out of the cave, shirtless and muscular as an old sailor. He took one look at us, and suddenly brandished a long, wicked axe. "Where do I keep the Macallan?" he asked in a threatening growl.

I stared at him, and then burst out laughing. "Nobody fucking knows!"

His hard look slowly faded, and a faint smile replaced it as he lowered his weapons. But he looked exhausted, on his last legs. To emphasize this, he leaned on his axe for support, waving us closer.

My friends approached as I turned to the horses. "Watch our asses. From the sky."

Pegasus turned to me, frowning somehow. "You're going into the cave. It is physically impossible to watch your ass... from the sky... through a fucking cave."

Grimm snickered.

I glared back. "Just watch for invaders or anyone shady. Kill them if you must, but try to stay out of sight if you can. We shouldn't be long," I snarled, turning my back on them. Gunnar was pestering Mallory, but he only gave vague responses, staring at me instead.

I tried to bury my anger, which was getting hotter and hotter. Probably from unease over that strange sensation still tugging at me and this fucking place being so bizarre on even the best of days, not even considering the recent anomalies. "Yes. She's fine, but you cannot enter yet!"

Gunnar froze, frowning at Mallory in confusion.

Mallory was still staring at me, and slowly, each of the others did the same.

I slowed, frowning. "What's going on, Mallory?" I asked, my shoulders itching.

He met my eyes and gave me a nod. "Wylde is your leader. I grant him leave to enter first, as is his due. Without him, none of you would have been able to come here."

I nodded. It made sense. The Fae were odd about customs, and since I was the leader, it was my right. Still, I had expected an eye roll or a growl from Gunnar, but everyone just looked fucking tense. What the hell was going on?

I resumed my pace, walking up to Mallory and extending a hand. He grasped my forearm and shook once. "I've missed you... Nate."

I nodded, and then wrapped him up in a quick hug. "Thank you for saving her, Mallory," I said, loud enough for all to hear. "Once Gunnar sees her safe, I'm sure he'll personally thank you as well. Profusely," I warned, glaring at Gunnar, who wilted guiltily, so obsessed with seeing Ashley that he hadn't even considered thanking the man who had saved her in the first place.

I did wonder why they hadn't left yet if Ashley had been healed, but I was sure I was about to find out, and that I wouldn't like the answer.

I entered the cave. Gunnar was about a millimeter behind me, waiting until I crossed the invisible line that marked the cave proper, and then he tore past me. I smiled faintly, studying the walls around me. Ashley stepped out of the shadows, looking weak, but healthy. She was in her Wulfra form, wearing the Nemean Lion Cloak that Gunnar had given her. She whined as she saw her fiancé, her knees buckling. Gunnar dropped his Rarawk antler and swept her off her feet, burying his face into her neck with a growl. Then he carried her deeper into the cavern, where I noticed hallways leading off into smaller crevices – bedrooms.

Faint lights glowed on the walls, illuminating the space, and I realized it was much larger than I had thought from the outside. I heard a door slam and blinked, staring at where Gunnar had taken his fiancée. Then I slowly turned, arching a brow at Mallory, who was watching me intently.

"You installed doors?" I asked. "Or did you just happen to find a cave with all the modern updates?" I pointed at the lights. "And Stonelights, no less. Those are rare. And valuable. How has no one discovered this place?"

Mallory glanced at Talon, who was trailing a paw along the wall, studying what looked like drawings on the stone. He looked troubled.

"No one knows about this place," he finally said. "Consider it a safe-haven."

I nodded absently, not really caring. Alucard and Yahn sat down with weary sighs before a glowing orange rock. I held out a hand towards it, frowning. "It's warm," I said, surprised. "Is that... lava or something?" I asked.

"It helps keep the cave warm when the breeze rolls through the back."

"What do you mean?" I asked, noticing that Alucard and Yahn were leaning back, taking a break, and talking in low tones, leaving me to chat with Mallory in private. It was good to see them talking rather than fighting over the Reds – although I knew that would eventually happen.

Mallory motioned me deeper into the cave. "Follow me. I'll show you around." He sounded incredibly tired.

"Keep an eye out, guys," I said to Yahn and Alucard. "And put some earmuffs on unless you want to hear what wolves do for fun," I added with a faint grin.

Alucard chuckled, waving a hand to shoo me away. Yahn glanced at the tunnel Gunnar had taken, looking thoughtful. Alucard quickly slapped him on the arm, scowling – likely remembering Yahn's interest in the Reds.

Mallory hadn't bothered to stop, simply walking away, so I rushed to catch up, studying the smooth walls. It was impressive. The place had been scoured flat, as if thousands of years of rushing water had formed a perfect home. But glancing closer, I noticed the stone had been worked by hand, not nature. Still, drawings decorated the walls, some more elaborate than others. I blinked, leaning closer to one. It was a rough sketch of the field below with the forest in the background, and three moons in the sky. It was good enough for me to recognize it, but crude enough to make me think of a child doodling with charcoal.

Mallory watched me patiently until I was ready to continue. I could tell he had a lot on his mind, and not that he just wanted to show me around the cavern. He was likely wondering what had happened in his absence. With the War.

He led me onward. "I had a feeling you would come for us," he said softly, almost as if regretting that he had been right. "We decided to stick around a bit longer just in case."

I grunted, knowing there was going to be more to the story. The tunnel angled sharply to the left, revealing three more doors bolted into the walls.

One was a kitchen, but the others looked like bedrooms. "Hell of a find," I muttered curiously. I reached out to Wylde, wondering why he was still hiding from me. Perhaps the cave reminded him of his home – the one I had made for him when first establishing our connection.

As we rounded another corner, I froze, my breath catching as unexpected wind buffeted my clothes. I stared out at an ocean of rolling stone thousands of feet below us. An open cliff leaned out over it, and I saw thunderstorms on the horizon – great green and black clouds with purple flashes of lightning in their depths. The air felt damp and sweet, not salty as I had expected.

I turned to see Mallory smiling at me sadly.

"This is beautiful," I whispered, shaking my head. "Imagine sitting here with a cup of tea and watching a thunderstorm," I murmured, smiling faintly. "My father would have loved it."

Part of me still felt uneasy, though. As if waiting for an attack. This place generally messed with you, but since we hadn't experienced an all-out war like I had expected for the last few weeks, it was almost like I had been running on adrenaline and was finally running out of steam.

Mallory let out a long breath. "Aye, he did…"

I nodded absently, trying to shake off my unease, and then his response registered in my brain. I slowly turned to see him pointing at the wall. I followed, and my heart skipped a beat.

A very crude *Temple Industries* logo was sketched on the wall beside a stick figure family of two adults, a young boy, and a cat. I struggled to breathe as my vision began to tunnel out until all I could see was the drawings. I shook my head, my mind straining under the impossible image. Mallory stepped up beside me, tears streaming down his cheeks.

"Welcome home, Wylde…" he whispered.

The world tilted crazily, as a great roar of pain erupted from deep within my soul. Wylde was screaming. A dam broke in my mind, and a lifetime of memories slammed into us, drowning us.

Firm hands caught us – caught *me* – as my world folded in on itself.

CHAPTER 33

I came to with a start, gasping and scrabbling with my hands, remembering that I had been standing near a cliff with a thousand foot drop into a stone ocean, and that I had fallen down.

"Easy, lad. Easy," Mallory murmured, squeezing my leg reassuringly.

I sat up and realized we were backed against the wall, a good ten feet away from the drop-off. Mallory had placed a blanket over me, and tucked a pillow underneath my head. I stared at him, my hands shaking. "I don't... this is impossible," I rasped, jerking my gaze to the wall with the Temple Industries logo. It had obviously been drawn with a more skilled hand than the stick figures, and as my gaze swept the wall, I noticed several variants for the logo.

I shook my head, grasping my temples with a groan.

Flashes of memories hit me like hammers, and my head *ached*.

I... remembered.

A storm raged as I drew on the walls. "His is better, Calvin," a familiar voice teased. "Let him design it." I glanced up, smirking at my mom. Her hair was braided back, and she had soot on her nose from her time in the kitchen, cooking dinner.

My father and I had decided not to tell her about the smudge, giggling at our private joke.

"And what's wrong with mine, Makayla?" my dad growled at her playfully.

She rolled her eyes. "Which one?" she asked sweetly, indicating the dozens of other logos he had drawn on our walls over the last few months.

My dad sighed, leaning back on his heels, cocking his head as he inspected the drawing before him. "I think this one's it, but if Wylde wants to give it a try, I'm open to it."

I looked at it, considering, and right when I was about to draw, a furred paw slapped the charcoal out of my hands. I snarled at the furred face that met mine. He grinned back. "Tag!"

I shrieked in mock anger, chasing my best friend through the cave, ignoring my parents' warnings to stay close to home. Talon was going to—

I gasped, snapping out of the memory, and rounding on Mallory. "Talon?!" I hissed, eyes wide in disbelief. "Fucking Talon... *lived* with us?" I all but shouted.

Mallory nodded, pointing his thumb to a darkened corner of the room. I glanced up to see a pair of silver eyes staring back at me, and I instantly grew angry, struggling to climb to my feet and toss the furry bastard over the cliff.

Mallory latched onto me, not letting me move, and here, in this place, it was literally no effort for him to restrain me. It felt like I was manacled to the floor. "He didn't remember," Mallory growled. "Much the same as you. It was as your parents... intended," he grunted.

I saw Talon lower his head, staring down at the floor. Then, with a soft sigh, he scooted closer, enough for me to see. His cheeks were wet, and I realized that he had been crying. He wouldn't meet my eyes. Not out of shame, but as if it were the last thing on his mind. Because... he was in the exact same position as me. Learning that his life had all been a lie.

I slowly turned to glare at Mallory's hand. He removed it, returning my stare.

"I think it's past time for you to start fucking explaining," I warned, realistically considering killing him. Wylde grumbled deep within me, also wanting to kill something.

Mallory stared off into the ocean, as if gathering his thoughts. The storm was much closer now, and I realized that the horses were still outside. I opened my mouth, glancing back, but Talon spoke. "I told them to come in. They searched for miles and didn't find a living thing."

Mallory grunted. "No one would dare come here. Couldn't even find it if they tried."

168

I studied him, frowning. "Why not?"

He fidgeted with a pebble in his hand, staring down at it. "Your father warded this place. For miles. Anyone not part of your family could only enter the vicinity by accident."

I grunted. "Wow. That's... actually very clever. Anyone looking for him couldn't find him, and any visitors that did make it here would have no idea who he was..."

Mallory nodded, a faint smile on his face. "He was a clever son of a bitch, that's for sure."

I sighed, remembering I still had my satchel on me. I reached inside for my canteen and took a healthy drink. I passed it to Talon, but he waved it away, watching the approaching storm in silence. But his ears were swiveled towards Mallory, waiting expectantly.

"Calvin and Makayla were two very ambitious wizards. The two friends came here in search of something," Mallory began. "They had heard about the Invitations the Fae used to grant to Makers, but since they were only wizards, they snuck through a back door."

"With a fucking child? How the hell did they make it through the entire Land of the Fae with a child? And why would they *do* that? This doesn't make any sense..." I argued.

He tossed his pebble out over the edge, sighing. "They weren't even *together* back then, just two friends. You definitely weren't part of their lives yet. Just let me finish. All will become clear soon. I swear it," he muttered, sounding frustrated. While sympathetic of my position, he also wasn't used to being interrupted. "They found a way to cheat the system. They broke into Fae as thieves, and stole something very, *very* valuable, which obviously put the entire land on high alert. But the Fae – no matter how hard they tried – couldn't find them. To this day, they still don't know who took their treasure..." He glanced at my satchel for some reason before continuing. "But the two friends couldn't find a way back... And they were forced to hide here, on the edge of the map while they tried to figure out a way back home." He glanced up at the walls, smiling nostalgically. "By this time, their wild sides had truly taken over. They barely made it here in one piece, only able to survive by working together. Then they put up their wards, and were finally able to relax, confident they were no longer being hunted."

"How do you know all of this?" I asked softly.

"Oberon asked me to help him find the thieves since he had been unsuccessful in doing so himself, but I'll come back to that. Your parents used to laugh about this next part..." he added, chuckling at the memory. "Now, remember, they were just two friends doing what they could to survive, trying to find a way back home. But they spent *months* here, all alone... And, as is often the case, they grew... fond of each other. When two people are locked in a cave on the edge of a hostile world, a baby can be born. A baby Manling, born in the Land of the Fae..." he whispered reverently, as if reciting a prophecy.

I realized I was leaning forward, my jaw hanging open. Talon was actually pressed up beside me, having scooted closer, no doubt waiting for his part of the story.

"I... was *born* here?" I said slowly, shaking my head in disbelief. "I don't..."

Mallory nodded, meeting my eyes. "It was you who brought them closer together. Reminded them of their humanity. You... *saved* them. Made them a family. You were the missing link. You reminded them how to *love*, because through falling in love with you, they soon fell in love with each other. But you spent years here. You grew faster than anyone thought, reaching your teens in only a span of years—"

"Wait," I interrupted. "That doesn't make sense. That would have resulted in *centuries* passing in the real world..." I argued, shaking my head.

Mallory held up a finger. "It very likely should have. But remember that they came here to steal something... And in their time here before you were born, they triggered that prize." He jerked his chin towards my satchel. "And you just brought it back. Still active. It's why we chose not to leave yet."

I blinked, glancing down at my satchel. *"What?"* I asked, bewildered.

Mallory sighed. "The hourglass, Nate. And all of Fae knows it's here by now. That was the cause of the alarm."

A very icy chill shot down my spine. "The hourglass..." I repeated dumbly, staring at my satchel. "The one from my father's statue."

Mallory nodded. "I put it there for him. As I promised I would. Never to be used again unless in the greatest of emergencies." He leaned forward, studying me thoughtfully. "My question, is how the hell did you find out about it?"

I shook my head. "I... guess by accident," I admitted. "I remembered seeing the Hand of God in her hands, and figured that since it had been so important, that the other thing must have been important, too. I thought they had left it for me as a gift. What does the hourglass do?" I asked.

"It controls the time shift between the worlds. So that they could spend as long as they wanted here without ill effect in your world. It was paramount to their plans. To go places and steal things unseen. It masked their thievery as they stocked up the Armory."

I stared, dumbfounded. Talon watched the two of us, looking impatient to hear his part of the story. "They just told you all of this? Even though you were hunting them?"

"Ah, well," he said, chuckling guiltily. "I wasn't too honest with Oberon. I was fascinated with the story that two humans had outsmarted the Fae so profoundly. So, I found them by not looking for them. I just wandered the land. I figured they were using some kind of magic to stay hidden, and if the Hunt couldn't find them, I surmised it was because they were trying too hard. I sought out a place where I could be in solitude, undisturbed, and to consider the solution. I knew everyone else was emotionally charged, so to find the thieves, I needed to be detached. I stumbled upon them quite by accident, actually."

CHAPTER 34

*H*e glanced at Talon. "I found your village in the Realm of Glass. It had been destroyed in a raid from a warring tribe. I found you, the only survivor, huddled up to your parents' bodies. I don't know how the invaders overlooked you, but they did. I took you with me, knowing that any place had to be safer than a smoldering village. Weeks later, when a storm was rolling in, I saw lights in the distance, and decided that shelter sounded preferable to a soaking. That was an uncomfortable meeting, to say the least. Your mother took one look at me at the steps of her secret cave and froze in terror, no doubt recognizing me. But I didn't know her from Eve, of course. No one did.

"Then you came running out from behind her, all of seven years old, it seemed. You took one look at him," Mallory said, pointing a thumb at the furred creature beside me, who had stopped breathing a few minutes ago, "and asked me what his name was. I told you he didn't have a name, and you decided that wasn't acceptable. *'Of course, he does. It's Talon the Devourer. Anyone can see that,'* you said with all the self-importance of a philosopher. Then you scooped him up, and took him into your room. Your parents were too stunned to stop you, staring me down warily. And that was when I realized that they weren't Fae, and that they probably had a very interesting story to tell. It took me a few days to coax it out of them, to learn that they were the thieves I had been asked to find. But I'll admit, seeing a seven-year-old child with them prevented the thought from ever crossing my mind. They made me swear to always keep you safe before they would speak a word. After I did so, your parents finally spilled the beans. And that was when our long con began," Mallory said, grinning. His shoulders looked lighter, as if he was relieved to finally get it all off his chest.

Talon suddenly gripped my shoulder and I turned to look at him. His eyes were very wet now, and he opened his mouth a few times, no words coming out. Streams of wet fur were visible down his cheeks. "You... *named* me," he finally whispered in awe. "And you gave me a *life*..." he said, turning to Mallory. Then he wrapped me up in an almost bone-breaking hug, purring as he nuzzled into my neck.

Something was wrong with my eyes, because I suddenly felt emotional, too, squeezing back just as hard, and patting his back affectionately.

Talon finally pulled away, shaking his head in wonder. "I remember you, now, Wylde..."

I nodded, grinning, although it all felt so strange. "I think I do, too. Do you remember a fort?"

"Oh! Yes!" he all but shouted. "I do!" And then he was laughing, shaking his head. "This..." he frowned after a moment, and then turned back to Mallory. "How did we not remember? I lived here for years, but Wylde wasn't in my memories..."

Mallory nodded sadly. "It was part of the price for the Temples to escape Fae. We couldn't very well have you blabbing about the only Manling ever born in Fae, and we also couldn't have Wylde on earth talking about his life as a teenager with his bipedal feline best friend. We had to wipe your memories. I put you in service to Oberon, and told him I had been unsuccessful in finding the thieves, but that I had found him a warrior to employ. An orphan."

I nodded absently. Not a pretty answer, but nothing was pretty in the Fae. "How was I so powerful when I came back the first time? I had memories of Wylde, but as a much more powerful version of myself than a teenager playing with his friend."

Mallory sighed, sounding uncertain. "I'm not quite sure about that part. You're the first Manling ever born here in Fae. Perhaps you were envisioning what you could have been? Some part of the land speaking to you?"

he offered, shrugging his shoulders. "I just don't know." His eyes latched onto my satchel. "Where on earth did you get that?" he asked very carefully, but I knew him well. He recognized the brand.

"You know Darling and Dear?" I asked.

"Everyone who is anyone knows Darling and Dear, but I wasn't aware you did." I decided not to take that personally, letting him continue. "Customers are strongly discouraged from sharing the information. Otherwise everyone would go to them, and pretty soon no one would need them. When did you meet them?" he asked. "Have I been gone that long?"

"Callie bought it for me. I've never met them. You've only been gone a month."

Mallory flashed me a very wide grin. "Did she now..." he chuckled. "Mind if I see it?" he asked, all but rubbing his hands together greedily.

I passed it over to him. He studied it curiously. Then he burst out laughing. "Fuck those glorious psychopaths! They never cease to amaze. This is incredible!" he hooted, grinning at me.

I blinked. "What?"

"Don't you know what it does?" he asked. "Didn't Callie tell you?"

I slowly shook my head. "It... *does* stuff?" I asked uneasily. And I'd just been walking around with it?

Mallory grunted. "It can hold anything. All the things. You can put as much in here as you want, and it will never change weight. Consider it your own pocket dimension." He frowned at it suspiciously. "Dean's not in here somewhere, is he?"

I burst out laughing. "Are you serious?"

"Yes. You could put the entire contents of the Armory in here. Well, as long as it fit through the opening, that is."

I frowned. "How would I dig through all that stuff to find what I want?"

He handed the satchel back to me. "Don't look. Just think of the hourglass, and then reach your hand inside."

I did, and instantly felt it. I frowned. "I don't have much else in there."

Mallory folded his arms, sighing dramatically. "Take your hand out and think of something else you put in there. Then put your hand back inside. I bet it's the first thing you touch."

I did, and then shoved my hand inside. It came out with an apple. I blinked in disbelief. I shoved the apple back inside and tried a few more times. It worked every time. "That's insane," I said, shaking my head. "Why didn't she tell me this?" I said, more to myself.

"Well, you were in private, so none of us could answer that for you," Talon chuckled.

"Oh?" Mallory asked, leaning closer. "Do tell…"

I stammered an argument, but Talon overrode me. "He used the tree to shield their activities. But I'm guessing he showed her his inner…" his eyes latched onto our surroundings. "Caveman," he laughed.

I growled. "I wish…" I muttered, leaning back with a growl.

Mallory watched the two of us, looking nostalgic. Then he waved a hand at my satchel. "Do you mind showing me the hourglass?" he asked.

I shrugged and took it out, handing it over to him. He let out a breath, shaking his head as he studied it. "What Oberon – or the Queens for that matter – wouldn't give to have this back. It gives the wielder control over their world, in a fashion. They hate that it's been missing for so long. Not that they ever used it. But the Fae love their power, and knowing someone stole from them bothers them greatly. I would say you are very lucky to have traveled this far with it. If anyone found you with this, all of Fae would turn against you," he said, face serious. "Keep it hidden in your satchel."

"What if someone took his satchel?" Talon asked curiously.

Mallory was already shaking his head. "They would reach inside and find nothing."

Talon frowned in disbelief, so I handed him the satchel, tucking the hourglass back inside. Talon thought for a moment, and then reached his paw inside. Then he reached deeper, all the way to his shoulder, frowning. He looked up in wonder. "I can't find anything in here…"

Then he handed the satchel back to me. I reached inside and pulled out the hourglass, handing it back to Mallory. He blew on the hourglass, and the stone encasing it simply vanished. I blinked in disbelief. He indicated a dial on the side. "Pretty simple. *Forward*," he said, motioning one direction. "*Backwards*," he said, motioning the other way, although he didn't actually turn it.

"Wait…" I said, considering it in a new light. "If it's already activated, does that mean that no time has passed between our worlds?"

Mallory nodded, a very dark grin marking his features. "Aye, Laddie."

I jumped to my feet. "It's time to be a hero!" I hooted, but banged my head on the low overhang. "Gah!" I grouched, rubbing my head and crouching.

"Yeah, that shouldn't become a thing, Wylde. Please," Talon chuckled.

I glared at him, motioning for them to follow me. "Let's go talk to the others. This shit's crazy, and I need to spread it around a little bit. And we probably shouldn't overstay our welcome since everyone knows this thing is here right now…"

CHAPTER 35

We sat around the orange stone, eating dried… something. It was meat, but I didn't ask for details beyond that. It was smoked and cured, so I tried my best not to guess. Which wasn't hard, since it tasted like nothing I had ever eaten before. Like a dried, herbal fruit.

Everyone was doing their best not to stare at me, especially at my ears, as if they would see points growing from the tips at any moment. All that attention was enough to make me twitch.

Mallory growled. "He's not a fucking fairy. He's something…" he trailed off, finally waving a hand uselessly.

"Else," Yahn offered.

"He's our fucking friend," Talon growled, eyeing the rest of the gang with slanted eyes. Gunnar frowned at him thoughtfully, almost a flicker of jealousy, as if wondering who was my best friend, now. Like a jilted girlfriend.

I threw a pebble at him and he flinched. Wulfra chuckled, squeezing Gunnar's arm affectionately. "It's not a pissing contest, boys…" she soothed.

Gunnar grunted. "Sorry. I guess it's the only part of the story that I can relate to," he said, then winced at how that sounded. "Sorry, Nate."

"Wylde," Talon spat. "Here, he is *Wylde*. Get used to that, because if shit goes down and you forget to treat him like the king he is, you're going to be whispering that name while choking on your own blood. Names have meaning, here, *Wulfric*," he emphasized the last word in a hiss.

Gunnar looked territorial and angry, but finally backed down, nodding. "No disrespect meant, Talon," the werewolf muttered, shaking his head. "It's like I'm two different people right now. Trying to pick which one is most important is… difficult."

Yahn shrugged, seemingly more interested in his hand as he held it up to the light, admiring the translucent crystal flesh. Talon tensed, spotting a reflected rainbow, but I placed a restraining hand on his forearm. He flinched, then dipped his head in embarrassment. I grinned at him, shaking my head for him to let it go. Fucking cats and shiny things. No matter how bloodthirsty the feline, they see a shiny and lose their shit.

Luckily, Pegasus and Grimm were away from us, near the entrance to the cave. They had been taking turns scouting the night – which had fallen like the drop of a hat, startling the living hell out of everyone but Talon, Mallory, Ashley, and myself. Now that I thought about it, sitting here in this cave, experiencing the sudden change from day to night was actually nostalgic.

Which sent a strange feeling to my fingertips. I had been… raised here.

Alucard let out a breath. "That's…" he struggled for the right words. "I don't know if something can be beautifully terrifying or not. But, what I'm trying to say is that it's incredibly sweet to hear about your parents, but understandably unsettling to wonder about what it all means."

I nodded, glancing up at Mallory. His eyes were distant, and for some reason, he still looked uneasy. As if not all had been shared yet. I didn't think it wise to press him on anything in front of the others, but you could bet your ass I would corner him in private. If he was uneasy to tell me something else after what he had already shared, how freaking bad was it?

Yahn cleared his throat, then sprawled out on the stone, eyeing me. His gaze was entirely troubling. Not because he looked so different, but because those eyes were just so… absolute. Much different than the incessantly nervous weredragon I had brought here. "What does that make you, Wylde?" he asked respectfully.

I opened my mouth to fire off a quick retort. That I was the same as I had always been.

But… what exactly *was* that? Was my birth the cause of all the strange stuff that happened to me? How I so easily adopted my Beast, accepted my wild side from Fae, killed a god, and been offered a Horseman Mask? It was something to ponder.

I turned to Mallory, letting him know I had the same question.

He sensed everyone's attention, and snapped out of it. "Nobody knows what – exactly – you are, Wylde. No one. Not your parents. Not me. Not the Horsemen. Not the Gods." He met my eyes, looking very savage and... concerned. "No one..."

I frowned, not upset with him, but upset that I didn't have an immediate answer. "Is this why I pick up so many... afflictions?" I asked, ticking off fingers as I spoke of the various powers I had wielded in recent years.

Mallory sighed wearily. "It must be. No one has been able to do what you have. Ever. You make other beings concerned. And I'm talking beings that are *never* concerned."

"Gods?" Alucard sniffed. "No offense, Mallory. The other ones."

Mallory snorted. "There are gods, and then there are Gods..." he said, enunciating the difference.

I sat up, blinking. "Excuse me?" I asked.

He sighed. "We are about to have a visitor, and I don't think any of you are going to like it, but it must be so," he said, brushing off his hands.

Talon jumped to his feet, hissing and spitting as his tail trebled in size, hair sticking straight up. A millisecond later, Grimm skidded into the cavern, his horn tearing through part of the low-hanging ceiling, not causing him any discomfort, just annoyance. What the hell was that thing made of if it could simply break solid stone and not cause him to blink? "One man approaches. He's holding up a leaf."

The rest of the gang jumped to their feet, now. Wulfra and Wulfric slid up to either side of the cave entrance, ducking back into the shadows, despite their size. Alucard and Yahn stepped up before me, squaring their shoulders, one gold, one crystal. I couldn't see their faces, but I could imagine.

Talon stood beside me, a step ahead, actually, suddenly gripping his spear. He could make it appear and disappear at will. I wondered where he had gotten it, and if I had been there.

Because as much as some memories had returned, I hadn't exactly caught up on decades worth of my childhood in the span of an hour. It came back in bits and pieces that didn't seem to make sense, and in no particular order. Eating with my parents and Talon, watching storms together over steaming mugs of tea. Playing games in the tall grass. Even hunting in the woods. Learning magic from my parents.

I gasped.

Not... magic. They had tried to teach me wizard's magic.

But... I had responded with the Fae form of magic, like I had seen Wylde use. At the time, I had been too young to realize the difference, simply assuming I had succeeded in their request. But now, seeing it as a memory, I was able to remember the looks on their faces, and of Pan studying me nearby, leaning forward intently, face pale.

I shook off the feeling as I heard Mallory call out in a booming voice. "He comes in peace, or he leaves in pieces..."

My friends grumbled approval, and I heard a very familiar voice respond.

"Oh, I come as a friend. To one who has done me a great service, how could I come as anything else?" Oberon asked. I glanced, well, *through* Yahn to see the Goblin King standing a dozen paces before the entrance, one hand held high with a large single leaf. His other palm was low, open, and facing us.

Pegasus called out. "He comes alone. Which is very brave..."

He sounded disappointed that he wasn't going to be able to kill something yet.

The air was tense and silent as they waited for something, I wasn't sure what. Then it hit me.

"He may enter," I said neutrally. "If he offers his word of safekeeping for all those present."

Oberon chuckled. "I mean no one any harm, here. Least of all, you. You've done me a service, as you said you would. You could call me surprised, and a little frustrated that I must come to you as a beggar to repay you... But I do have questions." His eyes locked onto Mallory. "And we need to talk about your entrance into my realm. This is not a threat, but there must be payment. We had an agreement..."

Mallory nodded. I squinted at him, this being the first I had heard of any payment owed. Mallory owed... rent for coming here to save Ashley? Why hadn't he said anything to me about that? And why didn't he look very concerned?

"Enter," I commanded, and my bodyguards relaxed.

This should be fun.

CHAPTER 36

*O*beron strolled past the invisible line marking the cave entrance, and the wolves casually stepped out. Oberon didn't even flinch, merely speaking under his breath as if he had known they were here all along. "I lured some… well, they're more lethal than the deer you're used to back home. But they might provide you some entertainment while I speak with your leader." Wulfric sniffed the air instinctively, but his eye never left Oberon. The Goblin King smiled, placating. "Or you are more than welcome to stay here and listen in. Consider it a peace-offering. I haven't heard of many skirmishes, even after the alarm, and you need to keep your beast fed during your first visit to Fae. Suppressing it is not good."

Then he walked on. Gunnar shot me a look, and I waved him off. "We'll be fine. But you're more than welcome to stay…" I said, sensing the feeling of hurt from him. I sighed. "I value your insight, and would love for you to stay here…" I said, letting my offer stand for a moment as Oberon situated himself between Alucard and Yahn, directly across from Mallory and I. "But I would appreciate you giving some time to Wulfra even more. Cherish your time together. Remember why you came…" I said.

Which was a double warning.

Not only should he do exactly that for the obvious reasons – that she was his fiancée.

But that he needed to feed that human side of his heart. Hunting would feed both. Sating his beast, but doing so with the woman that he loved. She had survived this place already. Spending private time around her would let him drop his guard a little around the woman he trusted most in this world. Being around me right now would only keep him on edge and defensive.

A dangerous combination when struggling to merge with his wild side for the first time.

And keeping him away from Talon was also smart, because that feeling of jealousy between them was still alive and well. I hoped it shifted to a mutual camaraderie soon, because I didn't have time to deal with pettiness. We were all friends.

This wasn't the bestie Olympics.

Wulfra nipped at Wulfric playfully, and then darted from the cavern. Wulfric snarled back in amusement, shot me one last look, and then slipped away, too. I reached out to Grimm.

Look alive.

I heard a very tired sigh in my mind. *You know that your snippets of conversation mean literally nothing to me more often than not. I always look alive. Because I am alive.*

I growled back. *Stay alert for threats. Ambush. Trickery.*

That snapped his humor off immediately, and a sense of wariness entered our bond. Then he faded from my mind, taking to the air to make sure we were safe and that Oberon hadn't led an army here in disguise.

I finally turned to Oberon. He was studying Talon thoughtfully, even scratching his clean-shaven face. He looked at once annoyed, curious, and concerned.

I snapped my fingers. "I'll cut to the chase, since letting you two lead the conversation is just going to give us all a headache." Mallory snorted, and Talon purred approvingly. Oberon simply shrugged, turning his attention to me. "You mentioned that... Pan came here uninvited and owes you something for that. Elaborate. Because you could have approached him at any time to make good on that. But you arrive just after we do."

Oberon studied me, as if debating how to answer. Then his eyes swept over the cave, and he scratched at his arms, frowning. "What is this place? I can honestly admit I've never been here before. Nor been aware of it. And now that I am here, I sense faint residues of magic. Something that had been blocking this area from sight..." he trailed off, studying each of us in turn, even Yahn and Alucard. "And of all the places I find you, Nate, it is in such a place…"

Mallory cleared his throat. "I needed privacy. A mutual friend was dying and I needed time to heal her. This was my last and only option for success."

I noticed he had very carefully avoided Oberon's questions. And that this conversation had many fatal pitfalls. Oberon had once set his brother Pan to find my parents, and I wasn't entirely sure how we had gotten away with that, or what Pan had told Oberon. He obviously hadn't mentioned this cave… But why? If it was all over and done, why keep this place safe? Why not just destroy it? Wash off the cave drawings so that none would ever tie it to me?

"You and Talon once came to me after a very long journey. A journey where I hadn't been able to track you…" his eyes snapped to the cavern around us. "And I can track anyone in Fae…"

"Do you two need some privacy? I thought we were here to talk about you owing me?" I asked in a low growl, leaning my elbows on my knees.

Oberon snapped his attention back to me, nodding in agreement. "Yes, quite right. You took the Hatter away from this place, after hundreds of years of captivity. I don't believe you considered how incredibly dangerous that was to your people…" he smiled sadly at me, but I kept my face blank, not wanting to agree. "But that isn't my problem any longer, thanks to your actions. He is gone. You have done all of Fae a service. Granted, he was far enough away that only a handful ever crossed paths with him, but killing a few is a short price to keep a secret. I still wish I could learn who started the first rumors about him…" he said harshly, punching a fist into his other palm.

I nodded, pretending not to notice his talk of murdering the few who had found Matthias Temple and his white island. But I wasn't about to get into that. "What's my prize?"

He grunted. "Prize signifies a contest. You performed a service, not a challenge."

I studied him. "Is there really a difference? I know you pride yourself on word games, but I don't see how semantics is going to change anything."

He thought about that, and then smiled. "Habits," he admitted. I shrugged, motioning for him to continue. He, again, studied the cavern, frowning as he rubbed his arms. "Thought we covered that part…" I warned. "We do have things to do, and lucky for your world, they don't involve us sticking around, so you needn't be concerned."

He nodded absently, then studied each of us. "Just a strange feeling..." he said after a time, and finally shrugged. "Brings back memories..." his eyes flicked to Talon and Mallory one last time, but he soon shifted his attention back to me.

I kept my face studiously blank, because I had a sudden concern. Was he sensing the hourglass? That would be bad. Very, very bad. And what if he happened to recognize the company logos drawn on the walls in random places?

He cleared his throat. "I have turned off the call to arms. The alarm that alerted every Fae in the land to hunt, torture, and destroy the intruder who set it off not too long ago."

I blinked. "We, uh... did all that? Just because we came here?" I asked, sheepishly. I had hoped that it wasn't that kind of an alarm. Maybe like a Fae doorbell instead. Just letting everyone know they had guests. Not a dinner bell.

Oberon looked very uncomfortable, and then he sighed, shaking his head. "This really is the perfect chain of events..." he muttered, sounding troubled. "Your entrance here," he said, jerking his thumb at Mallory, "made many of us very concerned, but we couldn't find you." Then he turned to me. "Then you arrived and set off the call to war. Which meant you brought something over here that you shouldn't have had ownership of..." he said, staring at me patiently.

I tried not to squirm in my seat, like I didn't have a flashing *guilty* sign above my head.

"But... since you took out the Hatter... I find myself in a very unique position. I cannot retaliate against you. I can only demand payment of my... brother." He leaned forward. Not angry, but very, very serious. "Just know that if I hadn't been the first to answer the war call, all of Fae would be after you to reclaim what you brought with you..."

I swallowed audibly, and then nodded, extending my hand. "I accept your payment of keeping our secret safe from your subjects, and also for your discretion – even though it was not intentional, and likely does not sit well with you. This only makes it all the more valuable, and I will hold you to it."

He sighed after a long silence, and then shook my hand. "Clever..." he muttered. I nodded, trying not to smirk. Because I had just solidified that he couldn't tattle on us the moment he left. "Now that I have made my intentions clear, it would only be proper to tell me the truth."

I folded my arms, turning to Mallory, who looked very, very uneasy. "We will tell you the truth if you promise not to retaliate on any of us... now, or in the future."

He grimaced. "That is... a hard bargain," he said.

I smiled this time. "I wasn't even finished. This will clear Pan's debt to you as well."

He frowned unhappily. "And what if that does not sit well with me?"

I shrugged. "Then you can remain in ignorance. Truth is expensive," I added. This made him frown. I held up a finger. "I'll give you this for free. Those guilty have paid the ultimate price..."

He studied me, eyes calculating. "You know I could have an army here in a blink..."

"But you are a man of your word, and I could have us out of here in a heartbeat. You would also be seen as attacking someone you just paid a favor to..." He grunted unhappily. "And not to put too fine a point on it, but you really don't want to risk what I would do to any army I found too close to me right now," I all but whispered, allowing Wylde to stare through me at Oberon. The cavern grew significantly darker for a moment, and Oberon stilled.

"Let's not resort to threats. I'm sure the three of us have significant cards up our sleeves that would result in many deaths." His eyes met mine, and he very pointedly didn't look at my friends. Lucky for him. Still, they sensed it, and Yahn...

Belted out in laughter.

Alucard tensed, eyeing his partner askance. Then he smiled, turning back to Oberon, who was turning from one to the other on either side of him. Yahn was leaning forward, rubbing his hands excitedly, and Alucard – between one second and the next – suddenly looked like an entirely different person. His fangs slowly grew from his golden lips, and the ground beneath him began to smolder, his eyes pulsing with golden light.

Oberon grew very still, reconsidering his position.

Mallory muttered something unintelligible, but finally leaned back, folding his arms.

"We're all badasses. Agree or disagree, brother. None of us have time for anything else."

The cavern was silent for about thirty seconds before Oberon spoke. "For the price you mentioned, I want to actually *see* what you brought with you – what I am pretending not to have had within my grasp. The item that set off our alarms." I waited for Mallory to nod before agreeing. "I also want to know about this place, and what happened between you two before I first met Talon," Oberon said, indicating Talon and Mallory. "In essence, I need to know the full story if you are asking me to risk my name by ignoring the warnings that all of Fae heard. I will not pretend I am unaware when I don't know the full truth. And I believe I am owed the full truth, considering it involves me." His savage eyes met mine, "I'm guessing you're involved somehow as well, since you hold the artifact…" he muttered.

Then he leaned back. I reviewed my agreement, wondering if there was any risk to spilling the beans. But part of me felt like this was owed. "One last thing. I want you to give me your honest, unfiltered thoughts after… No deviation. I want what you *know*," I said.

He studied me, looking as if he was about to salivate. "Deal," he finally agreed, sounding both excited and frustrated. His curiosity was literally too aroused to ignore any longer.

I finally nodded, pointing at Mallory to cut loose.

With a deep breath, he did, and I spent my time studying Oberon for even a sign of stomach indigestion, in case our world was about to burn to ashes or a horde of goblins were going to rappel down the mountain behind us.

Oberon's face paled as his brother came clean, and his mouth opened wordlessly several times. But Mallory was only just beginning, telling the story of my birth, and everything else he had shared with me so far.

CHAPTER 37

*O*beron stood and began to pace the cavern, muttering under his breath. Mallory held the hourglass in his hands as proof. Oberon hadn't liked that one bit, especially when we refused to hand it over to him. I could tell his mind was running faster than it ever had. Trying to find a loophole in the story, but also trying to find a way to get an advantage out of it. He couldn't retaliate, but he had never promised not to find a way to profit from it.

I also knew he would give almost anything to have that hourglass back, but without knowing more about it, I wasn't about to consider that. My parents had sought it for a reason, and I wasn't sure if the Armory had been their ultimate purpose. Not entirely. Because I knew how my father thought. He always had schemes within schemes.

I cleared my throat, a new thought hitting me. A topic not as heavy as my birth story and the theft of all thefts. "What's the deal with Robin Good-fellow? Are you three the same person? And how are you both here right now? I thought that wasn't possible, considering Pan wouldn't enter last time he was here."

Mallory shook his head. "It wasn't that I couldn't come here with you, *ever*, but that the Invitation didn't concern me. Meaning, I was explicitly told not to interfere. And... I agreed with that, fearing the consequences should you fail. Also, Oberon," he said, jerking a thumb with an eye roll, "would have charged me an arm and a leg to remain by your side." Oberon grunted, but Mallory was smiling faintly.

The two acted like... two brothers ribbing each other.

"Why do you charge him rent to visit? That's not very... brotherly," I said, amused.

"I would do the same if he wanted to visit my world," Mallory admitted, giving me a very serious look. "And I think you should be thankful for that..."

I nodded, thinking about it. Kind of like a checks and balances system. "You didn't answer the other question. About Puck..."

Oberon finally sat down. "It... is complicated. We are not *entirely* the same. But we are similar enough that there is bleed over..."

Mallory nodded, eyes distant. "Our stories share many aspects, and since stories are our source of power, sometimes we must learn to share in order to... well," he sighed, sounding frustrated, "live, I guess. To keep our power, we sometimes lend each other power. When one waxes, another wanes, so we keep each other charged up. To put it in terms your tiny brain could understand..." he added drily.

I rolled my eyes. "Got it. But now I have this dreadful headache." They smiled at that, and then the silence returned. "So, what... am I?" I asked Oberon in a low tone.

The Goblin King studied me, eyes a million miles away. "A Manling," he finally said, sounding frustrated. "Who can wield Fae magic, but also your own magic."

"And you've never heard of this?"

"I'm not going to say you are the first Manling born here, but..." he looked resigned, almost guilty as he continued, "you are the first to survive to adulthood, thanks to your parents."

I nodded. "Is this the reason for my other... affinities?"

He shrugged. "Who the hell knows?" he almost whispered. "If the Queens knew of this... If they knew *I* knew of this..." he met my eyes, looking concerned for the first time. "I might have to pay whatever Pan charged me to relocate to your world," he admitted flatly. Then, realizing he had admitted a weakness, he straightened his shoulders. "They stole the hourglass for this Armory... But that can't be the only reason. I mean, perhaps, but there were other ways to achieve their ends. There had to be another reason..."

I turned to Mallory, giving him a questioning look. He shook his head. "That's what they told me," he said offhandedly.

I kept the brief sensation of shock from my face, masking it with a look of frustration. He was hiding something…

Oberon was too busy muttering to himself to notice, thankfully.

Talon finally spoke up, making me jump. He had been dozing, not wanting to remind everyone that he had played a part in this. Although unaware of the story, he had owned a piece of it, and hadn't wanted to risk Oberon's displeasure. Understandably. "My apologies for the deceit. Although I don't know if I would have changed anything if I had been aware of it, the apology still needs to be said."

Oberon froze, and then slowly lifted his head to study Talon. He looked very… grateful. As if Talon had just stroked his ego. Talon dipped his head one time, and then curled back up to leave us in peace.

I almost grinned. With that statement, he had disarmed a potential retaliation in the future, and redirected the conversation.

"I take it you are leaving immediately?" Oberon asked, eyes latching onto the hourglass.

I debated answering, but wanted to deal with him in good faith. "I might stick around for a bit, or return later…" I said, waving a hand at the cavern. "I want to spend some time here. You must understand that this is just as much of a shock to me as it is to you. I want to get a better grasp on my roots… and my powers, apparently. I'll likely visit from time to time, and I expect no retaliation for that. I certainly don't mean anyone here any ill will."

Oberon looked troubled. "If the hourglass returns, the alarms will go off. Any future visits should be done naked… I cannot make this agreement last forever. One time might go unnoticed, but I can't pretend nothing is happening if the alarms keep going off on a regular basis…"

I sighed wearily. "Right."

"And I don't think sticking around for very long is a good idea…"

My shoulders tightened, and Mallory slowly climbed to his feet, as if expecting a threat.

Oberon held out his hands in a peaceful gesture. "I came alone. But I'm not in the Queens' good graces. I wouldn't be surprised if they had someone tailing me." Seeing the looks on our faces, he held out his hands, calming us. "I swear on my name that I haven't betrayed you, and I never saw anyone following me. But I *know* them. It is something they would do… And if they discovered you here," he said, staring straight at me, "whom they hate with a fiery passion, and connected your arrival with the alarms, no powers will keep you from their fury," he whispered. I nodded, skin pebbling. He was being sincere, and I had a sudden desire to get the hell home.

Oberon met our eyes. "Something else is off about this place. I think you should very much return to figure out what it is. I will keep the place warded. Because, to be honest, I'm not sure if it's a danger to my people, or to *me*. Knowing the depths of your parents' schemes, I fear to discover it, but I definitely don't want any unlucky Fae stumbling onto whatever it is about this place that sets my arms to itching." He grinned guiltily. "Then again, if you wait too long, my curiosity may get the best of me, so I would encourage a speedy return." Then he climbed to his feet, brushing off his hands.

I locked arms with him in a respectful gesture. "Thank you, Oberon. Really."

He nodded, looking distracted. Likely at the number of things he had to lie about soon. He appraised me. "I'm not entirely sure how to address you. As a local – of indeterminate power – or as an enemy in my land…"

"Always better to err on the side of caution…" I said in as light a tone as I could manage.

He grunted after a few moments. "For now. Let me be the first Fae to welcome you."

With that, he dipped his head respectfully, and then embraced Pan in a tight hug, and left.

Not moments later, Wulfra and Wulfric returned – having likely been hiding just outside the cavern, listening the whole while. Which was fine. They could have walked in for all I cared. It hadn't been a secret meeting, but I was distantly pleased at the sign of respect – to not interrupt midway through a conversation with two kings and a god.

I turned to Mallory. "Spill. What else were you hiding from Oberon?" I asked.

CHAPTER 38

$\mathcal{M}$allory sighed. I turned to everyone else in the room. "Sharing time is over. Everyone get some rest. I want to talk to him in private, first. Set up a watch to give the horses a break."

Alucard and Yahn jumped to their feet. "We'll go first."

I arched a brow at Mallory. "Is there a more private room for Wulfra and Wulfric? I'd like to get some sleep at some point," I added drily.

"We don't mind," Wulfra said. "But there will be howls tonight..." she growled, rubbing her head into Wulfric's chest, which puffed out considerably at the prospect.

"No red rockets for me. I'll never be able to get that out of the old mental library. You guys get first pick," I said, shaking my head.

Talon didn't even stir, either already asleep, or accepting the fact that he would be sleeping first, and hopping to it with alacrity.

Mallory motioned for me to follow him outside. The horses were speaking with Alucard and Yahn, and after a brief discussion, they nestled down to get some rest. Alucard and Yahn walked away to put some distance between themselves and the cavern.

Mallory led me around the cavern towards the cliffs overlooking the ocean.

After about fifteen minutes, we reached the edge, and he sat, staring out at the moonlight reflecting off the waves of magma far, far below us.

"Your birth changed your parents. I only learned this much later, but your parents knew of an upcoming war. They found some very ancient texts in England speaking of an All War. They considered it their duty to safeguard weapons, because they didn't trust the Academy or the Syndicate with certain items. But they also knew that one would come who would be a *Catalyst*, as they called it. They didn't know if it would happen in their lifetimes, but that this person would have ties to Heaven and the Fae..." he trailed off, his silence significant.

I stared at him, taking it in, trying not to throw up. I had both of those things... "Is that why they really came here? Not just for the hourglass, but to gather stories on the Fae? To see if this person was already born, and perhaps building an army?"

Mallory nodded. "Aye." He turned to me, face pained. "Then you were born. And... when you started growing so rapidly, and showed an affinity for Fae magic, while also showing the spark for a wizard, they changed their plans slightly. I won't say that they presumed you to be the Catalyst they had sought, but they didn't discount the possibility, either, knowing how prophecies can sometimes be self-fulfilling. If they hadn't heard about this Catalyst in the first place, they may never have come to the Fae World..."

I nodded, my throat dry. "And I would never have been born..." I finished for him.

Sensing my distress, Mallory produced a hip flask of booze. I snatched it from his hands eagerly, uncorking it and taking a whiff. Absinthe. Some of the good stuff from back home, judging by the smell. I took a very liberal drink. Then I motioned for him to continue.

He took a drink, staring down at the flask, reliving the memories. "You were such a curious child. You and Talon came home scraped, bruised, and bloody so often that it became expected. Talon taught you the lessons of his people. Of war. And you, all by yourself, began to show talents at tapping into the powers of the land itself. You had the spark of a wizard, but were too young to – or simply chose not to – reveal your skills at wielding it. But born and raised in this place, you displayed... darker tendencies. This was why your parents began to trust me. They wanted to give you *time*, to see what kind of person you would become, knowing you needed to learn powers here before going back to your world.

"Because if you were raised as a human, and then learned about your Fae talents, they feared the power would go to your head. They considered it more natural for you to learn it from youth, from *living* it. And then, if they didn't consider you a danger, to wipe your mind and take you back home, to experience life as a wizard, raised in your world, with no living memories of this place. Until a later date, when they hoped that the two would combine, and not corrupt you too severely."

I shook my head very slowly, mentally forcing myself not to lash out with my power. Part of me now understood my parents' position, but part of me still hated them for it. "And if they decided I was dangerous…" I muttered, knowing the answer, "Uncle Pan would take care of it…"

Mallory sighed, nodding his head in shame. He didn't dare meet my eyes as he spoke. "I won't justify it, but consider the fact that there was quite literally no one like you. No Manling who wielded Fae magic. Raised in their world of *might is right*, where power literally called out to you from the very land itself. Like you were a god. Power corrupts…"

"And absolute power corrupts, absolutely…" I finished the saying.

We sat in silence for a time. I let the anger wash over me, feeling the elements around me calling out, begging to be used by me. In order to kill Pan.

I listened to them with an open mind.

And I let their wild, instinctive power roll through me, fueling me. I let the power build up, and then I lashed out at the ocean. A wave of invisible force – a merging of all the Fae magic coursing through my heart – struck the ocean far below like a meteor, sending a geyser up into the air, easily a thousand feet tall.

I let out a shaky breath, and then turned to Mallory, who was watching me warily. "And what kind of man have you deemed me to be?" I managed.

A slow smile crept over his face. "The man worthy to receive a final birthday gift from your parents…" he said, sounding very sad. He pulled out a cube of solid rock, the size of his fist. He set it on the ground before me, and muttered a word.

A stone block the size of my torso suddenly sat before me. I gasped in disbelief. It had to have weighed hundreds of pounds, and Pan had carried it around in his pocket?

I met his eyes. "I know not what it is, but that I promised to either give you a… blade through the heart, or this block if you ever returned here…" he admitted, sounding disgusted with himself. "Your parents said the Catalyst would need it someday…"

Instead of inspecting the stone – although I was itching to do just that – I closed my eyes, reaching out to the powers around me. They replied, eager to be used again, especially after tasting destruction only moments before, even though it had only been to make a splash in the ocean. Instead, I used those powers to assess Mallory. "Give me your hand," I heard myself say.

He reached out, clasping mine, and let out a deep breath. I called out to Wylde, checking that he had heard everything tonight, because he had been strangely silent. In shock. My parents had essentially broken me into two entirely different people. Leaving part of me here as a wandering spirit, full of memories and unable to inhabit a body. That spirit had wandered the Fae world, likely learning, studying, watching, growing into a man – but a man with no morals.

And no body.

When I had come here the first time, we had been reunited, and had both struggled to control the other. Only through a joint agreement had we realized we could be stronger together. And then we learned the truth tonight.

That we had always been the same person. Victims of a trauma.

But now, we were reunited. And decisions needed to be made. Namely, I needed to get Wylde's take on Mallory.

The other half of my soul reached out, and tentatively embraced him.

And memories rolled over me.

CHAPTER 39

*S*itting on Pan's lap, listening to him tell me stories about Manlings, and how they weren't as terrifying as Talon had made them sound. Talon sat beside us, amazed at this knowledge.

Pan showing us how to hunt, and how to beat the most dangerous of foes in combat.

Pan helping my mother clean up after dinner.

Pan talking my father down after an argument with my mother, while Talon and I leaned against the door, listening, spying.

And hundreds of other moments – shards of a life long forgotten.

Pan was… like a grandfather to me. An example of manhood when my stubbornness prevented me from seeing the same in my father – like all children did at one point or another – only realizing too late that what fathers preached oftentimes made perfect sense later in life, even though it had only made us angry at our first hearing of it.

And through him, I felt things I had never seen as Wylde.

The utter torment as Pan watched Talon and I sparring with sticks in the field before the cave, crying softly as he watched me, shaking his head defiantly as he muttered to himself, *I can't do it, I can't do it, I could never kill this special, beautiful boy...* over and over again like a mantra.

Pan's epic argument with my parents, where they had made him promise to kill me if I turned bad. He had understood their position, but he kept staring down at his hands, where I had painted a crude feather on the back of his wrist, telling him he was the best old man I had ever met.

My parents were openly sobbing as well, telling Pan that they couldn't be trusted to do it. Their love would prevent it, and they would try to stop Pan, but that he must do it anyway.

I snapped out of my focus when I heard low, rough sobs from Mallory in the present, hand visibly shaking as he stared down at his feet. He was thumbing the back of his hand, not even aware of the motion. I placed my hand over it, halting his motion, and he flinched. Then he slowly lifted red-rimmed eyes, and his other fingertips glowed with golden light as he smudged the back of his hand, revealing...

A duplicate of the feather I had drawn so long ago.

I met his eyes, my heart breaking.

He nodded, smiling in embarrassment. "I had it permanently tattooed there, later. As a reminder... Of both the good and the bad," he added the last in an anguished whisper.

I let out a breath, and leaned back on my hands, trying to stop my arms from shaking.

I stared down at the rock, frowning.

"A rock," I finally said, breaking the silence.

He grunted. "Apparently, but I'm sure it's something more. They said only you could see it, and this in itself was a test..." he answered, frowning down at it.

I pondered that, not even angry that – of course – my parents had another test for me. Even from beyond the grave they continued to test me. Not only had I been forced to prove to Mallory that I wasn't a sociopath, but my reward for *that* was that I was given *another* test.

So, how would this pertain only to me? Surely, anyone could strike it and break it open to discover its secret.

"It's impervious to harm. I tested the corner of it," Mallory admitted, reading my thoughts. I arched a brow at him, and he shrugged guiltily. "You can't ask someone to hold something for twenty years and not grow curious..."

I grunted, completely understanding that. I would have lasted a day or so before attempting to crack it. Well, *maybe* longer. But probably not.

Which pretty much left me with the obvious answer. If Mallory had tried breaking it open – unsuccessfully – then the only thing setting me apart from any other badass was my Fae juice.

Any ideas, Wylde?

He was staring at the stone through my eyes, feeling very uneasy.

Then I felt my hand slowly reaching towards it, guided by Wylde. I let him, not knowing what to do myself. Plus, Wylde *was* myself. I wasn't about to start having trust issues with my own inner psyche. That would mean that Mallory had made the wrong decision, and that would be the end of my story.

My fingers hesitated before the stone, as if asking permission. I grunted agreement.

Then my fingertip gently touched the stone, and it… rippled.

With an earth-shattering crack, the grass all around us flattened in an instant, and Mallory grunted as he fell onto his back.

I remained motionless, unaffected by the sudden force all around me, and I stared in wonder at the stone cube, suddenly reminded of the items in the Mausoleum – how they had been encased in stone, camouflaged from view.

But this didn't turn into a smaller, prettier cube.

The rock simply washed away like wet mud, to reveal a raw, stone encased hammer.

And when I say hammer, I mean a one-handed, godly son of a bitch. Power vibrated from it, pulsing into me, and I saw that Mallory was visibly holding himself, as if in pain at the proximity of such raw power.

The handle was about as long as my forearm, and wrapped in aged, braided leather, with gold and silver wire interweaving between the strips. The haft ended at a large, stone block, that seemed to pulse with golden light from deep within. The stone of the hammer was rough, not smooth – as if the discarded dream of a someday great weapon. As if the weapon-smith hadn't yet decided on the final look, and had left the stone raw instead. But that golden light shone from within, looking like faint, obstructed runes, and I felt a very small shiver as I noticed a single word carved into the stone by a crude hand.

Birthright.

I slowly turned to Mallory, my eyes wide. "That's not…" I whispered faintly, unable to say it out loud.

His eyes darted from me to the hammer, face contorted in confusion, as if having never met me before. "That... can't be possible..." he rasped, studying me and then the hammer again.

"You haven't lied to me about anything, right? About my mom maybe hooking up with the milkman, or... a guy selling thunderbolts cave-to-cave, right?"

Mallory shook his head violently. "No," he stammered. "I swear it—"

I heard grass rustling behind us, and instantly grasped the hammer, shoving it behind me as I spun on the ground. Alucard rounded the hill, eyes latching onto us. He looked relieved to have found us. "You guys okay? Something exploded nearby. And something else blew up in the ocean not long before that..." he eyed Mallory, and then shot him a guilty grin. "To be honest, I kind of hoped not to see you here. That maybe Nate had given you a gentle shove."

Mallory stammered in confusion. "What?" His eyes were wild, as if struggling to wrap his head around what he had just seen – as well as Alucard's words.

"I bet Yahn that Nate had thrown you into the ocean." He shrugged, feigning disappointment.

"We're fine, Alucard. We're not finished speaking, though. Thanks for checking up on us."

He watched us for a few moments, face blank, and then he nodded, turning away.

We remained frozen for a good five minutes, shooting silent looks at each other.

Then I spun back to the hammer, and hefted in in my hands. My palm thrummed with immeasurable power from the hilt, even though the weapon wasn't fully uncovered – still encased in stone.

"I think you should hide that motherfucker in your satchel for later," Mallory breathed.

I arched a brow at his choice of words, especially considering my last question to him, about Odin getting jiggy with my mom at some point. Too soon.

He flushed, realizing from my smile that he had said something inappropriate. "Not what I meant," he breathed, shaking his head. "But my advice still stands. Perhaps uncovering it sent off another alarm. We need to get out of here. Back to safety. We needed to anyway – what with Oberon's warnings, but..." his eyes locked on to the hammer again. "Especially now."

I nodded, and shoved the hammer inside my satchel.

What the fuck kind of crazy, acid fairy trip had my hippie parents been on when they decided to come here, and where the hell had they gotten the idea?

Mallory had mentioned texts from England. Where I had just sent Baba and Van…

I climbed to my feet. "Let's round up the gang. I'm suddenly opposed to sticking around here any longer. Even though I have a million questions…" Mallory agreed, and we made our way back in relative silence. I did say one last thing. "Did I tell you that I spoke to Odin yesterday? He told me to keep valuable things locked up at home…" Mallory actually fell over, but I didn't slow down to help him, simply continued on, shaking my head. What had he meant?

Someone was going to pay for this shit. Seriously pay.

CHAPTER 40

*A*lucard snarled, his fangs catching the orange light from the lava rock. "Let them come," he snarled hungrily, eyes pulsing faintly with the same glow as his fangs.

Yahn yawned, entirely unconcerned. "When will we return, exactly? A minute after we left? Or..." he trailed off, tapping his lips with a finger, glass on glass. *Ting, ting, ting.*

Wulfra spoke up. "We do not know how far we can trust Oberon. Remember what happened last time..." she growled, meeting my eyes briefly.

I nodded, sighing as I combed my fingers through my hair. "She has a point," I admitted.

Mallory sighed. "I don't know how he could wiggle around his oath, and judging from our shared... consciousness, I don't believe he wants to risk the backlash of what may happen if he reneges on his commitment, even though the consequences if caught will be severe. The Queens will be none too pleased." He glanced at me pointedly. "With either of you."

Wulfric stepped forward, glancing down at my satchel. "I don't think keeping the hourglass here is a good idea. We don't know how long the wards will stay up, or if they are entirely up right now. Oberon said they were weak. And carrying that around is like tossing a steak on our backs. Even though Oberon said he wouldn't snitch on us, there are many factions in Fae, and I could imagine they would be more than happy to catch you and prove Oberon a liar with one act. Possibly gaining the Queens' favor…"

I muttered angrily under my breath. We had come here, saved Ashley, and found everything in the best possible light. The things we had come here for, anyway. But we hadn't anticipated the extra drama, namely, the history lesson.

But did it really change anything? Was I blowing things out of proportion? Not that it wasn't vitally important information, but was it time sensitive? After all, if Matthias and Castor took me out, would any of it really matter? Wylde murmured his agreement, although his heart didn't sound in it. Tactically, it made sense, but he was deeply troubled about the news that he was a broken off part of me, and not his own person.

"Makers first. We'll figure this Fairy crap out later," I finally said. "Be ready to leave in ten."

Everyone departed except Talon and Mallory, who didn't have anything to pack. Mallory had relied on the things he found here to nurse Ashley back to health. Talon had his spear, and his old friend, Wylde. That was all he needed.

I approached them, speaking softly. "How do we get out of here? I could probably wing it, but I don't want to accidentally leave anyone behind. Did my parents have a convenient backdoor in this cave? How did we leave the first time? I doubt we traveled across the Land of the Fae if we were trying to avoid attention."

"They had love. It let them leave."

He discreetly jerked his thumb at Wulfric and Wulfra – Gunnar and Ashley. "They're taken care of in that regard." He studied the rest of my friends, who were scrambling about, hiding evidence that anyone had been here.

"The horses can come and go as they please, and you two should be able to do the same."

I studied the last two people. "Which leaves Yahn and Alucard…" Mallory nodded.

"I can take care of them if you are unsuccessful." I opened my mouth to tell him that he should just take care of it himself, then, rather than me risking failure. He shook his head, reading my thoughts. "You should try. Get used to this ability of yours. I have a feeling it will be important later, if you really are what your parents thought you were. The Catalyst. A Manling born in Fae. There has to be a reason for that…"

I sighed, seeing the truth in it. "So be it," I muttered.

In short order, everyone was ready. I stepped out of the cave, eyes focused inwards, not acknowledging the gestures I received from my friends. They didn't shoot me friendly looks, but respectful nods. They weren't privy to everything that had gone on recently, but had heard enough to have questions. Knowing that pushing me too far here was a bad idea, they let it go. But I knew their questions would drown me once the dust settled.

If we didn't scare the hell out of everyone when we returned to Chateau Falco so quickly.

I stood entirely still, staring out at the night, and took a deep breath, beginning to reach out to Wylde for assistance. He responded tentatively, not wanting to give up his place at home. I realized something for the first time. I wasn't temporarily taking him back, away from his home. I had literally returned to Fae, told him he had been missing from my soul for decades, and then basically commanded him to come back home to a strange new world.

Like inviting Tarzan to live in the city, where people like him were supposed to live. Except… I needed his help to accomplish it.

"We aren't finished, here…" I said out loud. The others shared looks, not speaking, but wondering if I was addressing anyone in particular. "But it's time to—"

Grimm slammed into the earth beside me, wobbling on his hooves and bleeding from several arrows embedded in his side. "Enemies approach," he wheezed, growling in both pain and anger. He wasn't down for the count, but he was injured.

My friends fanned out on instinct, not even waiting for my command, and I heard Pegasus screaming in the distant skies. We stared, and I pulled deep through Wylde, only to realize I was chuckling darkly under my breath. I wasn't sure if that was me or Wylde.

Or both.

"Help me, Wylde. We are the same," I murmured, closing my eyes. My mind was silent for a time, and then I heard a very deep, dark chuckle slowly building up from deep within. And power washed over me, filling me to the brim, the land speaking to me, begging to be used. I opened my eyes just as a line of monsters stepped into view about a hundred yards away. I spotted several flyers circling above fighting Pegasus, archers filling the air with bone arrows.

The creatures before us were a mix of every sort imaginable. But one thing set me to grinding my teeth. Every single one of them that leaned more towards human wore armor made of bark, vines, and foliage.

Hatchetmen – who worked directly for the Queens.

I shot a cold look at Mallory.

He returned the glare, shaking his head. "Oberon wouldn't betray us. Especially not so soon. And we had the horses scouting the skies. They would have *seen* something."

Grimm growled, obviously in pain, but stubbornly ignoring it. "Not Oberon…"

I continued staring at Mallory for a long moment. "Heal Grimm," I finally said. He nodded, and set to work immediately. I wasn't angry with Mallory, but I was considering consequences for my next decision. The Queens had arrived, and looked to have brought enough warriors to do the trick, unlike the last couple times when they had underestimated me.

I cleared my throat, catching everyone's attention as the army began to advance with bellows of outrage, hunger, and fury. Horns filled the air, but I shouted over them, somehow still sounding like a dark whisper. "I think it's time they met some St. Louis monsters. Agreed?"

Wulfra and Wulfric howled, a truly bloodcurdling sound, but I don't know how I heard it over my laughter. Wulfra tugged her Nemean Lion Cloak on, setting the hood over her head so that it looked like she was erupting out of the lion's open mouth.

I glanced at Mallory, arching a brow. He was finished, and Grimm looked right as rain. "You allowed to play? Because I intend to make this night memorable…"

In response, Mallory suddenly exploded into his ten-foot-tall form – a goat-legged man-creature with spiraling horns on either side of his head. Pan, the Wild God. "For this, I'll make an exception," he growled. "Consequences be damned." Then he lifted a set of pipes to his lips, and began to toot that motherfucker.

With an explosion of glass, Yahn abruptly shifted into his dragon form, and launched up into the sky with a shriek that faintly sounded like *toe-tah-leeee!* Yahn reached his peak, directly between the army and the moon, and sudden spears of white fire hissed into the front lines like lasers, ripping dozens in half.

I blinked, realizing that Yahn hadn't actively *done* anything. The spears had been formed from the moonlight shining through his body, but instead of rainbows, they created laser arrows of murder.

Toe-tah-lee cool, I thought to myself.

I shot a look at Grimm and Talon, reminding them of their earlier interest in catching those tiny rainbows. They looked suddenly apprehensive, lips tight. I grinned, and then turned back to the army, waiting.

"Disco Ball of death!" Yahn roared, and then hurtled himself towards the enemy flyers pestering Pegasus.

I turned to Alucard, grinning expectantly. He met my eyes for a few seconds, and I remembered our conversation on the roof. That single look let me know he was ready to cut loose. Sure, he had accepted his beast, but until this moment, he hadn't fully given in, fearing what it would make him. I smiled encouragingly, murmuring a single word with only my lips.

Reds...

His eyes flashed, throbbing with golden light, and wings exploded from out of his tattered robes, slicing through the purple grass around him, where it burned to ashes in an instant, leaving him in a smoldering crater, the smoke rising up to meet him. Then he smiled, and his fangs dripped molten gold, hissing and smoking where it struck the ground at his feet. Then he turned to the oncoming horde, flexing his fingers, which suddenly erupted into inches-long golden claws. Streamers of smoke drifted from their tips, literally hot enough to melt the freaking air.

And he flipped off the front line of the advancing Fae.

Wulfric winked over at him. Or blinked. I sighed. Whatever. He looked happy.

Talon stepped up beside me, glaring out at the army with utter hatred. When he spoke, he didn't turn to look at me. "My people have a tradition," he began. "When the chief is chosen, the most dangerous out of the remaining tribe becomes his Shadow – his protector." Before I could state the obvious, Talon scratched my arm, drawing blood. Then he held the claw up to the moonlight, revealing the crimson stain on the tips.

My instinctive anger faded as I watched his next action in horror.

He sliced through his own face with that claw, basically inserting my blood directly into his face, from above the eye down to about the center of his cheek. Then he did the other eye.

He turned to look at me, silver eyes flashing as he licked his lips, the two wounds bleeding slightly. Lucky for him, he hadn't sliced his eyes out on the way down his face. He dipped his chin once, and then spoke in a clear tone. "You gave me a name. I give you my life. I am your Shadow until death, Wylde Fae."

Then he slammed the butt of his spear into the earth, crouching lower in a ready stance, because the fight was almost upon us.

"Give us a tune, Pan!" I howled, my arms pebbling with the excitement of battle. He did, and I sprinted at a troll trying to shove through the front line, swinging a giant club in one fist.

"*This* is where the wild things are!" I shouted at the top of my lungs.

His giant misshapen teeth opened back in a snarl, and I felt Wylde pull through me, yanking the ground out from under him like a rug. He flipped up into the air, horizontal, back to the ground. Faster than I could blink, Talon was there, his spear propped up directly beneath him. The troll fell, impaling himself on the spear, his innards exploding with white fire as he screamed.

Just in case, Talon gripped him by the head with both paws, and jerked him down until his back slammed into the earth with a heavy thud. The spear was pristine, poking up into the air like a flag. Talon jerked the spear free and bowed to the Fae staring back at him, dumbfounded.

Then he began spinning, slicing, tearing, and cleaving.

And then he began to sing, a haunting battle chant. "Talon kneads the flesh, rakes the flesh, presses the flesh, rips the flesh, to make the perfect dough for our Lord Wylde's favorite pie!"

Not wanting to miss out on the fun, I joined him, unleashing my trusty whips, letting them remain fire and ice – one liquid lava, and the other chips of razor-sharp ice that broke off and reformed as needed when I struck, so that each crack of the whip either slashed or splashed the opponent with droplets of lava or shrapnel frost.

And I realized for the first time that this was appropriate.

Fire and Ice.

Summer and Winter.

Life and Death.

Balance.

Like the Queens had once taught me.

I truly was a man in the middle. A man of opposites. Contradictions.

A Catalyst.

But I made it look damned sexy.

Death rained down on the Fae, and the Manling and his friends had the time of their lives.

CHAPTER 41

*W*hat felt like an hour later, I realized that Talon and I were momentarily clear of any immediate threats, giving us time to catch our breath. But I didn't feel tired. I felt... *alive*. As if each enemy's cry, whimper, or splash of blood had been fueling me.

Talon was actually strutting, coated liberally in both blue and red blood, licking his paws fastidiously. Despite the gore covering his body, his spear was still perfectly white.

But there were still so many enemies left on the field.

Wulfra and Wulfric fought back to back against a skulk of purple-eyed foxes. They were small – only about waist-height – but there were dozens of them, and they wielded hatchets as if born with them in paw. They also wore expensive-looking silver muzzles, complete with purple jewels down the top of the nose. This jewelry prevented them from opening their jaws, which I found... odd. Why prevent them from using their teeth? But Wulfra and Wulfric didn't really care about their flashy bling. They were too busy murdering them to death.

The two fought like one being, seamlessly merged with their inner savages and each other. When Wulfric's diamond claws tore through flesh – even if not a fatal blow – the victim screamed and smoked, the wound spreading through them as it turned to ashes, crumbling away to fill the air with a thick, pungent scent like charred meat. Piles of silver muzzles littered the ground.

Wulfra abruptly darted away from the pack as if fleeing, drawing the foxes after her and away from her one-eyed wolf king. But I realized she hadn't been running away from the foxes – she had been running *towards* a twelve-foot-tall, pot-bellied ogre – a real ugly son of a bitch. The ogre spotted Wulfra in her Nemean Lion Cloak, blinked in momentary confusion as if unsure whether she was a lion or a wolf, and then decided to bash whatever she was with his club.

But instead of rolling away, Wulfra swung her fist in a full-bodied uppercut directly at the club – which was easily as wide as her entire body. The club splintered on impact with her furred fist, pelting the pursuing foxes with splinters as large as arrows. Half a dozen dropped dead, but the others jumped over their fallen brethren without concern. The cute factor of their bushy, orange and white tails was slightly diminished by their brandished hatchets winking in the moonlight. The ogre blinked at Wulfra in surprise, bleeding in several places where the club had pierced his own thick hide. Then she climbed up onto the ogre's knee, jumped up onto his shoulders, and then began tearing at his face with her razor claws. The ogre howled, caught by surprise, but the foxes weren't about to let their chance to catch her from behind go to waste.

They lunged into the air, directly at her back. As if having a sixth sense, she sprung backwards in a flip, directly over the foxes. They slammed into the ogre, hatchets buried deep into his face and chest in a dozen blows. He grunted in shock, crashing to the ground, thrashing back and forth as he rolled in agonized screams, crushing or injuring most of the foxes.

Wulfra calmly walked up behind them, snapping their necks before turning back to Wulfric.

He hadn't budged, simply watching her with folded arms – he must have lost his Rarawk antler club at some point. He may have grunted back at her, but that glint in his eyes was the very definition of pride. They reconnected, embraced, checked each other rapidly, and then sought out new foes.

A roaring shriek made me glance up to see Yahn beating his wings in the skies. Three flying beasts flew at him – their archer riders launching arrows as fast as they could draw them. The projectiles struck him and ricocheted away harmlessly. Yahn beat his wings once more, tucked them into his body, and then flipped backwards into a double flip. The flyers stared at him, unsure if their attack had harmed him.

But Yahn's wings snapped out again and he spat a wave of glass spears at the attackers, impaling them all several times over. Both flyers and riders screamed in anguish, falling down to the earth in sickening splats. Yahn cackled, and resumed his sweep of the skies. I glanced back to see Pan healing Grimm and Pegasus behind us.

But the things I had seen those two doing to their foes... I shivered, forcing it from my mind. They probably had the highest score if we had been competing for number of dead Fae.

"Come to me!" A honeyed, southern drawl laughed. I spun to see a glowing Alucard standing in a slight depression in the field, surrounded by a circle of at least two dozen Hatchetmen.

"Enough talk, vampire. I don't care if you *are* a Daywalker. It's night time, and that's when *we* feed," a helmeted voice shouted back.

Talon took a few stealthy steps toward them, but I grunted, holding up a hand. He frowned at me, but finally nodded, looking uncertain.

The immediate area was silent for a moment, and then Alucard spoke again. "Do you have enough men to guarantee victory?" he asked in a soft voice.

I frowned at his tone. It didn't sound powerful. In fact, it sounded saddened, and I began to wonder if maybe Talon had been correct to offer help. But the choice was taken from me as the crowd swarmed him from all sides.

Alucard's response was as sad and final as a prayer over a grave, his face one of sorrow, regret, and forgiveness. He didn't even try to move.

But when the first attacker on either side was within arms' reach, he abruptly shifted like liquid metal. The two attackers slammed into each other, impaling the other on their blade. But Alucard wasn't even looking. He dipped, ducked, dodged, and adjusted like a cobra, letting the Fae kill each other as he moved like a silk ribbon in a hurricane – harmless, but untouchable. Then I heard a chiming sound, and his wings snapped out, ripping entirely through a dozen attackers. The tops of their bodies simply fell to the ground, smoking where his wings had sliced them in two.

Only then did he begin to laugh, and his claws stretched longer, as if he was holding four swords in each hand.

"I wanted to introduce myself!" he shouted in a clear, crystal voice. "My name is Alucard Morningstar, and I'm a Fae-o-holic. Because I'm addicted to your *blood*." He sighed, shaking his head sadly as he casually decapitated another Fae with one of his wings, not even looking. His devilish smirk slowly returned as he stared down the survivors, who looked suddenly uncertain. "I'm the one your parents told you stories about. I'm a Manling monster. And it feels *soooo* good to say that out loud," he chuckled darkly.

Then they tried to run.

And he killed them all in a tornado of laughing, golden blades.

After only a few seconds, he was entirely alone amidst a circle of smoking, groaning bodies. He assessed the bodies with a casual look, a light smile on his face, and then his wings stabbed down, each sword-like feather impaling anyone who made a noise, until all was silent.

He turned to me and licked some blood off one claw, moaning in delight. "I guess I fell off the wagon," he admitted, licking his lips. "Oh, well. Zero days without an incident."

I burst out laughing. Terribly inappropriate – but the best one-liners usually were.

And then he walked over the bodies, the forms erupting in fire under each booted step. His tattered robes seemed to absorb the blood, the crimson color climbing up higher on his clothes as he moved. Then he was clear of them, staring outwards, looking for a fresh drink.

I realized that the Fae army had retreated behind two royal palanquins. Great, four-legged monsters as large as elephants – but resembling feathered warthogs – who stomped their feet impatiently, forced to carry their Queens into battle.

Two utterly nude women stood from their respective seats atop each platform, faces tight with anger. "Nate Temple is to be tried and judged for his crimes of invading the Fae, and stealing one of our most treasured artifacts. Submit or perish," they said in unison.

I stared back at them, and then began to laugh. "Nate Temple isn't here right now," I called out, spreading my arms wide for all to see as I spun in a slow circle. "Please leave a message."

Then I began to walk closer, my friends slowly angling behind me into a V formation with me at the point, well within range of their archers. Yahn screamed from the sky, reminding anyone who might be trigger-happy that it wouldn't end well for them.

The Queens shared a look, frowning. "We see you, right before us, wizard. We followed Oberon here, sensing something was not right when we found his Hunt abandoned. The call was raised for war, letting us know our precious artifact had returned, but the Hunt sat idle."

I managed not to grin in relief. Oberon hadn't given us up. At least, they made it sound that way. "Oberon was forced to make a deal with me," I said in a calm voice.

The Summer Queen – her hair flashing in the moonlight sniffed. "No agreement with a mortal – and a thief, at that – could bar him from his duty. Only those from Fae could bond him so."

And a very dark, hungry smile split my cheeks as I slowly nodded back at them, relieved that I had guessed this correctly. I mimed a finger gun, pointed at her, and said, "Pew! Pew!"

Their army actually flinched, lifting their shields in alarm. Talon burst out laughing.

I lowered my deadly finger gun and took three steps closer. "Behold!" I shouted, drawing from Wylde's natural talent for authority. "A Manling, born in Fae."

The army grew utterly silent, many shaking their heads in disbelief as my words seemed to echo throughout the land. "What ridiculousness is this?" The Winter Queen demanded, her purple nipples standing out in sharp contrast to her ivory skin. "You are a wizard, not a Fae."

I sighed. "I'll give you a demonstration for free. But if you want details, you're going to have to request an appointment." I pointed a thumb behind me. "And my receptionists are gigantic assholes."

And without further warning, I opened up to Wylde, letting him cut loose. With a roar, he began moving like a force of nature. He snatched the darkness from the sky and slammed it down on top of the army like a lead blanket, smothering their muffled cries. Then he plucked three stars from the sky, and tucked them underneath the Shadow blanket. Three muffled flashes incinerated anyone caught too close. My legs were shaking from the effort of moving so much power so rapidly, but I kept my face devoid of any strain.

Ashes drifted up from the earth where a large chunk of the their army had stood.

The Queens hissed in disbelief, and their surviving army began to break.

With my last bit of power, I coaxed Wylde to call out to the earth itself. The vines and foliage used to make the Hatchetmens' armor erupted to life, and they screamed as trees suddenly erupted from the earth, growing centuries old in a span of seconds, trapping the bodies inside their trunks. Soon, all was quiet. The leaves dripped blood, swaying slightly in the breeze.

The rest of them simply ran screaming, shedding their armor like Autumn leaves, not wanting to risk becoming a permanent woody.

"Your allies have taken gifts that do not belong to them," the Summer Queen snarled.

"We shall retrieve them now," the Winter Queen promised. And they both lifted their arms.

My friends began to scream, falling to their knees in agony. I spun to see what looked like fish hooks tearing the souls from their bodies, and the fishing line led right back to the Queens. Wylde lashed out to either side, slicing the lines with what looked like gray fire, and the souls slammed back into my friends. The fishing lines whipped back into the Queens and they shrieked in a primal cry, their jaws suddenly elongating like snakes.

They rounded on me and flung out their hands again, but Wylde groaned in exhaustion, unable to fight back. Pure willpower struck me, knocking me onto my ass. The same spiritual fish hooks ripped into my chest, and latched onto my soul, lighting it on fire. I wheezed, grunting and groaning as I tried to fight back, but my power ebbed, growing weaker with each passing second. My satchel sat on my lap, and as my mind began to splinter, I saw a haft protruding from the opening.

Before their attack could drown me, I jerked my torso with every ounce of strength I had left. My unresponsive arm flipped up over my body and my hand hit the handle of the war hammer.

Their attack winked out as if it had never been, my soul slamming back into me. I let out a shuddering breath.

And then a maelstrom of lightning erupted from deep within the depths of my being, crackling up through my body like a bag of popcorn in a microwave.

Wylde screamed in ecstasy, laughing and crying simultaneously.

I climbed to my feet, small arcs of electricity zapping out of me, striking nearby blades of grass. I slowly lifted my gaze to stare back at the army. Then I opened my mouth to speak.

"I… am… Wylde Fae," I whispered.

And a hundred bolts of lightning flew from the hammer into every single Fae before me.

The Queens flung up their hands and dove off their mounts – which was the only thing that saved them. Somewhere in the back of my mind, I knew how dangerous it would be to kill them, but I hadn't tried to *do* anything. I'd just... *spoken*.

The army exploded in a single *boom*, and the earth rocked as if struck by a meteor – bodies and huge clods of earth flipping up into the now incredibly warm air. I heard my friends shouting behind me, scrambling as they struggled to keep their balance, but I stood as solid as a boulder in a river. The ground around me was perfectly flat in a wide circle. But beyond that...

Was a landscape of ruptured earth with rivers of blood flowing like tributaries.

When the dust settled, I was panting, the war hammer hanging forgotten in my fist.

I saw the Queens peering out from behind the carcasses of their mounts, eyes wide with fear and outrage. And then they simply disappeared.

I turned back to my friends, dropping the war hammer.

And passed out before I could even open my mouth.

CHAPTER 42

I awoke to the sound of splashing water and just knew that a giant god was taking a giant piss near my tiny head. It just goes to show you that things can always get worse, and that my level for shock was pretty high.

I peeled open my eyelids, which felt crusted with too much sleep.

"He's awake!" a low purr announced.

"Rest... Wylde," another familiar voice responded, as if choosing the name purposely. "Rest. You're safe. I've put a healing balm on your wounds."

I sat up with a groan, eyes finally focusing enough to separate blurs into familiar shapes. I was on the floor. The air was humid, and I realized I was in the Sanctorum inside Chateau Falco, right beside the waterfall – *not a golden shower, then, praise Odin*. I tried to talk, and instead dove into a coughing fit.

I wiped my eyes and Pan hissed a warning, grasping my forearm before I could do it again. "The balm," he reminded me. "You had burns."

I frowned at him, and realized that his face looked very, very concerned. Talon handed him the compact mirror from the nearby desk – something I had found buried in one of the back drawers from hundreds of years ago. Pan handed it to me, showing me my reflection. My face was slightly red as if I had just finished a long run. Not serious burns, but definitely noticeable. My skin felt tight, and it shone from Pan's magical balm.

"Why..." I coughed, clearing my throat. "Why didn't you simply heal me?" I rasped, pocketing the mirror clumsily.

He studied me, debating something that he didn't share out loud. "You were... unpredictable. I didn't want to cause you concern if you woke up and sensed magic touching you."

I slowly nodded, but I must have still looked confused, because Talon piped up helpfully. "You know, from when you killed an entire battalion of Fae and sent the Queens running."

I turned to look at him, my memory returning. Then I realized we were alone. "We have to go back! The others—"

"Are fine," Pan said soothingly, placing a hand on my chest. "You've been out for sixteen hours." He held me down more forcefully, sensing my sudden panic at hearing how long I had been asleep.

Talon spoke. "We showed up seventeen minutes after everyone saw us leave," he said, making sure I was paying attention. "We anticipated much worse before we left. Days, weeks, months. It hasn't even been a full day. We're still ahead of the Makers."

I grunted, still anxious.

"Only Dean, Carl, Tory and the Reds know we're back. That's it."

"I think he imagines that trumpets herald his arrival wherever he walks," Pan muttered.

I shot him a glare, but seeing the smile on his face, I finally relaxed enough for him to remove his hand from my chest. "What happened... at the end?" I asked, my memories still spotty.

Talon was shaking his head wonderingly. "You... made a name for yourself. Killed *so many* people. It was truly breathtaking..."

Pan cleared his throat. "You... used the hammer. The one I told you to hide."

"It wasn't like he had much choice," Talon argued hotly. "They tried to take away our wild sides – and almost succeeded. But whatever you did stopped them. It was..." his voice trailed off into a whisper, and I saw the faint scars from forehead to cheek, through each eye. "Glorious..."

I let out a nervous grunt, head jerking to the side. Pan placed his hand on my thigh, catching my attention. I looked up to see him pointing towards the Round Table. I followed his hand to see my satchel sitting there, and I let out a sigh of relief.

"I don't understand what I did..." I admitted. "I just reacted. They almost had us. Even me."

Pan nodded, face distraught. "They tried to take away the gifts the Fae World had given your friends. For a moment, they were as they entered – still dangerous, but not strong enough to fight off the horde before them. Then you cut their power off somehow, so they tried to take away your wild side. After that... you kind of... well, used the hammer to share your feelings..."

I blinked back at him, not remembering. Really, up until seeing the Queens, I was clear-headed. But after that was just frozen images, like strobe light memories. "What do you mean?"

"They hit you with their power, trying to take your savage side. It hurt you, but didn't work as intended. Because it *couldn't*. You *are* Wylde. Then you touched the hammer and laid waste to... pretty much everyone. You took your name in fact – *Wylde Fae*. The world exploded in lightning and everyone died. Except the Queens. I still don't know how they made it, but I'm glad they did. As much as I despise them, the world needs them," he said in a lecturing tone.

I nodded absently. "I agree. They told me about that once..." I said, trying to remember what had happened before I had woken up. "Everyone is okay?"

Pan nodded, a faint smile on his face. "More than okay, considering." Knowing me well, he continued. "They maintained their... gifts. The Reds were quite taken with Yahn," he said.

"Which Alucard absolutely *loved*," Talon purred, practically salivating.

I tried to smile, but my face felt too tight, sensitive to the touch, and even the slightest of movements hurt. "Well, I think I'm good. Mind healing me? I'd rather not look like the world's worst sunburn victim."

Pan was watching me warily. "I'm not sure that's wise. The power that came out of you... It should have simply melted your body. But all you received were topical burns. That's..."

I grunted. "Not possible. Yeah," I sighed. "I'm hearing that more and more often."

When it was obvious they intended to sit beside me until I went back to sleep, I cleared my throat. "I need to speak to Death." I had a request for the bastard – one they didn't need to know.

That was absolutely the opposite of what they had expected. They both tried to argue, but I raised a hand. "Either you get him here, now, or I call Grimm and find him myself."

Silence stretched for quite some time before Talon grunted in displeasure. "As you wish."

Which left Pan and me alone in the Sanctorum. He avoided direct eye contact, pretending to do small tasks around the room. I watched him, not giving him a moment of respite.

"God's balls, boy. What?" he finally snapped.

I smiled faintly at his turned back, considering what I wanted to ask. "I'm not Thor."

He flinched, slowly turning to face me. His face was blank. "Okay."

"I'm not Thor," I said more forcefully.

"As you just said," Pan said carefully.

"I'm not—"

"I think he heard you, boy," a voice as cold as winter frost interrupted, and I actually felt snow striking my eyelashes. We both spun to see a, tall, gaunt, hooded figure standing beside a bear of a man with one eye. My fingers subconsciously shot to the necklace at my throat, and I felt a wave of relief as I touched the wooden disc. My Mask. I focused back on the newcomers.

Death and Odin.

I glared at them, forgetting Pan's advice to stay in bed as I yanked back the blankets. After a quick look, I yanked the blankets back into place, scowling at Pan this time. He shrugged, and then turned to the two guests. He dipped his head respectfully, and then left the room.

"Hey. How are things?" I asked, my voice clipped.

They grunted noncommittally, seeming more interested in studying me from different angles as they began circling me in silence. I fidgeted slightly, trying not to look at Odin – who wore a silver eyepatch this time – while trying to make eye contact with the hooded figure, but the depths of his cloak were impenetrable.

"I can pull back the blanket again if you need a closer look, but turn down the snow-blower effect. I need to maintain some of my dignity," I muttered to the Allfather.

He grunted, but didn't speak, seeming to stare right through me. Then he turned to Death, staring into the hood. "Satisfied?" he asked. Silence filled the room as they stared at each other for a full minute. Finally, Death nodded.

I opened my mouth to demand an explanation, but they were suddenly gone, leaving me entirely alone. "What the living *fuck?*" I shouted, punching the stone floor beneath me. It cracked, which almost made me pee a little in surprise.

I glanced down to see my fist glowing with golden veins again, and the stone beneath it was cracked, leaving a small crater where I had struck.

The long litany of curses I shouted into the room next did not exactly go together.

But it was an impressive attempt.

CHAPTER 43

I had managed to find some clothes, and even put them on mostly correctly. My muscles were jelly, so it took some time to get them to respond to basic commands, but I'm a survivor.

Once confident I could make it across the room – I verified this by squinting my face and eyeing the distance with one eye for a full minute – I hobbled over to the Round Table.

With a very real sense of unease, I reached into the satchel, expecting to find everything missing, despite what Pan had shown me about it. Because my memories of the fight had returned, and I remembered that I hadn't put the war hammer back in the bag.

But I let out a breath of relief as I felt the haft. I didn't dare grab it directly – I used a wadded-up cloth to handle it and set it down on the table. Then I pulled out the rest of the items I had put inside. I set the hour-glass and the stone pyramid beside the war hammer, and then sat down before the table, propping my chin in my palms as I studied them.

They had all been encased in stone at one point.

All entirely different.

All given to me by my parents… with absolutely no instruction manual.

I started at the beginning of the line. The stone pyramid that was a replica of the Hand of God Indie had used to wake up Athena. I picked it up, inspecting it curiously. I was pretty sure it wasn't actually a Hand of God, because there were a limited number of them, and it sounded like all of them had been accounted for.

So, what was it? Remembering how I had freed the war hammer from the stone, I reached out and touched it with a finger, drawing on Wylde. Nothing happened. I scooped it up and wandered over to the waterfall, holding it under the stream. I was surprised when the stone casing simply washed off, revealing a hollow, glass pyramid.

I stared at it for a few seconds, noticing a small hinged cap at the tip. I flicked it open with my thumb, waiting for the world to end. But nothing happened. I frowned at it and then made my way back to the Round Table, reaching into my satchel again. I pulled out the small bag that contained the dust from the real Hand of God, my hands shaking as I hefted it absently.

This was probably a very stupid idea. But no one was here to confirm that, so I carefully dumped the dust into the glass pyramid. It filled it up to the brim, and the crown snapped shut. The entire pyramid flashed with light, momentarily blinding me, and then all was silent. When I peeled open my eyes, the hinge was gone – not a seam in sight – and the glass pyramid was closed around the dust. I frowned, tapping my lips.

Had I just remade the Hand of God Indie had used?

I set it down nervously, scooping up the hourglass instead and leaning back into my chair. It wasn't unusually heavy, but hearing its origin story made it feel like solid lead. An ancient artifact that had been in possession of the Fae. They valued it highly enough to start a war to retrieve it, but... did it truly belong to them? My parents had been in the business of retrieving dangerous or stolen items and storing them in the Armory.

So...

The obvious question was why hadn't they stored the hourglass there? Why had they entrusted Mallory – Pan – to put it on their statue in the Mausoleum? Was there a specific reason? Did they know something would happen to the Armory? Was the hourglass even meant for me, or had they simply wanted to diversify their hoard a little, hiding a bit here and a bit there?

One thing I knew, it helped distort the time suck between worlds.

The first time I had gone Fae Side, I had been there during one night and day, but about seven weeks had passed in the real world. This time? I had been gone about the same length of time, I think... and only seventeen minutes had passed in my world.

Something about that bothered me.

Seventeen minutes…

Such an exact number. I frowned, mentally poking my brain to jog it like a primer button on a gas lawn mower.

Then it hit me. That was the exact amount of time that the Armory had remained open per visit before I had accepted stewardship of the place. Well, stewardship over Pandora, who actually ran the place. Once I had accepted that responsibility, the time-limit had dropped. But… the hour-glass had never been inside the Armory, had it?

Then I thought about that a little more. Maybe it *had* been in the Armory. But someone had removed it at some point… maybe right after I had agreed to supervise Pandora. Maybe the hourglass had enforced the seventeen-minute time limit up until then. Which meant Mallory had then moved it to the Mausoleum for some reason. It was possible.

But that begged the question… what the living hell? Why?

I sighed, shaking my head as I turned the hourglass over in my hands. I tried to recall any mention of an hourglass from the various myth lore I had studied over the course of my life. I could only think of Father Time.

I sighed, shaking my head, not coming up with anything that seemed to fit – or at least nothing that gave me any solid answers. Maybe it was a Fae design, but I had never heard of it. At least it wasn't anything obviously horrific that they had stolen centuries ago.

Then again… why had my parents needed to steal it so badly if it wasn't that important or dangerous? The short answer was… they wouldn't have.

I set it down carefully and moved onto the last item.

Instead of touching it, I stared at it. Despite the chaos it had unleashed against the Fae, it still resembled a crude hammer with a quality haft. As if the true weapon had been covered in concrete. Faint golden light still shone through in cracks, but I wasn't about to test it by hitting it.

I didn't think Falco would appreciate a detonation inside her soul. I realized my hand was hovering over it without me consciously choosing to do so, and that my veins were glowing with golden light again. The light within the hammer seemed to be glowing brighter in response.

I hissed, yanking my hand back with a nervous breath.

Instead of studying the hammer, my vision was locked onto my skin. The light had first appeared after I killed Athena, but I had received no answer on it. It had also seemed to be fading over time, only coming back when I was particularly angry. I also hadn't heard the voice, or felt those dark sensations encouraging me to do bad things.

But near the war hammer, it seemed to be back in full force.

I stared at the word carved into the stone. *Birthright.*

My phone buzzed, startling me. It was sitting on a nearby table where I had left it before heading to the Fae. I climbed to my feet and answered it, recognizing the number.

"You found something?" I asked excitedly, glad for the distraction.

Van grunted. "Possibly. To be honest, I thought this was going to go to voicemail, but I wanted to give you an update just in case anyone was checking your messages. Haven't you left for Fae yet?" he asked, sounding eager.

"Back already. Successful mission," I said. "What have you found?"

He was completely silent, as if not comprehending my reply. Because it didn't make any sense. I should have been gone much longer.

"Hello?"

He grunted, still struggling with my answer. "We're scoping some things out, but it looks promising. We've been tracking names like you asked, and well, I don't want to get your hopes up, so I won't share details, but we think we found one of them. I'll keep you posted."

I grinned excitedly. To score a win on something that wasn't life or death made me so happy. Just once, I was ahead of the game. Even though there wasn't really a game, but with Pan mentioning a tie between my parents and England, I was suddenly unsure I wanted to find out what they had been looking into.

My parents hadn't known about this room with the round table, so whatever they found couldn't have been tied to it. But still. I had a sinking feeling. My parents had found something in England that had sent them off to Fae for the hourglass, resulting in my birth, and full-circle, giving them the other thing they had been looking for. The Catalyst, as they had called it.

Me.

But I also didn't want to share that with Van and Baba Yaga. Not because I didn't trust them, but because the fewer people who knew about it, the better.

"Just be careful over there. I know you're a badass, but if you even get a whiff of something feeling off, I need you to run and observe from a distance. We really don't know what we're doing here, or even if there's anything to do. But you can bet your ass we aren't the first to go looking for clues. Secret societies come to mind."

Van grunted and I could hear Baba in the background, giving Van hell for something. "Yes, mother. You were right, I was wrong," he muttered to her. I grinned. She had been listening in on the conversation and had warned him as well. Good. Meant I didn't need to convince the both of them.

"You still have the copper rings I gave you, right?" I asked, hoping he hadn't arrogantly decided to leave them behind.

"Yeah. I'm not a fan of being tracked, though," he complained. I had given them rings to let me know where they were, just in case I needed to get to them in a hurry. Or on a more macabre note, if I needed to retrieve their remains.

"Just wear them. I'm paying you well for this, so humor me."

"I know. Just chafes. Anyway, we'll keep you posted. Chicken foot sends his love," he added, and then hung up as Baba squawked at him in the background. I smiled, shaking my head as I set the phone down.

"You called?" a familiar voice spoke from directly behind me.

I jumped, falling back into the desk to see Death had arrived. He wore tight-fitting black jeans and a *Morningstar is my Mayor* shirt. I glared back at him, trying to calm my racing heart. "You need to wear a bell or something. You can't just sneak up on people without warning," I scolded.

He blinked, and then arched a brow, lip curling into a smile. "Oh, really..."

I frowned, realizing how stupid my comment had been. That was kind of his job description. To arrive unannounced at the moment of one's death, and take their souls to the Underworld. "I'm still getting you a bell," I muttered, accepting his outstretched hand and letting him pull me to my feet. "What's up with the wardrobe change?" I asked, walking away from him and the table, trying to organize my thoughts.

I realized I didn't hear him following me, so glanced over my shoulder to find him standing where he had helped me to my feet. He was frowning. "I beg your pardon?"

I slowly turned to face him, but seeing the concern in his eyes, I suddenly felt very, very concerned myself. "That... wasn't you..." I whispered.

"I just arrived after Talon interrupted a meal I was sharing with Othello," he said, walking closer, eyes troubled at the look on my face.

I raked my hands through my hair, replaying the encounter with Odin and the hooded figure. Then I told Death about it. He blinked a few times, and then let out a breath. "That wasn't me."

I wanted to hit something. "Of course," I muttered. "How many hooded guys do I kn—" I cut off, shooting him a sharp look.

"Let me check with my brothers," Death said, and was suddenly gone.

I paced as I waited, hoping he was about to return laughing about Famine playing a joke or something. He returned without fanfare a minute later, shoulders tense. "They didn't visit you."

"Great..." I growled. "Since when has Odin been able to just waltz in here? And how did he get a free guest pass?" I said, more to myself than anything.

Death didn't answer, so I turned to look at him. He was staring at one of the upper levels, where a depiction of my family crest was carved into a large wooden shield that hung on the wall, easily ten feet tall. A jagged lightning bolt split the shield in half, and one side of the shield showed a feather, the other two mountain peaks.

Two polearms – one a scythe and the other a glaive, or sword-bladed spear – angled out from the top corners, and each had a ribbon below the blades. The scythe's ribbon said *Memento Mori* – *remember you are mortal* – and the spear's ribbon said *Arete* – *become the best possible form of a thing.* A large fist rose above the shield, symbolizing mastery over all, and the words *Non Serviam* sat below it – Latin for *I will never serve.*

But I knew what Death was staring at.

On the butt of each weapon sat a large raven, and their names were even written underneath.

Hugin and *Munin. Thought* and *Memory.* Odin's ravens.

I stared at it harshly, and then glanced at Death. "What does it mean?" I asked him.

He shrugged. "Not sure. But I don't like coincidences..." His eyes noticed the hammer on the table with a studious frown, but he didn't comment.

"Looks like I need to bake a raven pie..." I promised.

Death winced uncomfortably. "Or you could just talk to them first. Don't start off with the pie idea," he offered.

"Any idea who was with Odin?" I asked.

Death was very, very still, considering. "It could have been anyone. Hoods aren't very specific. But it was obviously someone recognizable if they wished to conceal their identity."

I decided not to comment on that, since Death was most often found in a hooded cloak. He and his brothers. Which reminded me. "Conquest swung by before I left..."

Death nodded absently. "About time. They all want to get to know you better. War won't stop talking about you," he muttered, sounding amused.

"Right. Any particular reason? You guys already offered me the job."

Death nodded, eyes distant, considering how he wanted to answer. "One should know one's brother. And you must remember, we've spent millennia around each other. We very soon learned what we were, and once the fourth was chosen, we pretty much closed our circle. No one ever said anything about a Fifth Horseman of the Apocalypse..."

I frowned. "It wasn't like I applied for the job. You guys offered it!" I argued.

Death nodded slowly. "Yes, well... we're not quite sure where that idea came from. It was almost as if someone spoke through us. Everything says *Four* Horsemen, so why would we all suddenly agree that we should consider a *Fifth* Rider?" he asked, sounding deeply philosophical.

I shrugged, my temples beginning to ache. "You should think on that. I don't have the brain power to add another question to my list. If you haven't noticed, I'm kind of drowning in them."

He nodded, eyes drifting to the Round Table and its contents again. Then he turned back to me, waiting patiently. I waved him on to inspect them. "Feel before you touch. Just in case one blows you up and solves our Four Horsemen conundrum," I grouched.

His hand stilled before the hourglass, as if very seriously considering my comment. I frowned at that. Death was scared of... Death?

On that note, I decided I deserved a drink. I had a lot I wanted to talk to Death about, and one big old demand, but it all depended on what he gleaned from the items spread out on the table. I had a feeling it was going to be a long night.

CHAPTER 44

I scowled as I stormed through the halls of Chateau Falco, shouting for Dean as Bob Marley played on full blast through the entire house. The music had woken me up from a dead sleep that I had sorely needed. Thankfully, I had woken to find my burns gone. Pan was good at healing, whatever that balm had been.

Since when had Dean listened to Bob Marley first thing in the morning? I knew no one else did. Techno or something European would have meant Yahn, but reggae?

"Dean!" I shouted, nearing my office, already annoyed about my conversation last night with Death. I wasn't pleased with his answer, but it wasn't like I could do anything about it.

Rules were rules.

"Dean!" I shouted again.

"Right here, Master Temple. I've been searching for you," he called out, hustling up the steps with a black package in his arms.

I frowned, forgetting my anger at the music as he reached me. "What's that?"

He slowly held it out to me. "I… don't know. It was on the front steps."

I smiled instinctively, shaking my head as I took it. "Callie again?" I asked, untying the silver ribbon wrapped in a bow around the package. I opened it and found a single card inside.

Meet at the Arch tonight or thousands will die.

I blinked, dropping the box. "Who sent this?" I rasped.

Dean's face went pale at my tone. "I do not know."

My hand shook. It had to be one of the Makers. Castor or Matthias. "Get the others. Have them meet me in my office. Now," I said in a cold voice, walking past him, my mind racing.

I heard him stammer a response, but my thoughts were elsewhere. I remembered hearing about some big event at the Arch, but since I hadn't expected to be in town, I hadn't paid much attention. Some kind of fundraiser with the mayor. Shit. That meant crowds.

Thousands will die, the note had said.

I reached my office, throwing open the doors to shut the damned music off since the stereo was housed there. Which meant I was caught totally off guard to find a naked Egyptian-looking dude sitting in my favorite Chesterfield leather chair, grinning as he faced me with legs spread wide.

"Gah! Who the hell are you?" I snapped, trying to keep him in view without staring at his twig and giggleberries. "That *used* to be my favorite chair..."

His bronze skin glistened faintly as he nodded in time to the beat. "I am Kai."

And I froze, dropping the card. I studied him warily. His dark hair brushed his shoulders, and light gray eyes only seemed to draw you in. He was handsome, well-chiseled, and not overly large, but something about him was very... imposing.

And I'm not talking about his flagpole.

"Why are you out of the tree?" I asked, closing the doors behind me and picking up the card.

"I wanted to listen to some nice music," he said, pointing a thumb behind him. "Took me a bit to figure it out, but this is pretty cool. Way better than my tree."

I nodded dumbly. I thought he had been kind of restrained to the tree. Not permanently, but I hadn't expected him to just start walking around in the flesh, either.

"A warning would have been nice," I said, walking closer. "You... okay?" I asked, sitting opposite him on the couch, my shoulders tense.

Because I was sitting face-to-face with a Beast – a creature of unimaginable power. And he was free. Just plopping his naked, immortal ass in my favorite chair, listening to Bob Marley.

He leaned forward. "I think we have a problem…" he said.

"I have a lot of problems, Kai. The biggest one being that two Makers want me dead so badly that they're willing to kill—" I cut off abruptly at his smile. And then he gave me a slow nod.

A small shiver shot down my spine, but it wasn't all fear. It was also anticipation.

"You have any ideas about that?" I asked tentatively.

His grin was wolfish. "Thought you would never ask…"

CHAPTER 45

I studied my assembled friends, idly clicking a pen open and closed, waiting for the backlash.

"This is the stupidest idea you've ever had," Gunnar grumbled, giving me a very slow clap.

I shrugged, not rising to the bait. I hadn't told them everything. Not much, in fact, but enough to get their hackles up. Alex stood beside the Huntress, watching everyone. No one had attacked overnight, or in the whopping seventeen minutes we had been in Fae. But we had really been gone for quite a while, and had encountered so much that it was hard to come to grips with the fact that we had returned so soon. I had spent *weeks* fearing for their safety in my planned absence.

But everyone was fine. In fact, they seemed more startled that we had returned so soon than we were to find everyone safe. But the sight of Ashley soon had everyone in tears. Especially their wolves, who had been discreetly brought into the mansion by Gateway, so as not to alert anyone possibly watching Chateau Falco.

Because the wolves had needed to see their leaders.

But we needn't have bothered, because the Makers obviously knew we were here, or had assumed we never left. Which sent an icy shiver down my spine. What if we had still been gone? Would I have returned from Fae only to hear that thousands had been killed at the Arch?

Both the mysterious package and my talk with Kai had made up my mind. I was playing things differently this time. I was handling this alone.

I had brought my friends into every fight lately, and dozens had died or been injured as a result. Hell, I had asked them to fight a war not even a month ago, and then I sat back to watch them die. Even though it was against my ex-fiancée. That had been important, though, to keep them safe in the long run, because the world had needed to learn to fear my friends, not just me.

Like in jail. Pick a fight with the biggest person on your first day, and hope that you made enough of an impression that others would think twice about bothering you.

And it had worked. My friends had made names for themselves during the war. Especially Ashley, who had slain Hercules. And now she was back.

Still, my friends weren't too keen on my plan right now. You could say I had given them a taste for chaos, and part of them kind of liked it, or were at least addicted to it.

Ashley cleared her throat as the murmur of protests began to lean towards Gunnar's view. She was back in human form, as was Gunnar, but they both had that faint glimmer in their eyes, as if only a heartbeat away from turning into savages. Gunnar, surprisingly, wore this look well.

When I had met him, he had been the noblest, calmest, most honorable person in the world.

It wasn't that he no longer had those traits, but... he had definitely *changed*.

The wolves forming a small semicircle around her backed her up in a warning growl, and the room quieted. They were not in human form, and had decided amongst themselves that Gunnar and Ashley would have permanent bodyguards from now on. I knew Gunnar didn't like it, but Ashley had nodded in approval, because she could understand the tactical reasons better than Gunnar. She didn't let her pride get in the way like he did. Gunnar was more concerned about watching over his people, and was confident in his own abilities to protect himself, and considered having bodyguards as only placing his subjects in danger.

Ashley saw them as a shield.

For the good of the pack.

And she was the only wolf that could successfully argue with him.

When all was silent, she spoke. "Nate is right. Much like we had to prove ourselves in the war, now it is Nate's turn to make a point. Not that he hasn't numerous times already, but these two... men," she said with a look of disgust on her face, "will destroy everything in their way to get to him. Even use those nearby as distractions."

The Huntress was nodding absently, but I could tell she was secretly glad that her task was to watch over Alex. She had been attacked at the end of the war when Matthias tried to sucker punch me, and she hadn't stood a chance. Alex was all that mattered to her now.

Well...

Tory sat in a chair before her, looking frustrated. She understood the point, but didn't like the solution. The Huntress placed her fingers on Tory's head, gently massaging the scalp, and a slow, pleased smile replaced Tory's concern as her eyes rolled back into her head and she snuggled closer to the touch.

The Reds shot a smirk at their adopted mother, Tory, but their interest was soon switched to Yahn, who sat in my leather chair, legs wide open to reveal an impressive mooseknuckle. What was it about that chair that made one flaunt their magic stick? Alucard, watching the Reds like hawks, sensed their attention, and kicked Yahn's knee hard enough to slam his legs closed.

He grunted, but a faint smile remained on his face.

He was like a new person. A bad boy.

The Reds liked this.

Alucard did not.

He continued to scowl at the dragon, not even bothering to voice his opinion on the subject at hand, which was just as well. I hadn't wanted him to take me excluding him personally. I was excluding everyone.

"I'm glad that's settled. But I want everyone on high alert. Secure behind doors with an escape plan in place. You should all have a handful of my tiny balls..." I said drily, waiting for their grins, "to get you out in a blink if necessary. If things go sour and I need help, I'll know where to find you." I leveled the room with a stare. "Because you will all be in your prearranged places, away from Chateau Falco. Don't take any risks. These guys make Indie look like a joke. Because, well, she was," I admitted, frowning to myself, remembering the glass pyramid sitting in my satchel. Ashley's lips thinned, and Gunnar squeezed her thigh affectionately, nodding one time. "They've both had centuries to hone their skills," I added. "And Castor, especially, doesn't like to play fair. He will have a backup plan in place, which is why I need you all safe. I can't deal with him or his goons kidnapping one or all of you."

Gunnar shot me a look. "Are you trying to remind us of how stupid your plan is? Let me—"

I held up a hand, especially as I noticed Alucard suddenly paying attention, almost looking hopeful. "No, just me. If I took anyone it would be Alucard." The vampire flinched, a wide grin suddenly splitting his cheeks as he leaned back into his chair self-importantly. Gunnar, on the other hand, looked hurt. "You have a pack to look out for." A small smile crept onto my face. "And I'm disappointed in the lack of screams you two made back in Fae. You acted like it was your parents' basement, when I had assumed you would wake all of Fae with your sexy time," I muttered, winking at his suddenly crimson cheeks.

Ashley sighed, nodding faintly, which set the wolf bodyguards to chuckling softly. Gunnar shot them a look, silencing them. Ashley placed a hand on his shoulder, smiling. "We have time to practice..." she promised in a dark tone.

I clapped. "Not here! Don't make me whip out a squirt bottle."

The Reds burst out laughing.

"I have a few things to take care of before I leave," I said, hoping they got the hint.

Really, I just wanted to clear my head and solidify my plan.

"You should go to the Academy. Make sure the Syndicate is locked up," Tory said firmly.

I nodded. "I already called them. The Syndicate are safe."

"You sure they'll use the event at the Arch? It sounds too public, too obvious," the Huntress asked, ruffling Alex's hair this time. Her eyes latched onto the black package on the desk.

I nodded. "Yes. They want a show. Not just to break me, but to let the city see it happen."

The room grew very silent as that settled in, because it meant in all likelihood that their secret was out, too. If I fought these two with magic in downtown St. Louis, someone was bound to catch it on camera, and with all the coverage the event was going to get, that meant some of those cameras would be news crews.

"I don't really have a say in the matter. If I don't show tonight, they say they'll kill thousands."

"Do you have any idea which one sent you the message?" Tory asked.

I shook my head, wondering. I really had no idea.

"It doesn't really matter, does it? I need to kill them both, unless by some miracle I can convince Matthias that I didn't kill his son," I said, knowing I had no chance of that.

Alucard stood, shooing the others from the room. Tory watched him curiously, sensing his new level of confidence, no longer a melancholy vampire. She shot me a brief smile, silently thanking me for whatever I had done.

I shrugged, returning the look.

All I had done was let him be a monster. Told him it was okay to be himself.

That we had loved him when we first met him, so he had never needed to change.

Still, I wasn't going to stop teasing him. I just wished the religious thing was still a problem to him. That had been good times. I realized I was laughing in an empty room and cut off abruptly.

A form slithered off one of the bookshelves, hopping onto the back of a chair, purring with his tail arched up high. Then he suddenly shimmered into a bipedal cat. Talon the Devourer.

He sat facing me, silver eyes thoughtful and hungry. "You didn't tell them."

I shook my head, not speaking.

"Why?"

"They wouldn't understand..." I sighed, shaking my head.

"They should know the dangers of what you plan. Or, at least the potential for danger."

I stood, turning my back on Talon angrily. I wasn't mad at him, exactly, but I didn't want to think about it. I stared out the massive floor-to-ceiling window, studying Kai's tree through the enchanted glass. The glass reminded me of Carl.

I wondered where he was, and then realized I was stalling.

I turned back to Talon. "No one knows what could happen. The powers could cause an explosion. They might not mix. They might cancel each other out. There are a dozen potential ways for this to go wrong. At *least* a dozen..."

Talon nodded, looking sad, but resolute. "Yet you must do this to stand a

233

chance…" he said firmly. Then he held an open paw to his chest, the claws digging into his flesh enough to scratch the skin. I realized I had returned the gesture. It meant undying loyalty. I nodded faintly, the light in the room catching the scratches down his face where he had sworn to be my Shadow.

My guardian. The only one I had shared my plan with, other than Kai.

"And I will be with you at the end, Wylde…" he promised.

I realized I was grinning as well. Not at the prospect of my death, but at the look in his eyes. Mischief and danger.

Like we had done countless times before. Even if I was only recently aware of it.

Despite my fear, I was eager to flex some muscles tonight. To see what I could do. I wasn't sure how the night would play out, but I had a few options.

Which face did I want the world to see?

A Godkiller wielding a war hammer imbued with lightning.

Wylde Fae and his unique definition of physics.

The Horseman of Hope.

Nate Temple, the wizard.

Or… maybe a splash of all *four*.

The possibilities were endless…

But against two Makers, I knew I couldn't hold back.

CHAPTER 46

I had wandered the property, checking on everyone, making sure all was well and that everyone was accounted for. Carl and Tory had kept everyone safe in my brief absence, not that they'd really had anything to do in such a small window. They were currently rounding everyone up to leave the property a few hours from now. Grimm and Pegasus had already left. I was no longer concerned with being seen, because either Matthias or Castor – or both – obviously knew I was back. Maybe they hadn't even known I had left in the first place. Which could be an asset.

So, I had walked my property. I decided to take one of the ATVs out into the woods, checking the old trails I had used as a child, where Gunnar and I had played – shooting slingshots, practicing our powers, and getting into trouble.

Just like I had with Talon, but in a much more dangerous place.

Which was kind of cool. I had gotten to live two childhoods, and as the hours went by, the memories were slowly folding over each other, settling into place, as familiar as a favorite shirt. They weren't all back, many gaps still filled my life from Fae, but enough to get a good picture.

Although my parents had been bastards to keep that life from me, they had tried to make up for it as best as possible. By helping me find a replace-ment for Talon, my best friend. They had likely known that even though I wouldn't remember him, that I would probably feel depressed, some deep part of me remembering that something was… wrong. A part of me was missing.

Enter Gunnar, stage left.

I let out a laugh as a new thought hit me, and I climbed off the ATV, killing the engine as I spotted an old fort Gunnar and I had built so many years ago. I had always considered cats vile creatures, and had preferred dogs. Was that because some deep part of me felt betrayed by my best friend, Talon? Then when Gunnar appeared, showing me he was a were-wolf, I had jealously latched onto him instead of my unknown memories of Talon?

"We did some pretty stupid stuff, here," a voice growled, coming from a nearby stump. I flinched in surprise, not having seen him. Then I relaxed as I recognized Gunnar's blonde hair. He turned to face me, smiling faintly as he pointed a thumb at the fort, which was now crumbling and falling apart.

"Yeah," I said, smiling as I walked up to him. I studied the fort, shaking my head. "You think they're still—"

Gunnar burst out laughing, interrupting me. "I wondered the same, but the dirty magazines are so much pulp now," he sighed, shaking his head as he nudged a plank with a boot.

"Damn. Kathy Ireland…" I said nostalgically.

Gunnar made the cross over his chest, nodding.

"You okay?" I asked. "Ashley okay?" Because it was strange to find him here, as if also reminiscing on our childhood.

He nodded, smiling. "Better than okay. It's just…" then his face colored as he turned to me. "Sorry, I keep thinking about what you went through, but all I focus on is how…" he trailed off, not saying what I knew to be the truth. "I never stopped to think about how you feel."

I nodded. "Weird. The memories are there. Not all of them, but a lot of them. Random flashes. Enough to know it's the truth. I remember Talon and Pan," I said, shaking my head.

"I'm not jealous," he said, not looking at me.

I bit back a grin. "Okay."

"No, really. I'm…" he let out a rush of air. "Maybe a little." He turned to me, scowling. "A fucking *cat*? Really?" he finally spat, throwing his beefy arms up.

I chuckled, shrugging. "I know. I was just thinking the same thing."

He was silent for a time. "Think your parents hooked us up on purpose? Somehow?"

I sighed, and then finally shrugged. "I don't know, man. But... I'm glad they did."

I noticed a sharp intake of breath, but didn't look at him. "I'm not crying, you're crying," he said in a low tone, sniffing once.

"Probably all the deadly mold spores from our fort. Don't worry about it."

"What's your real plan?" he asked, crouching down into a squat to lift up a plank. The words *Chateau Defiance* were crudely painted onto it, and Gunnar grinned, pointing. I smiled at it, remembering the debate we'd had when coming up with the name.

But his question made that memory short-lived. "I have a general idea, but the main objective is to make an example of them. I'll try reasoning with Matthias, but from the last time we saw him, I don't think that's in the cards. He won't listen long enough for me to say it, let alone prove it. And I don't know how to prove it anyway. He won't believe anyone who was there to vouch for me, so it's not like I can bring in a witness. And even if Athena was still alive, I'm sure she wouldn't be willing to give me an alibi."

"You're probably right. And he wouldn't listen to Talon either. Because every witness is a friend of yours..."

"And I killed everyone who wasn't. Athena and Indie."

"That fucking bastard," he cursed. "Do you have any idea how he got in past your wards?"

I sighed. "That's what makes me nervous. One or both of them have. I'm not sure if it's because the wall is still broken or what. Maybe the wall is part of the magic in the wards, and it's not working without it. Like a broken circuit."

Gunnar grunted. "Makes sense. How much longer till Danny and his brothers are finished?"

I turned to him, shrugging. "We can go check. It was on my list of things to do anyway. Before I sent them away for the night."

Gunnar nodded slowly, as if checking his schedule. Then he shoved me, almost knocking me over the planks on the ground. "I'm driving," he shouted, turning to sprint towards the ATV and hop into the driver's side.

I rolled my eyes, glad I hadn't fallen down.

I climbed in beside him, and let my shoulders relax, trying to enjoy the moment with my best friend, and not think about my fight tonight.

Gunnar hooted as he drove across the overgrown paths, tearing over obstacles so that I had to grab onto the dash rather than falling off the ATV.

We cleared the forest and tore across the manicured lawn, Gunnar swerving as he drove wildly. I realized I was laughing, the cool wind biting at my eyes, making them water. He skidded to a halt near the gate, and the bewildered crew stared at us, hammers and tools in hand.

We hopped out and approached, still smiling. Danny stepped forward, shaking his head.

"How goes it?" I asked him.

He glanced back at it. "A few more days, I think."

I blinked. "That's impressive."

He shrugged, admiring his work. "We're good at what we do. That wall could hold back an army if necessary. Unless they have bombs. Not sure about that," he admitted. But then he pointed at a nearby griffin statue perched atop the wall. "We tried to move that, but it wouldn't budge. It's not cemented down, so it must weigh a ton." He turned to look at me. "Leo told us to leave it alone," he added, pointing a thumb at a worker who stood apart from the others. The man hadn't turned at our approach, but had instead continued to place his stones, slathering them with mortar. He was a big son of a bitch, his long dark hair falling down his shirtless back. Gunnar studied him with one eye, grunting as he picked up a large stone, setting it in place.

"It's fine where it is," I told Danny, still eyeing the newcomer, Leo. I remembered Danny mentioning the new help, but was curious about his comment on the Guardian. Had he recognized it as a griffin, or had he just been making an idle comment?

"We should be ready to leave in a little while," Danny said, no doubt wondering why I had asked him to call it quits for the day.

"Introduce us to Leo," I said. The man's shoulders tensed, and my curiosity piqued.

Danny led us over to the man. "Leo, this is Nate Temple," he said. The man turned to face us, nodding respectfully, only making brief eye contact. He didn't look shady or anything, more as if he was just a loner, a drifter, and not comfortable with social interactions. He had a thick beard, neatly cut into a square below his jaw, and his chest rivaled Gunnar's bulk.

"Thank you for letting me help, Master Temple," he said, still holding his trowel.

"Thank Danny," I said, not taking my eyes from Leo. I tried to remember his last name, but it escaped me. Danny said something and left the three of us. "You've seen one of those before?" I asked, indicating the griffin statue.

He nodded slowly. "I saw it hiss at one of them when they weren't looking. I know they don't like to be moved..." he said uncomfortably, still not meeting my gaze. I grunted, wondering about his story. Again, despite his obvious familiarity of magic, I didn't feel even a hint of bad vibes from him. I felt quite the opposite, in fact. That he was unbelievably trustworthy and loyal, but had preferred not to make his awareness known. Which made sense when his coworkers were Regulars. He would sound like a crazy person. Not good for the new guy on a job. "You have remarkable control of your beasts," he said in the uncomfortable silence. "Last time I worked a job where we unknowingly tried to move a griffin, the thing almost tore the worker's leg off. But that was at night, so we were ready for it. Danny and his brothers... well, I thought it easier to keep the truth a secret. I'm the new guy," he said with a shrug.

"They're more like family, not beasts," I admitted, glancing up at the Guardian griffin. It winked at me, not moving the rest of his body, but Leo noticed it.

"I see," he said slowly. "Maybe you can let it know that we meant no harm."

"He can hear you. Don't worry. How do you like the job?" I asked, changing topics.

He smiled briefly. "Feels nice. I miss this stuff. Regular walls are so boring." His eyes flicked up to mine, as if wanting to say something. "Heard about the other day. What you did to the bastard who tried to take your kid," he growled. "Fucking coward. I hope he suffered."

Gunnar grunted. "One thing you never do is piss off Nate, or try to take his toys."

I nodded, straight-faced. Leo glanced up at Gunnar, nodding at both the words and the werewolf's undertone. "Understood," he finally said. "Maybe we could grab drinks sometime?"

I laughed sharply. "I may be a billionaire, but Danny and his brothers look like they could do some damage at a bar," I said, grinning. "I'm not that flush."

Leo chuckled, nodding his agreement. "True, but I was just talking about me. I hear your name a lot, from the other side," he said cryptically, implying the magical world.

I sighed. "Yeah," I admitted. Not really feeling like sharing stories about my exploits over drinks. Especially when I had a lot on my plate tonight. The saga of Nate could very well end by my own relative killing me.

"I've got a few stories I bet you've never heard," he said in a careful tone. My shoulders suddenly twitched at a new sound. A car had pulled up to the drive and parked. Achilles climbed out of the car, saw me, and waved before jogging over.

"We'll talk soon, Master Temple," Leo said, sounding as if he had over-stepped his bounds.

He turned to take a step, and a spear slammed into the dirt at his feet. He didn't even flinch. I spun, surprised to see Achilles grinning as he pointed a finger past my shoulder. "You sneaky son of a bitch! How long have you been in town?" he roared. And suddenly the two met in a violent bro-hug, with great back-patting. Leo looked both ecstatic to see an old friend, but also guilty that I was witnessing it, the two emotions warring with each other on his face.

I turned to Gunnar, frowning. He shrugged, watching the two men. "We don't look like that, do we? Is that a European thing?"

The two men turned to me, and Leo looked very wary.

Achilles was beaming. "Why did you hire this sack of shit to build a wall? He's terrible at it."

Leo growled. "It's what I do, now."

Achilles grunted, shaking his head. "You need to come to my bar. I know just the thing for your obvious boredom." The other workers were watching us, as if surprised to see the new guy was so popular.

I furrowed my brows, turning from one to the other. "That sounds... nice. What have you been up to lately?" Leo asked carefully.

Achilles waved a hand. "I run a bar on the side, but Nate helped me and Asterion set up a Fight Club. We should get the old gang back together," he said, eyes dancing with unrestrained excitement. He studied the wall, frowning. "Well, after you finish this, I guess."

"Gee, thanks, Achilles," I muttered, but I couldn't keep my eyes off Leo. Achilles had mentioned Asterion, and there was no mistaking the flash of eager recognition on the man's face.

"Leo…" I said, thinking. Then I took a step closer, my breath catching as I recalled his last name. "Vasilias…" I shook my head, staring from him to the wall. *Vasilias* meant *King* in Greek. "No. You've got to be shitting me…"

Gunnar folded his arms, not looking happy. "Who the hell are you?" he finally asked.

Leo sighed, lowering his eyes for a moment. But when he lifted them again, they were full of an inner fire, a self-confidence that reminded me of Achilles. But his were different, as if weighed down by a sense of duty – more like Gunnar. "Leonidas… of Sparta," he finally said, turning to me. "I didn't want to tell you at first, wanting to earn the job on my own merit rather than my history. I don't play in that world anymore. Too much politics," he admitted, squaring his shoulders as if to accept a beating. "I'm sorry for the deception—"

I took two steps and gripped him by the shirt, shoving him into the wall as I stared deep into his eyes from an inch away. The workers suddenly found important things to do near their vans.

I tried to control my breathing. "Swear on your name that you have never betrayed me or mine. Ever. Not even in the slightest," I hissed, suddenly wondering just how convenient it would be for Castor or Matthias to hire this legendary Spartan to infiltrate my home, possibly thwarting my walls, making me believe them to be safe when in reality they were dysfunctional.

Leo met my eyes without blinking. Not happy about the situation, but understanding my position entirely. "I've only done service to you, none other. Only Achilles knows who I am. All else think me dead or forgotten."

"Achilles?" I asked without turning my head, ready to incinerate Leonidas' head if he so much as farted.

"It's true. He doesn't play well with others. Too much betrayal in his past."

"You've had no contact in the last year… two years," I corrected, "with anyone knowing who you really are?"

Leo shook his head. "None. I swear it on my name."

I let him go, still angry at how easy it could it have been for one of my enemies to slip someone into the crowd.

"You really, *really* should have told me, Leo," I muttered. "Finish the wall. We'll talk later. Achilles," I said, turning to face him. "This better be important. I have an appointment."

241

I wasn't angry with Achilles, and he knew it. But he also knew I was still a little raw from the war, where he had been on the other side, playing a double agent.

"Just coming to check on the place. I thought you were going to be gone longer." He assessed me thoughtfully. "You look less... crazy this time." Then he turned to Gunnar with an expectant grin. "Have fun?"

Gunnar growled, showing his teeth as he smiled.

"I can't wait to hear about it." He turned back to me, shrugging. "Like I said, I planned on checking the place regularly, just in case you were gone a while. I didn't have anything to tell you," he admitted. Then he let out a breath, holding up a hand like a Boy Scout. "I swear I haven't betrayed you, switched sides, or done anything to cause you a headache." He glanced over his shoulder at Leo who had gone back to work without a word. "Well, anything other than accidentally recognizing Leonidas. In fact, you could say I did you a favo—"

"Okay. Thanks, Achilles. I need you to leave. Now," I said, feeling annoyed. I didn't have time to play games or joke around. My good humor had been washed away entirely by my sudden fear that I had already been invaded or betrayed.

I turned away, not bothering to be polite. I heard Gunnar speaking to him, letting him know I hadn't meant to be rude, and likely explaining my situation tonight.

I didn't have time for distractions. I needed to be cold. A killer.

CHAPTER 47

I slipped through the mass of people, everyone drinking cheap beer and even cheaper processed food that not even vaguely contained any real nutritional value – even though it was delicious. I was too anxious to be hungry, though, so the smells and cheer just made me grind my teeth.

My satchel was tucked tight against me, but still clicked with each step as the leather bumped against my hip. I hoped I wouldn't have to use anything inside, but I was pretty sure I would have to make a decision tonight. One I wasn't eager to make. But I wasn't exactly sure how everything was going to play out tonight, and I couldn't afford to hold back.

The crowd was much more packed than I had hoped. The event was supposed to last through tomorrow, culminating in giant banners of silk rolling down from the top of the arch all the way to the ground, turning it into a giant rainbow-colored flag to celebrate Equality – which was awesome. But I had hoped that the crowd would be smaller today, most choosing to attend the ceremony tomorrow instead.

But like the Field of Dreams movie, *if you provide food trucks and booze, they will come.*

Worse, it looked like the City Council was holding a private banquet on the grounds beneath the Arch. Because election season was coming up. That wasn't good. Not at all.

For multiple reasons. Because it meant cameras, and that the crowds weren't likely to leave any time soon. And I was pretty sure that this was exactly what the card had intended. To put me in an impossible situation. Fight and reveal my powers in front of the entire city. Or just die. I tugged my baseball cap lower, not wanting to be recognized, because I was kind of a celebrity in town. A reckless, billionaire playboy with a penchant for trouble.

Allegedly.

As I slipped through the crowd, I tried to get a full picture of the scene, keeping an eye out for my two enemies, and hoping they didn't simply start unleashing fireballs to get my attention.

I needed to find a way to get everyone out of here. Just for a minute. Because although I hadn't expected to find so many here, I had come up with something that would help keep the innocents safe. It was a real whopper of magic, but then again, if my plan worked, I wouldn't need to rely too much on my magic to beat these cock-beards. I just had to rope-a-dope.

For quite a while.

But first, I needed to clear the area. After scanning the numerous banquet tables – which held a higher quality of food, large ice-sculptures, and bowls full of champagne bottles – I made my way back to the streets away from the Arch. I needed to do this next part fast, out of sight.

And it needed to be loud and horrifying.

I scanned the streets, and found the nicest three cars on the block, ignoring the ones that looked like they belonged to families.

Essentially, I targeted the politicians' cars, those fancy two-seaters with nothing inside – because I double checked. I wasn't going to choose one that had a car seat or other evidence of tiny humans. Also, this might fit a narrative that seemed to be plaguing America these days.

Terrorism. Political unrest. It made me feel like a bad person, but the alternative was worse.

I checked for witnesses, and seeing no one in immediate sight, I...

Fire-bombed them to Kingdom Come. I did this very rapidly, one after the other, making sure the gas tanks blew, and then I screamed and shouted at the top of my lungs in case anyone had somehow missed it. I immediately hauled ass into a nearby alley as the three six-figure-price-tag cars exploded. Then I Shadow Walked a block away, closer to the Arch, and waited.

Screams filled the night, and sirens abruptly wailed in a chorus as everyone panicked, jumping to my hoped-for conclusion – Terrorism. I walked through the alley, careful not to step on anything that might make a noise, and peeked around the corner. Everyone had fled the fancy tables, leaving the lawn before the Arch fairly clear of people. Not wanting to risk everyone deciding to corral into the open space and out of the streets, I sprinted towards the tables.

I hurdled one, clipping an ice sculpture and a bowl brimming with champagne bottles, sending them crashing to the ground, but not tripping me up, thankfully. Then I fell to my knees, closed my eyes, and drew as much magic as I possibly could, faster than was advisable.

The air began to vibrate, and I felt my arms shaking as I drew in more and more. Since my eyes were closed, I didn't have to worry about my vision tunneling, but I knew that was just a warning sign anyway. I already knew I was doing something stupid. I didn't need a reminder.

That I was holding way too much power for one spell.

But I drew deeper, my skin seeming to catch fire, drying the blood in my veins.

Magic rocked through me, beating at my skin from the inside, wanting to burst out.

With a great expulsion of air, I finally obliged, sending the power deep into the earth.

Walls of purple fire screamed up from the ground, tearing through the manicured grass, sending clods of dirt and rock into the air, as a good hundred-yard square area was suddenly walled off from the general public. I fell back, panting as I turned my head in each direction, verifying that we were entirely enclosed.

It hadn't been perfect, because I heard screaming nearby as a lone family rushed to escape the cordoned area. The father halted his family in front of the purple wall of light, tore off his cap, and threw it through the shimmer of light. It sailed through without harm, and I saw him eagerly usher his family through with a look of relief.

They instantly passed out on the other side, collapsing into a pile.

I sighed, shivering in exhaustion. This had been the only way I could think to make it as safe as possible. If I made the walls lethal, I could have killed innocents – or trapped them inside where chaos raged between me and my enemies. Also, any ambitious cops trying to break in could have been harmed. This way, they just went to sleepy land instead, not seeing anything that would give them nightmares for the rest of their lives.

I stared through the wall back towards the crowds, and saw several cops test it for themselves. Seeing no harm from the light, they jumped through, and instantly passed out on my side. I saw their boss waving his hands frantically on the other side, halting his other officers from attempting the same.

I climbed unsteadily to my feet, and snapped my fingers. The walls of light grew suddenly opaque, so those outside could no longer see through. I froze as I spotted a figure in a black turtleneck and black pants staring directly at me. But the reason I stared was because he wore a glimmering candy skull, and it didn't look like a mask. It looked like a literal skull. Then I saw another at the opposite corner of my wall. Then another in the third corner.

All identical.

They abruptly winked out of view and I let out a nervous breath, turning to check the fourth corner. But I found a man standing before me, staring at me with disgust. He wasn't one of the candy skulls, momentarily making my head spin. Who the hell had *they* been?

"Nate Temple," Castor Queen snarled, eyes dancing with hatred. "You think that wall will keep them safe?" He looked much the same as when he had stood on my property during the war. Totally nondescript, and somewhere in his later years. Not old and frail, but definitely wise with age. He wore gray slacks and a red dress shirt, but he wore them casually as if to fit into the crowd after a day at the job. I shoved the candy skulls from my thoughts, focusing on the now.

I shook my head. "No, but it will make you divert energy to get to them, all while I'm kicking your ass from behind."

He grunted dismissively. Then he began to circle me like a wolf. I slowly spun, always facing him, my face blank. He stopped, folding his arms. "Well? I assume you invited my old pal, Matthias as well?" he muttered. Then he shrugged. "Saves me time. Kill two birds with one stone."

I blinked back as I felt a wriggling sensation in the pit of my stomach.

"I didn't invite you here…" I finally said.

He squinted, assuming I was lying.

"I received a box. Black with a silver ribbon. I thought one of you sent it…" I said, watching his face carefully.

His breathing slowed, and then he nodded. "I received the same. With a letter…"

I nodded. "Me, too."

"Fucking Matthias!" he cursed. Then he shrugged. "It doesn't really matter. I'm going to kill both of you anyway. I don't care how."

And he began to advance, eyes dancing with glee. "Well, what if he set a trap?" I asked desperately, backing up at the same pace, maintaining our distance.

He shrugged. "I don't care. He can come out whenever he's ready to play. But right now, it's just you and me. Did you like what I did with Ichabod, the sniveling brat?" he asked.

My face flushed with anger. "Don't get me wrong, I didn't like the guy, but what kind of fucking coward can't even take responsibility for what he did? Making it look like me? Are you that scared of the Mad Hatter?" I asked, lacing my voice with disdain.

The ground erupted in a swath of fire, and I jumped to the side, barely avoiding it.

His face had reddened, but he didn't stop advancing. "Just a little fun. Twist the knife. But you… are going to pay for taking my Syndicate away. They were *mine*!" he snarled.

"Well, what's left of them, I guess. Kind of a sorry lot if you ask me. I had them quaking in their boots. Hell, I even recruited them for a war. That must have stung. Seeing your dogs lick another master's han—"

Before I could finish my sentence, fire abruptly appeared between us, screaming as it threatened to roast my face off. There hadn't been a clear trajectory of fire leaving his palms, just the fire suddenly a few feet away, likely so he could have a moment to see the fear on my face before I was burned alive. Because he very literally could have just lit me on fire with a thought.

Fucking Makers.

I didn't even have time to retaliate. I just held up my palm, the universal sign for *stop* as the flames roared over me, along with Castor Queen's laughter.

CHAPTER 48

I heard Castor's laughter cut off as my palm flared with ice.

The palm with the Temple Family Crest branded into it.

The flames winked out, and I stared back at Castor, trying to hide the stunned disbelief from my face. I very pointedly didn't look at my palm, but I felt that it was still ice cold.

Then I heard a very familiar female voice in my head.

Kill this goat-fucking son of a bitch, Falco snarled in my head.

An ear-splitting grin split my cheeks, and I took a step closer to Castor. I definitely hadn't planned for this – hadn't even known it was possible. Tonight might have just gotten a whole lot easier. Castor's eyes were wide, and he sputtered desperately. "That's... not possible. You're just a wizard. Not a Make—"

"Shut up," I said in a very calm voice, flinging out my hand. A green shield – a depiction of my Crest – rippled into existence, the air warping around it. It struck Castor like a truck, and I heard his skin sizzle on contact.

He screamed as he flew back a dozen feet.

I strode up to him, grinning darkly. This man had set my friend, my ancestor, my only living relative – after hundreds of years of a false prison sentence, which Castor had *also* caused – against me. And I was about to make good on that disrespect to the Temple name.

Falco purred warningly in my ear. *He is very strong, and I am very far away... Make this quick, or continue with your original plan...* she warned.

Oh. Well, shit.

Castor was whimpering, climbing to his feet, his face raw with wet, singed flesh.

"I will *kill* you, FALCO!" he roared, spitting as he screamed. I hid my shock that he recognized Falco's aid.

"Come on, Queenie. Show me what you can do. I've still got to deal with Matthias, and I don't particularly enjoy your company, believe it or not."

"Y-yeah! Leave him alone, b-bully!" a very tiny voice squeaked from near one of the tables.

Castor's eyes shot past my shoulder and he abruptly disappeared. I lunged to the side, expecting Matthias about to kill me from behind, but I saw nothing and cursed. Castor had used the *made you look* trick on me? The steaming shitwaffle. Just another reason to hate him.

But what the hell was a kid doing standing up against Castor to protect... me?

Hadn't he just seen our exchange? The magic? The chaos?

I spun to locate the kid, only to find Castor staring him down from a dozen paces away. He very easily could have scooped up the kid, but as he glanced my way, I realized his game.

He wanted to *hurt* me. To give me the illusion of a fighting chance.

The kid quivered, panting in fright as he stared at the man who had suddenly appeared before him. I took a step closer, but Castor held up a hand, a ball of flame hovering in his other palm, and I knew that no matter what juice Falco lent me, I wouldn't be fast enough to save the kid.

"What's your name, child?" Castor asked in a grandfatherly tone, which was all the worse because I could see the primal look behind those eyes, that he would very much enjoy slaughtering this child if it meant harming me.

Because I had taken away his Syndicate – the one thing he had already sold his soul to steal from Matthias Temple. And then along comes Matthias' descendent, hundreds of years later, to take it all away again, and then free his nemesis.

"Xander," the boy answered, voice shaking. "And I'm not s-scared of you."

"Oh, dear, dear boy, you really should be," he said, leaning forward to flash a predatory grin.

"It's t-time to be a h-hero!" the boy stammered, and his face bunched up with determination as he threw a bottle of champagne at the Maker.

My heart broke, knowing that I had no chance to save him. "Xander! No!" I screamed.

The bottle didn't even make it to Castor, shattering in the grass. Castor burst out laughing as he took a step forward, turning to meet my eyes as he lifted his hand.

Then he gasped as his hand was suddenly sliced off, the flame falling to the ground.

I didn't waste a second, sprinting closer. "Xander! No—"

Castor snarled, flinging a fireball at me. I threw up my hand, but tripped and fell on my ass as my feet tangled together. Castor quickly grasped his stump, trying to halt the blood. With a muttered curse, he sealed the wound with fire, the sudden smell of burning flesh hanging in the air as he growled in outrage and pain. Then his eyes latched onto Xander.

Or, the person beside Xander.

Because Sonya crouched next to the kid, squeezing his shoulder and smiling proudly. "You did well, Xander. A real hero. But now I need you to get out of here. Go hide over there, okay? We'll take care of this, douche—" she changed what she had been about to say, "bully."

Xander nodded, running away clumsily. Sonya stood, turning to face Castor with a blank face. "Want me to lend you a hand with that?" she asked deadpan.

Castor sneered as he finished cauterizing his wound. Any other time, I would have smiled at her comment, but she had just made everything much worse for me. Now it wasn't an unknown stranger in danger, but a friend. And she hadn't listened. I had told everyone to stay out of this.

Which meant that if I survived, Tory was going to kill me. This kind of ruined my motivation to win. Also, I was distantly pissed that Xander had nailed my line. *It's time to be a hero.*

Sonya stood no chance against Castor. And she had to know that. Her red horizontal pupils flickered into view, daring Castor to make a move.

"One little weredragon. What hope do you have against a Tiny—"

"Phew," she said, sounding relieved. "I was hoping I wouldn't have to use that line."

Castor laughed, shaking his head as Sonya's eyes grew suddenly intense, pulsing brightly. "Did you really think you could use your mind control power on me? One dragon? Pah!"

Then he grunted, laughter abruptly cutting off as he warily scanned the area. Aria slipped out from under a nearby table, licking a bloody talon on her partially-shifted red dragon claw. I blinked. She had been the one who sliced his hand off? "You taste delish, Tiny. But make that *two* hot-ass dragons," she said, licking her lips.

He snarled dangerously as they both stared him down, trying to use their mind control power on him. I did my best to discreetly creep closer. If they could distract him long enough, I might just close the distance. I didn't dare draw any magic, because he would sense it. But I might just get an opening to at least knock him away while they kept him occupied.

Castor chuckled, but it was abruptly cut off. His eyes flinched wildly, scanning the area, even behind him, eyes frustrated. "How many of you little fuckers are there?" he demanded.

I hesitated, because Sonya and Aria looked just as surprised as Castor.

Which made four surprised people in the glowing purple square of death.

"Enough of this! I'll pay you back for my hand later, but right now, Temple and I have business," he warned, shooting a look at me.

"You heard him," I quickly agreed. "Thanks for trying to help, but I need you to get out of here. Now," I commanded, eyes begging for them to listen. Worst case scenario I could hit them with my magic, knocking them through the barrier and to safety.

As long as I could do it faster than Castor attacked. They didn't even look at me.

"No," Aria said.

"I haven't gotten to taste him yet," Sonya complained, frowning.

Castor Queen grinned as I opened my mouth to shout at them, but I wasn't fast enough. He unleashed a barrage of power – tri-colored light that I just knew would kill them in a horrifying way. I flung up my hand, unleashing a blast of air, using my wizard's power to knock them clear.

But the damndest thing happened.

As the two blasts of power flew at the Reds, the fucking ice sculpture on the table behind them exploded, and a thousand-piece cloud of shrapnel erupted between the Reds and Castor's spell. A massive crystal dragon chock full of awesomeness and protective outrage slammed into the earth directly in front of them, roaring out at Castor, hurling spears of glass at him before folding his wings into a defensive shield.

Yahn had disguised himself as an *ice sculpture?*

The tri-colored bar of light lost much of its momentum in the explosion of shrapnel, but a very strong bit still struck Yahn's wings right as my force of air did the same – and rang out with a twin chime like a struck bell followed by the sound of crunching glass. A heartbeat later, Yahn's spears grazed Castor's shoulders, because he was too stunned to try and dodge them.

Poor luck that one hadn't killed him.

I was running as his face contorted in rage, and a ball of utter darkness roared to life before him. I could tell that his injury bothered him, because the spell was messily made, and looked to almost fall apart as I ran on tired legs, unleashing my whips to trail behind me as I prepared to slice something he valued off his body.

But I wasn't fast enough. The orb of power rippled like a ball of oil, seeming to suck the light into it, eating it, and then it flew at the three dragons in utter silence.

Then, I shit you not, a *fourth* motherfucker ninja-flipped out from another of the banquet tables, landing directly before Yahn.

This was just getting *ri-god-damned-diculous!*

I really needed to brush up with a management skills book, because my failure at issuing simple orders was going to get my friends killed.

Alucard stood to his full height, and then erupted into a pillar of golden, flaming light, bright enough to make me wince. I struggled to stare off to the side so that I could use my peripheral vision, since staring directly at the Fae-touched, flaming vampire was out of the question.

I saw a vision beautiful enough to make me weep.

Alucard stared down at Castor Queen, gold-bladed wings spread wide and pointed into the air. His golden face was merciless and emotionless, a blank slate, and his stained robes hung below his feet, which I suddenly realized were a good pace off the ground, since he was hovering. The crimson on the bottom of his robes dripped blood to the earth, catching fire as it struck the grass. The incoming orb of darkness puffed to nothingness in response to his explosion of light.

Castor gaped. "Who the hell are you?"

In a voice like a struck bell, Alucard replied as cold as ice. "I'm the monster they let out of the cage. And you aren't harming them. *Any* of them," he said, mercilessly.

But what hit me in the feels was the fact that Alucard hadn't stepped out to protect the Reds. He might have intended to, but Yahn had interrupted that, risking his life to keep the Reds safe.

And in return…

Alucard had manned the fuck up.

Stepping in front of *Yahn* to keep *him* safe.

I still didn't want to be anywhere nearby when Yahn came a-knocking to take one – or both – of the Reds on a first date, but it was touching to see Alucard defending Yahn, convinced of the glass dragon's feelings by the sudden decision to potentially sacrifice his life to save theirs.

But what the hell were they all *doing* here? Was anyone else sneaking around, disobeying my orders? I didn't have time for distractions. Matthias could show up any minut—

Without speaking, Castor pointed his nub, and three cords of midnight nothingness shot out from his hands, each as thick as my torso. Right at my Glampire.

Alucard screamed, flaring brighter as the world around us seemed to suddenly dim.

And then brighter as the light from the moon seemed to pale.

And he grew still brighter, seeming to become the only source of light in the world. I couldn't even see Castor or anything around us, other than Yahn's glittering skin, and thousands of rainbows reflecting off his scaled, glass wings, which were still folded up into a wall behind Alucard, cracked and dented in places, but still looking functional.

The cords of power hammered into Alucard, striking him in the chest with a resounding metallic sound. His body folded inward at the force of the blow, but I gasped as I saw the cords of power ignite like fuses on a firework, racing back towards Castor faster than they had flown at Alucard. The Maker tried to release the cords, but it happened too fast for him to react.

The fire washed over him in a great *whoomp* of napalm flame, erupting in a ten-foot circle around him, and the darkness evaporated as Alucard fell – Castor's pillar of flame replacing Alucard's glowing form. All I heard were screams from within the fire, but they abruptly cut off.

I raced over to Alucard. He lay on his back, breathing shallowly, and his chest smoking where two of the cords had struck him. I skidded to my knees, grabbing his golden wrists eagerly.

The crystalline dragon leaned over him, snarling as tiny beads of glass rolled from his eyes to land on the Glampire's chest. The Reds were suddenly leaning over Alucard, sobbing, crying, and begging him to wake up.

Yahn dipped his head lower, nudging the vampire's cheek with his massive glass snout.

Alucard's eyes flickered open and he groaned, throat raw from screaming.

The Reds folded into Yahn's side, sobbing and hugging each other. Yahn let out a big snort, sounding relieved as he nudged the vampire again, this time affectionately, a gesture of thanks.

"What the hell are you guys all doing here?" I whispered, wrapping the Reds up in a tight hug, and kissing their heads. "You could have been killed!"

Sonya met my eyes, unflinching. "We wanted to help. We didn't care what you said or how mad you would be. We wanted to be close in case you needed friends. In case he brought goons or something."

Aria nodded forcefully. "I wasn't going to let you walk into a trap. You… showed us how to live, Nate. You're family. And no one fucks with my family. Not anymore."

I smiled, squeezing them tighter, their words squeezing my heart like a vise. Then I shot Yahn a look. I was both angry and happy at the same time, which I think showed on my face, because no one seemed to take it personally. He grunted dismissively. "The Reds left, so I followed them. I wanted to make sure they were safe."

Not knowing what else to do, since he was too large to hug, I patted his snout. "Thank you." I shot a quick look at the flames behind us, making sure Castor wasn't about to swoop in for the kill. I didn't hear him screaming anymore, and the fire was far too bright for me to see anything through the flames.

I knelt beside Alucard, smiling as I shook my head at him. "You stupid, stupid bastard," I muttered, gripping his shoulder. "What the hell are *you* doing here?"

"The Reds and Yahn disappeared, and Tory was frantic. I knew they would come here, so I followed the chaos." He smiled at Yahn, giving him a nod of respect. "You saved my girls…"

Yahn snorted, as if to say, *Yah. Toe-tah-lee.*

Alucard smiled faintly, wincing as he shifted. I glanced down, but other than the charred circles, I didn't see anything fatal. It didn't look to have pierced his skin. Sure, it had caused some serious damage, but it hadn't stabbed through him or anything.

Which I simply couldn't explain. I scanned our surroundings, muttering. "Where the hell is Matthias?" I growled, frustrated.

Alucard grunted as he gripped my wrist forcefully. I met his eyes, and saw they were panicked, as if I had reminded him of something. "He isn't here, Nate. Van called me. Or, Matthias *let* him call. The bastard tracked them to England and took them. Van sounded like seven days of hell, and told me under no circumstances were you to come after him. I heard Matthias shout at him angrily before the line went dead."

I slowly climbed to my feet, feeling Wylde ignite with rage. I had kept him muted during my encounter with Castor, not wanting the Maker to suspect my backup source of power. But I no longer cared about that since he was dead or dying. And Wylde roared up out of me, furious.

But it was different this time. It didn't feel so much as another being inside of me, but as if I had broken down a wall – a part of myself I had long ago locked away.

Kind of like when someone does something out of anger, and then promises themselves they will never again let that happen, and they wall it away deep down, becoming the nicest pushover in the world.

But at hearing that Matthias had taken two of my friends, and that he was coincidentally in England brought back memories of my parents, and that instant spark of anger was enough for the wall to crumble to ashes.

I didn't have an instant influx of memories as Wylde, but I suddenly felt of one mind with him. No longer two halves, but one single whole. And I decided I was about ready to see what he had learned in Fae over the past few decades.

"Go home. Now," I said in a distant voice. "Not to Chateau Falco. Anywhere but there…" I said, walking away from them and towards Castor. I flung out a hand, and the fires instantly winked out. I heard my four friends speaking urgently together, and after a loud sweep of wings, I glanced up to see Yahn carrying the three on his back – Alucard propped up between the two Reds. Then they vanished from sight as Yahn activated his stealth-mode.

I stared down at the circle of charred earth and saw a mess of greasy ashes. Castor's hand was just beyond the charred circle. I decided to leave it there as I closed my eyes, focusing on the rings I had given Baba and Van.

I found them, and in my mind's eye, I knew exactly where they were.

Because I had been there before. Stonehenge. I glanced down at Castor's remains with a disgusted sniff. At least I would only have to fight Matthias one-on-one.

The Colonial heathen, Nate Temple, flung out his hand to open a Gateway back to his homeland, to put an end to his ancestor once and for all.

Yankee-Fuckle-Dandy.

CHAPTER 49

*I*didn't bother with trying to plan a cool, stealthy entrance. Instead, I cast a barrage of lightning through the portal, ripping up the earth for dozens of feet.

And then I stepped through. "Honey, I'm home!" I called out.

Matthias stepped out from behind one of the stones, smiling. "I'm so glad you disregarded his warning, my boy. We have unfinished business. Shall I put the kettle on?" he asked in a dry tone.

I shrugged. "If you prefer a cuppa before I rip your asshole out through your mouth."

My eyes tracked to see Van, Baba, and her Familiar each tied to a separate stone with silver, glowing cords. They had gags in their mouths, and their faces were bloody as hell, but they were thankfully alive, shaking their heads for me to run while I still could.

I tried to reach out to Chateau Falco, but the distance was too great, and to be honest, I wasn't sure if using her was a good idea. Because she had once served Matthias, and he knew a whole helluva lot more about her Beast than I did. Maybe there was a loophole that he could take advantage of if I tried. And I didn't want to risk that.

The same could be said about my Mask. Because Matthias had freaking gifted it to me.

Which pretty much left me my wizard's power against his Maker's power. Which was no contest. My only other option was Wylde or the strange golden power in my veins. The power I had seen after killing Athena.

Or I could use my new war hammer, but it had knocked me out when I used it against the Queens, and I couldn't risk that. I didn't let anything show on my face.

I turned back to Matthias, enjoying his angry snarl.

Then I frowned at Stonehenge. The moonlight pierced the cloudy sky in places, illuminating the area clearly, but the blue runes weren't glowing.

"They're clever, I'll give them that," Matthias said. "They found one, much to my surprise. At first, I tracked them to use them as leverage to get you to crawl out of my home," he growled, implying Chateau Falco. "Imagine my surprise to find them looking into my old research. Of course, things are much easier these days, what with your... *internet*," he said the word strangely, as if reciting an ancient incantation. "They had piles of printouts from numerous websites. Information I had never found nor heard of in my day," he said, shaking his head in wonder. "Why your kind hasn't taken over the world is beyond me. It would be so *easy*..." he said, chuckling. "But you're too stupid to know what to look for. But now that I'm back, I'll rectify that. After I punish you for killing my son," he said in a low snarl.

I turned to look at him, wondering what to address first. He had been researching the Round Table in his day? I had been doing it more out of curiosity than anything. Because I wanted to know if it really was *the* Round Table that King Arthur and his bros sat at with Papa Merlin.

Why would Matthias care about any of that?

And did it have anything to do with what my parents had found over there? The reason they had gone to the Fae? The text about the All War and the Catalyst?

"I don't know what proof you require, but I swear that I didn't harm your son. I even swear it on my power." I frowned, then let out a brief chuckle. "Well, *powers*, I guess," I admitted.

Matthias snarled. "You think I'll fall for that? Even swearing on your powers is a trick I learned to break. As a child," he added, shaking his head dismissively.

I blinked at him. Well, *that* could have been useful fucking knowledge to have about a dozen times over in the past few years. I wanted to kill him just for that. To so nonchalantly mention that breaking oaths sworn on your power was no big deal.

It also explained how Castor had slipped around the oath to obey me when he had been disguised as a lowly Syndicate wizard during the war. I had never learned how he had done that.

Apparently, I was a total noob in the magic department. Maybe Matthias was onto something. My generation had a lot to learn from our past.

But I'd rather just kill him. Because he had hurt Van and Baba.

"I'd rather not kill you, Matthias. But I will if you make me. Is there anything I can say that will make you believe me? Some third party? A Horseman? Maybe I can wrangle up a God or two to give me an alibi. But, of course, I already killed the best alibi. Athena—"

"Enough!" he snapped, breathing heavily. "I won't believe a thing you, or any of your friends, say. You told me time and time again that my son, Ichabod, was your enemy. That you intended to kill him unless he relented. Then, in his moment of tribulation, when he had decided to give up his cause, you killed him in cold blood. Right as I was reaching for him." His bloodshot eyes met mine, and I involuntarily took a step back at the madness dancing there. The madness that had brewed for hundreds of years, at one point convincing himself that he was actually the Mad Hatter, in fact. "You will die horribly," he whispered.

"Well, that sounds miserable." I indicated Stonehenge and my tied-up friends. "Mind telling me what this is all about, first? I literally have no idea, and I feel kind of stupid pretending."

He shook his head. "Fucking kids. You saw the Round Table in the Sanctorum, and you sent these *babies* to look into it without knowing *why*?" he asked incredulously.

"I guess that about sums it up," I admitted.

He stared at me in disbelief. "My, how far the apple falls…"

Which pissed me off. "You're kind of being a condescending dick right now," I warned, my pulse increasing dangerously. "Plus, if it's *anyone's* fault how far the Temple family has fallen, you might just take a gander in the mirror," I said, and tossed him the compact mirror from his old desk – which I had kept in my pocket for some reason.

I think the shock of seeing the familiar item again was what prevented him from lashing out in a wave of death at my words. He caught it with a sharp intake of breath, staring down at it.

"Because it was your excellent parenting skills that brought us to this," I added with a snarl, and I reached out with Wylde just as Matthias' face contorted in rage.

I grasped the moonbeams piercing the clouds, corded them together with a flick of my wrist, and then flung a net of lunar fire at Matthias. The web wrapped around him and began to constrict. His eyes shot wide in disbelief, but I didn't waste any time. I Shadow Walked over to the captives and freed them with surgical slashes of fire, luckily eating through whatever power Matthias had used. Then I opened a Gateway behind them, glancing over my shoulder urgently. "Go, go GO!" I shouted, keeping my eyes on the Maker.

They scrambled to obey, not even caring where I was sending them. "You need to kill him, Nate. The bastard took him right from under our noses," Van wheezed.

"What?" I asked, still staring as Matthias struggled to break free of the slowly tightening web. I urged it on, not wanting to cast any more magic at him unless it counteracted whatever the hell I had done in the first place.

"The Knight. He's still where we found him, but he's restrained. You can't let Matthias get his hands on him," he pleaded, voice rough.

"I'll, uh, do my best. Make your way back to the Knight, since I have no idea where that is. I'll take care of the Hatter."

"Nate, this is big. *Really* big—"

"I got it!" I snapped. "It's a big fucking deal. Now get the hell out of here!" I shoved him through the opening just as Matthias broke free from the net, shaking his head.

The Gateway winked out of existence before Matthias could see where I had sent them. I had only sent them a mile away, but I doubted he would consider that. He would either think I had sent them back to this Knight that everyone seemed so concerned about, or…

"I'll leave the porch light on for you," I cackled as he turned to glare at me. And I made a Gateway back to Chateau Falco, making sure our ancestral home was visible through the opening. I jumped through and let it wink shut behind me.

Rope-a-dope time.

CHAPTER 50

*A*s planned, Dean had moved the furniture to the exact spot I had requested. With a heavy sigh of relief, I sat down in my favorite Chesterfield leather chair, and lit up a new cigar I had been meaning to try. An Absinthe Infused monster made by Alpha Cigar.

If my plan worked, it would be a victory smoke.

If it didn't, it would be a remembrance smoke.

Either way, I wanted to enjoy at least a taste of it.

I puffed contentedly, absorbing the flavor. It was excellent. I appreciated the momentary silence around me. It was a strange sensation after so many months of the property being full of hundreds of people. Now, it was just me. Unless Dean had *also* ignored my orders to leave.

I pondered the situation, wondering exactly what had ignited it all tonight. Someone had invited us to meet at the Arch, and it seemed like that someone was Matthias – all so that he would have a minute to do whatever he intended with the Knight that Van Helsing had found. Whatever that was about, it had made Van very nervous, and Matthias very excited.

But… Matthias had tried to lure me to England, so that didn't make any sense.

I shook my head as a Gateway ripped open the air underneath the giant white tree, directly before me. Matthias stepped out, and let out a growl as he stared me down.

"Might want to move to the left a few steps," I offered, puffing my cigar until a cloud of smoke surrounded me. I reached into myself until I felt that strange, golden power fill me, illuminating my veins, and making the cloud seem to glow.

Then I smiled, knowing my eyes were also glowing as I stared through the cloud at a frowning Matthias.

"That's where Icky got... well, *smoked*," I elaborated, shrugging with a light laugh.

Matthias' face purpled as he took an angry step closer, eyeing my chair with a frown. It *was* rather bizarre to be sitting in a chair in the middle of the grass with no one else around.

I let him stew on that.

"Where is Castor?" he asked, eyes darting about, anticipating a trap. "I know you're working with him."

I stared at him for a few seconds, and then burst out laughing. "Why in the living hell would you think *that*? He wanted to *kill* me!"

Matthias grunted doubtfully, and then he cut off, his eyes locking onto mine. "*Wanted*?" he asked, noticing my emphasis on the past tense.

I nodded. "I took care of him before I met up with you. But you know all about that, sending us those boxes with the cards," I added, waving a hand as if that was unimportant.

But I watched his eyes. And they looked... concerned.

"You got one as well?" he asked, sounding surprised. "It must have been Castor..."

I shook my head. "He thought it was you, since you didn't show up at the Arch."

He frowned. "Mine didn't say to go to the Arch..."

My skin grew suddenly cold. What exactly was going on here?

"It doesn't matter. It's time for you to pay for what you did. You killed my so—"

And with a thunderous cawing sound, two giant ravens swooped down from the titanic white tree, slamming into Matthias and knocking him into the trunk.

I jumped to my feet, stunned. "What the fuck?" I shouted.

"What the fuck, indeed," Castor Queen rasped, appearing out of thin air a dozen paces between Matthias and I.

I flinched in horror, staring at him. He resembled a discarded collection of barbecued ribs. Bone showed through in several places, and what was left of his skin was blackened or oozing. Like a fucking zombie. But even as I watched, he was struggling to heal himself, the skin slowly – ever so slowly – growing back.

Some places on his body were beyond repair, too much of him simply missing.

For example, he had a hole in one of his cheeks, revealing his molars. The skin had healed around it, but left the gaping hole. I shivered, wanting to simply put him out of his misery. I heard bones cracking, and he spasmed occasionally as he turned from me to Matthias, who was lying on the ground, panting. The ravens were standing on his chest, and screaming at him, but he didn't wave them away.

Instead, he twitched, moaned, and rocked, writhing on the floor at the base of the tree.

Castor glanced back at me. "Should have seen that coming. You're tied to Odin," he said, jerking his chin at my palm. "Like your Crest."

I glanced down at it instinctively, but didn't say anything. I was pretty sure I wasn't tied to Odin, because those asshole birds showed zero respect for me, and neither had Odin. If my family was tied to him, I had never heard about it, and after meeting him recently, I was pretty sure he would have told me if I owed him forgotten allegiance.

"Either way, I'm going to kill you much slower than I intended. Because some of this is permanent," he snarled, pointing his nub at his face.

"Which part is permanent? I didn't see which finger you were pointing with," I said, motioning at his stump. He snarled, taking an aggressive step forward.

With a shout, Matthias jumped to his feet, eyes wild. They locked onto mine, and I held my breath. He didn't look harmed, but he did look homicidal. What the hell had Hugin and Munin done to him?

"You… were on the Pavilion…" he whispered, tears streaming down his face as he stared at me in utter disbelief.

I swallowed, not wanting to do a single thing to interrupt this cobweb of a chance. I very slowly nodded, realizing what Odin's ravens had done. *Thought* and *Memory* had shown Matthias the truth. Because they had been on the pavilion when I fought Athena. They knew I had been nowhere near

Ichabod, and since they were about as unbiased as one could get, Matthias just might buy it. Also, I was hoping that since they were on our Crest, that he possibly held a mystical sense of superstition about them. That they were tied to our family, and were possibly intervening before Temple accidentally killed Temple.

Or his mind was about to break at the complexity of it all, and we were all going to die.

Pick one of those.

His head swiveled to Castor Queen, and his face was as blank as a tombstone. "How could you?" he whispered.

Castor – someone who I was beginning to believe was more than one-hundred-percent asshole – suddenly let out a deflated sigh, and his healing abruptly stopped. "The Syndicate was mine. He took it from me. I wanted him to hurt for that. I knew you'd eventually come after me, so I turned you against each other."

"I've got a question," I said, frowning at Castor, wondering why he had stopped healing. "How are you still alive? Not just now – although that's fucking with my head a little – but in general. I didn't think Makers were immortal."

He shook his head as if disgusted that he was even having to talk to me. "Makers can be whatever they want. It all depends on how you work with your Beast…" He let out a long, tired breath. "For example, like I have these past few hundred years. I never fully merged with him, but it had a side effect you're about to witness."

Matthias sucked in a breath. "You didn't…"

Castor gave him a sad nod. "I had a good run, but now it's time for him to taste freedom." Matthias hissed as Castor turned to me. "You see, in exchange for a long life and help in taking control of the Syndicate, I promised my Beast that he would be freed upon my death…" He glanced down at himself, pointing out that his healing had stopped. "I tried to heal myself. I really did," he muttered, glancing at Matthias with another sad smile. "It was wrong, I know, but you always got all the credit…"

"Castor, you *fool*," Matthias cursed, seeing his friend for the first time. "How long do we have?" he asked.

"What the hell is going on?" I snapped.

The two old dudes ignored me. Castor looked up at Matthias, coughing up blood. "Not long," he sputtered, coughing more violently.

Matthias turned to me, his eyes wide with terror. "When he dies, his Beast will be free. You better have one hell of a weapon on you, boy, or neither of us are going live to see the sun rise."

CHAPTER 51

I slowly turned to Castor, watching him die before my eyes, and realizing that I *done fucked up*. He had turned himself into a martyr – a suicide bomber. I could tell that Matthias wanted to rush to his old friend's side, despite their past, but he didn't dare get close to the bomb that was about to blow. I wasn't entirely sure why they were so scared of Castor's Beast being freed, because I had freed mine, and the world hadn't imploded.

Still, when Makers were scared of something, it was best to listen.

For example, Hugin and Munin were suddenly hauling ass, screaming as they flapped as hard as they could, as far away as possible from me and the two Makers. Which didn't fill me with a whole lot of confidence.

Castor crashed to his knees, coughing violently. He struggled to speak, and managed one last phrase that made my blood curdle.

"The one thing he wants over all else is…" he hacked nastily, spitting up something, "Falco."

Then Castor Queen died, and all was right with the world.

The end.

Well, okay, not really. Not at all, in fact.

As Castor's body crashed to the ground, a dark stain rose up from his corpse, a shifting, smoky apparition, the color of a deep bruise. It lifted its

WAR HAMMER

arms high above its head as if stretching. Then it began to laugh. A deep, sinister, foreboding giggle of profound glee.

Which doesn't sound like it would be scary.

But a giggle can make you ruin your pants if employed by the right kind of psychopath.

And this one must have been practicing for a few thousand years.

Because I almost had to call a *time-out* for a wardrobe change as the sound made my arms instantly pebble with gooseflesh.

Matthias didn't move an inch, staring in horror at the rising form of Castor's Beast – which was easily as large as Gunnar had been on the Fae Side. It turned from Matthias to me, eyes of white fire against the purple bruise color.

"Oh, this shall be fun. The Temples, offering up their sacred Beast. Falco…" he purred, staring past me toward the house, eyes flaring brighter for a moment. "You will be—"

He cut off abruptly, and stopped moving. *Completely stopped*, as if I was looking at a two-dimensional picture of what I had seen only a moment ago.

"*SHE. WAS. MIIIIINE!*" he suddenly roared, and I had to clasp my hands to my ears to prevent my head from exploding like a melon.

The form was suddenly moving, sliding back and forth as if pacing, cursing and muttering in a language I didn't know. Then he froze, and his eyes locked onto the tree.

I knew he was staring at the tree, because Matthias had instantly Shadow Walked a dozen paces away, expecting an attack, and the Beast's gaze didn't follow him.

I frowned.

"You…" Castor's Beast snarled, eyes flashing dangerously.

To be completely honest, this next part was improvisation. Sure, I had originally schemed with Kai, but I hadn't anticipated anything like this. But since the situation suddenly seemed even worse than we had anticipated, I took this as my cue.

"The bullshit stops when the hammer drops!" I shouted, and threw my war hammer with every iota of power I could muster, directly at my tree.

It struck the massive trunk like a grenade in a pond, ripping entirely through it.

267

And Kai exploded out from within – not in human form – but as a green cloud infused with golden glitter – drawing the power from my war hammer.

Kai flew at Castor's Beast and the earth sunk a good foot lower for a dozen paces on impact as the tree erupted in flames and began to fall. It crashed to the ground in an explosion of embers as flames roared to life, burning much too bright and fast for any normal fire.

Because I had remembered one thing about the tree. It doubled as a Gateway to Fae, and I hadn't really wanted that on my property anymore, just in case the Queens held a grudge about me annihilating their army. But it had been Kai's idea. He had known I wouldn't stand a chance against two Makers and had wanted to help in any way he could.

I stared, transfixed as the two clouds of light slammed into each other with great peals of thunder filling the skies and shaking the earth.

Two entirely free Beasts going head-to-head.

"She was to have my child!" Castor's Beast raged.

"She chose better, Maru. But anyone would have been better than *you*," Kai's voice boomed back – like laughing thunder, not sounding remotely afraid.

Maru… the name of Castor's Beast?

And then physics grew kind of… *fluid*, and I Shadow Walked to a really safe distance as the two Beasts began flinging magic around like I had never before imagined, and I had seen quite a bit in my day.

Even the part of me that had been Wylde stared in wonder, like a child seeing a magician for the first time. But magic that was so beyond your scope of understanding that your mind kind of fragmented to even accept the fact that what you were seeing was real, let alone *how*.

Great big monsters, twenty feet tall, suddenly appeared, tearing into each other, matching the color of their masters. Maru's bruise-colored challenger sliced down, missing Kai's gold and green construct, and instead tore a dozen feet down into the earth as if it were made of paper. Then the two began to fight in earnest as Kai and Maru let their creations do as they would, literally ripping each other – and my beautiful lawn – to shreds. The tree roared with flame behind them.

Kai cast a ten-story pillar of flame at Maru. The bruise-colored apparition winked out of existence for a second as the flame roared through where he had been hovering, burning itself out after scorching a ten-yard swath of my lawn.

Maru reappeared and flung out a hand. The two warring creatures exploded into a bazillion fragments that disappeared just as quickly as they had been shattered.

And then... flashes of light, dark, colors, explosions... Listen, I can't even find the words to describe it because the human language doesn't possess them.

I lost track of what happened before me, and I would have immediately worshipped any god who strolled by – promising to worship him or her until the end of my days – if they could guarantee that the last few minutes were wiped from my mind.

Unable to comprehend what was going on, I just stared, eyes vacant, choosing merely to observe rather than understand what I was seeing.

After an indeterminable amount of time watching the titans play, Kai's gold and green form tore through Maru, and the earth cracked for a hundred paces all around them at his death scream.

One of those chasms reached me, the earth splitting between my legs, opening up into nothingness, and I began to fall.

A fist latched onto my shirt, tugging me back from the crevice.

I crashed on top of him, and rolled away, eyes wild to suddenly find myself involved in the chaos. Matthias stared back at me, looking surprised that he had saved me. Then he climbed to his knees, staring past me. I turned to see ribbons of the bruise-colored Beast floating up into the air, disintegrating the higher they rose. I stared at the ground below it to see the dark-skinned Egyptian dude from earlier lying motionless on the grass.

Kai.

I scrambled to my feet, and was running towards him without considering the consequences.

I skidded to a halt, staring down at him. He was battered to hell, and covered in blood. Where his wounds were most grotesque, I didn't see organs inside his body, but instead only gold and green smoke against a black background, like I was staring into some celestial body. Kai grunted, staring up at me. Then he smiled.

"Took care of that bastard," he grunted. "Our plan almost went to hell at the end, but it all worked out." Then he glanced over my shoulder, face grimacing. I turned to see Matthias staring down at Kai with profound sadness in his eyes. "Temple shall not harm Temple," he commanded.

With barely a hesitation, Matthias nodded.

Probably knowing that even as wounded as he was, Kai could make short order of him if he chose to do so.

"You did well, Kai," I whispered, trying to kick-start my brain. "I didn't expect any of this, but your plan was solid. We'd all be dead without you," I admitted.

"Thanks to your War Hammer," he grunted painfully. We had planned to lure the Makers here, where hopefully Kai or Falco could finish them off if I couldn't do so myself. Beast versus Beast in the cage-match of the century.

I hadn't known it would literally come to that, though. And now my friend was dying. "What was he talking about with Falco, Kai?" I asked. "And what do you need? How can I help you?"

Kai grunted, coughing violently. "I'm done for. Don't worry about that." He took a breath, closing his eyes as he smiled. "I... *got it on*," he whispered, sounding like the smuggest son of a bitch that had ever existed.

I blinked at him, and then arched a brow at Matthias, hoping he had understood. He shrugged, frowning down at Kai. "What?" I asked, turning back to him.

"The love song," he admitted, opening his eyes to stare at me. "I was trying to woo *her*." I felt a presence behind me, and turned to see a silver mist pouring out of Chateau Falco, quivering in agitation. "I wish we could have had longer," Kai told the mist. "But you will carry my name with you, now..." he said breathlessly.

I blinked, brain emitting weak sparks of confusion. "Falco?" I whispered.

Yes... she said in an anguished voice.

Matthias stared in awe, as if seeing God for the first time. I even spotted a tear on his cheeks. He had grown up with her, spent his life with her, but I guessed he had never seen her with his own eyes before.

"What are you talking about, Kai?" I asked nervously. When he didn't answer, I turned, fearing he was already gone. He had tears in his eyes, and each of those drops throbbed with golden light, like mini universes. Like my veins. And my War Hammer.

"Falco's pregnant. I always wanted a child of my own..." Kai said wistfully. "You have a baby Beast on the way, Temple. Take care of him for me?" he pleaded, face full of pain.

I nodded, feeling tears of my own streaming down my cheeks. "Of course... Falco and I will take care of your son," I promised, even though I had no way of knowing if it would be a son.

Let alone how I was supposed to care for a baby Beast.

He nodded in relief, my promise allowing him to finally let go of his tentative hold on life. "It's why they don't want us freed," Kai whispered, closing his eyes. "They don't want us to fall in love. To make new Beasts, born *outside* of the cycle of servitude..."

With a faint expulsion of breath, he died, and a gold and green swirl of mist slowly rose up from the ground. It split into two separate clouds – a golden cloud raced back towards the burning tree and my War Hammer, and a second green cloud floated high into the sky. I stared up at Kai's green cloud for a long time, hoping that he explored the galaxy before he went to... wherever he was going. Hell, maybe that was where he was from. I remembered someone recently saying something to me, but couldn't for the life of me remember who had said it. *There are gods, and there are Gods...*

Matthias placed a hand on my shoulder, and I climbed to my feet, wiping my cheeks as I faced him. I saw Falco drift back into the house, the door closing with a faint click. I felt a deep sadness from my home, and decided to let her grieve in peace.

"So..." I said, kicking a rock with my foot, glancing at the cracks covering my property.

"That was..." he trailed off. I looked up to see him shaking his head. "I think I'm pretty much done with all of this," he finally whispered. "I almost wish you hadn't brought me back, or that one of you had killed me..."

I nodded, kind of understanding him. He had lost everything. And then saw two Beasts kill each other. Beasts just like the one inhabiting his own body, giving him his power. He probably had a whole lot of introspection to do, wondering if he was possibly at fault for imprisoning his Beast. Then again, unleashing your Beast could be deadly.

A lot to consider.

"Yeah..." I replied lamely.

"I'll be back someday, but for now I'm going to go somewhere no one can find me."

I nodded, wanting desperately to question him on the Knight thing, but knowing that this was the worst possible time to do so. Hell, we hadn't even really made amends.

"I'm sorry, Nate," he said, sounding like the saddest person in the world. And then he Shadow Walked away, not even giving me the time to respond.

Not wanting to go inside my home, I walked over to my chair and sat down wearily. The tree burned before me, having caught up several of the bushes as well, but they weren't close to anything important and looked to be finally dying down, so I ignored them, staring up at the heavens.

Searching for Kai, and thinking wizardly things.

At some point, Talon approached on silent paws. He set a lawn chair beside me, something he must have found in the garage. He dropped something heavy beside my chair and I glanced over. The Hammer rested at my feet, a cloth wrapped around the handle where Talon had held it. I grunted uneasily and turned back to the sky. We sat in silence for a time before he spoke, even though he didn't need to say anything.

"I... didn't think I could be of any help, Nate. Not when it escalated so quickly. I'm sorry..."

I coughed in disbelief. "I don't blame you, man. Jesus..." I said, shaking my head. But I did place a hand on his shoulder, squeezing once before pulling away.

We watched the stars in silence for a while.

"What's next?" he asked.

I hesitated. "Well, I think I'd like to relax for a while. Enjoy this thing called life."

Talon nodded absently, letting the silence grow. "And when we get bored of that?" he asked.

"I made Death promise to take us to Hell. To talk to my parents. Should be dangerous."

Talon was quiet for a little while, and then he began to laugh loudly, the sound echoing around us. "Oh, yes..."

I nodded, closing my eyes. "Thought so."

I wondered many, many things as I watched Kai's tree burn like a funeral pyre, wondering how I was going to break the news to Alex. But... a baby Beast was on the way, whatever that entailed. Because Kai had apparently banged Falco behind my back, the sleazy scoundrel. I shook my head, a faint grin on my cheeks at the possibilities.

I was very concerned who those candy skulls had been at the Arch. Castor's goons? They sure hadn't helped him during our scrap, so I was guessing not.

And who had the hooded guy with Odin really been, and why had the Allfather asked if he was satisfied?

Who had sent the three of us the cards, telling us where to go tonight?

What was I going to do with the Knight that Van and Baba had found?

I didn't even want to think about my various powers or my childhood in Fae.

I let out a long breath, dismissing it for tomorrow or a year from now. "This is going to be nice. No immediate threats. Take a break. Relax."

I smiled at Talon's disgusted groan. "I'd rather go down to Hell," he said hopefully.

"Maybe I'll even go visit Kansas City for a while..." I said, smiling to myself. I continued to watch the fire burning, truly realizing the magnitude of the friend I had lost. Since the tree had burned so fast and hot, it was running out of fuel and beginning to die down very suddenly.

Then I squinted, leaning forward with a frown. I nudged Talon, grunting and pointing.

"Is that... the treehouse Kai made for Alex?" I asked in an incredulous whisper. "Why is it entirely unharmed?" Because it was as pristine as ever, as if freshly built, sitting in the center of the dying coals, not a mark of soot or flame touching it.

Talon sighed. "This place is almost as trippy as Fae..." he muttered.

I simply nodded, staring at the baby house...

~

*N*ate Temple returns in **NINE SOULS**... Turn the page for a sample! Or **get the book ONLINE!**

TEASER: NINE SOULS (TEMPLE #9)

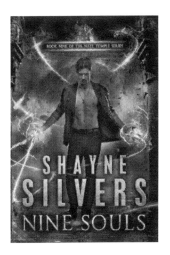

I fidgeted with the cuffs of my dress shirt, staring at the most beautiful woman in the room. She stared back, a faint smile on her pale cheeks. Her white hair was shorter than when I had first met her, now brushing her jaws in a jagged, messy line that she somehow made look sexy and dangerous. She wore a silver dress that hugged her frame like a frosted candy coating.

I tried not to imagine myself licking it off her to see what lay underneath. But her growing smile told me she had read my mind. Was her smile amusement or... inviting?

"Just *do* something with her already," Alucard complained in a low growl. "Cradle robber."

Which was enough to snap my mind out of the gutter. I shot him a dark look, but I didn't need to defend myself out loud. Callie Penrose *was* younger than me, but only by a handful of years. We had spent a lot of time around each other recently, not as much as I wanted, but neither of us had taken that last step – possibly fearing what would happen the next morning. Two wizards with ties to Heaven playing pre-marital confession under the sheets could have all sorts of consequences.

I turned to the hard-looking man sitting near her. His eyes assessed the room out of habit. At least his eyes weren't glowing red at the moment. Roland Haviar, ex-Shepherd, now vampire.

As was usual now, Roland was flanked between two stunning brunettes with Callie sitting next to the unlikely trio. They wore playful smiles as they noticed my gaze drifting back to Callie.

"Are they taken?" Alucard murmured softly, discreetly gesturing to the two brunettes.

Roland had been a Shepherd – a warrior wizard priest who hunted monsters for the Vatican. But all that had changed months ago when he had been turned into a vampire. He and Callie had gone to the Vatican to save the two brunettes – fledgling werewolves – from a false murder charge. That act had broken the Vatican Shepherds, revealing both a traitor and Roland's new... affliction. The wolves had instantly become Roland's loyal companions – like every bad vampire cliché ever. His two familiars or something. I hadn't decided if the relationship was romantic or not. It was really hard to tell sometimes. They were very... clingy with Roland.

Long story short, none of them considered themselves employed by the Vatican any longer.

"You don't want to play with Paradise and Lost," I warned him, finally breaking eye contact with Callie to study the two brunettes. They had dressed to impress, proudly displaying their cleavage in tasteful but revealing crimson dresses. They knew they attracted attention. Paradise was taller, and Lost was shorter, but both could have been sisters.

The Reds – two teenaged weredragons – sat near them, studying the two wolves as if taking notes. Yahn, a tow-headed dragon shifter sat between them, much like Roland, and there was definitely some sinning going on somewhere in that triangle of teen angst, but I'd be damned if I knew exactly what it was. Yahn was either dating one or both of the red dragon sisters.

I let the thought go, not wanting to know. Especially since Alucard – the Daywalker vampire standing next to me – was their adopted father. Alucard and I stood elevated above the seated guests, who were mostly chatting back and forth with each other, and thankfully not staring at our every move.

Yet.

"Just ask Gunnar's pack. A few of them tried to play red rocket with Paradise and Lost." I shot Alucard a meaningful look. "It didn't end well." The two stunners turned to me as if they had heard me say their names – the names they had given themselves after all the chaos they had been through. They licked their lips at Alucard, their smoldering eyes practically inviting him to try his hand.

He coughed pointedly – whether at my crude reference or their hungry eyes, I didn't care.

My eyes flicked from place to place about the room, wary for threats. "Everything is fine," I murmured, letting out a breath. "Nothing is going to happen."

Alucard grunted beside me. His eyes caught a ray of the setting sun from the glass window behind us, flashing for a moment. He looked relaxed, at peace. Of course, the sun hitting him was like a constant battery, charging this new breed of vampire that didn't need blood to fang out. "Except a man is about to lose his life," he reminded me.

I nodded soberly. "It was bound to happen sooner or later. I'm surprised it took this long."

"Do you think we could have prevented this if we had been better friends?" he asked softly.

I felt Tory glaring at us from a few paces away on the modern-day execution block. The Huntress stood beside her, looking beautiful, but uncomfortable in her dress. I averted my eyes from her as I replied.

"No. Death comes for us all."

"He does," a new voice said. My sphincter tightened enough for my entire body to flinch at the arrival of the stranger. I let out a breath and shot the newcomer an anxious look. He was cleverly disguised in a well-fitting black suit, but no clothing could have hidden the depths in those eyes. His three *Brothers* watched over various points around the room, alert for dangers.

Of *any* kind.

"Little early. The body isn't even cold," I whispered to Death – Horseman of the Apocalypse.

He rolled his eyes. "So dramatic. It happens to everyone. Well, many, at least."

"What are you doing here?" I asked.

Gunnar, the Alpha werewolf of St. Louis, sensed the sudden arrival from a few feet away. He shot a panicked look at us and then swept his lone eye over the small gathering, checking exits for threats. Seeing nothing, he still didn't look relieved, almost as if he was about to approach and demand answers to why the Horseman of Death had arrived so suddenly. I waved a hand at him discreetly, mouthing *I'll handle it.*

He gave me a stiff nod before turning away to speak to the last person on the execution block.

"I have something to tell you, of course," Death murmured dryly.

"Well, wait twenty fucking minutes. We're about to start."

"It cannot wait. Your request has been answered. Three may enter, but three shall not leave. You have two days. Meet me at the Arch at Noon." I almost popped a button on my suit as I spun, but Death only stared back with an immortal grin – not of pleasure, but of... something. "Oh, and you might want to remove that before..." he indicated a few spaces away with his chin before waving a hand at the gathered crowd and the door at the far end of the room.

I glanced down where Death had indicated. Gunnar was busy talking in low tones with a woman in front of him. A dead mouse had been placed behind his foot. I frowned at it and then turned back to Death, but the Horseman of the Apocalypse was gone. I saw him stalking the perimeter of the seated guests, hands clasped behind his back, hyper vigilant. The woman speaking with Gunnar briefly glanced at me and then tracked Death's gait thoughtfully. Othello was no doubt wondering what her *kind-of-sometimes-boyfriend* had been doing on the stage where a man was about to be executed for the oldest crime of all time.

Alucard grunted beside me, his eyes noting the dead mouse. "I guess Talon wasn't as pleased with his role in this as we thought."

Organs abruptly belted out in a rehearsed melody, preparing the gathered crowd for the dark ritual only moments away. Everyone seated before the stage turned in their seats to see the doors at the far end of the room open. I used the distraction to swoop in and scoop up the dead rodent by the tail. I flung it behind me, aiming for a few potted plants near the wall.

Othello stared at me with wide eyes, but she was in no position to ask questions as she stood beside Gunnar on the elevated stage. I gave her a crooked grin, turning back to stare down the aisle between the seated witnesses – where the Executioner would soon appear. Gunnar's stone eyepatch glinted in the sunlight from the windows as he faced his death with a brave smile.

A young girl appeared at the open door. She flashed the crowd a smile, a mockery of the horror about to unfold.

And then she began to walk down the aisle, tossing flower petals to the left and right.

A beautiful Maine Coon wearing an ornate blue bow with shells of some kind woven into the silk ribbon followed the girl. He stalked with feline grace – that strut that wildcats had used to prowl the darkest corners of the world throughout history – as if considering how best to slaughter the young girl with the petals. His fur had been combed and his long, furry ears pointed high in the air, swiveling now and then to catch sounds none of us would have noticed, alert for dangers. He was easily fifty pounds and walked on all fours taller than many dogs. His tail twitched back and forth with agitation.

I tried not to smile as I dipped my head at him in gratitude.

"Jesus. He looks like he wants to kill us all…" Alucard breathed.

I let out a breath, taking in Talon's mercurial eyes. They did indeed shine with murder, but no one else seemed to notice. Gunnar deferentially lowered his beard at the feline, a silent *thank you*. Talon's eyes swept the ground at his feet, searching for the mouse I had just removed. Then he shot me a look and…

Winked. Which is weird as shit. Cats weren't designed to wink. Especially intelligently.

Gunnar frowned, glancing down, sensing nothing. But he did sniff the air, as if only just sensing the small death that had been there. He shot me a look and I shrugged guiltily.

"Maybe the dead mouse was a sign of what this is going to cost us..." Alucard whispered.

"Nah. Cats leave dead things behind for their owners all the time. It's like a..." I searched for the word, and then smiled. "An offering. A present."

When I heard no response, I glanced over to see Alucard frowning at me. "I don't think it was a present, Nate. Look at him. He wants to kill us. All of us. You, too."

"He won't kill me. Maybe you, Sparkles, but I'm safe. He's my Shadow. My guard."

"If you two can't shut the hell up for two minutes, I'm going to kick you out, no matter what Han Solo says," Othello warned in a growl loud enough for us to hear, but soft enough to be hidden by the *oohs* and *aahs* of the crowd as they fixated on the procession heading our way. Gunnar shot an anxious glare at us, hiding it from the crowd.

Othello was running this dark ritual, and she took her job very seriously.

I nodded, murmuring one last thing to Alucard as I watched Talon stalk closer to us, the cloth bundle at the base of his throat swinging back and forth. "He asked what he could do to strengthen the relationship between my other childhood friend. Ring bearer to Gunnar's freaking wedding sounded like a great idea."

But watching Talon now, and considering the dead rodent... I began to have doubts. Because Talon wasn't really a cat – that was just one of his shapes. He was naturally a bipedal feline Fae warrior – like a Thundercat. He had chosen his less threatening form for this event. And three things in this life made Talon the Devourer truly happy.

Murdering anything with a heartbeat.

Getting high on Fae catnip.

And chasing reflections of light on the ground.

Talon stalked up the steps toward the Alpha werewolf of St. Louis, and I held my breath.

He finally stepped to the side and sat down between Tory and Gunnar, turning out to face the crowd, and I let out a breath of relief.

"Are... those mouse skulls woven into the ribbon?" Alucard whispered from beside me.

I subtly glanced at Talon to see him licking his paw. He *did* have skulls woven into the ribbon, almost too small to notice. They gleamed wetly as if freshly acquired. He sensed my attention and turned to face me, paw still in the air. His lips curled back in a predatory grin.

The music changed to a different funeral dirge, and I turned, plastering a smile on my face. If Talon wanted to add some skulls to his ribbon as a small show of defiance, oh well. It was better than killing the flower girl.

"We're almost done. Nothing has happened yet. It's all going to work out fine," I told myself under my breath.

Then the executioner appeared at the end of the aisle, as radiant as an Angel of Death.

A collective breath went up as the audience stared at her with awed joy.

Ashley truly did look radiant in her wedding gown.

So why did I have a very bad feeling in the pit of my stomach?

We had enough guards here at Chateau Falco to prevent a war. Horsemen, werewolves, Odin's Ravens, the shifter students from Shift, even a few Kansas City Freaks.

We were safe.

But that feeling didn't go away...

~

Get your copy of NINE SOULS online today!

~

Turn the page to read a sample of **UNCHAINED** _- Feathers and Fire Series Book 1, or_ **BUY ONLINE**_. Callie Penrose is a wizard in Kansas City, MO who hunts monsters for the Vatican. She meets Nate Temple, and things devolve from there..._

(Note: Callie appears in the Temple-verse after Nate's book 6, TINY GODS... Full chronology of all books in the Temple Universe shown on the 'Books in the Temple Verse' page.)

TRY: UNCHAINED (FEATHERS AND FIRE #1)

*T*he rain pelted my hair, plastering loose strands of it to my forehead as I panted, eyes darting from tree to tree, terrified of each shifting branch, splash of water, and whistle of wind slipping through the nightscape around us. But... I was somewhat *excited*, too.

Somewhat.

"Easy, girl. All will be well," the big man creeping just ahead of me, murmured.

"You said we were going to get ice cream!" I hissed at him, failing to compose myself, but careful to keep my voice low and my eyes alert. "I'm not ready for this!" I had been trained to fight, with my hands, with weapons, and with my magic. But I had never taken an active role in a hunt before. I'd always been the getaway driver for my mentor.

The man grunted, grey eyes scanning the trees as he slipped through the tall grass. "And did we not get ice cream before coming here? Because I think I see some in your hair."

"You know what I mean, Roland. You tricked me." I checked the tips of my loose hair, saw nothing, and scowled at his back.

"The Lord does not give us a greater burden than we can shoulder."

I muttered dark things under my breath, wiping the water from my eyes. Again. My new shirt was going to be ruined. Silk never fared well in the rain. My choice of shoes wasn't much better. Boots, yes, but distressed, *fashionable* boots. Not work boots designed for the rain and mud. Definitely not monster hunting boots for our evening excursion through one of Kansas City's wooded parks. I realized I was forcibly distracting myself, keeping my mind busy with mundane thoughts to avoid my very real anxiety. Because whenever I grew nervous, an imagined nightmare always—

A church looming before me. Rain pouring down. Night sky and a glowing moon overhead. I was all alone. Crying on the cold, stone steps, and infant in a cardboard box—

I forced the nightmare away, breathing heavily. "You know I hate it when you talk like that," I whispered to him, trying to regain my composure. I wasn't angry with him, but was growing increasingly uncomfortable with our situation after my brief flashback of fear.

"Doesn't mean it shouldn't be said," he said kindly. "I think we're close. Be alert. Remember your training. Banish your fears. I am here. And the Lord is here. He always is."

So, he had noticed my sudden anxiety. "Maybe I should just go back to the car. I know I've trained, but I really don't think—"

A shape of fur, fangs, and claws launched from the shadows towards me, cutting off my words as it snarled, thirsty for my blood.

And my nightmare slipped back into my thoughts like a veiled assassin, a wraith hoping to hold me still for the monster to eat. I froze, unable to move. Twin sticks of power abruptly erupted into being in my clenched fists, but my fear swamped me with that stupid nightmare, the sticks held at my side, useless to save me.

Right before the beast's claws reached me, it grunted as something batted it from the air, sending it flying sideways. It struck a tree with another grunt and an angry whine of pain.

I fell to my knees right into a puddle, arms shaking, breathing fast.

My sticks crackled in the rain like live cattle prods, except their entire length was the electrical section — at least to anyone other than me. I could hold them without pain.

Magic was a part of me, coursing through my veins whether I wanted it or not, and Roland had spent many years teaching me how to master it. But I had never been able to fully master the nightmare inside me, and in moments of fear, it always won, overriding my training.

The fact that I had resorted to weapons — like the ones he had trained me with — rather than a burst of flame, was startling. It was good in the fact that my body's reflexes knew enough to call up a defense even without my direct command, but bad in the fact that it was the worst form of defense for the situation presented. I could have very easily done as Roland did, and hurt it from a distance. But I hadn't. Because of my stupid block.

Roland placed a calloused palm on my shoulder, and I flinched. "Easy, see? I am here." But he did frown at my choice of weapons, the reprimand silent but loud in my mind. I let out a shaky breath, forcing my fear back down. It was all in my head, but still, it wasn't easy. Fear could be like that.

I focused on Roland's implied lesson. Close combat weapons — even magically-powered ones — were for last resorts. I averted my eyes in very real shame. I knew these things. He didn't even need to tell me them. But when that damned nightmare caught hold of me, all my training went out the window. It haunted me like a shadow, waiting for moments just like this, as if trying to kill me. A form of psychological suicide? But it was why I constantly refused to join Roland on his hunts. He knew about it. And although he was trying to help me overcome that fear, he never pressed too hard.

Rain continued to sizzle as it struck my batons. I didn't let them go, using them as a totem to build my confidence back up. I slowly lifted my eyes to nod at him as I climbed back to my feet.

That's when I saw the second set of eyes in the shadows, right before they flew out of the darkness towards Roland's back. I threw one of my batons and missed, but that pretty much let Roland know that an unfriendly was behind him. Either that or I had just failed to murder my mentor at point-blank range. He whirled to confront the monster, expecting another aerial assault as he unleashed a ball of fire that splashed over the tree at chest height, washing the trunk in blue flames. But this monster was tricky. It hadn't planned on tackling Roland, but had merely jumped out of the darkness to get closer, no doubt learning from its fallen comrade, who still lay unmoving against the tree behind me.

His coat shone like midnight clouds with hints of lightning flashing in the depths of thick, wiry fur. The coat of dew dotting his fur reflected the moonlight, giving him a faint sheen as if covered in fresh oil. He was tall, easily hip height at the shoulder, and barrel chested, his rump much leaner than the rest of his body. He — I assumed male from the long, thick mane around his neck — had a very long snout, much longer and wider than any werewolf I had ever seen. Amazingly, and beyond my control, I realized he was beautiful.

But most of the natural world's lethal hunters were beautiful.

He landed in a wet puddle a pace in front of Roland, juked to the right, and then to the left, racing past the big man, biting into his hamstrings on his way by.

A wash of anger rolled over me at seeing my mentor injured, dousing my fear, and I swung my baton down as hard as I could. It struck the beast in the rump as it tried to dart back to cover — a typical wolf tactic. My blow singed his hair and shattered bone. The creature collapsed into a puddle of mud with a yelp, instinctively snapping his jaws over his shoulder to bite whatever had hit him.

I let him. But mostly out of dumb luck as I heard Roland hiss in pain, falling to the ground.

The monster's jaws clamped around my baton, and there was an imme-diate explosion of teeth and blood that sent him flying several feet away into the tall brush, yipping, screaming, and staggering. Before he slipped out of sight, I noticed that his lower jaw was simply *gone*, from the contact of his saliva on my electrified magical batons. Then he managed to limp into the woods with more pitiful yowls, but I had no mind to chase him. Roland — that titan of a man, my mentor — was hurt. I could smell copper in the air, and knew we had to get out of here. Fast. Because we had anticipated only one of the monsters. But there had been two of them, and they hadn't been the run-of-the-mill werewolves we had been warned about. If there were two, perhaps there were more. And they were evidently the prehistoric cousin of any werewolf I had ever seen or read about.

Roland hissed again as he stared down at his leg, growling with both pain and anger. My eyes darted back to the first monster, wary of another attack. It *almost* looked like a werewolf, but bigger. Much bigger. He didn't move, but I saw he was breathing. He had a notch in his right ear and a jagged scar on his long snout. Part of me wanted to go over to him and torture him. Slowly. Use his pain to finally drown my nightmare, my fear. The fear that had caused Roland's injury. My lack of inner-strength had not only put me in danger, but had hurt my mentor, my friend.

I shivered, forcing the thought away. That was *cold*. Not me. Sure, I was no stranger to fighting, but that had always been in a ring. Practicing. Sparring. Never life or death.

But I suddenly realized something very dark about myself in the chill, rainy night. Although I was terrified, I felt a deep ocean of anger manifest inside me, wanting only to dispense justice as I saw fit. To use that rage to battle my own demons. As if feeding one would starve the other, reminding me of the Cherokee Indian Legend Roland had once told me.

An old Cherokee man was teaching his grandson about life. "A fight is going on inside me," he told the boy. "It is a terrible fight between two wolves. One is evil — he is anger, envy, sorrow, regret, greed, arrogance, self-pity, guilt, resentment, inferiority, lies, false pride, superiority, and ego." After a few moments to make sure he had the boy's undivided attention, he continued.

"The other wolf is good — he is joy, peace, love, hope, serenity, humility, kindness, benevolence, empathy, generosity, truth, compassion, and faith. The same fight is going on inside of you, boy, and inside of every other person, too."

The grandson thought about this for a few minutes before replying. "Which wolf will win?"

The old Cherokee man simply said, "The one you feed, boy. The one you feed..."
And I felt like feeding one of my wolves today, by killing this one...

∾

Get the full book ONLINE!

∾

*Turn the page to read a sample of **WHISKEY GINGER** - Phantom Queen Diaries Book 1, or **BUY ONLINE**. Quinn MacKenna is a black magic arms dealer from Boston, and her bark is almost as bad as her bite.*

(Note: Full chronology of all books in the Temple Verse shown on the 'Books in the Temple Verse' page.)

TRY: WHISKEY GINGER (PHANTOM QUEEN DIARIES # 1)

*T*he pasty guitarist hunched forward, thrust a rolled-up wad of paper deep into one nostril, and snorted a line of blood crystals— frozen hemoglobin that I'd smuggled over in a refrigerated canister—with the uncanny grace of a drug addict. He sat back, fangs gleaming, and pawed at his nose. "That's some bodacious shit. Hey, bros," he said, glancing at his fellow band members, "come hit this shit before it melts."

He fetched one of the backstage passes hanging nearby, pried the plastic badge from its lanyard, and used it to split up the crystals, murmuring something in an accent that reminded me of California. Not *the* California, but you know, Cali-foh-nia—the land of beaches, babes, and bros. I retrieved a toothpick from my pocket and punched it through its thin wrapper. "So," I asked no one in particular, "now that ye have the product, who's payin'?"

Another band member stepped out of the shadows to my left, and I don't mean that figuratively, either—the fucker literally stepped out of the shadows. I scowled at him, but hid my surprise, nonchalantly rolling the toothpick from one side of my mouth to the other.

The rest of the band gathered around the dressing room table, following the guitarist's lead by preparing their own snorting utensils—tattered magazine covers, mostly. Typically, you'd do this sort of thing with a dollar-bill, maybe even a Benjamin if you were flush. But fangers like this lot couldn't touch cash directly—in God We Trust and all that. Of course, I didn't really understand why sucking blood the old-fashioned way had suddenly gone out of style. More of a rush, maybe?

"It lasts longer," the vampire next to me explained, catching my mildly curious expression. "It's especially good for shows and stuff. Makes us look, like, less—"

"Creepy?" I offered, my Irish brogue lilting just enough to make it a question.

"Pale," he finished, frowning.

I shrugged. "Listen, I've got places to be," I said, holding out my hand.

"I'm sure you do," he replied, smiling. "Tell you what, why don't you, like, hang around for a bit? Once that wears off," he dipped his head toward the bloody powder smeared across the table's surface, "we may need a pick-me-up." He rested his hand on my arm and our gazes locked.

I blinked, realized what he was trying to pull, and rolled my eyes. His widened in surprise, then shock as I yanked out my toothpick and shoved it through his hand.

"Motherfuck—"

"I want what we agreed on," I declared. "Now. No tricks."

The rest of the band saw what happened and rose faster than I could blink. They circled me, their grins feral...they might have even seemed intimidating if it weren't for the fact that they each had a case of the sniffles

—I had to work extra hard not to think about what it felt like to have someone else's blood dripping down my nasal cavity.

I held up a hand.

"Can I ask ye gentlemen a question before we get started?" I asked. "Do ye even *have* what I asked for?"

Two of the band members exchanged looks and shrugged. The guitarist, however, glanced back towards the dressing room, where a brown paper bag sat next to a case full of makeup. He caught me looking and bared his teeth, his fangs stretching until it looked like it would be uncomfortable for him to close his mouth without piercing his own lip.

"Follow-up question," I said, eyeing the vampire I'd stabbed as he gingerly withdrew the toothpick from his hand and flung it across the room with a snarl. "Do ye do each other's make-up? Since, ye know, ye can't use mirrors?"

I was genuinely curious.

The guitarist grunted. "Mike, we have to go on soon."

"Wait a minute. Mike?" I turned to the snarling vampire with a frown. "What happened to *The Vampire Prospero*?" I glanced at the numerous fliers in the dressing room, most of which depicted the band members wading through blood, with Mike in the lead, each one titled *The Vampire Prospero* in *Rocky Horror Picture Show* font. Come to think of it…Mike did look a little like Tim Curry in all that leather and lace.

I was about to comment on the resemblance when Mike spoke up, "Alright, change of plans, bros. We're gonna drain this bitch before the show. We'll look totally—"

"Creepy?" I offered, again.

"Kill her."

~

Get the full book ONLINE!

MAKE A DIFFERENCE

Reviews are the most powerful tools in my arsenal when it comes to getting attention for my books. Much as I'd like to, I don't have the financial muscle of a New York publisher.

But I do have something much more powerful and effective than that, and it's something that those publishers would kill to get their hands on.

A committed and loyal bunch of readers.

Honest reviews of my books help bring them to the attention of other readers.

If you've enjoyed this book, I would be very grateful if you could spend just five minutes leaving a review (it can be as short as you like) on my book's Amazon page.

Thank you very much in advance.

ACKNOWLEDGMENTS

First, I would like to thank my beta-readers, TEAM TEMPLE, those individuals who spent hours of their time to read, and re-re-read Nate's story. Your dark, twisted, cunning sense of humor makes me feel right at home…

I would also like to thank you, the reader. I hope you enjoyed reading *WAR HAMMER* as much as I enjoyed writing it. Be sure to check out the two crossover series in the Temple Verse: The **Feathers and Fire Series** and the **Phantom Queen Diaries**.

And last, but definitely not least, I thank my wife, Lexy. Without your support, none of this would have been possible.

ABOUT SHAYNE SILVERS

Shayne is a man of mystery and power, whose power is exceeded only by his mystery...

He currently writes the Amazon Bestselling **Nate Temple** Series, which features a foul-mouthed wizard from St. Louis. He rides a bloodthirsty unicorn, drinks with Achilles, and is pals with the Four Horsemen.

He also writes the Amazon Bestselling **Feathers and Fire** Series—a second series in the Temple Verse. The story follows a rookie spell-slinger named Callie Penrose who works for the Vatican in Kansas City. Her problem? Hell seems to know more about her past than she does.

He coauthors **The Phantom Queen Diaries**—a third series set in The Temple Verse—with Cameron O'Connell. The story follows Quinn MacKenna, a mouthy black magic arms dealer in Boston. All she wants? A round-trip ticket to the Fae realm...and maybe a drink on the house.

Shayne holds two high-ranking black belts, and can be found writing in a coffee shop, cackling madly into his computer screen while pounding shots of espresso. He's hard at work on the newest books in the Temple Verse—You can find updates on new releases or chronological reading order on the next page, his website or any of his social media accounts. **Follow him online for all sorts of groovy goodies, giveaways, and new release updates:**

Get Down with Shayne Online
www.shaynesilvers.com
info@shaynesilvers.com

facebook.com/shaynesilversfanpage

amazon.com/author/shaynesilvers

bookbub.com/profile/shayne-silvers

instagram.com/shaynesilversofficial

twitter.com/shaynesilvers

goodreads.com/ShayneSilvers

BOOKS IN THE TEMPLE VERSE

CHRONOLOGY: All stories in the TempleVerse are shown in chronological order on the following page

NATE TEMPLE SERIES

FAIRY TALE - FREE prequel novella #0 for my subscribers

OBSIDIAN SON

BLOOD DEBTS

GRIMM

SILVER TONGUE

BEAST MASTER

BEERLYMPIAN (Novella #5.5 in the 'LAST CALL' anthology)

TINY GODS

DADDY DUTY (Novella #6.5)

WILD SIDE

WAR HAMMER

NINE SOULS

HORSEMAN

LEGEND

KNIGHTMARE (TEMPLE #12) — COMING SOON…

FEATHERS AND FIRE SERIES

(Also set in the TempleVerse)

UNCHAINED

RAGE

WHISPERS

ANGEL'S ROAR

MOTHERLUCKER (Novella #4.5 in the 'LAST CALL' anthology)

SINNER

BLACK SHEEP

GODLESS (FEATHERS #7) — COMING SOON...

PHANTOM QUEEN DIARIES

(Also set in the Temple Universe)

COLLINS (Prequel novella #0 in the 'LAST CALL' anthology)

WHISKEY GINGER

COSMOPOLITAN

OLD FASHIONED

MOTHERLUCKER (Novella #3.5 in the 'LAST CALL' anthology)

DARK AND STORMY

MOSCOW MULE

WITCHES BREW

SALTY DOG

CHRONOLOGICAL ORDER: TEMPLE VERSE

FAIRY TALE (TEMPLE PREQUEL)

OBSIDIAN SON (TEMPLE 1)

BLOOD DEBTS (TEMPLE 2)

GRIMM (TEMPLE 3)

SILVER TONGUE (TEMPLE 4)

BEAST MASTER (TEMPLE 5)

BEERLYMPIAN (TEMPLE 5.5)

TINY GODS (TEMPLE 6)

DADDY DUTY (TEMPLE NOVELLA 6.5)

UNCHAINED (FEATHERS... 1)

RAGE (FEATHERS... 2)

WILD SIDE (TEMPLE 7)

WAR HAMMER (TEMPLE 8)

WHISPERS (FEATHERS... 3)

COLLINS (PHANTOM 0)

WHISKEY GINGER (PHANTOM... 1)

NINE SOULS (TEMPLE 9)

COSMOPOLITAN (PHANTOM... 2)

ANGEL'S ROAR (FEATHERS... 4)

MOTHERLUCKER (FEATHERS 4.5, PHANTOM 3.5)

OLD FASHIONED (PHANTOM...3)

HORSEMAN (TEMPLE 10)

DARK AND STORMY (PHANTOM... 4)

MOSCOW MULE (PHANTOM...5)

SINNER (FEATHERS...5)

WITCHES BREW (PHANTOM...6)

LEGEND (TEMPLE...11)

SALTY DOG (PHANTOM...7)

BLACK SHEEP (FEATHERS...6)

GODLESS (FEATHERS...7)

KNIGHTMARE (TEMPLE 12)

Printed in Great Britain
by Amazon